EARTH A TONE

ENTERPRISES

TM

T0204227

Eartha Watts Hicks

LOVECHANGES

Edited by Grace F. Edwards

Paperback Fiction
PUBLISHED BY EARTHATONE ENTERPRISES

EARTHATONE ENTERPRISES
244 Fifth Avenue, #2643
New York, NY 10001, U.S.A.
Copyright © Eartha Watts Hicks, 2013

Earthatone Paperback Fiction Newly Revised Edition 2015
Earthatone name and logo is a trademark of Earthatone Enterprises
Printed in the United States of America
Designed by Eartha Watts Hicks
Illustrated by Rakim Villanueva

ISBN 978-0-991-48921-3
Library of Congress Control Number: 2010936925

$\mathcal{F}$or my mother, Renee H.

You are my oldest and dearest friend. Thank you for giving me life, for being my angel in times of trouble, and for teaching me as best you could.

Author's Note

This is a work of fiction. Any references to actual events, real people, living or dead, or to real locales are intended only to give the novel a sense of authenticity. Names, places, incidents, titles, characters, and dialogues are either products of the author's imagination or they are used fictitiously. These scenarios, however realistic, are not to be construed as real.

Acknowledgments

To God be the glory. He has blessed me with abundant grace, the gift of creativity, as well as the encouragement of family, friends, mentors, and a network of fellow writers and musicians. I am grateful for my children, Miraque and Hector, who have been more than I could ask for and have been so patient with me through this process.

I thank my editor, Grace F. Edwards, my copy editors, Monica West and Sonja Noll. The staff of Eternal Beauty of New York, Alice E. Wattley of Ascend Financial Management, Steven M. Baxter of The Gannon Funeral Home, Inc., and Lenny of Lenny Heyward's Realty all took the time to help me research, filling me in with details I couldn't uncover on my own. I thank Moreh Yashoshua ben Yisrael and Michael Warner for their music contributions. The advice and assistance of Olivia Whiteman, Patrice Shaye Allen, Yona Deshommes, Mary Yost, Mark Stewart, Knowledge McKnight, Charles Brown, Marie L. Martin, Monique Martin, Charles Finelli, Toni Cross, Claribelle Loubriel, Carol Hill, the Callender family, and my uncle, Charles Watts, have also been a blessing.

I thank my mentors, Valerie Wilson Wesley, Chris Abani, Marie-Elena John Smith, Sheree Renée Thomas, Jacqueline Johnson, Margaret Irby, and Bernice McFadden. I thank Pastor Chris Mietlowski, Neil Criste Troutman, Lulu Paolini and Gustavus Adolphus Lutheran Church; Reverend Fletcher Crawford and Union Grove Baptist Church; the Harlem Writers Guild; the Frederick Douglass Creative Arts Center; the Hurston-Wright Foundation; the Center for Black Literature; Daniel Middleton and Scribe Freelance; Daniel Tisdale and Harlem World Magazine; Simone Monet Wahls and Future Executives, Inc.; Lois Reddick and Cultivating Our Sisterhood International Association; as well as Althea Burton, Helen M. Tomlinson, Renee Cofer, Bridgette King, Diane Williams, George Williams and Project Enterprise. I also thank Angela, Akkida, and Erica, members of my Artist Way support group who have cheered me on. I have benefited from workshop experiences and the feedback, especially that of Iquo Essien, Aldora Britton, Laura Brown, Femi Lewis, Amy Moran, Tacuma Roeback, Miriam Kelly-Ferguson, Nicole

Goodwin, Betsaida Velez, Neil G. White, and Cecilia Falls.

I thank my closest friends, Karen Vanderburg, Miss Mary Maybank, and Eve Robinson; my sisters Erin, Alexis, and Charise; my cousins, Leslie, Teaira, Brian, and Yolanda; and my mother-in-law and my sister-in-law, Laney, for their continued support. I thank all the Verizon employees who read this novel before it was even completed.

I thank my stepfather, Aaron Hill, and my aunts Michele Williams and Gail Adams. I especially thank Aunt Carole. Because she asked me to write her into the story, I had no choice but to try my best to make it a good one. I thank my Aunt Eartha Mae Quintano-Dessaso, for whom I am named; she pushed me to the finish line, but God called her home before I could actually hand her a bound copy.

So many people have supported me along the way that I can't possibly list everyone by name, but I am grateful for my family and friends, as well as their prayers and encouragement. I am so grateful that God has blessed me with all of you.

⁵For your maker is your husband—
The Lord Almighty is his name—
The Holy One of Israel is your Redeemer;
He is called the God of all the earth.

Isaiah 54 (NIV)

1995

*M*OMMY NEVER MINCED WORDS. INSTEAD OF saying hello, she stood on my welcome mat, greeting me with an insult. "You don't look good. You're not getting enough sleep."

Sleep. What was that? I'd had fifteen weeks off, but maternity leave was no vacation. I spent the entire time nursing, changing diapers, grocery shopping, cooking, cleaning, doing laundry, and running back and forth to doctors' appointments. Not to mention dealing with Spider. If Tee-Bo wasn't crying, Spider was calling; they tag teamed me. I opened my apartment door all the way, yawning, "I haven't slept since March."

Mommy waved her finger in my face. "Talk to your boyfriend. He helped make the baby. He should help take care of him." Seeing Tee-Bo strapped to me in the harness carrier all ready to go, she asked, "Are you going out or just getting in?"

I was actually on my way to the laundromat, which is only empty on Tuesday nights. Last wash is at seven, so I looked her straight in the eye and said, "Just getting in." Half the time she left me no choice but to lie or argue, and since I didn't have time to argue, I urged myself: *Focus. Keep my answers short and sweet. Don't volunteer information. Whatever I do, don't mention anything about having keys to Dr. Snyder's brownstone.*

Mommy breezed by me. Her hairstyle was different. Bangs stopped at a scab. The back tapered. A pixie cut. Judging by the curling iron burn, she was probably at the salon this past Saturday, but her curls were still crisp; Mommy always did know how to sleep pretty. She wore the same "red raspberry" shade on her lips and nails. A pencil skirt and pantyhose showed off the long, curvy legs. The white, tailored suit was spotless. Her snakeskin heels made quiet steps into the

3

living room, but the keys to the new Volvo rattled until she stuffed them inside the Louis Vuitton hanging off her arm. She then felt my chaise, rubbing the fabric as if to determine whether or not the pattern was printed on.

The upholstery was ivory Jacquard. The blue carnations, woven. "This one *is* a little busy." I then pointed to the adjacent camelback loveseat, solid ivory. "But, that one adds balance."

Mommy dusted off her hands, staring at the silver mirror covering the wall over the loveseat. The scroll and leaf detail was intricate. The antique frame was gleaming. When I bought it, it was all black. A polishing cloth couldn't get into the crevices, but I remembered how my Nana used to clean her silver in the sink with salt, baking soda, and aluminum foil, so I lugged the mirror to my bathtub. After soaking one side at a time, there wasn't a speck of tarnish. Mommy grunted and turned. The bachelor's chest wasn't a coffee table, but it was a cute substitute. On it, I had my stack of *Modern Bride* magazines all spread out, and on opposite ends, the decanter and fluted vase were both cobalt blue.

"The one closest to you is Mikasa. The taller one is Lenox. Hallmarks are etched on the bottom." Now I was beaming, not because of the brand names but because of the way I used color to draw eyes to the center of the room. I tried to find matching material for throw pillows, but the match I found was expensive silk. At Goodwill, I found curtain panels that I cut into squares and stuffed, costing me next to nothing. Beige linen paled in comparison, but it worked out better that only the crystal was this bold blue. That pop of color was actually the effect I wanted.

Mommy gravitated in that direction. Then, as if changing her mind, she drifted to my bistro table, first drumming her fingernails on its glass and then tugging on the edge so hard; the bowl of lemons on it slid around. Three wrought iron chairs with heart shaped backs surrounded my little round table. She looked down, and then back at the wall. The periwinkle paint matched the cushions perfectly. I took a swatch to Sears; they mixed the can while I waited. Watching her tip one of the chairs back, I admitted, "I covered the seats myself with a power stapler. Would you like something to drink?"

No comment. She was ignoring me. Oh well. Anyway,

there wasn't much more. To the left, the arch and twelve linoleum tiles marked off my stove, sink, refrigerator, and ten inches of counter space. It's the smallest kitchen ever. And down the hall, my bedroom was so tight that we had barely enough walk space between our king-sized bed and the dresser. This was the Bronx, not Hoboken, and my two and a half rooms on 167th Street were nothing compared to Mommy's condo. In fact, this whole apartment could probably fit in the backseat of her Volvo, but it was finally furnished, and I had done it myself, even if these were thrift store finds. Now I knew Mommy was scrutinizing, because she's a buyer for a furniture chain. She used to design showrooms so I was hoping she'd comment on the décor, but she zipped her purse by the padlock and sat it in the chair. She didn't utter a word. Her face contorted. I twisted my own face, following her favorite fragrance, Poison.

Mommy kicked off her heels. Draping her folded blazer across the chaise, she asked, "How was work?"

How was work? I couldn't help but just seal my lips and blink. I worked for a collection agency. Translation: I called people, demanded that they pay their debts, threatened to take them to court and sue for the money they didn't have, all while hoping that I annoyed them into making payments, but that's what I did...all...day...long. No matter how many times I heard, "You can't get blood from a turnip," I hassled them. Even those who were honest enough to confess, "I just don't have it," I hassled them too. I didn't exactly "harass" them, so to speak, with repeat calls minutes apart or with empty threats. No. That, I didn't do. But I did badger them. I had to. I had to demand payment, otherwise the debtors wouldn't commit. I had to make a certain number of calls per hour, and a certain percentage had to follow through with their promises, or else I'd get written up. Enough write-ups, they'd fire me. And those supervisors, they hovered over us like vultures, bloodthirsty vultures, circling, with clipboards and number two pencils, filling in circles. The ones that didn't were in the back office wearing headphones bigger than earmuffs, monitoring our phone conversations, hanging on our every word, "This is an attempt to collect a debt. Any information obtained will be used for that purpose. This call is also being monitored and recorded for quality assurance. My name is Miss Love. I'd like to start by verifying the last

5

four digits of your Social." I could say that in my sleep. Day in and day out, I had to stick to the script and all the other bullet points of the collection process: identifying the original lender; stating the reference number; demanding the balance in full, even if debtors insisted they could only make partial payments; demanding payments by the preferred methods, Western Union or check by phone, when debtors could actually mail their checks in. And, of course, golden rule number one: verifying all information; making sure I got their work number, if they had one, so that we could garnish their wages if we needed to; and verifying the home addresses and phone numbers so that we could put liens on their homes. All this or I'd get written up. The fact that I was so good at my job is what made it so awful. Most debtors were already depressed or had recently experienced some personal tragedy. I performed like their sob stories didn't affect me, when the real deal was I could relate. Even though I was a bill collector, I was one paycheck away from hardship myself.

Mommy unfastened her gold clip-ons and dropped them in her pocket. She then stood upright, massaging her earlobes. "Ah! My goodness! That feels good. Beauty has its price." She looked at me. "Well?" she said.

"Seventy-two degrees and sunny, that's great weather for the end of June, right? Don't you just love sweater weather? By the way, you look *good* in white."

"Mmhmm. Now, how was work?"

"Can we talk about something else? I hate that place."

"Be grateful. That's a good job, and you have no degree," she said.

"Mommy!" I took a deep breath to calm myself. And I counted backwards. Didn't work. "Today was only my second day back, and my supervisor caught me nodding off. Did I make quota? Yes, actually I doubled it. Did he take into consideration that I have a baby that isn't sleeping through the night yet? Nope. He wrote me up! Then, he wrote me up again for lateness when I made it in this morning and signed the time sheet at exactly seven fifty-two. I logged in, not realizing my computer froze. I logged back in, but the clock said two minutes after." That reminded me. Time check. Six twenty-two. My elevator was broken. I had to use the stairs with Tee-Bo *and* the shopping cart. If I was going to make it to the laundromat on the other side of the Concourse, I needed to leave in no less than eight minutes. I looked. Mommy was walking up the hall. When the bathroom door closed, I called her. She didn't answer. So, to save time, I went to the linen closet and stuffed the detergent, bleach, fabric softener, and everything else I needed into the top of the laundry bag. Now, all I had to do was drop that into my shopping cart. I glanced down. Flats were on my feet, but climbing four flights of cracked steps, they'd feel like stilts. I changed into Reeboks.

Mommy was still in the bathroom. I pressed my ear to the door. Hearing only my pulse, I was about to knock, but then, the toilet flushed. Mommy yelled, "Why didn't you tell him to check the sheet?"

Tee-Bo twitched, but the noise didn't wake him. His legs flopped like a rag doll's on my way back to the living room, where I called out, "I did. He said time sheets don't matter. If that's the case, why is there a time sheet?" With the second hand still spinning, I stopped watching it, but anxiety had me counting in my head. The faucet ran, but I couldn't think of one single solitary thing to say or do in order to rush out of here in the next few minutes without her tagging along.

The door opened. She came out smiling, crumpling a paper towel. "It happens." She tossed it in the wastebasket and then approached, extending her arms. "I came to see the baby. Hand him over."

"He's asleep."

"Hand the baby over."

"His name is Tobiah." At this point, I didn't even put up a fight. I just took Tee-Bo out of his harness and passed him to her. She sat, looking him over. Then she looked at me tight-lipped. I knew what she was thinking. Before she could say it, I told her, "I *am* using the cream."

"No one in our family has eczema."

"No one in Spider's family either."

"What could it be? You're hand washing, I hope."

Mommy grew up scrubbing laundry with her knuckles at five in the morning. So, of course she had stressed the importance of hand washing Tee-Bo's clothes since he was born. But, between catering to Spider and taking care of Tee-Bo, especially now that I'd returned to work and had to express enough breast milk to fill eight bottles, how could she expect me to still have time and energy? I shrugged and shook my head.

"You are washing this newborn baby's clothes in those nasty machines?"

"He's not a newborn anymore."

She raised her voice and repeated herself. "In those nasty machines?"

"He's three months old now."

"I know how old the baby is. Stop washing his clothes at the laundromat!" Now, here she was hollering at me, and I was almost twenty-six years old.

I hollered back, "I'm saving for a washing machine!"

Mommy squeezed her left eye. When we were kids, we knew: once she squinted, duck. "Did you just lose your mind?"

I nodded and spoke like I had some sense. "Sorry, I'm saving for a machine."

Her face relaxed. "What are you going to do in the meantime?"

So much for the laundromat. "I guess I'll have to use Dr. Snyder's."

"You shouldn't get too comfortable in that woman's home."

"I'll be there, anyway. I have to sign for a package on Friday, and I have to run an errand for her next week." I smacked my forehead almost as soon as those words slipped out.

Mommy didn't even hesitate, "Why doesn't her out-of-work son run her errands?"

"Spider is not out of work. He's an intern."

"That's no job. You two should have a mutual exchange."

"We do."

"Sexual favors don't count!"

"Don't bad mouth Spider in front of my baby." I reached, grabbing Tee-Bo at his waist.

Still, Mommy would not let him go. She tightened her grip and cut her eye at me. "He's asleep, Mia."

"Can he sleep in the room while we have this conversation?" I asked, but she pulled him even closer. "Mommy, *please*," I begged. After a few seconds, she laid him in my arms.

As soon as I reached the cradle, I laid Tee-Bo on his back. Tiny, red bumps covered half his face. I knew the stages. In a few days, the redness would fade, but not the bumps. His hair—jet-black like Spider's—swirled in the sweat on his scalp. He looked like a Kewpie doll, even if his skin did look like tapioca pudding. I reached for his cream, applied a dab to the side of his face, and then kissed his forehead. His skin cream smelled like bleach, but I was getting used to it.

I'd been dealing with this for over a month. I looked all through Dr. Snyder's medical journal. None of the rashes in the pictures had pointed tips like Tee-Bo's, but after looking in that big book, everywhere I went, I saw hives, prickly heat, bug bites.

On my way into Manhattan this morning, the man nodding off next to me was wearing a short sleeve shirt and had what looked like psoriasis. Not only was it red, it was covered with white ash. Seeing that man this morning hit so close to home, I almost broke down on the D train. This rash was spreading. I should've known that would set her off. I kissed Tee-Bo again and wiped off some of his sweat.

I know once my mind is set on something, it's almost impossible to convince me otherwise, but I was glad I had an excuse not to bump my shopping cart down four flights, especially now that my surge of adrenaline had fizzled out. I was exhausted all over again. I wasn't going anywhere. I yawned and stretched my body. This harness carrier was pointless. I took it off and laid it across the diaper bag.

At my knees, lace hung past the hemline of my black skirt. There was no elastic left in my half-slip, and the knot at my waist untied. I should've pinned it, but my only safety pin was keeping my skirt's zipper from sliding down. Stepping out of the slip, the ankle strap from my high-top caught onto the lace. When I separated them, the Velcro tore the slip all the way across the bottom. I held up the slip and examined it. Besides the rip and not having any elastic, it had more runs zipping through it than an old stocking, but a raggedy slip is not the same as a raggedy pair of stockings. Slips are functional. This slip served a purpose. My skirts didn't have linings. Debating whether or not to remove the lace trim from it entirely, I carefully folded it and placed it in my night table drawer. From behind me, I heard, "Well, now I've seen it all." I turned and caught a glimpse of Mommy leaving the doorway.

I expected her to get started on Spider all over again as soon as I walked into the living room, but she was seated, leaning on the arm of my loveseat. She straightened up and I looked into her face. She wasn't squinting, tightening her lips, or drawing up her nose. Her forehead was crinkled. That meant she was worrying, but I knew what I was doing. I had to at least try to convince her. I thought for a moment. Then, I made my voice as sweet as possible. "Mommy, you've always taught me I've got to give a little to get a little, right?"

"What's your point?"

"My point *is* I give my all to Spider."

"Don't you realize giving your *all* to your boyfriend leaves you with nothing?"

"Spider's all I want. I can't live without him."

Mommy jumped up, grabbed me by the shoulders, and shook me hard. "I told you before. Don't say that! Mia, Mia, Mia." She pulled me over to the mirror. I wondered why. I didn't see any streaks. But then again, seeing the light from the window bounce off, I did notice some fingerprints. I pulled my sleeve and reached to wipe them with my cuff but she pulled me back, pointing me into the mirror. Punishment. I already knew that the pocket of my white Oxford shirt had a milk circle. When my supervisor handed me my write-ups, I sucked my teeth, and my breasts leaked. I scratched away the crusty stuff, but this was a protein stain. I needed to soak it in cold water. The second button from the top was reattached with grey thread, only because I ran out of white, and with two top buttons open, I felt naked. My collar was wearing thin, because bleach was eating away at the fabric. This blouse may have been worn out, but at least it wasn't dingy.

She brought her cheek to mine. This was torture. Bad enough she tanned bronze, and my brown skin was turning blue from the neck up since I didn't have a coupon for sunscreen, but she was standing here in all this black mascara, eye shadow, and liquid liner, when she never needed any of that. Mommy's eyes were beautiful all by themselves. Even if mine weren't bloodshot and didn't have the dark circles underneath or the bags from lack of sleep, she would still be Nefertiti, and I would still look like a locust, standing next to her with my big, bug eyes. I've tried squinting and batting them, practiced smiling and half-smiling, bleached my skin with Ambi, baked it back with cocoa butter, and when none of that helped, I mailed dollar bills and coins to P.O. boxes for all kinds of goop, believing testimonials, but nobody ever asked me for mine: *If it's in the back of a magazine, it doesn't work.* $12.95 plus $2.00 shipping and handling never made me love what I saw in the mirror. Mommy was almost twenty years older than me, and I still would've traded faces. Why didn't she just spit me out the way she did Dawn? All our other features were somewhat similar. Why wasn't I a clone, too? Why did Donald Jackson's genes have to be this strong? I would've loved to look like her. She pinched one of my hairs and stuck it into my bun. Then, finger-combing, she blended more fly away strands. In the mirror, we made eye contact. She squeezed my arms and said, "You can have any man you want. Don't waste your time."

I didn't know how to respond to that, but looking into her eyes, I had to sound confident. "We *will* get married, Mommy. Spider gave me his word."

"Mia, for heaven's sake! Should I go shopping for a blue dress? Should I buy a ten-pound bag of Uncle Ben's?" I didn't answer, at least not right away. I never knew how to respond to her rhetorical questions, so I just folded my arms and stared down. Determined to make her point, she twisted me around and tilted my face toward hers. "Should I call Reverend Earl?"

"Spider's an atheist, Mommy. It's been so long since I've set foot in church, I doubt Reverend Earl even remembers who I am."

"That's not the point! The point *is* no one's going to be throwing any rice at you anytime soon."

"Maybe not, but—"

"No buts! That man should already be married to you! It's been ten years, and he's reaping all the benefits. You pay his bills. You just gave him a baby. You dropped out of college twice for him!"

"I transferred."

"For once, will you *please* be honest with yourself? Instead of knocking yourself out trying to pay for your pretty boyfriend's master's, let his mother, "the doctor," pay for it. You best believe if his mother's a surgeon, that boy ain't broke. He has some money stashed somewhere. The only question is how much. So take that which is rightfully yours, and get your *own* degree! I worked three jobs to get us out of those projects! And I didn't keep you in private school all

11

your life for you to be anybody's fool!"

"I'm nobody's fool!"

"Then I must be! I paid college tuition for four, no, five years and then went out and spent a hundred and twenty-seven dollars on a frame for that diploma!"

I screamed, "I know! Enough already! Gee whiz! So what, I don't have a degree for you to show off to all your friends! That was three years ago, Mommy! Get over it!"

The next thing I knew, I was holding my stinging face. I didn't see the swing. I didn't even see her squint. I was dazed for a minute, trying to figure out what triggered the slap. The last time she had done that was ten years earlier because I was "smelling myself." But I wasn't a sixteen-year-old sneaking out in the middle of the night with roller-skates anymore. I was a grown woman. "I can't believe you just did that. I can't! I can't believe you just slapped me!"

"Shut up, and stop overreacting," Mommy said. No remorse whatsoever, but she was calmer. "I don't care what folks think. My concern, Mia, is you and the baby."

"His name's Tobiah."

"I know! Tobiah Osbert Love!"

"No! His last name is Snyder, Mommy!"

She froze. Staring. She didn't even blink. Then, she politely collected her suit jacket, hung it over her arm, and slid her pedicure into her pumps. "Goodbye."

"Does this mean this *talk* is over?"

"Why should I stay here and talk to a wall? I got walls at home."

"Now this is *my* fault?"

She yanked her purse from the chair and gave me that look. Her one squinted eye was now wet at the corner. "I tell you time and time again, but you don't listen. You just don't listen! And when you don't listen..." Her voice quivered, "...you suffer. Mark my words. Keep doing what you're doing, Mia, you'll keep gettin' what you got. Absolutely nothing."

"Mommy," I said, rearranging my throw pillows. After I gave them each a karate chop, I glanced back at her. "All this look like nothing to you?"

"Mia, look around! Anything in here child friendly? Once the baby starts crawling and walking, he'll be in everything. The lamps, the vases, all that is placed low. This seating is right next to where you eat. Even if a professional comes in here with Scotchgard, in a year's time, I'll still see it covered in grape juice and spaghetti handprints. And that's not even the worst of it!" She tapped her fingernails on the bistro table's glass. "This top isn't tempered! And it's a tip-over hazard! It has no suction cups, no gripping pads, nothing securing it to the base, nothing to keep it from sliding off!"

"Nothing's wrong with that table! You're nitpicking!"

"Am I?" Mommy pushed down on the table's edge. The glass overturned, and the opposite end went straight up, sending the wooden bowl crashing to the floor and lemons rolling across my living room. The glass top came back down with a bang but didn't break. She looked at me. "Need another demonstration?"

Now that my heart was in my throat, I could only manage to shake my head.

"That table can topple if someone so much as puts an elbow on it, let alone a toddler trying to pull himself to stand. And your walls...are sheetrock. That mirror has got to weigh a hundred pounds. That's *another* accident waiting to happen."

I turned, wiping the fingerprints off it with my cuff, "I don't think so."

"Of course not! You haven't learned to think for your child yet." She walked away. "All *you* think about is your boyfriend's curly hair and hazel eyes." She faced me when she reached the door. "Remember what I told you. And another thing: that's your boyfriend's mother and all, but don't make yourself too comfortable in that woman's home. You can have keys and still be an outsider."

That said, she snatched the door open and stepped out. "Kiss the baby for me."

2

$\mathcal{S}$PIDER AND I STARTED GOING TOGETHER WHEN I was in the tenth grade. He was still in the ninth, but he was only a few weeks shy of his fifteenth birthday. His mother was hardly ever home, so we spent a whole lot of time lying in his twin-sized captain's bed, staring up at stucco as if it were stars. I'd say things like, "When we get married, I'll make you breakfast in bed every Saturday," or "I'll make your homemade ice cream just like my Nana's." Spider was never talkative, but he'd always respond, "Sounds good." Daydreaming back then, it seemed like we were talking about some point eons into the future, but the years flew by.

We started "shackin," as Mommy would say, in 1992. At that time, we were about seven years into our relationship. Spider was in graduate school full-time, and Tee-Bo wasn't even thought of when we found this apartment in the Bronx. We started off looking for something on the Concourse near the courthouse. Cheaper rent brought us six blocks over. From the get-go, Spider wasn't too keen on the neighborhood. I had to come see it for myself. I lit up when the gypsy cab turned onto 167th Street. Everything was on 167th Street. A 99-cent store, subway station, supermarket, bodega, hardware store, laundromat, and even a check cashing place.

When the cab turned onto Sherman Avenue and stopped, I spotted the new building with the surveillance camera out front. Immediately, I bounced up and down. "That's it, Spider! That's it!" I dropped a ten-dollar bill through the chute and jumped out. Standing out front with my issue of *Bronx Apartment Listings*, I flipped the pages, searching for the circled ad with a pass code to open the gate. I found the page, but there was no code number. I looked up. A security guard was on her way down the steps; Spider had pressed the zero-button.

"Who are you here to see?" she asked.

15

I smiled, showing her the ad.

"Wrong building." She pointed across the street.

Our building wasn't only off by one digit. Spider and I looked across the street. Cardboard was duct-taped to every window on the first floor. I sucked my teeth, but we walked right in through the open gate. Spider tried to pull it closed, but the gate creaked back until its corner lodged into the sidewalk. He looked at me. What was I supposed to say? Plus, I didn't want to open my mouth. Something somewhere was rank. I held my breath as we headed up the steps, swatting away horseflies. Three big ones. Spider stopped at the landing and turned to me, raising his brows. "Are you sure about this?"

I shrugged. "This is the best I can do for now...until you find work."

"Whatever." He reached over to the top button and rang for the superintendent. Nothing buzzed, beeped, or made any other kind of noise. And with this place looking the way it did, it was safe to assume the intercom was broken. Spider shook his head, so I rolled my eyes and stepped across him. Black paint and rust peeled off the door. Someone had popped the lock. A knotted rope looped through a hole where the knob should've been. I looked at it, thinking. *Why didn't they just replace the knob?* But, I pulled the rope and opened the door.

After ringing almost every bell on the first floor, we found Rafael, the superintendent. Rafael was about Spider's complexion. He had a dark Afro but his sideburns, mustache, and beard were silver. I looked down as he stepped out of his apartment. He dragged his right side, bracing himself with an orthopedic adjustable cane. Stunned, my gaze went from the rubber tip of that cane, to his ashy hand gripping the handle, up past the blurred, green tattoo on his forearm that read "Santo Domingo," to his wrinkled, paint-streaked shirt, and to the cigarette, shaking as it dangled from his lips. With a jittery right hand, he removed it. Blowing smoke in a stream as thick as his accent, he said, "Stroke." Now, I knew exactly why this building looked like this.

The apartment was on the fourth floor. We waited for the elevator, because Rafael couldn't climb the stairs. When it finally came, Spider pulled the gate aside for him. We all

16

piled in, but the elevator did not move. Spider looked at me. I looked at Rafael. He took a pull from his cigarette and said, "You gotta pull the gate back."

Okay, I admit. This was not the Taj Mahal. But I was willing to make a few sacrifices for cheap rent.

Anyway, right after we moved in here, these kente wedding invitations started coming in the mail. The trend that year was Afrocentric weddings and after jumping the broom, buying a house in Atlanta, North Carolina, Maryland, or Virginia. I was in a wedding in May, in June, and another in September. My girlfriends were hightailing it south with these guys they either barely knew or had met in college. So when I turned twenty-three on December 5th, it occurred to me that by the time my mother was this age, she had already been divorced three times. I started to wonder what was up with Spider, why he and I never had a formal conversation about marriage or set any date.

The first person I thought to ask was Romell. We've been friends as long as I've been alive so I knew he'd give me his honest opinion, but he went off, "Mia! You're rushing! What the fuck you rushin' for? We're young!"

Hearing the thug come out of him caught me completely by surprise, but Romell has always been my window into the male psyche. It seemed logical to me that if Romell reacted this way, Spider would probably react the same way. I decided to take Romell's advice and give Spider time to broach the subject on his own.

Before I knew it, almost two years had passed. I was putting the finishing touches on the craft project I had been working on for I don't know how many months: my quilt. I couldn't find anything affordable. Since I loved quilts and was in the habit of recycling scrap material anyway, I decided to make one myself. I sketched out my own pattern on graph paper, cut the fabric, and, every night after work, I painstakingly hand-stitched each section until the day I flipped the quilt right side out, stuffed it, whip-stitched it closed, and snipped that last thread.

When I carried it into the room, Spider was hunched forward in the chair by the window in khaki shorts and his John Starks throwback, cleaning the threads of his wax forty-five records. Spider was so into what he was doing that I only saw the top of his head. His jet-black, shiny curls always left me wondering whether his hair was wet or dry. I loved that, but now, I was eager to see the expression on his face, so I called to get his attention.

"Spider! Come here." When he didn't budge, I tried a different approach, lowering my voice and batting my eyes. Not that he noticed.

Without looking up, he said, "It's fine." His normal baritone sounded hoarse, as if a cold was sneaking up on him.

Perfectly measured blocks bordered my quilt in lime green. The orange and lemon yellow patches were sewn into two sets of larger blocks in a pattern of alternating triangles that rotated inward like vanes of a windmill. The only quilt I saw that was even remotely comparable was in Macy's with a three-hundred-dollar price tag, so I said, "Spider, will you look at it?"

He stopped wiping the wax threads of his Isley Brothers record long enough to look at me. His hazel eyes were intense, especially because of his thick eyebrows, but he rolled them and twisted his pink lips to the side before feigning chills, saying, "Oooh! Silk?"

I sucked my teeth. "For your information, the green is silk. The yellow is satin, and the orange is...I don't know, maybe...rayon or polyester."

"Where did you get all that?"

"The white satin for the underside I got from a sample sale, but the whole top is made from all my old bridesmaid dresses."

Spider grinned, and I now saw every perfect tooth. Then, he dropped his head, and with that goofy laugh, "Huh-ha," he went right back to wiping his record.

"What?" I asked. I don't know why, but I did.

Spider laughed again. "Lotta weddings," he said.

I glanced at his end of the dresser. In a picture frame that was so old that half the seashells had fallen off, Spider and I posed beneath a blue and white balloon arch with eighties hair. Maybe because he was wearing a tuxedo or maybe because my prom dress was white, but right then, it hit me: we were no closer to being married now than we were then. I blew up.

"Lotta weddings?" I snatched the quilt off the bed, balled it up, and threw it at him. He struggled out from under it, like it was a parachute. After he dropped it on the floor, he slid back in his seat with his legs spread, pretending to focus on the record he now spun around his index finger. So I continued, "Did it ever occur to you that maybe...just maybe...*I'd* like to get married? All my friends are getting married. I would *love* a church wedding."

His jaw grew tense. His eyes averted away from mine. No comment.

I folded my arms and stared at him. He stopped spinning the record and started tapping his foot, but otherwise remained silent. Noises from outside filled the room, though: giggles, cars passing by, thumps of a basketball bouncing high, dribbling fast, and then bouncing high, again. When I couldn't stand his silence anymore, I yelled, "Say something!"

Straightening up, Spider reached over to his night table. The forty-five slid off his finger onto the five-inch stack next to his suitcase record player. He shrugged. His response wouldn't have hurt me any more if he spat in my face. "I don't believe in marriage."

He was always an atheist, but the fact that he didn't believe in marriage, this was news to me. I marched over and snatched him up by the number three on his Knicks jersey, even though he had a body that could easily play point guard in their starting lineup. "Excuse you?"

He grabbed my wrist tight enough to loosen my grip on his chest hair. Then, glancing around the room, he said, "That piece of paper don't mean a thing." And then, all six-foot-five inches of him stood and brushed by me.

I went after him. In the living room, I ran right into his back. As soon as he turned to face me, I said, "Don't you think I'd make a good wife?"

"Can I breathe?"

"Don't you think I'd make a good wife?"

"If you say so," he said, looking everywhere else. After I folded my arms across my chest, he took a deep breath and looked into my eyes. "You'd make a great wife. Now, drop it. Okay? Drop it!" Then he took off back up the hall.

I stomped after him and felt something jab into the sole of my foot. Bare feet and old wood floors didn't mix. We didn't have a stitch of furniture in the living room then, so I hopped over to the windowsill. I didn't need tweezers. In the light coming through the window, I carefully plucked the splinter out. And then, just sat there a moment, remembering how I used to practice signing my name—Mia Love, Mia Love-Snyder, Mia Snyder—on the cover of all my binders. Prom night Spider gave me a large, diamond initial ring. He bought this by saving his Stop-One stock boy money for weeks. Besides that, I couldn't even begin to count the number of times he'd called me his wife. So, I had always assumed that we'd someday get married.

I caught up as he was on his way to the bathroom with the bottle of rubbing alcohol tucked under his arm. I stopped him in the hall. "If that's the case, what's the problem?"

He backed into the bedroom, plopped on the mattress, and tossed up his free arm. "Problem? There's no problem! Everything's fucking peachy! Okay? Now, will you leave me alone?"

"Well, exactly how long do you expect me to wait on you?"

"Mia!" He threw the alcohol bottle down. "If I'm going to stay with you, I'm going to stay with you! What more do you want?"

"Don't be throwing shit in my house! Who do you think you are?" I grabbed the bottle from the floor and placed it next to his cologne bottles. Then, I exhaled. "Don't act dumb," I said calmly. "You know what I want."

He took a deep breath. "Yeah, it ain't happening. And a church wedding definitely ain't happening."

"Why not? Give me one reason! Just one!"

"You want a reason. You want a reason!" He flew to his side of the room and snatched his drawer open. The whole thing fell. Forty-fives slid off his night table. He got down on his knees, digging pictures out of the pile, flinging them. One hit the wall; the other, the ceiling. "There's two!" He jumped up, snapping one of the records. He then grabbed his basketball and did a three-hundred-sixty-degree spin. After looking every which way, he looked at me, and asked, "Where are my keys?"

I nodded toward the armoire.

"I'll be back." He squeezed by, trying to avoid touching me and bumping into the dresser. The mirror wobbled back and forth until it tilted to a stop.

I knew I needed to tighten those loose screws. "Almost broke my mirror, you must be crazy!" I shouted. "Don't you know a broken mirror means seven years of bad luck?"

He snatched his keys and mumbled on his way out. I was listening closely to make sure he didn't let the wrong words slip. He knew better. Now that he'd left, I dumped the stuff back into the drawer and stacked the records back on the night table. It figured that out of all the records, the one that broke was the only one that belonged to me. It cracked right down the middle. That was an old jam from 1986 that I hadn't heard on the radio since. I loved that song enough to listen to it over and over until I had all the lyrics written down on loose-leaf. There was probably no chance I'd ever hear it again. I slid the cracked record between my mattresses and went for those pictures.

Once I saw them, I had to sit down for a minute. They were his parents' wedding photos. I didn't even know these pictures existed. His parents looked as young as we did in our prom picture. In one, they were walking hand-in-hand through stone columns, maybe at the Cloisters. In the other, they were among some trees. Mr. Zach had his arms wrapped around Dr. Snyder's waist; his chin rested in her veil. She smiled so hard; her eyes were closed. Mr. Zach's smile was Ultrabrite white, but he left her seven years later, when Spider was a baby.

I stared at the pictures for a while, before returning them to the drawer. I still couldn't figure out what Spider was trying to imply. Whatever his logic, we were not his parents. I started feeling like maybe this relationship was nothing but a waste of my time and energy. I cried, but I accepted how he felt.

For the longest time, Spider never acknowledged that his father existed, but they had recently begun to hash out their differences. It was Mr. Zach who gave him the pictures. He told me nothing. Sometimes Spider could be eerily quiet. Because he bottled his feelings, I usually had to run him down or corner him to get him to open up. Either that or I had to wait until he was in one of his rare talkative moods. So, at first, he wouldn't tell me a thing about what he and his father discussed, but one day, he broke down. He was so upset; I overheard him talking to himself, "I hated that man all my life, because I only heard the negative things about him. Come to find out, he's actually a decent guy." A few days after that, while crossing the street on his way to work, Mr. Zach collapsed and died of an aneurysm. He was 48 years old.

After that, Spider withdrew. For weeks, he wouldn't speak at all. The most he'd do was nod or shrug. Gradually, he came around, grunting, giving me one-word answers here and there, until finally, one day, I noticed a glint in his hazel eyes. Silly me, I thought it was my constant affection that was bringing him around, and things were finally returning to normal, but that night, as I was reaching for my diaphragm, he said, "Let's make a baby."

I froze. I wanted so badly to help him feel better, and I thought I would do anything. At that moment, I realized I did have my limits. So, as hard as it was, I grabbed my diaphragm and excused myself, until I was fully protected. That was the first night.

Spider persisted every single night, "Come on. Stop playing. Let's make a baby."

After two weeks of that nonsense, I couldn't take it anymore; I broke, "No! I don't make babies with *my* last name!" I then grabbed my quilt from the foot of the bed and rolled myself in it like a burrito, thinking that would be the end of it.

But, he kept nudging me. When he said, "All right, then. I'll marry you after our baby is born," I finally sat up.

I gave Spider this Negro-you-must-think-I'm-some-kind-of-fool look.

He didn't flinch. Instead, he pulled the covers away, planting his soft lips on me. My body sank into the pillows. Lying there, in his arms, I couldn't help but respond. We were both all over each other. I lost my head until I felt my panties slide. I clamped my knees together, sat up, and opened my mouth to object. But, he pressed his finger to my lips. I looked up and saw him squinting with tears collecting in his eyelashes. Tears, just as we were about to do the nasty. I never saw that before. I started tearing up myself. He saw my tears, and he broke out into deep, deep sobs. I held him close and rubbed his back. I loved him more than life itself, but I had to stay firm. After a while, I grabbed the quilt and tried to wrap myself in it again.

He snatched it back. "Do you love me?"

I nodded.

"Do you *really* love me?"

I nodded even harder.

He pulled me close. "I'll marry you...after," he whispered. His fingers started stroking my feminine parts. My stomach knotted up. Maybe it was butterflies, but then again, it was probably nerves because my hands were trembling. His grief was taking its toll on both of us. Part of me thought maybe a baby *was* what we needed to bring some joy back, but I didn't know if I wanted to laugh, scream, or cry. I had to admit, though, Spider settled on this apartment. And I knew for certain he didn't want to. He just went along with what I wanted. Besides that, he was clearly going through something right now. So, I made a conscious decision; I nodded. I should've gotten it straight exactly what he meant by that "after" part, but right then and there, that wasn't on my mind. Spider slipped my nightgown over my head, and I went with the flow.

Tee-Bo was born on March 13, 1995. Spider's first name is Spence. I named our baby Tobiah after his grandfather. Reluctantly, but to appease Spider's mother, I also gave Tee-Bo Spider's late great uncle's middle name. I made sure the spelling was exact, even though I was afraid saddling my child with a name like Osbert could make him the brunt of jokes. But as much as I hated that middle name, it didn't bother me as much as the fact that my last name was still Love. Now, whenever I hear anyone refer to Spider as my "baby daddy," I cringe. I had it all fixed in my head that by the time I became a mother, Spider and I would have long since been married. I swore up and down that that moniker would never apply to any man of mine.

But now here I am. I've learned that I can't dictate where life will lead. I can only hypothetically say what I will and will not do. Dealing with emotions and urges is hard enough. Add a crisis to the mix. Do I follow my heart or listen to common sense? Despite all my lip action, I let go of reason. My "baby daddy" had his offspring, and I was left hanging on, waiting for him to decide to marry me, the whole time worrying if he would or if he wouldn't, wondering if I could keep this up, and if so, for how long. And just when I needed a reason to feel good about myself, my "baby daddy's" mama handed me a set of keys off her desk, smiled and said, "These are for you. Now, you can drop by whenever you'd like." *Hello!*

Now I know that key ring was not an engagement ring, but I needed something concrete to make me feel that I, Mia

23

Love, was an exception. The "baby mama" stigma didn't apply in my case, because I was the woman Spider's mother would give a set of keys to. Having Dr. Snyder's keys was something. Something was better than nothing at all. And, even though I felt like telling the world, I didn't want it to get back to Mommy. I could trust Romell, so I told him. I only told my sister Dawn because this time, she swore she'd keep her mouth shut.

3

*D*AWN WAS BORN WITH A CURLING IRON IN HER HAND. The only time she burned people was when the gossip was juicy enough to whisper. I should've known the moment I spotted the forehead scab—Mommy got her do done and her update at the same time. Thanks to my sister, Mommy heard about the keys. That's why she was on a mission.

I already knew why she believed the laundromat was nasty. Once, when I was pregnant, Mommy went to the laundromat with me. There we saw the most conspicuous fixture of my neighborhood with his strawberry birthmark over his eye and matted red hair. On any given day, he could be found parked around the corner from my building, twisting locks in his beard. Everyone avoided his side of the street. On this particular Tuesday night, Red Beard dragged his overstuffed garbage bag right into the laundromat. He then commenced to load his rags into a washer. The stench was intense. I couldn't tell if it was coming from the man's laundry or him. "C'mon, Mia," Mommy said. "Let's wait out-side."

Once we were under the streetlight, I could clearly see she had that look in her eyes that could bore holes through steel. I smiled to ease the tension. Mommy rolled her eyes. "This is ridiculous! Don't do your laundry here again! Get your own machines."

Times were hard and money was tight. Those machines had to wait. I didn't stop going to the laundromat, but I did get into the habit of thoroughly spraying the machines with disinfectant before I used them. Still, I knew there was no convincing her that Tee-Bo's rash was not caused by the laundromat. I tried to tell her that the rash appeared before I started going, that I sprayed the machines well, and I always washed his clothes in hot water, but that wouldn't make a difference. Really though, I questioned whether Mommy's tirade had anything to do with Tee-Bo's rash or the laundromat. My mother meant well, but I still wished she would take her advice back to South Cackalackie.

Mommy clearly loves Tee-Bo, even though she was so disconnected from him that she called him "the baby." She was obviously disconnected from Spider and his family; she always called him "your boyfriend," Jackie "your boyfriend's sister," and Spider's mother she called "that woman." I tried to avoid giving her any details about them, but conversations with Mommy were like quicksand, the harder I tried to wiggle my way out, the deeper I sank. I guess my being stingy with info only made matters worse. She'd wind up saying something that left a scar. That's why I shifted my attention by engaging in projects.

After she left, Tee-Bo was sleeping peacefully, so I broke out the shoe polish and started with my sling backs. Next, my leather espadrilles and gladiators. Before I knew it, I was surrounded by leather, pleather, and patent leather. The t-shirt I was dipping into a cup of water was old but served its purpose. I ran it over the loafer I'd just coated in black shoe wax, stopped, and inspected the shine. It was on the dull side. I could still see scuff marks. I knew how to fix that. I dipped a Q-tip in liquid dye and dabbed them away. Once the dye dried, I placed the shoe between my knees, wrapped my rag around my hand, and buffed like the shoeshine man outside Grand Central Station, the only person I'd ever seen put a smile on a pair of shoes. Spider couldn't put his best foot forward with scuffed loafers. I buffed until my frown reflected. At least the shine was perfect. Nothing compared to a spit shine. Technically, it wasn't spit. The thought of spitting always disgusted me. Besides, I had no projectile skills. Dribble always landed on my chin. But, whether the shoes were shined with spit or not didn't make a difference to Spider; he couldn't care less. His favorite shoes were parked right in front of me.

Spider's Hush Puppies had holes in the soles, a split across the toe crease, and the Dr. Scholl's in them had shriveled from ten years of sweat and caked up foot powder. But for some reason, Spider could not part with them. Well, I was not about to waste any polish. That was it for now. I slapped the loafer in my hand down and glanced around.

26

Most of our shoes looked brand spanking new, but I didn't feel any better, especially since I had been inhaling fumes for the past hour, and my hands and thighs were all stained from the polish. I even had that black gunk caked up under my fingernails. They were the longest they'd ever been, because I was still taking the horse pills, better known as prenatal vitamins, so I didn't appreciate that. I decided to do something better.

I put my rag down and grabbed the phone. I could talk to Romell about anything. What I loved most about him was, unlike my sister, he didn't repeat a word I said to anybody else, not even the deep stuff. So, when he picked up, I don't think I even gave him a chance to open his mouth. I said, "Can we switch mothers?"

"Dawn told her about the keys, huh," Romell laughed.

I know he thought I was stupid for telling her. Dawn's mouth was bigger than her behind. But with all my girlfriends out of state—and me with no long distance carrier—who else would I call about girl stuff? Mommy? I sucked my teeth. "Are you a psychic friend?"

"Nah, my advice is free. Next time, save yourself the trouble. Tell your mom from the get-go like I suggested."

"Whose side are you on?"

"Chocolate, when it comes to you and your family, I blow the whistle and wear the stripes. Now, hold on. I have someone on the other line." The phone line clicked twice, but the call switched back to me. Romell's voice had turned to syrup. "Yeah, Akasma. Like I was saying, I feel real bad. I really do, because you and I have a lot of fun together. But, I've got to be honest. We don't have much in common. So, I guess—"

I cut Romell off, doing my best to imitate his voice but sounding more like Cookie Monster, "It's best that we just be friends." I got a chuckle out of him, so I kept it up. "The last thing I want to do is waste your time. I'd still like us to hang out once in a while, if that's okay with you." I closed by saying, "And the Oscar goes to...."

Romell's voice was just above a whisper but it had bass— that combination could lull me right to sleep or wake me up from it. Even though I didn't sound a bit like him, I knew I had the script down cold, because he was still laughing when he said, "Trust me, Chocolate. If I ever give you something stiff, bare naked, and about that size...it won't be an Oscar. Now, knock it off. She won't buy it, unless I'm composed."

I never bought into any of his flirting. Romell and I were just friends. Actually, Romell was my closest friend. An investment banker, big and built, bald, brown, and dimpled, but he was a mess. Not only did he collect women like he did luxury timepieces, he remained unattached and had absolutely no time for "sistahs." He even had the nerve to have very specific taste. His type was blue-eyed, with big lips, hips, boobies, and black girl booty, courtesy of Stairmaster.

Romell was back on the line with me sooner than I expected. "Okay, what's the story?"

"Do you want the whole story or the abbreviated version?"

"The truth, Chocolate! Don't add any plot twists or cliffhangers. Just tell me what happened. I know how you are."

"Well, first of all, Mommy shows up here unannounced and uninvited. She doesn't even bother to say hello, right? She just pushes past me, gruntin' and complaining. 'Hmmh, you look tired. Hmmh, this place is disgustin.' And I'm tryna be nice. I'm like, 'Hi, Mommy. You look great. Would you like something to drink?' She ignores me, walking all through here like she owns the place, turning her nose up at everything."

"Okay, that's nothing new."

"Wait, let me finish. It gets better. She snatches Tee-Bo from me and starts yelling, 'He looks horrible! What kinda mother are you? You ain't doing nothin' for his rash!' And then she starts calling Spider all kinds of broke bums, while she is holding my baby. So I try to take him to put him in the room, and Mommy is snatching him from me, and we are having a tug of war with my baby. Tee-Bo is screaming at the top of his lungs. Finally, I pry him from her *vice grip*, take him back in the room, and calm him down. I come back and Mommy starts shaking me like I'm a two-year-old, pointin' to the mirror, saying 'Hmmh, look at you. You're busted! Ain't no man ever gonna marry you! I don't know why I wasted my money on your education! You ain't nothin' but a fool!' And then, she hauls off and slaps me!"

"Whoa, time out!" Romell whistled. "Chocolate, come on now. That's foul!"

"What? You think I'm lying?"

28

"I know you're lying! I'm just trying to find the nugget of truth in this gold mine of yours."

"I'm telling you the truth, Romell! Mommy slapped me right in my face!"

"No way! What did you say to her for real?"

"Nothing! I was going out of my way to be nice. All I said to her was that she looked good, and I asked her if she wanted something to drink. That's it! Mommy just went nutsy-cuckoo for no reason. I'm lucky she didn't bruise my face."

"Why don't you come over here, so I can kiss your boo boo?"

"I don't know where your lips been!"

"You and that mouth! Now, I know you said something to your mom."

"I'm sorry. I'm upset. Can't you tell I'm upset? She slapped me, Romell, and that's not all. When I told Mommy I gave Tee-Bo Spider's last name, she really went ballistic. She flipped my glass table over and almost broke it!"

"Why would his name upset her like that?"

"I promised Mommy that he would have our last name until Spider and I got married."

"Okay. So, why doesn't he?"

"Because of you! Does this sound familiar? 'I'm having a baby, and I'm naming him Tobiah Love.'"

"You can't buy love." Romell laughed. He stopped, and a few seconds later he repeated himself, "You can't. You can't buy love," and laughed even harder.

"Hello, I'm dyin' here!" Just as I said that, Tee-Bo stirred in his cradle, tightening his little fists and scrunching his diapered bottom. I peeked over; he didn't wake. Sad to say, but Tee-Bo was used to noise. Because I tended to get loud at times, he wasn't a light sleeper, but I now knew the volume was getting too loud for him. I took a breath, held it for a moment, and then continued, "Don't you get it, Romell? I'll be twenty-six years old. How would you feel if your mother barged in your apartment and slapped you up?" That made him burst out all over again. This time I understood. That thought was ridiculous. Mrs. Goodwin wouldn't smack a roach off the wall. But still, waiting for his laughter to die down, I was getting aggravated. "Are you done?"

"Okay, okay. Maybe your mom was extreme, but you know as well as I do that Miss Anne has the gift of gab. She tells it like it is. I'm sure if you think back on what she said, you'll realize she's right. Here's what you really need to do...."

I didn't hear a thing he had to say after that. I placed the receiver back in the cradle. It was the beginning of summer, but that didn't matter. I dragged the heap of boots to my side, grabbed one of my ankle boots, and slapped some polish on it. The two things in this world I never got from Romell were sex and sympathy, so I should have known better. *Gift of gab.* Mommy's gift of gab was packed with sarcasm, wrapped with an "I told you so," and tied with a string of reminders of all the shit I should've done, so I expected that from her, but Romell should've known me well enough to know this was no time to agree with her.

Spider said he was going to marry me, so he was going to marry me. I had held up my end of the bargain. I knew Spider was broke. I wasn't expecting him to go to any by-appointment-only jeweler. But I had to admit, by now he could have gone to any one of the jewelers on Fordham Road with the dookey ropes and crucifixes in the window. It wasn't like I was particular.

4

*T*HURSDAY AFTER WORK, I PICKED UP TEE-BO from Aunt Carole's. As soon as we made it home, I nursed him and played peek-a-boo, until he started yawning and rubbing his face. That was my cue. I changed him into his yellow nightgown and laid him in his cradle the way I always did, on his left side against a rolled blanket. White cotton with turquoise and hot pink stripes, it was one of those receiving blankets I had *borrowed* from the hospital's nursery. When we were discharged I tucked so many in my overnight bag that I was surprised security didn't cuff me and haul me off. Receiving blankets were expensive. Newborn babies are expensive, period. I read somewhere that it costs sixty thousand some odd dollars a year to raise a baby. I didn't even make half that. Thank God for family.

This hand-me-down cradle was oak, and if you pulled the brass pins out of the front and the back, it rocked back and forth. I kept the pins in though. Tee-Bo loved to be rocked but would spit up if I rocked him in that thing. The cradle was smaller than standard, but all five of Aunt Carole's children slept in it until they were able to roll over. Tee-Bo was nine pounds when he was born. At three months, he had put on another seven. He was outgrowing this thing. Lying in it now, he reminded me of a walnut in its shell. Even with baby shower gifts up the ying yang, he needed a crib like yesterday. I had exactly three hundred dollars to my name, only because I was saving for a washing machine.

It had been a couple of days since Mommy and I spoke. And even though I didn't see things her way at first, a thought occurred to me during one of my 2 a.m. feedings: *Why am I nursing our three-month-old with no ring on my finger?* So, I made up my mind to approach Spider about us getting married. Not because Mommy put pressure on me, either. I was too headstrong and independent for that. No, I thought for myself, just like I took care of myself and handled my own responsibilities. I didn't need anyone's help, approval, or permission to do anything. I was now deciding to speak to Spider about us getting married for the first time since before Tee-Bo was born. I usually ran topics like this by Romell first because I was interested in hearing what he had to say, but I ultimately made my own decisions. I was grown.

I knew there was a chance he was still mad at me because I had hung up on him, but Romell was never angry long. I pulled the hairpins out of my bun and let my hair loose. Two long, fuzzy braids fell down past my breasts. I unraveled them. My split ends were as rough as straw from my trying to straighten my hair myself with my blow dryer and the brush attachment. What I really needed for this bush was a rake and a hoe. I was in desperate need of a deep conditioning and hot oil treatment too, because now my scalp was itchy. Greasing it with coconut oil didn't help, I dug my fingers in, scratching from my hairline back to the nape of my neck. I scratched like there was no tomorrow. After having those hairpins stabbing me in the head all day, this felt better than sex. Now, I could think straight. I reached for the telephone and dialed. Romell picked up on the first ring and said "Hello" in his usual velvet tone.

"You know I love you, right?"

"Who doesn't? What's up, Chocolate?"

I smiled and sank into my bed. I knew Romell wasn't upset; I'm always "Mia" when he's pissed. But he did have his sideways comment. "You called to hang up on me again?"

I giggled and turned onto my side. Opposite my night table, my breast pump was calling me. It was electric. "No, I called to tell you I am going to speak to Spider about getting married. So, buy a tux."

"What for?"

"You'll either be going to my wedding or Spider's funeral."

"Tell you what, Chocolate. Let me know which one I am going to, and I'll be sure to show up in the right jeans and t-shirt."

"You know, Romell, you might like Spider if you tried to get to know him."

"Why ruin a good thing? Anyway, call me back, Mia."

Mia? Romell called me Mia, *and* he was cutting our conversation short. I knew what that usually meant. That's why I lit into him. "Romell Ulysses Goodwin!"

"What?"

"The booty can't wait?"

"What booty?"

"The booty you're rushing me off the phone for. Who is it?"

Romell laughed. "Someone who doesn't hang up on me."

"Oh, now you're a comedian? Don't make me hurt you."

"Nah, Chocolate. It ain't that kinda party. I'm just here playing chess with Jun Ko."

I looked down and poked my breasts. My bra was damp with sweat, and they felt like rocks. Yup, my milk was in again. Now that I was nursing, my bra size was a DD, and I couldn't find one in any store to save my life. I had to order from a maternity catalog, but all nursing bras must be hideous. It's in the Constitution. No lacy demi-cups, mesh underwires, or push-ups in a rainbow palette for us lactators. Just white cotton, straps, flaps, and hooks. Oh yeah, mine had criss-crossed back support—how sexy. My breasts looked like they were wrapped in gauze, but they were full. I pulled the electric breast pump out of the corner. I didn't always have boobs. I was flat as a pancake until I got pregnant. But Jun Ko was a crêpe. That's why I said, "Yeah, chess but I doubt they're Jun Ko's."

"A *game* of chess with Jun Ko. She's today's victim. Here, see for yourself," Romell said. I heard the phone fumble for a moment.

Then, I heard, "Hi, Mia!"

I rolled my eyes. It was Jun Ko's squeaky voice, all right. Even though I wasn't exactly eager to speak to her, I tried to fake it. "Hey," I said. Then, I unsnapped the flap on my bra, placed the suction cup over my nipple, and pressed the power button on and off, and then on and off again. It didn't start.

"How have you been? I haven't seen you in ages. I'd love to see the baby! When are you coming back to the spa?"

"Beats me," I walked over to the outlet and plugged in the pump.

"I improved the cream!" She was obviously proud of that.

Too bad I couldn't share her enthusiasm. I was busy propping my pillows up against the headboard. When I was done, I gave her a dry reply, "Good for you," and sat back.

"I know. I know. Now it leaves the skin *so* much softer. Why don't you come down?"

33

This time I gave her an I-don't-know moan. Hooking myself up to my pump once again, I had an idea, so I said, "*Hey*...you guys are playing chess?"

"Yeah."

"Who's winning?"

"Do you need to ask? Goodness gracious! I would love to beat him, just once!"

In the background, Romell talked trash, "Too late for prayer, Jun Ko. Move already!"

I'm no Bobby Fischer, but I once kept a table in Washington Square Park for nine whole hours, playing against the clock and every old-timer that challenged me. One by one, I left them all picking their faces off the floor. Now Romell was a sore loser and a poor winner; I'd known that ever since we were kids. When he won, he would gloat until he plucked your last nerve. When he lost, on the other hand, his pouting was intolerable. And when he didn't pout, he'd flip the chessboard over. Romell was deluded—a chess master by default because I used to let him win, until I stopped playing him altogether. I jumped at the chance to let Jun Ko see that other side of him. "Pin his queen," I said.

"Huh?"

Pulling the breast pump closer, I switched the power on and watched my milk swirl through the tube and spray into the bottle. Manual pumps suck big time! At least mine did. There were parts missing. It was a nightmare ordering them. And when they finally came, the thing still didn't work. I'd squeeze that bulb for so long; my arms would cramp, and all I'd get would be a whopping ounce or two. A hospital-grade breast pump costs an arm and a leg to rent, but it was well worth it. They're sterile, easy to use, easy to clean, and I could hold a conversation while I filled my bottles. "Pin his queen with your rook," I explained, "Romell always plays the same game. He relies too heavily on his queen. Eliminate his queen; you can put that king in check, and use your knight to mate him."

"Wow! I didn't even think of that! I'll definitely give it a try. Now, Mia, you have to come back to my spa. Mani's, pedi's, and facials are on the house. Come on! Tell me when."

"I don't know."

"I won't take no for an answer."

I pulled the phone away from my ear, stared at it, and

rolled my eyes. Then, I answered, "Maybe next week."

"Great! I'll see you then. Here's Romell." She passed the phone back.

"Chocolate, when you find out what to do for Tee-Bo's rash, let me know."

"Why?"

"I have a rash on my chest, and I've wasted time with two dermatologists so far."

"Okay, will do." I said. I glanced at the mirror and couldn't help but sigh. "Romell, am I difficult?"

"That's a trick question."

I sucked my teeth. "Well, I don't think I'm difficult. All I ask for is love and respect. Any man would be lucky to marry me. Right?"

"Absolutely. Chocolate, I don't mean to be rude, but I do have company. Let me get back to this chess game, and I'll—"

"Romell," I interrupted. "I know you can't go into this now, but just answer me yes or no. Is Jun Ko gay?"

"Why is that relevant?"

"Because she keeps offering freebies, and when she gave me a pedicure, she insisted on rubbing me down with her cream. I admit it did leave my skin feeling like butter for days, but the massages are a *little* extra. Have you ever seen her with a man?"

"No."

"Well, I don't want that Japanese lady massaging me if she's just tryna feel me up. And, if she is straight, why doesn't she find herself a man? So, tell me. Is she straight or gay?"

"Bye, Chocolate."

"What! She's bisexual?"

"Good-bye, Mia!"

Romell met Jun Ko at Georgetown and stayed in touch after they graduated. I would say they'd been friends for five years. I used to think all Asian women were beautiful, with satin hair and porcelain skin, but Jun Ko was a troll. The roots of her hair were black. The rest was fried and dyed fuchsia, probably to match that bad case of adult acne that made her face look like strawberry oatmeal. But Romell, not only was he a fine, dark coffee-colored brother, he lived in a luxury high-rise in Midtown Manhattan. His car—even though he rarely drove it—was a black Jaguar XJ series convertible. And Romell held everyone and everything to these standards. Once he came into money, he made up his mind. He said to me, "I'm not wasting my time with anyone, unless something about her knocks my socks off." Ever since, the brother stayed barefoot. Aside from the fact that none of them were black, they were all flawless, exotic women, but to Romell, they were still just booty. Ergo my concern: Jun Ko was so far from flawless—why would he even spend time with her? Romell claimed they were "just friends." But, if that was the case, how was *she* knocking his socks off, if she wasn't knocking his boots? Why was *she* so eager to spend time with him? And why was *she* being so nice to me?

Jun Ko had invited me to the grand opening of Full Moon this past January. I walked in and saw the manicure stations to the left and to the right rows of black leather massage chairs with pink sinks at the base. I was seven months pregnant, my back was killing me, and my toes were nearly frostbitten. So, even though I was going to slip two pairs of thermal socks and my fur-lined boots back on my feet, I opted for the pedicure. Jun Ko said, "Take everything off your feet, and roll your pant legs up to your thighs."

Right then, I became suspicious, but I did as she ordered, saying, "Thanks, Jun Ko. You're the only Jun Ko I know. That name's so unusual. It must mean something." I sat in the massage chair.

Jun Ko nodded. "It does," she said and pushed the sleeves of her hot pink turtleneck up past her elbows. Then she hiked up her gray miniskirt and sat on a stool. After she filled the basin and added some blue antiseptic, she submerged my feet in that warm, soapy water. My whole body relaxed. Jun Ko pulled out one foot at a time, scrubbing with a pumice stone. She clipped, cleaned, and buffed my nails. And then she put them back in to soak and went over to what looked like a microwave. She came back with two steaming hot towels and wrapped them around my legs all the way up to the thigh, while my feet were perched on the edge of the tub. She left again and returned with a vat of green cream. She scooped out a handful, removed the towels and slathered this cream over my legs. She was rubbing in circles at first, but then she started squeezing and running her knuckles up my shins. She grabbed my foot and started working the inside of my arch down into the heel with her thumbs. While she was rubbing, I noticed I was feeling a little tingly. I thought it was because the water was kind of hot and the rest of me was still cold, or maybe because I was pregnant, my hormones were raging, and sex with Spider at that point was a distant thought, but on the wall to my left, there was a reflexology chart. I realized the part of my foot that she was rubbing, the center of my heel, was actually the point that connected to the genitals. It was obvious to me that she was taking the customer satisfaction thing a bit too far. So I excused myself, donned some brown paper slippers, and off I went to the back of the spa.

Near the ladies' room was a series of booths. None of the bamboo screens were pulled all the way, and all but two on my left were empty. In one, a heavyset redhead lay on the table, naked and facedown, with a sheet covering her behind. In the booth right before the ladies' room, there was a girl about my age with her legs cocked open, and a woman in a smock was smearing goop on her crotch with what looked like a tongue depressor.

I slipped into the ladies room. When I came back, Jun Ko started all over again, squeezing my toes between her fingers, and pulling them out individually. When she reached my calves, she said, "Ooh, tight," and started bopping them with the sides of her fist. Now, during my pregnancy, whenever I stretched in my sleep, I'd get a charley horse. My toes would spread out, my whole leg would lock, and I couldn't move a muscle until it passed. So, I'd try to combat that by consciously avoiding stretching out in my sleep, but then I'd wake with a knot in my calf that would ache for about a week. With Jun Ko massaging my calf muscle, I couldn't help but point and flex my foot, because that muscle was so sore. She looked up at me, batting her fuchsia, false eyelashes. "You feel good, don't you? Do you want a full body?"

That was my "aha" moment. "No thanks. I'm kinda in a hurry. Can you polish my toes now, please?" I grabbed the caramel colored polish off the station, shook it until I heard the bead rattle, and handed it to her. We were *not* going to become that familiar if I could help it.

She unscrewed the bottle and stroked my big toe with a dot of color. "Pure child," she said, and I thought she was referring to my unborn baby until she added, "*Jun* means pure.

Ko means child. My name means 'pure child' in Japanese."

After that day at the spa, I stopped making fun of her name. It's pronounced like *Junk-o.* As unsavory as that sounded, the meaning stuck with me. I was still sure she was gay; she had to be because she'd known Romell for years. She gave me a massage that made *me* feel a little conflicted. If Romell ever had one of her massages, without a doubt, he would've started sleeping with her, and that would've been obvious. Gay or straight, as far as I was concerned, Jun Ko was an unwelcome addition to our two-member club. I tolerated her for two reasons. One, she was his "friend." Never once did I notice Romell do that lip-licking thing he does when he checks women out. Jun Ko simply wasn't cute enough to catch his attention that way. And two, she was always nice to me. I still made faces behind her back, though. Every time Romell caught me, he called me petty. I didn't care; I was entitled.

Romell and I were friends forever. We grew up together. He and his mother had lived two floors below us in the same projects for years. We were almost family. Mrs. Goodwin was the missionary at our church, and we all went with her many Sundays. His mother was also my babysitter until we started kindergarten. Romell and I went to all the same schools. Even in high school, we were always in the same classes. He was a genius from birth; I was naturally competitive. Every time he did better, I did better, only because I refused to be outdone. We actually brought out the best in each other, and because of that, both of us remained at the top of the class until tenth grade.

Then, along came my fine freak of nature. Spider was modest, too, like he'd never seen a mirror. Romell thought of himself as the sun and all the rest of us as planets—*cocky.* Romell's arrogance was a problem from the moment he and Spider met.

♥　♥　♥　♥

The day I introduced them, I told Spider to wait in front of his homeroom because I wanted him to meet my "best friend in the whole wide world." I snatched Romell out of Geometry class and prepped him all the way there.

"I want you to meet that guy I was telling you about. He is *so* gorgeous."

"Enough, Chocolate. You told me that fifty times."

"I'm sorry. I just can't help it. He is just *that* gorgeous. He's light-skinned and—"

"Yeah. Yeah. Curly hair. Just for the record, I'm getting real sick of hearing that, too!"

"He's sweet, Romell. He's so sweet. So, you be nice!"

"You ain't got to tell me, Mia!"

Romell and I walked up to Spider, and I introduced them. I was grinning from ear to ear. Spider was such a sweet guy; I was sure Romell would be just as taken by him as I was.

Spider smiled, extending his hand. "I was expecting a girl, but nice to meet you."

Romell looked Spider over from head to toe and back again. He folded his arms, screwing his face up. Then he cocked his Jheri Curl to the side and snapped it back, dismissing Spider with the *fuck you* nod. "I'll catch you later, Mia," he said, and I watched Romell spin off on his British Walkers.

"What's that all about? Something going on between you two?" Spider asked.

"Not at all," I answered, smiling now because I was embarrassed. "Not at all."

♥ ♥ ♥ ♥

I later got Romell to apologize and arranged a "do-over," but after that, Spider wouldn't cooperate. There had been tension between them ever since. Romell never called me at home, and I only called him when Spider wasn't around. By keeping them separate, I kept myself sane.

Being with Spider was never easy though. I'd seen way too many pretty girls walk right into walls just to get an eyeful. Forget his hair, eyes, and complexion. Spider's smile alone was enough to make me forget my own damn name. So, once I had him, I was not letting go. I promised myself that no one would ever love him better. I would be his everything, even if it took all my energy. Romell didn't like that too much. He was always hootin' and hollerin' that I gave Spider too much attention. Maybe I did. Maybe Romell was right all along. Just this morning, after I ironed Spider's clothes and packed his lunch, I woke him up. He jumped in the shower and called for me to bring him soap, a washcloth, and a towel. I spoiled Spider. Now it was time for him to reciprocate and spoil me.

5

*I*T WAS ELEVEN THIRTY-TWO AT NIGHT. SPIDER still wasn't home. Beside his clock, five four-ounce bottles of breast milk lined my night table. I collected the bottles and stacked them neatly in the freezer. Completely topless when I returned to my bed, I flipped my pillows to the cold side. As hot as it was, I had to strip off that cotton contraption. Unlike the cool days that made it comfortable earlier in the week, today's high heat sweltered long after sunset. Sweat beaded on my forehead. Before the night was over, I just knew I'd be a puddle in the middle of my apple green sheets.

We braved two summers in our apartment with no AC by keeping the windows open, the lights switched off, and the fan on high, so I turned it up a notch. That gust of air tickled my face, but when I heard Tee-Bo sneeze, I changed it back and immediately felt for his temperature. He felt cool, even when I brought my lips to his forehead. Babies were hard to judge. No matter how hot it was, Tee-Bo always seemed cold. Even on a day like today, I turned the fan up, and he sneezed. So I kept a gown on him. Better safe than sorry.

With the fan on low, I was melting. Still, my moist skin tingled from the light breeze. I sat on Spider's side of the bed, listening to the fan's motor. It hummed over the noise from the street's traffic and the rhythm of salsa from the stoop below. By now, I was probably wearing a trail from the bed to the window, but I didn't even care. Once again, I shielded myself with one of the pillows, pulled the curtain aside, and leaned out of the window. Spider was nowhere to be seen. But there was that Afro with the silver sideburns. Our superintendent, Rafael, sat with a radio in his lap. Banging a conga on the arm of his beach chair, he sang in Spanish. The melody was so catchy; I wished I understood more than the word "*cho-co-la-te.*" I rocked in the window, until Spider's

41

voice from behind scared me so bad, I almost leaped out.

"Put some clothes on!"

I bumped my head, jumping back inside. I turned with the pillow pressed in front of me, and everyone in the building across the street had a full view of my bare back and ninety-nine-cent-store panties.

Spider clicked on the light and tossed his keys on the dresser, knocking over his cluster of cologne bottles. He didn't pick them back up, or even look at Tee-Bo as he dragged past his cradle, positioned himself at the foot of our bed, and collapsed as if he were shot. I walked over. He stared straight ahead like a corpse, so I had to ask, "Long day?"

He groaned as if speaking were painful.

He was usually tired when he came in. But, when he was dead-dog tired—like now—it was time to do a spot check. I straddled him, leaned down, and rubbed my cheek against his. "Stop, I had a long day," he said.

Gathering his purple t-shirt up to his armpits, I ran my nose along both sides of his neck. He smelled musty with only a hint of his *Obsession* cologne. I brushed the hairs on his chest with the backs of my hands and then walked my fingers down his cobblestones right to his navel. He grabbed my wrist. "Not now. I'm exhausted."

I twisted out of his grasp, unzipped his khakis, and slowly rolled him out, for the taste test. I could pretty much tell what he did during the course of his day by his flavor. He tasted like he needed a shower, but I was satisfied. As far as he knew, I was just kinky.

"Stop playing. Don't you understand? I don't even feel like moving. And it's too hot for you to be all up on me!" He twisted his body, until I slid off onto the mattress.

In the center of the dresser, between the bottle of baby wash and the bottle of baby lotion, sat a bottle of baby oil that was brand-new, never been touched. Rubbing Spider's belly, I said, "You know what I wanna try?"

He stuffed his limp penis inside his boxers and zipped himself up.

I was so sick of him. My gynecologist's exact words were that we could "resume normal sexual activity six weeks postpartum." Well, I was hoping for better than normal. It was thirteen weeks and hello, we'd only done it twice. He was always too tired or on his way somewhere else, so I had to wait until Saturday, because theoretically, he could sleep late on Sunday. But guess what? That wasn't convenient for me. Saturdays I did my running around, and I always did my grocery shopping first thing Sunday morning because that was double coupon day. Now that I was nursing, my nipples were supersensitive. I'd get excited every time something rubbed up against them, including my own blouse. It was like I was one big hormone all the time, and Spider wouldn't do a thing about it, which was unfair to me, especially since he wouldn't even touch me for the second and third trimester of my pregnancy. Why did I make him take me to that sonogram appointment? Spider seeing Tee-Bo's head and heartbeat on that black and white monitor meant the end of my prenatal sex life. That was my fifth month. So, count it off: six, seven, eight, nine, and Tee-Bo was one, two, three months old—that was seven months! And we only had sex twice, and one of those times didn't count because I was asleep. Right now, feeling the urge riding up through me, I was fanning my leg, having seedy thoughts about baby oil. I looked back at Spider. He was still staring up at the ceiling, not even the slightest bit interested in me or my fanning leg. I took a deep breath and shook my head. "Never mind, I'll wait until Saturday."

I piled some pillows next to him. Then, I pulled my bedtime braids back behind my shoulders, dug my elbows in, and just admired his face. I could tell he'd gotten some sun, because his smooth skin glowed. I brushed my lips across his strong jaw to his chin. He almost had a cleft. His jaw and chin were rugged, but not his lips. They were supple, didn't have a wrinkle or crease in them whatsoever. I ran my index finger across his bottom lip. He flinched. The corners of his mouth turned down in a frown, naturally. Other than that, his lips were...amazing, and even now, I still couldn't help but trace their shape.

He knocked my hand away. "Will you quit? You know that annoys the hell out of me! And stop staring at me like that!"

"Fine." I rolled onto my back. "When did you find your keys?"

"I copied yours."

"Spider, that's the third set!"

"My keys are in the office somewhere. They'll turn up."

"That's what you said last time. But anyway, how was your day?" I rested my head on his shoulder and wrapped my arm around the trunk of his body.

"Don't ask. This intern shit is some bullshit!"

"Spider, it couldn't have been *that* bad; you hang with celebs."

"I'm a go-fer! What do you know? You sit at a desk all day." He pushed me off and sat on the dresser. Then, he stared down, shaking his head.

"Spider, I'm sorry, but your job seems like fun to me."

"Fun? Mia, I do food runs for everyone else and I'm bringing in bologna sandwiches and a thermos of lemonade! That ain't fun!"

"Shhh!" I looked over; Tee-Bo was still asleep. Spider's voice was already Tone Loc deep. Why was he getting loud? Now, I admit my sandwiches weren't Blimpie's, but I did try. They were made with shredded lettuce, tomatoes, Muenster, and a sauce I made myself. I put my heart into those sandwiches. I mumbled, "And hello, those are Kaiser Rolls, *not* sliced bread. Dissin' *my* sandwiches."

He didn't hear me. He was too busy venting, "I spent most of my day copying stacks of reports and running to Dean & DeLuca for refreshments for the big directors' meeting. Do you see this?" He had McDonald's napkins rubber-banded to four of his fingers. He pulled them off and held out his palms. Dried blood stained his fingertips. "I have nine paper cuts...nine! And this one's from a FedEx envelope!" He flipped his hands and pointed to each and every one, but all I could think was, *I can't believe this ungrateful Negro just dissed my sandwiches.* Still, he went on, "I had to go to this dealer in Hell's Kitchen picking up whips for Butter's spread in *Honey.* Back and forth, back and forth, back and—"

"Hold up. You went to the kitchen for butter and honey. What's so bad about that?"

"I hate being teased!"

"Teased?" All I could think was, *first he dissed my sandwiches. Now, he's acting like I'm depriving him.* I screamed, "Honey's in the cabinet, and butter's in the fridge!"

"What? You lost me," he said.

"Why was that such hell for you? We've got whipped cream, too! And margarine!"

Spider shook his head, like he was trying to rattle his

brain. "Who said anything about margarine?"

"You did! Margarine! Oh, excuse me, you said 'butter spread,' since you wanna get technical!"

He looked at me. Then, his eyes rolled back and he laughed as if I tickled him. "No, Mia, not margarine. Butter. Not the kind that goes on bread, either; Butter's a person."

"What woman would name her child Butter?"

"I think his real name is Bernard, Bernard Burnett, but we all call him Butter. He's a video director. He's also a photographer and art director. Butter is doing a spread."

"What's that?"

"A photo layout for *Honey.* That's a project a writer friend of his is trying to develop into a magazine. The label is financing a test issue to use as a marketing tool."

"Oh," I said. "So why did he need whipped cream from the kitchen?"

"No, Mia. No. Not whipped cream. Whips," he said slowly, as if he were speaking to an imbecile, and he was making sign-language-like hand gestures. "You know...cars. I went to Hell's Kitchen, the far west side of Midtown, to pick up...cars."

What nerve! Every day, I'd ask him about his day, and every day he'd answer me. Since he started working at this label, it seemed as if he was speaking a different language. The entertainment industry was like a separate culture. Some days I didn't understand a thing he said. Sometimes I asked him to clarify, other times I nodded even though I didn't know what he was talking about because his condescending tone irritated the mess out of me. I used to be *his* tutor. How dare he try to make me feel stupid? I'd never heard of Hell's Kitchen, but I knew one thing. If he kept this up, I was going to give him hell in the bedroom. I rolled my eyes. "What cars?"

"A Bentley, a Rolls, and a Ferrari."

"What's so bad about that?" And then, I thought about it. "Oh, you dirty dog!"

"What's wrong with you, now?"

"You wish that Ferrari were yours because of all the attention from women?"

"No, Mia. No, no, no. Women are everywhere, and I don't need no Ferrari to get one, but I don't wanna drive the damn car if all I have in my pocket is bus fare. I'm tired of everybody around me eatin', when I'm starving!" He peeled his sweaty,

45

Howard U t-shirt off and threw it in the corner. Then he looked at me. "Did you ever type that?"

"No, not yet."

"I asked you to do that way before Tee-Bo was born. Why not?"

"Manual typewriter! No Correcto-type! Hello! Résumés have to be perfect. No mistakes. No whiteouts."

"Type it at work!"

"I keep telling you. Our computers only run collection software. My boss is the only one who has Word, and he locks his door. And your mother locks hers away, too."

"I really want human resources to have it on file. What if I got a computer?"

"With what money?"

"You know what? Forget it! Forget I ever asked!" His eyes rolled away and stared out the window.

Now, I felt bad. "No, I'm sorry. I didn't say I wouldn't type it. I will. I just haven't had time, Spider."

He faced me with his head tilted back and eyebrow raised. I hate that. When he looked at me like that, it made me feel like shit, even when I was right.

"That's interesting," Spider said. "You made time for Jackie when you typed *her* résumé. You made time for Dawn when you typed her complaint letter, and I don't know what you typed for Romell, but just the other week I saw you staple at least ten pages together for him."

"Whatchu tryna say?"

"I'm tryna do this for us!"

"Shhh!"

He took a deep breath and lowered his voice. "Joe Mason is the director of A & R, and he's leaving. I want them to have my résumé! Okay? Now, put one together for me, *please!*"

"Do you honestly believe they're going to promote you to head of A & R?"

"I'll have to work my way up, but yes, I do believe I *will* get what I want eventually."

Spider sounded so sure about that, and here I was so unsure about us. Feeling a twinge of sadness, I sighed, but I knew exactly how I was going to change the topic of this discussion. "Do you think the same is possible for me?"

"What?"

"That I'll get what I want...eventually?"

"When we believe, anything's possible. Why?"

"Because, Spider. I want to get married."

6

*S*PIDER DIDN'T SAY A WORD. INSTEAD, HE EASED over to the cradle. He looked down at Tee-Bo and I looked up at him. "Did you hear me?"

"I heard you," he said. Reaching into the cradle, he lifted Tee-Bo into his arms. The bedroom door squeaked as he made his way out of the room.

"I thought you said you were tired!" I scooted down to the foot of the bed, took a few seconds to allow my feet to search for my slippers, but then hurried into the living room without them. Spider sat on the radiator in front of the cracked window. But for the table lamp near him, the room was dim. The fern, suspended from the ceiling, dangled just above his head as he stared down at Tee-Bo. I stepped around the chaise, hand on my hip. "When will we get married?"

Still looking down, he shrugged.

I took a deep breath and stiffened my lip. "*Will* we get married?"

"Eventually."

My lips grew tight. I felt hot, angry tears welling up. At first, I stared at the ceiling, trying to fight them. They were ready to fall, but I looked back at Spider. When he looked up from Tee-Bo, I searched his eyes, "You said we were getting married after he was born!"

"I know."

"Then, what's the holdup?"

He shrugged again. "We have issues."

I folded my arms to keep from shaking. "What issues?"

"One: You know my job situation. I just got out of school. I am an intern. A man who can't provide for his family is less than a man. If I am going to be your husband, I have to step up to the plate and be the breadwinner. I am not in a position to do that right now. Two: What I absolutely can't stand is that you put everyone else ahead of me. I have to wait forever for you to do me a simple favor, and frankly, I'm tired of being last on your list."

"You are at the top of my list, Spider!"

"If I am, Romell is first, and that's another issue."

My jaw dropped, but I took a deep breath. Then I narrowed my eyes. "We had these same so-called issues before I got pregnant, right?"

"Yeah," he said.

"These issues didn't stop you then, right?"

"Right."

"So, why should they stop you now?"

"You don't wanna end up like your mother, do you?"

I placed both hands on my hips. "What did you say?"

"Do you wanna end up like your mother?"

Mommy had four husbands and never reached the first anniversary with any of them. Spider knew how much that bothered me. "Don't you dare throw that in my face!"

"Okay. I'll put it another way. If I do this marriage thing, I am only gonna do it once, and I'm gonna do it right, even if I have to take my time. I'm not gonna end up like my parents. My Moms and my Pops, they had that piece of paper; it don't mean a thing. My Pops and Lola had love. It's not about the promises you make; it's about the promises you keep. Love is not what you say. Love is what you do."

For a moment, I just stared at him. He didn't want to end up like his parents; I could identify. Dr. Snyder and Mr. Zach remained legally married, but had only lived in the same household for the first seven years. Mr. Zach wasn't married to Lola, but he lived with her until the day he died, nearly twenty-three years. Granted, given those circumstances, I could completely understand how Spider could be a bit of a commitment-phobe. But, why should we carry his parents' baggage? "This is *our* relationship," I responded. "Let that shit go."

He stared back at me. No comment.

I didn't know what else to say. And since there was no need for a staring match, I walked into the kitchen, poured some grape juice, and drank it. I washed my glass and put it away. Considering the fact that both our mothers spent most of their adult lives without a man, I couldn't figure out why Spider was giving me such a hard time. When I returned to the living room, he was looking down at Tee-Bo, who was now awake. He lifted Tee-Bo's leg, examined his feet and then his hands.

"I just clipped his nails yesterday," I snapped.

Spider unbuttoned Tee-Bo's gown and rubbed some of the white powder off of his chest with his thumb. He looked at it closely, then brought it to his nose and sniffed. So I explained, "That's cornstarch, Spider. It's supposed to help the rash."

He then held Tee-Bo's face between his thumb and index finger. He moved his head from side to side, looking more closely. "Are you paying attention to this rash?"

"Um, yeah."

"It's spreading."

"I know. He broke out on the side of his face a few days ago."

"Mia, this rash is all over his face."

"No, it isn't," I said. I knew I was tired when I picked Tee-Bo up from Aunt Carole's, but I'd had him for hours. Something like that, I was almost sure, I would have noticed. I rushed over to take a closer look and stared in disbelief. Sure enough, red tiny bumps had started to appear on the other side of Tee-Bo's face, too.

"You see?" Spider said. "It's probably that flour you rolled him in."

"That's cornstarch! Aunt Carole told me it would help clear the rash."

He shifted Tee-Bo in his arms and raised one eyebrow.

"Aunt Carole raised ten kids, Spider. She knows what she's doing."

"My mother's a doctor!"

"She's not a dermatologist!"

In one quick motion, I scooped Tee-Bo out of Spider's arms and held him to my shoulder. Spider jumped up, banging his head on the flowerpot. Without even turning around, I walked into the bedroom and reached for the phone. It was almost midnight. Office hours were over, and the pediatrician's service answered, "What is your message?"

"My son, Tobiah Snyder, is a patient of Dr. Rosenberg's. She's been treating him for a rash, but it's spreading. Please have her call me."

Spider walked into the bedroom with a Ziploc bag full of ice cubes pressed to the top of his head. As loud as it sounded when he hit that flowerpot, I was surprised he didn't have a nosebleed. He crawled onto the bed and turned to me, waiting for me to finish the call.

I hung up. "Dr. Rosenberg should be calling back any minute now."

He sat his "ice pack" on the night table. "Mia, you need to stop being so stubborn."

"I don't have a stubborn bone in my body."

"I'm going to pretend I didn't hear that." He reached over and rubbed Tee-Bo's hair. "Did you lay him on his right side?"

"No, on his left. Why?"

"When I picked him up, he was on his right," he said.

Realizing Tee-Bo must've rolled over, I sighed, "He needs a crib."

Spider looked away, nodding. I stared at him for a while, but he said nothing, so I took a good look at Tee-Bo's rash in the brighter light. It was all over his forehead, his chin, his cheeks, and in the folds of his skin. His scalp, ears, and his eyelids were the only places he didn't have bumps. They were not drying out at all. I reached into my nightstand, pulled out Tee-Bo's skin cream, and squeezed some onto my index finger. For something that didn't work, it smelled horrible and felt greasy and grainy on my fingertips. I applied it to his right cheek. Tee-Bo, feeling the rubbing against his cheek, jerked his head from side to side in search of my nipple. I held him close to my breast and made myself comfortable. Tee-Bo was nursing from the other breast by the time Dr. Rosenberg called back.

"Hello, Miss Love. You say the rash is spreading?"

"Yes, I've been using the cream, but it hasn't helped."

"Okay, I'll have to schedule another appointment. My associate is a pediatric dermatologist. He is in my office every two weeks. But..."

"Can I *please* get an appointment?"

"I'm sorry. He's booked solid until August."

"Can you squeeze me in?"

"No, sorry," she said. She paused for a moment and then said, "Wait. I do see an opening for tomorrow morning. Is that okay?"

"Tomorrow? No, but I'll take it."

"Okay, Miss Love. I'll pencil you in for this Friday, June 23rd, at 9:30."

"Thank you, Dr. Rosenberg." I hung up and shook my head. That appointment was a problem, but I had to take it. I was supposed to be at Dr. Snyder's that same morning, and there was no way I could be in two places at once. Dr. Snyder asked me over two weeks ago, and she kept reminding me. I sat there, trying to figure out what to do.

"What's wrong?" Spider said.

"Doctor Rosenberg could only give me an appointment for tomorrow. I don't know if I'll be able to take him."

"Aren't you off tomorrow?"

I took a deep breath. "Yes."

"So, what's the problem?"

"I told your mother I would sign for her package tomorrow."

He cut his eye at me. "What's more important? That package or Tee-Bo?"

"Tee-Bo!"

"All right, then. You know what you gotta do."

"Your mother is away at a convention. She will have a fit! Can *you* take Tee-Bo?"

"No."

"Can you sign for your mother's package, at least?"

Spider shook his head. "Tomorrow I have to set up for an album release."

"So, what am I supposed to do?"

"Learn how to say no!" Spider took a deep breath. "Just page my mother, and let her know you can't make it."

"I'll call her, but when she calls back, you talk to her."

He shook his head again. "We're not speaking."

"Why not?"

"Because I wanna know something, and she won't tell me."

That reply was vague, but I decided not to pry. "Okay then, I'll talk to her. But what if she can't find anyone else?"

He shrugged. "That's her problem."

"What if this is something important?"

"That's still her problem. Let *her* worry about that."

7

*I*T WAS WAY TOO LATE, BUT I PAGED DR. SNYDER. When the phone rang, my stomach started bubbling. I reached over and answered. It was her.

"Make it fast. I have a speech to memorize."

"Sorry, I just wanted to let you know, I won't be able to sign for your package."

"What?"

"Tee-Bo has an appointment with a dermatologist. Maybe Jackie could."

"I didn't ask her; I asked you! You mean to tell me you couldn't schedule this appointment for some other time?" She was screaming in my ear. Spider had to hear her from his side of the bed. I had given her my word and confirmed, so I completely understood why she asked, "When did you schedule this appointment?"

I hesitated, "About twenty minutes ago."

"Mia, my colleagues pay an awful lot to hear me speak, and they come from all over the world. You may not understand what that means, but believe me. I cannot risk my reputation depending on fickle people!"

Fickle? I looked over to my right. Beside me, Tee-Bo was sleeping peacefully. Spider stepped out of the bed and walked over to the fan. He turned the knob until it was so high the breeze blew the curtain horizontal. When he returned, he reclined and clasped his hands behind his head. Then, he crossed his ankles and shut his eyes. He looked comfortable, too comfortable. I sucked my teeth. "Dr. Snyder, I am not fickle," I said. "I had every intention of being there, but Tee-Bo..." I looked at Tee-Bo, lying on his stomach between Spider and me, sleeping peacefully, taking quick baby breaths. I sighed, "...his rash is getting worse." She was Tee-Bo's grandmother. I figured she would understand that.

"Is that the same rash you kept applying zinc oxide to,

weeks after I told you it wasn't diaper rash?" she said.

"Yes," I answered.

"The same rash you were smearing mometasone furoate on, even though I told you it wasn't eczema; it looked more like contact dermatitis?"

"Yes." I could feel myself getting irritated. Dr. Snyder was neither a pediatrician nor a dermatologist. She was an orthopedist, and she was not Tee-Bo's doctor.

"You should have done something about that rash a long time ago. Now, because you waited until the last minute, you've put me in a bind. Do you know where I am right now, Mia?"

"Yes, you're at the Scoliosis Research Convention."

"Do you know *where* that convention is being held?"

"No."

"Seattle! I am in Seattle!"

"Well, what do you want me to do?" I snapped.

"Don't trouble yourself!" Dr. Snyder hung up. I pulled the receiver from my face and stared at it with my mouth open. Then, I placed the phone back in the cradle. It rang immediately. I picked it up, and Dr. Snyder was back on the line. "Since you can't make it Friday, be there Saturday morning just in case they redeliver."

"Oh! Now, you need me."

"I need your help, not your attitude. Can I count on you or not?"

"Yes."

"Are you sure?"

"What do you need me to do, Dr. Snyder?"

"Sign for my letters."

"Letters?"

"Yes, letters! They're coming by Certified Mail."

I had to scratch my head on this one. Dr. Snyder only got this excited when she was expecting the surgical tools she special-ordered from some company in Santa Barbara. She was never home when they delivered them, though. Once it was an Osteon drill, another time it was an arthroscopic shaver, and about a month ago, it was #11 blades. The way she was carrying on, the last thing I expected was some measly envelopes. Had I known, I would not have put up with all this aggravation.

Dr. Snyder continued, "If they come, put them..."

"I know. I know. On top of the desk in the mail sorter."

"No. Sign for them and slide them under my bedroom door."

"Under your door? You usually..."

"Quiet! Spence is not in the room with you, is he?"

"Of course he is."

"Then don't say another word. Just sign and slide them *under* my door. Don't forget, and don't do anything else."

"Okay," I said. I hung up.

Anytime Dr. Snyder asked me to do something for her, I went out of my way to do it. There were plenty of other things I could do on my day off besides sit up in that brick oven and wait around. For two whole years, I used sick-time and vacation time to housesit while her contractors renovated, and the first time I have a problem doing something she gets stank? I always treated Dr. Snyder with respect. But if she spoke to me that way again, I didn't know if I could be polite. I shook my head. Then I looked at Spider, lying there like the poster boy for some mattress ad. That pissed me off even more. Now, I think "yo mama jokes" are ignorant, but I was ready to tell Spider about his. "Do you know what your mother said?"

"I don't wanna hear it," he said quickly.

I took a deep breath and started again. "Your mother had the nerve to call me fickle when I'm the one doing her a..."

"Didn't you hear me? I know she said her piece, but it's as simple as this: My Moms did what she had to do to take care of *her* children. Now, *we* gotta do what we gotta do to take care of our children."

I was not going to let Spider slip that one in and get away with it. He was not going to turn me into some kind of baby factory when I had yet to see a ring. "Excuse you!" I said, ready to give him a cussing that would have made my sister proud.

"I meant child," Spider said in the same tone.

I calmed down. "You said children."

"All right, then. Children."

I looked at him like he had three heads.

He sighed. "Mia, I'm not running away if that's what you think. We *will* get married, eventually. There are just a few things that have to be taken care of before we do."

I felt drained. It was late, and Dr. Snyder had worn me out. I didn't have any energy left to argue, so I reached up for the cord and switched off the light. "Fine, Spider. Now, turn down the fan. That's too much air on Tee-Bo," I said with a yawn.

"No, it's hot as hell up in here. You need to put him back in the cradle."

"*We* need to buy him a crib. He's sleeping with us until we do." After saying that, I climbed out of bed, over to the fan, and set it back to low.

8

IRST THING SATURDAY, DAWN WAS WAITING IN front of my building with the engine running. It made no sense for me to drag heavy laundry on the train, so I called my sister and asked her to drop me off at Dr. Snyder's on her way to the salon. With Tee-Bo strapped to me in his harness and a diaper bag across my shoulder, I carried the canvas bag up to her black Accord. Dawn didn't get out to help. Instead, she pulled her silver baseball cap further down on her head and popped the trunk. She remained in the driver's seat while I stuffed the laundry bag inside. I slammed the trunk shut, slid into the front seat, and slammed that door, too.

"What the hell is wrong with you?" Dawn asked.

"Nothing. Why?"

"Then what's wrong with your face?"

I patted Tee-Bo's bottom. "Oh, I'm just tired. Tee-Bo was in the bed with us the last couple of nights. I couldn't sleep at all. I was too afraid one of us was going to roll over on him."

"You look tired, but you look more like you're ready to kill somebody."

Tee-Bo's doctor's appointment came and went, and I was still pissed at Dr. Snyder for barking at me and at Spider for not intervening.

I chuckled. "That depends."

"On what?"

"How many years I'd get for wiping out a whole family?"

"When you're ready to take out Spider's crazy sister, I'll be your accomplice." Dawn laughed.

Dawn flipped her visor down and opened her vanity mirror. She had a mouth like a sewer, but the truth was she was too pretty to fight. I watched her seal her lips, blotting black lipstick. It was hideous, black and matte. Beneath the

59

bill of her silver cap, she had silver shadow on her eyelids. Dawn's facial features were like Naomi's, but she was pecan tan like Tyra. In my opinion, that wasn't enough to pull this off. "Android diva" was just another one of her drastic experiments. Her outrageous makeup no longer fazed me. She popped open the elbow-rest and held out what looked like a rolled-up magazine. "This should cheer you up."

I took it and then did a double take, noticing her claws were coated in shiny black polish. They were over an inch long, and they were hers. That's why they curved the way they did. How she braided with those things, I never knew. I shook my head and looked at what she handed me. It was all the Smart Source grocery coupons for the past three weeks. I bounced in my seat.

"Whoo-hoo! This almost makes up for you telling Mommy I have Dr. Snyder's keys."

"Oh girl, she dragged it outta me! You know how she is. But between you and me, you really hurt her feelings."

"How? What did *I* do?"

"You know what you did. Why did you call her a showoff?"

"That's not what I said!"

"And you said she doesn't care about you, and you never told us Tee-Bo had Spider's last name. Oh yeah, and Mommy's haircut, you never commented on it."

"Of course not, I hate it! She's bald. I liked it long, but I wouldn't tell *her* that."

"What about me? Notice anything different?"

"Yeah. Who wears black lipstick? You look like you're spittin' ink."

Dawn ran the back of her hand down her face. "Don't hate. This is still my money maker." Next, she removed her baseball cap. I screamed and then choked on my own saliva. A Caesar. The tiny waves left on her head were platinum blond. Dawn was turning her head from side to side, smiling. She looked in her rearview mirror, licked her finger and slicked down the one hair that was sticking up. Me, I'd always had a good length of hair. But because it was so coarse, and I had so much of it, beauty salons charged me double, so Mommy or Dawn would do it. It was cheaper to keep replacing straightening combs. After about a month or two, the teeth would either bend or curve or the comb would spin on its handle. Now Dawn, she was the one with the hair that laid flat with water, and she could sit on it, the only obvious trait inherited from the Cherokee Indian great-great grandmother we'd only seen in the tattered, old photo in the silver picture frame on Mommy's mantle. But with that head full of hair covering half her body, she shaved it all off? If I had been there I would've strangled her with those locks.

"Am I hot? Or am I hot?" she asked, raising eyebrows as dark and silky as her hair used to be.

I tried to answer, but I couldn't find my voice. I coughed some more and cleared my throat, but I only managed to eke out a hoarse, "Why would you do that to yourself?"

Dawn pulled her cap back down on her head. "What do you know about style? With your buns and Mary Janes, you still look like a fifth-grade schoolgirl. Now, where's this baby's car seat?"

"Why would I buy a car seat when I don't own a car?" I buckled my seatbelt, adjusting the shoulder strap underneath Tee-Bo's legs, and kissed him softly on the top of his head.

Dawn screwed her face up, looked into the side mirror, and then over her shoulder, saving her comment until she pulled off, "Because Mommy told you to, hardheaded!" Her stack of platinum bangles clattered as she turned onto 166th Street. They clattered again when she made another left and said, "Jackie called for an appointment again yesterday. This time it was an 'emergency.' You should've heard her begging. That girl can be real sweet when she wanna be."

"Jackie apologized," I said.

"So did I! 'Soo–rry, we're booked.'"

About a month ago, Jackie had gone to Head to Toe for a wash and set. She was half asleep when she asked Dawn to clip her ends, so she wasn't paying attention. When Dawn was done, she had lopped off about five inches. Jackie lost her mind and knocked over everything that was standing. All the styling products went flying off Dawn's station, and after Jackie leveled Dawn's Nexxus display, she walked out without paying a dime.

"Are you ever gonna let her come back?"

Dawn's screwed up face answered me. "Now, what's got you looking all evil?"

"Would you believe Dr. Snyder called me fickle? I was supposed to run an errand for her next week, but watch.

61

This will be the *last favor* this fickle person does for Dr. Mae Snyder."

"Yeah, right. If you weren't broke, I'd bet you. You are *too* eager to please."

"Not true. It just amazes me what she's accomplished while raising two children alone."

"Big deal. Single mothers do their thing all the time. Look at Mommy. With two kids and a GED, for years all she could do was pour coffee in the morning and drop French fries at night."

"Mhmm, at fast food restaurants, she still gives people hell when her fries are cold."

"Yeah, well. Now, she's a rising star in the corporate world. Did she tell you she's now buyer for the eastern *and* mid-Atlantic regions? That's over two hundred stores."

"Mommy picks out furniture. Dr. Snyder has received many, many, many awards for her pioneer research on the surgical treatment of spinal deformities." I held up my palms, pretending they held weights. "Spinal surgery. Sofas and chairs...sofas and chairs. Spinal surgery." I stuck my tongue out the side of my mouth. Tipping my imaginary scales, I said, "No comparison."

"You need to stop that! Stop worshipping that man and his family!"

"That's not worship! I *admire* her. Ain't nothing wrong with that! It's awesome that even though Dr. Snyder's husband left her, she still had it in her heart to pay his funeral expenses."

"What funeral? She cremated the man without a service!"

"Yes, but she made the arrangements and paid the bill. And I know for a fact her funds were tied up in her medical research. Mr. Zach was uninsured, too. There's no doubt in my mind; the woman's a saint."

"You're forgetting she's an atheist."

"She's Spider's mother, and that's what matters. I just wish he'd decide to hurry up and marry me." I knocked on her wood grain dashboard, noticing it was plastic.

"Be careful what you wish for. Speaking of your precious king, where is he now?"

"Home asleep."

"I still don't get it. What do you see in that man?"

"What? Spider's gorgeous! Hello! His skin and his eyes

are...mmm, like butterscotch. His teeth, a wall of Chiclets. And his lips remind me of...Hubba Bubba bubbles, *chile.* They're so round...and luscious!"

"Yeah, yeah, he's eye candy. I get that. Spider *is* entirely too pretty for a man, but tell me something I don't know, like what he does for you that you can't do for yourself?"

"There's nothing he can do for me that I can't do for myself."

"Then, girl, trade your eye candy for a sugar daddy!"

"There's nothing *anyone* can do for me that I can't do for myself. Okay?"

"Okay, so tell me. You want to marry this man...why?"

"I love him."

"Free love went out in the sixties, girlfriend. You got bills to pay."

"I pay my own bills, and I love Spider unconditionally."

"That's the problem. If a man doesn't have to earn your love, he will not work for it. Stop giving yourself away for free!"

"Dawn! You don't tell me jack about Kyle! Why are you all up in my uterus?"

"Fine! Keep clipping your coupons!" Instead of keeping her eyes on the road, Dawn gave me the evil eye, mumbling, "That man ain't rushing to get you down the aisle, no way." She stopped long enough to notice Tee-Bo's mint green plaid and denim outfit. "That's cute."

"Dior, baby!"

"You're lying!" Dawn stuck her fingers in the back of Tee-Bo's collar and pulled the label out. "Did Romell..."

"I bought this! Thank you very much!"

"Christian Dior? Not you. You're holding out. When'd you hit Lotto? Or did you finally decide to splurge?"

"Bloomie's had a Super Sale. I hit the clearance rack. My child will not wear his education. Trust me."

"Okay, he looks cute, but it's a shame you have to dress him up and bring him out in this hot, hot, hot summer heat, when *you know who* at home should be watching this baby."

"Didn't I just tell you to mind your business?"

"Yeah, but *you* made this my business! Now, why can't *he* help?"

"Dawn, Spider came in late last night, and when I left, he was out cold. I brought Tee-Bo with me because I know Spider

63

needs his sleep."

"He doesn't need his beauty sleep! You do!"

"Oh, now you're calling me ugly!" I pushed the power button on the radio and sang "Be Happy" aloud with Mary J., *"All I really want is for me to be happy..."*

"I wasn't calling you ugly! I was just saying."

I had turned the volume way up and was now screaming, *"All I really want is for me to be happy—"*

"I'll put you out, girlfriend! Don't try me!" Dawn smacked the power button. The next thing I knew, her car had screeched to a halt and the force had whipped us forward. The red Jetta in front of us had stopped short. She maneuvered to his passenger side. The guy rolled down his tinted window. A cloud of weed smoke wafted out. Dawn's power window came down, and in a hail of spit, she cussed that man out, "You blunt-smoking, no-driving...."

She had shut the radio off. I tuned her out regardless. My sister's the reigning queen of road rage. She told that man exactly where he could stick his blunt. Expecting her to speed off, I braced myself and held Tee-Bo close. While Dawn hit the gas, thrusting us backward, she hollered, "Good thing I look out for these idiots! That baby ain't in no car seat!"

Traffic lights were in sync down the Concourse. Dawn sped through the series of greens, until a red caught us at 138th Street. She pulled over, put the car in park, and said, "Backseat."

"Don't be ridiculous. Here?" There were three people on the block. All three looked like they had been in the same spot all night. Next to a bucket, a small German Shepherd was leashed to the lamppost maybe two feet ahead of us. I shook my head. "We're wearing a seatbelt."

"I said, 'Get in the back!'" Dawn cut the engine off. "These new cars have dual airbags. If I would've tapped that Jetta back there, we would've wound up in Lincoln Hospital crying."

"Even if we're wearing a seatbelt?"

She twisted toward me. "Mia, what would you do if something happened to that baby? You could make another one, but it wouldn't be Tee-Bo. Now, get your narrow ass in the back!"

I sighed, unbuckled my seat belt, and looked up. A strange man was heading our way. I kept my door locked and eased into the back between the bucket seats. I buckled us in, but this had to be the longest light in the Bronx. He crossed the street and walked right up to the car. Everything about him seemed gray, his clothes, his skin, his hair. He grabbed a squeegee off the ground and pulled a skinny bottle of Windex from his back pocket. Dawn was honking her horn and making all kinds of gestures, trying to signal him to stop. He ignored her, squirted her windshield, and then went ahead and ran the sponge end of the squeegee across it. We watched a stream of filthy water trickle down, and he scraped off every drop with the rubber end. Once he was done, he tapped the glass, holding out his hand. "Spare some change, sister?"

I asked Dawn, "You tippin' him or what?" When she shook her head, I dug in my bag.

She twisted her face. "No, wait! Here's his tip." The light turned green. She cracked her window, and as she turned the corner, she yelled out, "OTB, babe! Long Tall Sally! Fifth race!"

9

*D*AWN PULLED UP TO DR. SNYDER'S AND WAITED with me for the mailman. Tee-Bo stuffed his fist in his face, gurgling. He was teething; it must've felt good against his gums. The AC hummed. My stomach growled. Dawn was quiet. Something was occupying her mind.

♥ ♥ ♥ ♥

The last time Dawn was here she was dropping off both me and Spider. I was in the front seat, pregnant, due any day. Spider was in the back making love to his copy of *Sports Illustrated*. We had just crossed the 138th Street Bridge and hadn't heard a peep out of him so far, so I think Dawn forgot he was back there. She was telling me that Kyle broke up with her, and she didn't know why. Kyle bought her two pieces of Louis Vuitton luggage for her Valentine-birthday. He made dinner reservations for Tavern on the Green, so Dawn was getting dressed. She said Kyle carried the two large suitcases into her walk-in closet and came back out, looking like he'd seen a ghost. "How many bags do you have?" he asked.

"A hundred and twenty-seven," Dawn answered.

Without looking at her or giving her any explanation, Kyle walked out and didn't come back. He wasn't returning her calls, and she had no clue what was wrong with him.

Now Spider, quiet the whole ride, decided to dip in on our conversation. He asked, "How much does one of those bags cost?"

Dawn answered him, "About a thousand, give or take."

Spider laughed that goofy laugh, "Huh-ha," and he buried his face back in his magazine.

Spider and I had been together forever and a day, and the one thing I've learned is this: when Spider laughs that goofy laugh, don't ask him what he's thinking, not unless I want to get my feelings hurt. Spider wouldn't hurt a fly, but he would most certainly hurt some feelings. I tried to run interference, "Ooh, girl. This baby is pressing on my bladder. I gotta pee!"

Dawn wasn't hearing me. She pulled over so fast, the car jerked, and I banged my head on my window. She put the car in park, turned around in her seat, and faced Spider, "Okay, Spider Man. Come wit' it. You know something that I don't know?"

Spider looked at me, pleading with his eyes.

I jiggled in my seat. "Dawn, please! Talk about this later. I can't hold it!"

Dawn shut me down with an open palm to my face. "Well, Spider. If you got something to say, say it!"

Spider closed his magazine and sat back. He took a deep breath, "One hundred and twenty-seven bags at a thousand dollars a pop? It all adds up."

Dawn looked at him like he was crazy. "How you figure?"

"Do the math. At a thousand dollars a pop, this cat's either wondering how he's going to come up with over a hundred thousand dollars to keep you happy, or he's thinking, a hundred and twenty-seven bags, if he bought two, who are the other fifty-three cats." Spider's math was off, but he made his point. He's cold but honest.

At that, Dawn twisted back around in her seat, but her hands and knees were trembling. She had a smile on her face, but it wasn't the happy one. It was that smile she wore just before she exploded. I always used to say Dawn was mean for no reason, but right then and there, I realized that either my sister had matured, or she loved the hell outta me, because she didn't say a word. But when she dropped us off, she was so pissed she sped off with the back door still open. Had anybody else said that to her, she would've laid him or her out with four-letter words. Dawn and Kyle eventually worked things out, but ever since then, she never said more than two words to Spider.

♥ ♥ ♥ ♥

Now her bangles jingled as she ran her hand across her head, smoothing down peach fuzz. She was in deep thought, all right. She reached behind her seat for her satchel. Another new Gucci. This one was black leather and only had logos on the hardware. She sat it in her lap, pulled out a matching datebook, and sat that to the side. I heard her unsnap what I was sure was a matching wallet, because I soon heard her peeling off crisp bills that she more than likely stuffed in her bra before sticking the bag back behind her.

When I looked up, the mailman was making his way down the steps of the brownstone next door, so I stepped out of the car. Dawn popped the trunk and grabbed the laundry bag and detergents. I walked up to the mailman. "Please tell me you have Certified Mail for the Snyder residence," I said, wiping sweat and dribble from Tee-Bo's face. Tee-Bo still had his fist in his mouth and was busy sucking away. The mailman didn't answer, so I looked up at him. Something had his undivided attention. I followed his line of vision to Dawn's behind. Dawn had walked over to the stoop and placed the laundry bag on the bottom step. She was adjusting the ankle strap on her silver sandal with her big, visible, panty-lined behind up in the air, despite the many times Mommy told us, "Bend from the knees and not the waist." Dawn straightened and smoothed out her white tank top down over her gray camouflage shorts, but nothing could hide those curves. I couldn't help but feel disgusted. Here I was standing in the mailman's face; I probably had more hair on my knees than Dawn had on her head, and this man hadn't noticed me yet. He stared hard at Dawn. A thread of saliva hung from his open mouth. I was tempted to hand him Tee-Bo's washcloth.

"Hello! The Snyder residence," I repeated. "Do you have any Certified Mail for the Snyder residence?"

"I'm sorry," he finally said. "And you are...?"

"Mia, Dr. Snyder's...daughter-in-law," I said. It sounded better than son's baby's mama.

He rolled a rubber band off a small stack. I peeped the gold wedding band on his finger as he flipped through the mail. "The Snyders were next, but no certified."

"Were there any yesterday?"

"No, I didn't have any on my run yesterday, either."

"Okay, I guess. Since I'm here, can I please take today's mail? It gets caught when you put it through the chute."

"All that construction the doctor's been doing, she should go ahead and have a mailbox installed. It would be a lot easier on her mail," he said. We all told her that, but after having the brownstone exterior resurfaced and the door stripped, patched, and stained, Dr. Snyder still insisted a new mailbox wouldn't maintain the integrity of the original design.

I nodded as he removed the rubber band from another stack of mail, peeled off two envelopes, and handed them to me. They were Dr. Snyder's phone and cable bills.

"Thank you," I said, but he wasn't looking at me anymore. Dawn had walked up. Loose mail slipped through his fingers. He knelt but took his time picking them up. His eyes never left her legs.

He slowly stood and said, "Baby, you can have *all* my money!"

Dawn answered him, "Sure, babe. I'll spend that postal check," and with a wink, she grabbed the laundry bag and carried it up to the landing. The mailman was still standing there waiting for her as if she were serious. Dawn always had her pick of men, like Kyle. He had a mansion in the Hamptons. I thought the attention Dawn got would ease up now that she shaved her head, but here she was, baldhead and black lipstick, and I was still invisible.

I walked up the stairs, sulking, "You could hold out for sugar daddies. Me, I just blend in with the background."

Dawn's reply was, "I wish I could just blend in. You don't know how lucky you are to have the power to dress yourself up or down."

I sucked my teeth, "No matter how much I fixed myself up, sugar daddies never beat down *my* door."

She heard me. "It's not like you want them to. Trade your eye candy for a sugar daddy. *Somebody* has to be a sucker. Better him than you."

I ignored this and reached in the diaper bag for the keys to the brownstone, but I retrieved my own house keys. I stuck them on my thumb and reached back into the bag until I felt the other set. When I pulled them out, Dawn gave me a strange look. I shrugged. "What?"

"Why do you have so many keys?"

"These are the ones Dr. Snyder gave me," I said, shaking the smaller set.

"What about all the others?" Dawn said pointing to my crowded key chain.

"Yours, Mommy's, mine, and Romell's."

"Romell's? Doesn't it make more sense to keep his separate?"

"No. Why?"

"What if Spider decides to borrow your keys?"

I thought about it. "Good point," I said, quickly sliding Dr. Snyder's keys onto the link with my house keys and separating Romell's. When I was done, I looked at Dawn. I actually wanted her to hurry up and leave. Dr. Snyder recycled, and I wanted to go through the recyclables to see if she had any coupons left in her Sunday papers. Trash picking, but I was not about to let Dawn see me do it. "I can take it from here," I said.

"Okay. How will you get home? Do you need money for a cab?"

"No, I'm good," I said without hesitation.

"Are you sure?"

I smiled and nodded.

Dawn softly rubbed Tee-Bo's hair and then looked me in the eye. "Take care of yourself. You hear me. Get some sleep, and make sure you eat. You're losing that baby weight too fast."

"You sound like Mommy!"

"Hey! Mommy is almost always right, and she ain't never lied."

"Don't remind me," I grunted, "and don't worry. If I feel hungry, I have an apple in my bag. I may even stop at Pan Pan just to do something with myself."

"I was actually just thinking you need to get out. Do you feel up to partying tonight?"

"Not really."

"Well, I was invited to a movie premiere at Imax, and the after party's at Bentley's."

"Maybe next time. If I could sleep for even fifteen minutes tonight, I'd rather do that."

"Red carpet event, girl, wall-to-wall sugar daddies! If you change your mind, let me know, so I could put you on the guest list and do something to your hair besides that tired bun. And guess what, Mommy's loaning me the Volvo!" Dawn gave me a warm, sideways hug. "Luv ya," she said, and then waving, she bounced down the steps right by that mailman, who was still standing there, holding a strip of paper like a fool. She jumped in her car and drove off.

Grabbing the laundry, I bumped the front door open. As I stepped inside, I heard mail tearing beneath the door. I could've kicked myself. It had completely slipped my mind that Dr. Snyder wasn't there to collect her mail that week.

Now, I looked down at a whole bunch of letters scattered in the doorway. I carefully held Tee-Bo and stooped to gather them. Some were crumpled; the rest were ripped. The corner of one was ripped just enough for me to peek. It was patterned inside, a security envelope. I flipped it over. It was addressed to Jacqueline Snyder from Home Life Mutual Insurance Company.

I knew if it came from an insurance company in a security envelope, it had to be a check. *If there's one for Jackie, maybe there's one for Spider.* That was my first thought, but I caught myself. Since we had moved in together, Spider rarely received mail at his mother's. I shuffled through the envelopes to see if there was one for Dr. Snyder. There was, and right behind hers was one for Spider. Out of all the envelopes, Spider's was the one that had the least amount of damage. It was barely wrinkled. I fixed that; I balled Spider's up and ripped it across the top, so as not to damage what was inside. I zipped it down, creating a pocket large enough to allow me to peek. And when I saw what I saw, my heart nearly stopped. It was a check, pay to the order of Spence Snyder. Fifty thousand dollars.

10

T HE DOOR WAS STILL AJAR. "BROKE MY ASS!" I locked it, dragged the bags into the foyer, and threw my keys on the desk. Snatching open the mail sorter, I shoved everything in the first compartment and slammed it shut. Then I paced back and forth, wondering. Why was there an insurance check for Spider? He never told me he was expecting money. Then it occurred to me: I checked his mail at home, and it wasn't like this was mailed to *our* house. Maybe he purposely sent this to his mother's because he didn't want me to know. Maybe he wanted me to think he was broke, so that he could use that as an excuse not to marry me. I slumped in the chair, staring blankly at the return address. Then, I ran my finger across the raised ink, mulling over all the sacrifices I had made for Spider.

I had transferred from Bronx Community to go with him to Howard. He graduated and wanted to move back to New York for graduate school, so I left D.C., even though I still had a few credits left to complete. Right after he started grad school, Dr. Snyder put Spider out because she found out he had invited his half-brother to her home for a visit. I found us our apartment. I left my mother's four-bedroom condo in a brand-new building in Hoboken, where I was living rent-free, with AC, and cable TV. I left to move with Spider into an old, critter-infested, tenement building. Not only did I have to stuff all the holes with glass and steel wool and seal them with plaster to keep mice away, I had to squirt boric acid into the cracks at the baseboard of every wall to ward off roaches bigger than me. Once I saw that first cockroach fly, life was never the same. And I had no HBO or BET music videos to distract me. In fact, the only reception was on channels eleven and forty-seven. So I watched the WB until that singing frog danced in my dreams. Then, I watched the Spanish channel, until I had the soup commercial jingles memorized. *Y odio la sopa.* It was an unexpected bonus that my Spanish comprehension improved dramatically, but tele-novelas every day drove me *loco*, regardless. That's why now, we shut the TV up in the white console in the corner of the living room. My radio was my company. All this so Spider could bond with his half-brother.

And I didn't put up a stink about paying the bulk of the bills. Dr. Snyder had cut Spider off financially, and despite showing up at all the job fairs with his résumé and transcript, he couldn't find anything that fit into his class schedule. When he finally did find something, it was a retail sales position at Romeo Gigolo, a high-end men's fashion boutique. No benefits. The only perk there was the huge discount, but Spider had no need for high-end fashion. He'd be happy spending life in his Knicks jersey and khakis, as if that *faux pas* would start a trend. Anyway, he graduated and extended his hours at this place. I continued to be supportive, even though he came home on paydays with no money and a shopping bag, saying, "Sorry, Mia. All my clothes are out of season, and it's mandatory that I wear current stock." Here's the catch: Romeo Gigolo was barely paying Spider minimum wage, so their fifty percent discount didn't do doodly-squat. T-shirts in that place were two hundred. Clearance items were not an option, because that Village hot spot was more famous for its hunky sales staff than it was for its clothing line. Who needs mannequins? Romeo Gigolo had a bunch of dummies, and Spider was the biggest one. He complained every day about being ogled by customers, from the love-struck teenage girls buying socks to the drag queens who came in droves for the Avant-garde Collection's body shapers and shoes.

Around the time Spider's student loan bills started coming in the mail, I was about ready to tear my hair out, but then Mr. Burnett came into the store and gave Spider his business card, offering him that internship. Spider had reservations. "I have an MBA."

"You have no experience," I said.

Spider said, "I'm not going to spend a year of my life working for free."

He didn't see the logic, until I broke it down for him. "You're working for free, anyway! At least with the record label, you get your foot in the door of a GROWING

COMPANY. So, either you take that internship or go down-town and take that test for Transit."

Unlike Spider, I read *Black Enterprise.* I remembered the article in the September issue, "Independent Labels Take Record Industry by Storm." Ear-That-One Records could open up a whole career for Spider because I was the one who recognized the opportunity. Fifty thousand dollars and he wasn't going to tell me. Because of me, Spider went to that job every day and didn't have to worry about having a roof over his head, where his next meal was coming from, or taking care of Tee-Bo. So, the way I saw it, he owed me.

I picked up the phone and dialed home. No answer. And to think, I brought Tee-Bo with me so that Spider could sleep in. I dialed his pager and quickly punched in Dr. Snyder's number. Slamming the telephone down, sweat poured down my forehead. I wiped it off and looked at Tee-Bo; he was sweating, too. I took him out of the harness and wiped him with his washcloth. Dr. Snyder had closed all the windows before she left, and she didn't have air conditioning downstairs. During the renovations, the contractor told her that because her brownstone was a landmark building, he couldn't make the cut in the structure to install central air. I felt as if I was in a sauna. The mahogany wall paneling made the room dark. Turning on the lights would only make it hotter. Dr. Snyder had window units upstairs in the bed-rooms, but I had to put the wash in the machine first.

After dragging the laundry into the kitchen, I pulled the curtains aside and let some daylight in. Now the room had a bright, country feel even with the lights off. I knew by now Tee-Bo was probably wet. I checked his diaper. Sure enough, he was. I changed him, placed him in the infant seat we kept under the kitchen table, and sat it in front of me.

Pulling Spider's check completely out of the envelope, I wondered. *Was there a logical reason why he had had the check sent here? Maybe he wanted to surprise me.* I picked up the phone and paged Spider 9-1-1 again. *I never knew him to be sneaky. That just isn't like him, but how could he not mention something this big? He just finished telling me how broke he was. Why didn't he mention the check then? Was he lying to throw me off?* I decided to stop speculating and just ask him why he had this check sent to the brownstone, and let him explain for himself. It seemed like he was taking forever to call back. I paged him 9-1-1 again. The waiting was killing me. I needed to focus on something else. I pulled out the spot remover, bleach, detergent, and fabric softener. Then, I flipped the lid of the washer, grabbed Tee-Bo's laundry, and got started.

After a while, I noticed Tee-Bo was quiet, too quiet. I peeked over at him. He had opened his fist and was sucking his two middle fingers quite happily, so I fumbled inside the diaper bag for his frozen rubber pretzel and made a quick switch, but he was not fooled. He let out a squeak and then took deep breaths. I could see the tension mounting and his face going red, so I braced myself, knowing what was coming. His fists balled into knots; then he let out a deafening screech. I knew if he screamed long enough, there would be no stopping him, and I would soon have a headache that was a pill popper. Over all this noise, I heard the ringing phone; it was music to my ears. I answered it. "Hey, Spider,"

"Mia, I know you didn't page me 9-1-1 three times in a row just to say 'Hi.' And why is he crying like that?"

"He's teething, so he's cranky. Hold on a second." I unbuckled Tee-Bo from his infant seat, quickly unbuttoned my blouse and unsnapped the flap on my nursing bra. Then, I held him close. Tee-Bo latched on. The speckles on his cheeks contrasted with the smoothness of my breast. His forehead and eyelids were prickly, and now, even his scalp was turning red. I still didn't know where the rash was coming from. With Tee-Bo nursing, the room was now quiet, and I was able to speak. "Spider, why did you have this check sent to your mother's?"

"What check?"

I automatically assumed he was trying to play dumb. "This fifty thousand dollar check! The one that came...for you today...in your mother's mail."

"From where?"

I knew then he didn't have a clue what I was talking about. "Home Life Mutual Insurance Company."

"Never heard of them. Is the check real?"

"Very."

"I wasn't expecting any check. They must have sent it to the wrong person."

I looked at the check in my hand. It was computer generated. The signature was stamped but Spider's name was clearly printed on it. "Who else do you know is named Spence Snyder?"

"No one, but why would any life insurance company be sending me a check?"

"It says right here on the stub, that you're the beneficiary of a death benefit claim for Zachary Snyder. It has the policy number on it and everything."

"My father died more than a year ago, and he didn't have *any* insurance."

"Well, I guess he did because there are two more checks, one for Dr. Snyder and another for Jackie."

"Wait a minute! Let me get this straight. You're at my mother's house opening up my family's mail?"

Okay. I opened his mail at home all the time, but I realized this *was* his mother's house; I was way out of line. I needed to diffuse the situation. "Well, what had happened was...the mail, you know how the mail gets caught...under the door...and...rips. Well, this check ripped open."

"Don't lie to me, Mia!" After a deep breath, he continued, "What I would like to know is where did this insurance policy come from all of a sudden and why would they be sending us checks now, over a year later?"

"I don't know. Page your mother."

"I'm on a payphone, and there's no call-back number. Page her for me and ask about the checks."

"Spider, this isn't any of my business."

"You should have thought of that before you started poking your nose into other people's mail."

11

*T*HAT WAS IT. THERE WAS NO MISTAKE ABOUT IT. Spider was purposely trying to put me at odds with his mother. Dr. Snyder already thought I was fickle. Now, in addition to having to tell her that her certified letters never came, I had to ask her about the check that was in the envelope I had no business opening. *Why me?*

It only took a moment to realize that it was better that *I* asked Dr. Snyder rather than Spider. I could just hear him say, "Ma, Mia was opening your mail, and I wanna know; why the hell are we getting fifty thousand dollar checks when Pops had no insurance?" The drama would start at his mama and work its way through the whole family like yeast. At least if I sugarcoated the issue, there'd be more of a chance Dr. Snyder wouldn't get upset. If Spider brought it up, there would *definitely* be a problem. I grabbed the phone and paged Dr. Snyder. I figured once she saw her home phone number, she would call right back. That's exactly what she did.

"Mia?" she said.

"Yes, Dr. Snyder," I said in my most respectful voice.

"What's the prognosis?"

"The prog-who?"

"Tobiah's rash."

"Oh, the dermatologist thinks it's caused by the dyes in his clothing or maybe his detergent."

"Like I said, contact dermatitis. Mia, I'm sorry I was short with you the other night. I was just annoyed. I'm a surgeon, Mia; not just a surgeon, I'm one of only a handful of experts in my field. Those awards hanging on the wall in my den aren't just for show. My research on kyphosis alone is groundbreaking, yet you continue to doubt me, but accept the word of some Jewish doctor as the Gospel truth."

I thought about that. She was the head of the Department of

Orthopedic Surgery at her hospital, so with her credentials, maybe she did know a thing or two about rashes.

"I'm sorry if I made it seem like I didn't believe you. It's just that you were saying one thing and Dr. Rosenberg was saying another."

"Forget it, Mia. It's not just you. I've come to realize, as a black doctor, it's usually my own people who doubt my competence and give me the hardest time. But these are the people I've chosen to serve. Enough about that. What did this doctor prescribe?"

"Medicine in a bottle."

"A suspension liquid. Okay, can you be more specific?"

"I don't have it with me so I don't know the exact name, but it's an antihistamine."

"That sounds about right, but you still need to find out what's triggering the reaction."

"He said not to put dark colors on him."

"If that doesn't work, let me know. And keep a close eye on it, because if it spreads to his scalp, it can lead to seborrhea."

"What's that?"

"It's more commonly known as cradle cap."

"Oh, wow. Tee-Bo could lose his hair. I better get on the ball."

"Most certainly. Now," her voice turned cheery, "did you meet the mailman?"

"Yes, I did but he didn't have any Certified Mail today and he said he didn't have any yesterday, either."

"That's odd," she paused. "Well, I guess I'm going to have to contact the insurance company." She mumbled to herself, but I heard her.

"Insurance company?"

"Yes."

I had to ask, "Home Life Mutual?"

"How did you know?"

"Some mail did come from Home Life Mutual, but they came by regular mail."

"Regular mail? Someone must've made an error. Those envelopes are important. They're...my...my new homeowner's policy. Slide them under my bedroom door. I'll get to them when I return."

"Dr. Snyder, the mail caught under the door and ripped."

"Ripped? I don't care. Just slide them under my door."

"Dr. Snyder, there is a check here for Spider for fifty thousand dollars. It ripped...open."

She shrieked, "You didn't tell Spence about that check, did you?"

"Why?"

"It would be better if I explained a few things first. Now, did you tell Spence?"

"No."

She exhaled, a sign of relief. "Good. Don't."

"Okay, Dr. Snyder."

I hung up from her and paged Spider immediately. She may have thought it would be better if she explained a few things to her son, but I knew I had to give him an explanation right away. Then, I had to let him know not to say anything until he heard from her, which was easy enough considering he didn't want to speak to his mother, anyway. Tee-Bo detached from my breast, surprising me with one hell of a burp. Figuring there was probably more gas where that came from, I held him upright and gently rubbed his back, wondering. *Information on her homeowner's policy? Why did she lie? Why doesn't Dr. Snyder want me to tell him about the check? What is there to explain first? What does it matter?* I snapped out of it. Spider and I were in the money. I grabbed the telephone and quickly punched in a number.

As soon as I heard a voice say, "Yeah," I said, "Hi, is Dawn there yet?" Whoever answered placed the phone down. I then heard her shout, "Dawn, phone!" *Love that beauty salon professionalism,* I thought.

"Yeah," Dawn said.

"*Hey*, guess what!"

"What?"

"Spider's gonna be my sugar daddy."

"Humor me. How?"

"He just got a check for fifty *thou*, girl."

"Your broke boyfriend?"

"Yup, now, what kind of ring should I get?

"Tiffany's."

"Can you imagine me getting a little blue box?"

"Won't be the first."

"Dawn, that was Romell, and that was a bracelet."

"You're a fool. You should've kept that shit and had it

appraised."

"That's over and done. Now, we're talking about Spider. What kind of ring should I get?"

"Platinum! At least five-carats. Princess cut with trillion accents...in a basket setting."

"A what? Dawn, I said we're talking about Spider."

"I know."

"Then, you must want Spider to spend his whole check."

"All you do for him? Tell Spider he could put his change in a jar. And make sure he doesn't go to a check cashing place."

"Why?"

"They'll charge nearly a thousand dollars in fees; instead, he can use that for the inscription."

I laughed. "Okay, when the time comes I guess we'll deposit it."

"That'll take three days to clear, but if the bank it was drawn on is in the city, you can go directly to the branch, and get your cash the same day."

Dr. Snyder hadn't given us the check yet, and here my sister was advising me on the fastest way to cash it. "Thanks," I said. "Even though you seem to be forgetting this is not my money. I'm keeping my fingers crossed."

"Don't cross your fingers. Spread your legs, girl! Then it *will* be your money!"

I laughed. "Talk to you later, Dawn."

I held Tee-Bo up. He had only nursed from one side, but dribble was seeping from his mouth in bubbles; I should've known better than to have broccoli and garlic mashed potatoes last night for dinner. "Sorry, Sweetness. You're gassy, and it's all Mommy's fault," I said smiling. I carried Tee-Bo over to the wall jack. The ringing receiver vibrated in my hand before I could let go of it. I brought it back to my ear.

"Hello, Mia?"

I stretched the black coil back to the table. My shoulder pinned the phone to my ear. "Yeah, Spider," I said, rubbing Tee-Bo's back, now with deeper strokes.

"Where'd the check come from?"

"I don't know. As soon as I mentioned it, your mother asked me not to tell you."

"Why doesn't she want me to know?"

"Don't start me to lying. All she said was she wanted to

explain a few things first. Just act like I never said anything."

"Hell no! Somebody is gonna tell me something!"

"Spider, I already told your mother I wouldn't tell you. If you ask her about that check, I will look like a liar."

"You shouldna lied, then. Later."

"Spider," I persisted, but it was no use. I was talking to the dial tone.

When Dr. Snyder asked me if I said anything to Spider, I knew I shouldn't have lied. Bad enough that I opened their mail. I didn't want to admit that I had already told him, because I was clearly wrong on both counts. Now, it was too late for me to tell her that he already knew. My mother always did say I was a *people pleaser*. Every now and then, I reached a point where I realized I couldn't please everybody. This was one of those times.

12

A CHILL WENT THROUGH ME. WORRYING WHETHER or not Spider was going to question his mother brought a feeling in my stomach that was all too familiar, reminding me of something, but it was something I would rather forget. I sucked my teeth. Milk leaked from the full side, soaking my nursing bra. I'd triggered a let-down reflex. "I hate that!" I screamed. Tee-Bo squealed just as loud, reminding me that this was his time. I held him and smiled as I unbuttoned my blouse.

"Your mommy wants to cry, but I am not going to. I'm going to smile. I know when I start crying, you start crying," I cooed. "I don't want you to start crying, because I didn't bring my Motrin with me. These Snyders are silly pee-po. Why is your grandma asking me to keep secrets? And why is your daddy so honest? He's an atheist. What sense does that make? They're silly pee-po. I tell you, sill-lee pee-po. But, we're not silly, right Mommy's Sweetness?" Tee-Bo's eyes grew wide and glued to my face. His lips puckered and stretched into a toothless grin that melted my heart. It was probably gas, but it didn't matter.

I lifted Tee-Bo off my lap and placed him in the infant seat. Alert, his eyes followed me around the room. The washing machine buzzed—end of the cycle. I transferred the first load into the dryer and reloaded the washer. "It's too hot down here, right Sweetness?" I held him and headed upstairs to a cooler room—Spider's.

I stepped inside and immediately sensed something about the room was different. Spider's electric boogie blue walls were still plastered with his poster collection, Wilt Chamberlain and Dr. J in Afros, short shorts, and long socks. He still had the captain's bed near the window, the boom box with the twelve-inch woofers, the three-legged end table balanced on volumes 16 through 20 of the Encyclopedia Britannica. The Betamax and ColecoVision were on the dresser in the same place, stacked next to his army men and Mr. Spock. But on Spider's roll-top desk, the computer was not his Commodore 64. It was newer: some generic hybrid. I rested the infant seat and sat at Spider's desk. Next to the computer, staring me in the face, was a classic black touchtone phone. I picked it up. There was a dial tone. Spider never had a phone in this room before.

I glanced back at the telephone and realized I better page Spider again. I needed to let him know not to tell anyone else about that check before he spoke to his mother. If Dr. Snyder didn't want him to know about it, I didn't want him to call Jackie. Dawn was right about Jackie. Jackie could seem like the nicest person in the world at times, but as sweet as she could be, she could turn right around and be just as nasty. She was way too unpredictable. No telling what she would do. So I had no choice but to try to make sure Spider didn't talk. Otherwise, I'd be counting down until the moment all hell broke loose. I picked up the phone and paged Spider, 9-1-1. Five minutes later a loud piercing ring filled the room, startling Tee-Bo. I picked up before the second ring and heard what sounded like lips smacking.

"Hello, may I please speak to Spence." It was a woman's voice.

"He's not in. Would you like to leave a message?" I grabbed a pencil and spiral notebook from the desk.

"Yes," she said and made that smacking noise again, "Um, can you please tell him to call Asia? My number is—"

"What is this in regards to?"

"Oh, this is not a business call. May I ask who I'm leaving this message with?"

"Yes. His fiancée," I said politely.

"Oh, never mind. Thank you," she said and hung up.

This was nothing new. This happened all the time, especially since Spider—with that hair, those eyes, and that smile—was standoffish, giving off this vibe like he didn't realize a woman was hitting on him unless it was blatantly obvious: she threw her panties at him or something. But, even though it seemed he was oblivious, in the back of my mind, I had my doubts. I had a hard time believing anyone could possibly be that naive. I don't know why, but part of me couldn't help but think it was all an act and maybe, just maybe, he was the player of all players. And then another part of me believed he was so naive, he could actually fall victim to that breed of females who prey on guys who are taken. Spider was mine. He met friendly girls all the time but I questioned their motives, because it was always just a matter of time before they made advances or tried to play matchmaker, until he put them in their place. I knew Asia was only the latest, but that was no consolation.

Through the opened door, I heard the ring of telephones resound through the rest of the house. That annoying phone on the desk with the piercing ring was silent. I knew what that meant. It had to be a separate phone line. I picked it up. Sure enough, there was a dial tone and all the other telephones were still ringing. Now, I was pissed. I scooped Tee-Bo up in my arms and hurried to answer the closest phone.

"Hello, Mia," Spider said impatiently. "I wish you'd stop paging me 9-1-1 when there's no damn emergency."

"You lying, no-good—"

"What now?"

"Who the hell is Asia?"

"A friend."

"Don't play with me, Spider! Why did you add another phone line just for her to call?"

"Mia, not now. I'm with somebody."

"Do you think I care?"

"What's up, Mia!" I heard Spider's brother shout from the background.

"Tell Jeff I said, what's up."

Spider hollered out, "My wife said, 'hi'."

Wife? I pretended I didn't even hear that. "Spider, don't tell anyone about that check before you talk to your mother."

"All right, I won't tell anybody else," he said.

"Oh no! Please, tell me you didn't tell Jackie."

"I didn't tell her, but like I said, Jeff's with me. He knows what I know."

I sucked my teeth. "Well, make sure he *knows* to keep quiet. I don't want this to get back to Jackie, and I *definitely* don't want this to get back to your mother. I'll see you later. I'll talk to you about *your friend* when you get home," I said. "I love you, Spider."

"Yeah, I know."

He hung up, and now I was fuming. That girl was calling his mother's house like she expected to reach him there on a phone number I didn't even have, a separate phone line, on a day when I normally wouldn't have been there. No explanation, so my vivid imagination answered all my questions.

I made it back home, trembling. My adrenaline was pumping so much; I just couldn't sit still, not even after I put the folded clothes away. So I pulled out my bucket, rubber gloves, and an old toothbrush, and took my anger out on the grout in the bathroom. Where it was stubborn, I peeled my gloves off and scratched at it, pretending it was Asia's face. I already had a picture of her in my mind. She looked greasy.

When Tee-Bo fussed, I gave him formula. He took it. No problem. Normally, he would take a bottle from everyone else. From me, he would push it out with his tongue until I offered the breast. He finally took a bottle from me, but even that didn't make me feel any better. He was sated to the point of exhaustion, lying in a temporary substitute for a crib: his stroller. Once he went to sleep, I wheeled him into the bedroom, turned on the nursery monitor, and slapped a meal together.

It was way too hot to have the oven on, so I threw everything in the skillet on a medium flame. That took about twenty minutes. The aroma of garlic and wine sauce had my apartment smelling better than a Chock full o' Nuts. So, I pulled out a piece of my grandmother's fine china, set the table, and lit myself a couple of candles. The sun was beginning to set; the light in the room was dimming. The candle flames flickered from the slight breeze coming in through the windows. I sat in front of my plate and wine glass full of grape juice. Chicken Marsala, red potatoes, baby carrots, and tossed salad, a meal even prettier than the pink roses on the china pattern. I pierced some potatoes, lifted my fork to my mouth, and just held it there. I couldn't even force myself to eat. My stomach was in knots. I blew out the candles and pushed my plate away to lay my head down. My weight on the table tipped the glass top. My candlesticks and wine glass fell over. I pulled my chair out of the way and hurried back with the dishrag, sopping the juice spill that ran off the table to the floor, not even six inches away from my chaise. I decided, as much as I loved grape juice, this would be the last time I drank it in this apartment.

I stuck my plate in the microwave, and then massaged my throbbing temples. That whiny voice repeated in my head, that voice and her lip-smacking. Girls who smacked their lips when they talk were hoes, always. No, that's not exactly true. Dawn's friend Imani was a lip smacker, but she sucked her thumb; she was an exception. Not Asia, she sounded like she was ready for phone sex. With my head pounding, I could barely keep my eyes open. And to make matters worse, someone somewhere was hammering. It felt like I was being knocked upside the head. I ran to the medicine cabinet. I dumped a bunch of pills into my hand and counted them. There were twelve. I closed my fist tight. Then, I closed my eyes. I've made a lot of mistakes in my life, but I can't go backward. I've got to go forward. I dropped the pills back into the bottle, counting them off until I counted nine. I popped the other three and massaged my temples. I wished I could just scream, but I couldn't; Tee-Bo was asleep. And besides, screaming without Spider around was a waste of breath. He was out with Jeff, and this was Saturday, so that could very well turn into an all night thing, depending on how Spider was dressed.

I didn't know when those Motrin were going to kick in, but I knew exactly what to do to make myself feel better in the meantime. I picked up the phone and dialed the one person I always called to vent.

13

*R*OMELL CROAKED, "YEAH."

"Hey, sleepyhead." I glanced out the window; it wasn't even dark yet. I looked at the clock. "It's only eight forty-nine!"

"Who's this?"

"Who do you think?"

"Hey, Chocolate." After Romell finished yawning, he innocently said, "What? I can't have a nap?"

"Nap my ass! You just had some nookie, you garden tool! Pick one. Eeny, meeny, miney, moe. It ain't that hard."

Now he laughed. "Nah, a man can have more problems dealing with one woman than he can have dealing with ten."

I left that one alone. "Who is it this time?"

"You tell me."

"I'm having a hard enough time keeping track of my own man...and his women."

"Oh oh, here we go again," he said, and he listened. I told him all about the phone call from Asia and what Spider said, every detail.

Romell still wasn't convinced. "He probably didn't want to get into it in front of his brother."

"Pa–lease! Jeff ain't nobody. Jeff comes to our house empty handed and leaves with twenty dollars, toothpaste, and toilet paper."

"Yeah, but that *is* his little brother."

"Jeff's his *older* brother, two years older. To be exact, he's 27, way too old to be mooching! If it ain't food, it's clothes, the clothes *I bought* for Spider. And hello, Spider is six foot five. Jeff is about an inch or two shorter than me, and I'm five foot seven. Why doesn't he buy his own clothes that fit?"

Romell laughed, but I wasn't trying to be funny. "Well, even if—"

"Stop! Don't try to make excuses for Jeff. He's a leech,

broke, busted, disgusting—"

"Okay, okay, but your man still cares what he thinks. Right or wrong?"

"Spider cares what Jeff thinks? I don't think so!" I sucked my teeth. "That Negro just wants the extra time to get his lie straight."

"Chocolate, quit male bashing. It's only a phone call."

"No, you should've heard her voice, Romell! It's not what she said but how she said it."

"You're acting like you caught the man with his pants down. I'm telling you, it's nothing."

"Romell, please! That bitch was in heat, I know what I'm talking about!"

"Mia, enough already! Jeez! You're getting yourself all worked up over nothing, and if you're not careful, you're gonna make yourself sick!"

My jaw dropped; I was speechless, and that doesn't happen too often. That statement in and of itself was like he hauled off and slapped me. When I finally recovered, all I could say was, "Now Romell, I haven't done that in years. You didn't have to go there."

"I wasn't talking about *that*. You know I wasn't talking about *that*. I know you don't do *that* anymore, but I know how you get. I know you were so busy worrying about this other girl, you lost your appetite, didn't eat, had one of those hunger headaches, and the only water you had to drink, as hot as it was today, was a swallow with an aspirin. *One* aspirin. That's what I meant."

I didn't know if I believed him or not. He was talking entirely too fast and over-explaining. Normally, Romell was this suave, overly composed creature. He's tall and good-looking, but even if he weren't, his charisma alone had the power to win people over. I remember the one time Romell drove his car to pick me up from Dawn's salon. When he walked in, all conversation stopped cold and everyone focused on him, but that wasn't enough. Romell looked around at all the ladies, licked his lips, and said, "Mmh, somebody's perfume smells...*so* good."

When every girl in there screamed, "It's mine," he grinned at me and winked. Sometimes I don't know what I'm going to do with him, him or his dimples, but Romell is and has always been a flirt. He had women down to a science, and his lines were rehearsed. That's why he always knew what to say and when and how to say it. So, after just hearing him ramble, quite honestly, I was stumped. His excuse sounded good, but I couldn't tell if he said what he meant or if he said what I thought he meant. I let it go. Really, because I was afraid to ask. "Well, I took *one* Motrin."

"See what I mean? Keep taking those shits on an empty stomach; you'll be eating hospital food. That's what I meant."

I changed the subject. "How's your mother?"

"Why don't you call her back?"

"Because, I don't feel like going to church with her."

"Why don't you just say so?"

"I can't say 'no' to your mother!"

"You can't say no to anybody."

"What is this? Rank on Mia day!"

Romell laughed, "All right, you win. I don't want to piss you off now, especially since I need you Wednesday."

"For what?"

"I'm having a sofa delivered."

"Oh, come on, Romell! I just took yesterday off. Who else can you ask?"

"Nobody! I can't stand asking anybody to do anything for me. Most people will do a favor and throw that shit right back in my face later. 'I did this for you. I did that for you.' You never do that. Why do you think you're the only one I depend on? I don't trust anyone else."

"Aw, I feel special. But next time, give a sistah a heads up before you go buying shit! You can't just expect me to be at your beck and call all the time. I have a life!" I thought about it, but I was fresh out of suggestions. "Sorry, I can't help you."

"What if I pay your salary for the day?"

"Did you not just hear me?"

"What if I double your salary?"

"Romell! I just returned from maternity leave last week, and I took a day off yesterday. I can't keep taking days off. They'll write me up, and I could lose my job. You have a concierge; ask George. Or why don't you stay? It's your couch!"

"*Come on*, Chocolate. You know I need *you*. Help me out."

I had a soft spot for Romell. Usually, he could persuade me to do anything, but I was not about to risk losing my job, not even for him. "Look," I took a deep breath. "If you need me to run your keys to your office, I will do that, but I am not, I repeat *not*, taking another day off, Romell. If I mess around and get myself fired, then what? You gonna pay my bills? Not that you can't afford it. Anyway, how's your job situation? Any word?"

"Stevenson is still yanking my chain."

"At least he acknowledges the fact that you're doing a good job."

"Chocolate, don't insult me. Everything I do, I do well!" Romell has always been cocky. Sometimes he's even obnoxious so this was probably not the first time I heard him say that. Still, for some reason, I found myself turned off and on at the same time. Everything? How could I combat that? I just listened.

"My sector was just named the top-performing in the fund for the eighteenth consecutive month."

"I know. But, what about the last guy they promoted?"

"Henry Tanner Moore? Man, his numbers are in the toilet, but that doesn't matter when your uncle's a partner."

"Ouch!"

"Yeah, well, that's my dilemma. Let's face it. Livings & Moore Financial isn't ready for a managing director named Romell. That's why these clowns still have me cooped up in a cubicle."

"Don't worry. When you're senior partner, all this will be water under the bridge."

"Maybe, but right now, I just want my own damn door."

14

*R*OMELL'S PASSION WAS MONEY AND ANYTHING that had to deal with money. When he talked about it, his slanted eyes would glaze over and stare into space, like he was talking about sex. He'd use that same voice he used macking and words would just slide right off his tongue. Lip licking and all that. Of course, I'd try staring at his shoes, usually those Botticelli Oxfords. Anything to avoid eye contact. But I couldn't help but listen closer, so I'd close my eyes and concentrate. Then, I'd hear things like "P/E ratio," "cash flow," and "IPO." Once, he went on and on about liquid assets and DRIPs. It took me a good minute to realize this conversation wasn't kinky. The market was Romell's passion. If he could make me uncomfortable just talking about it, there was no doubt in my mind: he would have his "own damn door" right on Wall Street. Romell believed in himself, and just like Spider said, believing is half the battle. The question was whether or not that door would ever be available at his present firm.

The only black analyst there, Romell always arrived two hours early, never took a day off, never took lunch, and absolutely hated taking personal calls. He usually asked me to meet him at six or seven in the morning so that we could talk, like that was convenient for me, but even that was never a good time for him.

The last time I dropped by was the Friday before I returned to work. I had Tee-Bo strapped to my belly and was half asleep when I walked through the maze of cubicles to Romell. He was hovered over quarterly reports, a copy of the *Wall Street Journal,* and a cup of coffee, crunching numbers on his HP and Excel spreadsheet. He was so absorbed in the process of picking those companies apart and comparing them, that I was sitting there a whole ten minutes, sipping my smoothie before he said a word to me. To get his

95

attention, I had to ask about stock. "Doesn't this firm already provide you with a list?"

Romell dropped his mechanical pencil and sat so straight; his spine met the back of his chair and his starched shirt looked like it was on a hanger. He grabbed his throat. His solid gold bull and bear cufflinks glowed. They were probably 18 or 24K. And I noticed his French cuffs were monogrammed. With his mouth still closed, Romell winced.

"What's wrong?" I asked.

"My tongue is swollen, and it hurts to talk." He had a Mike Tyson lisp.

"Why'd you eat nuts?"

Romell shook his head. "I kissed," he said and then swallowed. This time, he winced so hard I felt his pain. He grabbed his throat again and finished his statement, "I kissed a friend of mine. She didn't tell me she just ate peanuts."

"Before you go kissing these women, maybe you should ask," I said. Romell stuck his tongue out at me. The top of it was white and had split, and the sides were red and puffy. "Ew! You sure that's not herpes?"

"Ha, ha, ha. You're comical," he said, and when he closed his mouth, saliva gushed from the corner. "Sorry, it hurts to swallow."

"You shouldn't be drinking anything hot. You need something cold to bring the swelling down. This might help." I took one last sip of my strawberry smoothie and held it out to him.

Romell shook his head. "I wouldn't wanna catch nothing."

I gave him a dirty look. "You'd be lucky to catch anything I've got. Now, drink." He cut his eye at me, but took a sip anyway. Immediately, I saw relief in his face, so I said, "Stick your tongue all the way out." When he did, it almost reached past his chin, but was swollen to the size of one of those tongues sitting in the supermarket's beef section. I reached into the diaper bag and pulled out the Ziploc bag of cotton swabs and the Baby Orajel. After squeezing a pea-sized amount onto a Q-tip, I held it up to his face, only to have him dodge it. I nudged him. "Will you trust me?" I said. Romell took a deep breath and opened his mouth. I then rubbed the Orajel on the top and sides of his tongue. "That's an anesthetic," I said, screwing the cap back on.

96

I could tell the exact moment that stuff took effect, because Romell said, "Mmm...ooh. Whew," and started smiling. "I could kiss you," he said in his normal voice. He then went on to explain his business, "My firm has been around since before the crash. We're one of the most prestigious, but here they recommend blue chips."

"Blue chips?"

"Stocks from companies with a history of steady growth, like IBM, Apple, and INTEL."

"Okay, what's wrong with blue chips?"

"Chocolate, I'm into wealth building." Now, he sounded like Tony Robbins. "I could push their turtles, but I'm not afraid of risks, I manage them."

"How?"

"I offset the risks of the dot-coms with the blue chips. But, mainly I keep a close watch on IPOs and other trends in the technology industry. My picks always see unprecedented growth. This firm has a legacy to protect. I'm the only black face at this level, but I produce like a machine, closing every quarter with record numbers. That's why they pay me the big bucks. But they can't hold me back forever. Nah, the way I see it, computer prices keep dropping. Soon there'll be one in every home. These Internet and software companies keep popping up. Soon I'll be the one raking it in, buying the jets and yachts. I can just feel it." Staring straight ahead, Romell took this deep breath that made his whole body swell and then he said, "If nothing else, I'm diligent. If I keep on the grind, in no time at all, I won't have to settle for the trickle down. I could retire comfortably and never have to work another day in my life. Right?" He looked at me.

I shrugged. "You're asking the wrong person; I'm a coupon clipper."

But this had long been a science to Romell. He began managing his money back when we were in high school. He worked afterschool in Livings & Moore Financial's mailroom. He was accepted to Georgetown on a full academic scholarship, graduated in three years magna cum laude with a degree in Economics, and then went on to earn an MBA in Finance from Columbia. Not bad for a kid from the projects.

Still, I could understand why Romell was discouraged now. Livings & Moore Financial was a very conservative firm. They were all probably wondering why he wasn't still in the mailroom. Those tight asses were not simply gonna just move over and make room for Romell to sit his black ass down. But after I hung up, I wanted to cheer him up. I pulled a new journal from the few I kept at the top of my bedroom closet. This one was a solid purple, fabric-bound with a white satin ribbon. It crackled as I opened to the first page. I wrote the number 32 inside the cover and scribbled the title of my next poem—Believe. Thinking about Romell, the words just popped into my head.

> Believe.
> When hard times get you down,
> You've got to believe.
> Things will all turn around.
> You'll see.
> You've gotta believe....

Once I was done, I slid the journal between the mattresses, realizing Romell had his problems, and I had mine. Here I was trying to encourage him, when I was so upset I couldn't even eat. I allowed myself to be sidetracked by a girl I never met and probably would never ever meet, when making sure Spider didn't ask his mother about that check, was way more important. I reheated my plate, poured a glass of water and proceeded to put some food in my stomach. My headache soon went away, but I couldn't get her voice out of my mind. I found myself pacing, hearing the same thoughts. *Calling my man sounding like some ghetto operator from 1-900-DIAL-A-HO, she must think I'm Boo Boo the Fool. Spider likes phone sex. Oh, I'll give him some phone sex.* Obsessing, I found myself once again dialing his pager number.

I walked into the bathroom and retrieved my makeup kit from the wicker caddy. I blew the dust off and stepped in front of the mirror. Dawn said I had the power. This was worth a try. I dotted my middle fingertip with Cocoa, dabbed at my face, rubbing in circles. I outlined my lips with Black Cherry and puckered for Surrender, which was really eggplant. After stroking Wine along my cheekbones, I stared at my eyes. These eyes needed minimizing. I closed one, grabbed the kohl and dragged it across my lid, extending just outside the corners, all the while hoping for a miracle.

I thought I knew what I was doing, until I stepped back and looked. What I saw was about as exotic as a clown mask. There was this unnatural looking line along my jaw where the foundation stopped. Plus it was too pale, even though the color matched when I bought it right after Thanksgiving. The lipstick was about as subtle as that inky stuff Dawn used. The biggest mistake of all was thinking I could make my big bug eyes smaller with eyeliner. Plus, I had that ancient Egyptian thing going on. Pulling my hair back with a banana clip, my feelings were hurt. I reached for the Noxzema and washed it all off. Blotting my face with my white towel, splotches of makeup still smudged it. So, I gave it a second scrubbing, this time paying close attention to my hairline and underneath my chin. I stood and again patted it dry.

Faintly, I heard the phone ring. I smiled when something I thought was provocative came to mind as I was walking into the bedroom. I answered the telephone, whispering, "What's hot, and wet, and has you and I all in it?"

"A bloody battle." Unmistakable, the Harlem twang was Jackie's.

15

"WHAT THE HELL IS GOING ON?"

"Oh hi, Jackie. Just trying on some makeup." I couldn't tell if she knew anything.

"Mia, who'd you think was calling?"

"Oh! Girl, I thought you were Spider."

"Never mind. I'm not even going to ask. Now, what's with you and the war paint?"

"I was trying to give myself a makeover."

"Let me guess. Another girl."

"Something like that."

"You need to stop. Where's your self-esteem? Have confidence."

"Spider doesn't tell me he loves me. How am I supposed to be confident?"

"Spence has *always* kept his feelings to himself."

"Tell me about it! Jackie, you probably know him better than I do. Please, tell me. *Why?*"

"Our mother never told us she loved us. She never hugged and kissed us, so he got it honest. And Spence, he's just always been quiet."

"No, he's guarded!"

"Maybe, but he's loyal."

"Jackie, that don't mean shit if he ain't marrying me!"

"What are you complaining about? He knows where home is!"

I sucked my teeth. "One day, he's going to come home and I won't be here! Either that or someone else will be in his place! You just don't know! I'm *so* tired of waiting on him!"

"Don't worry your pretty little head. He'll do the right thing. He always does. Who knows? Maybe one day he'll surprise you."

"I'll probably die first!" I took a deep breath, wiped away a tear, and lowered my voice. "No, forget I even said that."

"I know. You're frustrated, but—"

"No, I'm fed up! I'm trying to hang on, but it's hard. It's so hard. Sometimes, I wonder why I bother."

"If that's the case, why are you there? Why did you hook up in the first place?"

"Long story."

"Enlighten me."

I propped pillows up for support, yawned, and leaned back. Thinking about it, I had to giggle. "Well, I'll admit. Back in 1985, Spider *was* hot...."

♥   ♥   ♥   ♥

It was the start of my sophomore year at Sunshine Academy High School, right after second period; I was on my way to my friend Lisa's classroom to return her *Right On!* magazine. I had just turned the corner to cut across the long third-floor hallway when I noticed Spider at his locker. I saw those lips...those big, juicy lips and, for that moment, all time stood still. It didn't matter to me that we only had three minutes to get from one class to another. I still had to make it over to Lisa, and then all the way down to the other side of the first floor to get to where I was going, but I stood there gawking. I was frozen in the midst of all the other students around me rushing to class. Memorizing Spider from the curly hair on his head that was then cut into a shag, all the way down to the brand-new, brown Hush Puppies on his feet, I did not snap out of it until he closed his locker and walked away. I'd never seen him before, so I knew he had to be a new student. Judging by his height and because he looked about seventeen or eighteen, I naturally assumed he was a senior who came from another high school.

I was determined to get this "senior" to notice me. I made it a point to go past that same spot at the same time every day, even though that would make me late to my own geometry class. I wasn't bold enough to introduce myself and let him know point blank that I wanted to get to know him better. Instead, I tried getting creative with my appearance, which wasn't easy to do within the constraints of a private school dress code. But, I ditched my knee socks and Bass penny loafers for French Coffee pantyhose and heels. When that didn't seem to work, I started rolling my plaid pleated skirt until it stopped mid-thigh. Then, the deans noticed me. I spent a good number of days in detention back then, but Spider rarely even seemed to look in my direction.

A few months later, in December, Sunshine had School Spirit Day. That's when all students were supposed to come dressed in the school colors, navy blue and white, in support of the pep rally for the basketball team's first game of the season. I was keeping with tradition dressed in my navy blue sweater. But, when I followed my daily ritual of turning that third-floor corner after second period, I spotted him by his locker wearing a varsity basketball jersey with the name "Spider" across the back in large block letters. That confirmed what I already thought: he was a senior. As far as I knew, only juniors and seniors were members of the varsity team. But, later that day, the entire student body had assembly in the gym for the pep rally. The coach grabbed the microphone and went out onto the middle of the court. He called all the varsity players out individually and introduced them. The second player he called was "the talented new addition to the team, number eleven, freshman, Spence 'the Spider' Snyder," and Spider went running.

My jaw dropped. I couldn't believe it. *Freshman?* He was the tallest boy on the whole team and he looked like the oldest. Here it was, I thought he was this drop dead, gorgeous, unapproachable *senior,* and he was just another freshman. He was still cute and all, but now that I was aware that he was younger than me, he was just a kid.

"A kid?" Jackie laughed. "Mia, Spence is only a year younger than you."

"He's five months and ten days younger to be exact. His birthday is May 15th. Mine is December 5th, but back when I was fifteen, and he was only fourteen, our age difference converted like dog years. Anyway, back to how we hooked up...."

The mystique was gone. By no means did I continue to go out of my way to run up to the third floor just to catch a glimpse of *him.* I went about my business. I'd see him in passing, and I'd say, "Hi." He'd say, "Hi" in return. I knew his name; after a while, he knew mine. I'd wish him well in his next game every now and then. I'd also watch the team play every so often. When I didn't go, he would always let me know he didn't see me. That's how we eventually started engaging in small talk, but my fascination with him was over. I basically treated him like a little buddy until the start of the third trimester.

I volunteered to be an English tutor, because I was an honor student in the Advanced Placement class. It was a Monday when the English Department added my name to the list they had posted on the bulletin board in the main corridor. That Friday, I was walking down the hall when Spider tugged the sleeve of my cotton shirt. I looked up at him. In his raspy baritone, sounding like an older man, Spider said, "I've been asking around all week trying to figure out which Mia is Mia Love, the tutor. Is it big Mia, short Mia, or pretty Mia?" He then smiled the cutest smile I had ever seen in my life and asked, "What's your last name?"

I said, "I don't know. Which Mia am I?"

Jackie laughed.

But, I wasn't joking. Truth was: at that moment, I was so drawn in by Spider's smile that my only focus was to get one thing straight, and that was which Mia was which. My mind wandered. As far as I knew, there were three Mias in Sunshine. "Big Mia" was obviously Mia Singleton, the most popular girl in school, who was cool with everybody. There was no mistaking who she was. I figured "short Mia" was Mia Carson from the band, but even though she wore glasses, she wasn't bad looking at all. Then, the thought of all thoughts hit me. Of all the descriptions he could have chosen to identify me by, was he calling *me* pretty? Any number of other titles could have applied. I was thin. Why not call me skinny Mia? I was on the track team. Why not call me Mia from the track team? The most distinctive thing about me was my hair. Why not call me Mia with all the hair? Was the finest guy in Sunshine Academy calling *me* "pretty Mia"?

To understand how I felt at that precise moment, you'd have to understand what it was like growing up in the projects with Dawn as my sister. Dawn and I were known as the two "Love Sisters." Dawn was so incredibly pretty that when we were growing up, the kids used to distinguish me from Dawn in conversation by referring to me as "the ugly one." Up until then, I had kind of grown used to that. I spent a good part of my childhood wishing I were an only child or an identical twin. Now, here I was in high school, where I was no longer a "Love Sister." Dawn went to a different school, so for the first time in my life, *I* was "pretty Mia." And, what made this moment even sweeter was seeing *who* was calling me "pretty Mia." All of this was going through my head while I was staring up at Spider's pretty, white teeth. I snapped out of it, realizing what I had just said to Spider didn't make any sense. I tried to clean it up by rephrasing. "I mean, what difference does it make what my last name is?" I said.

Spider said, plain and simple, "If *you* are Mia Love, I want *you* to be my tutor?"

"Why?" I asked.

He smiled again flirtatiously, and in that sexy voice said, "Because, I want me a love."

I nearly melted, and I fell for him right then and there, but I didn't want to make a fool of myself by losing my cool. I asked him, "Why me?"

Spider backed away, smiling. His response was, "Why not?"

I became his tutor, even though he didn't need any help in English. That was evident in our first study session. Spider met me at the library to review Shakespeare's *Hamlet*. I arrived all prepared to decrypt Elizabethan grammar—line by line. But, he sat, flipped his paperback right to the soliloquy, and said, "'*To sleep perchance to dream.*' Ain't that kind of ironic? Suicide seems so appealing to this cat because of all he suffered through in his life. To him, life is cruel and death's a permanent sleep that might even be filled with sweet dreams. And, as far as I see, it's not even reverence for life that's stopping him; it's fear of the unknown." Then, he looked at me with those hazel eyes and said, "What do you think?"

I smiled and said, "I thought *I* was supposed to be the tutor."

Even with all the A's I'd earned in AP English, I hadn't analyzed that passage that deeply; I just understood that Hamlet was tired of living, but too much of a coward to do anything about it. Here I was, supposedly the tutor, but *Spider* had just enlightened *me*. And he needed to be tutored? It didn't take a genius to figure out what was going on. Tutoring was just his excuse to spend time with me. So, I leaned right in and kissed him. That sealed it. Our age difference no longer mattered.

"Wait a minute, Mia. This story doesn't make sense to me."

"What do you mean?"

"'I want me a love?' That don't sound like my brother."

"Well, that's exactly what he said. That's why I love him."

"And 'Pretty Mia'? That don't sound anything like Spence, either."

"He said that, too!" I didn't mean to raise my voice, but now, I was getting annoyed.

"Doubt it!" Jackie shouted. Then, she continued in her normal voice. "Spence thinks the whole world is superficial. He doesn't go around calling people 'pretty.' And I definitely can't picture him saying 'I want me a love,' especially not back then, because back then, all Spence cared about was basketball, ColecoVision, and making up those games on his Commodore 64."

I had to admit Jackie was right about one thing: in high school, Spider was obsessed with that Commodore 64. Once he learned how to program random functions and graphics in BASIC, he'd spend weeks typing codes just so his computer would perform simple card games. I remember when he finally got that Commodore 64 to run Spades. It took him nine weeks. Back then, we thought the graphics looked like actual playing cards, but they were only dots and characters. Spider hadn't yet learned to integrate color. Still, we were all amazed at what he could do on that thing. "What happened to the Commodore 64, anyway?"

"Spence replaced it with the new computer he bought. Why?"

"Just curious," I said, thinking where the hell did Spider get the money to buy a new computer. But, I didn't let on to Jackie that she told me anything I didn't already know.

"Listen, Mia. I called because I need a favor."

"Okay, name it."

"I need you to look after Joy. Mike and I wanna visit his timeshares. We're gonna spend four days in Hawaii and three days in Vegas."

"Jackie, I don't mind, but I can't keep going back and forth to Brooklyn to feed your cat. Can you take her to Dr. Snyder's? I can stop there on my way home from work."

"Mommy doesn't want her at the house anymore."

"Why not?"

"Joy clawed her old leather sofa last year when I was in the hospital. Remember? If you don't wanna come to Brooklyn, watch her at your house. You don't mind do you?"

"Is that animal declawed yet?"

"You know what, Mia? If you say another negative thing

about my brother or try to pump me for information one more time, I will personally crack your skull!" Jackie hung up.

16

$\mathcal{I}$ CAN'T STAND THEATRICS. THAT'S ALL THAT WAS, because as far as I could see, I didn't say anything wrong. Jackie's temperamental. Kind of like my sister, but the difference between those two was that Jackie might actually hurt somebody. She and I never came to blows, but I felt sorry for Mike. Jackie liked to throw things, and since he knew how to duck and cover, they were together almost as long as me and Spider. Good thing he had good reflexes. How Jackie managed to control her moods and earn a living as a social worker, I never knew.

This time, I didn't care if she was pissed off or not. Pet sitting in my apartment was where I drew the line. That couch Jackie called "old" was Dr. Snyder's button-tufted leather. She had it for years, but it was a classic, and it was in perfect condition. That sofa was burgundy. My loveseat was white and fabric upholstered. My chaise was upholstered in the prettiest pattern of blue carnations. My small swivel chair in the corner was brown leather. So was the ottoman. And Joy already had a thing for leather too? No way. Jackie would reimburse me for damage, but my furniture was worth way more than what I paid for it. I searched high and low for good quality, classic pieces, completely restored them myself, found coordinating fabrics, hand-stitched pillows, cushions, and window treatments just to tie all my furniture and periwinkle blue walls together in perfect, modern-vintage harmony. After all that trouble, her two-hundred-dollar compensation offer would only piss me off. Even if that was what everything cost me. Pet sitting? Not in my apartment. Not for her or her fat black tabby.

That established, I wasn't going to let her mood swing sway mine. I had other concerns. I just couldn't believe Spider bought that computer. That thought never even occurred to me. I was so preoccupied with the checks, whether or not Spider was going to tell his mother, and then that woman's call; I just automatically assumed Dr. Snyder bought that computer herself. Then again, when I thought about it, why would she? Dr. Snyder didn't buy crap. *So, why would Spider buy a computer without telling me? Why would he send it over there, when I was here pecking on a decade-old Smith Corona.* The phone rang, reminding me. *Hello! Phone sex. Get it together.* I picked up the phone. Making sure I didn't make the same mistake twice, I said, "Spider?"

"Yeah, I'm returning your call. What's for dinner?"

I moaned, "I'll tell you what's for dinner. What's hot, wet, and has you and I all in it?"

"Alphabet soup? Great. I'm in starvation mode right about now. I'll be home soon. What did you want to talk to me about?"

I hated him. "Nothing that can't wait until later. See you when you get home."

That wasn't what I expected, but I guess it didn't matter. He was on his way home. I grabbed my portable cassette player, plugged it into the outlet in the bathroom, hit play, and moaned for real. Rufus & Chaka's *Everlasting Love*, the right song at the right time could make me forget all about my problems for at least three minutes and thirty seconds. I turned on the faucet, running the water as hot as I could stand. That way the apartment would feel much cooler when I emerged from the bathroom. I'd brought my candles into the bathroom with me. I lit them, poured scented oil into the tub, and turned out the lights. Then, I undressed and climbed in. I loved my freestanding tub. It was long and deep. Now, with my eyes closed, I inhaled apricot steam from rising water so hot, my stomach muscles contracted involuntarily. When the water reached my chin and my feet floated, I cut the faucet off with my toes. This was my twenty minutes of bliss, so I just allowed my inner self to drift.

Lately, I didn't know what was going on with Spider. When we were younger he made me feel so special because *he* noticed *me*. For the first time in my life, I wasn't overshadowed or ignored. Back then, Romell only noticed pretty faces and exaggerated curves like...Dawn's. Bad example. More like the *Jet* magazine pin-ups he used as wallpaper. He wouldn't have noticed me if I were dipped in

110

purple paint. Maybe because we had taken baths together as babies, he just never thought of me that way. I don't know, but I guess because he was always right in my face, it was only natural that he'd be the first boy I looked at differently. I remember being about twelve and having a dream I kissed Romell. I spent the whole next day staring at his lips, even though they were so chapped, they were flaking. I think that had something to do with the fact that he had a mouth full of wire. Still, I was scheming to kiss him, crusty lips and all. We rode the subway together to and from school; he never picked up on it. In fact, on the way home, we talked nonstop almost the whole ride, until he pulled out his afro pick and began to "uh huh" me to death, picking his fro. He forgot all about our conversation. Some girl had walked in. She wasn't even that cute, but she was top heavy.

Another time, toward the end of the ninth grade, I remember curling my hair one morning, slicking my baby hair down with Vaseline, smearing on bubble gum lip-gloss, and stuffing my Cross Your Heart. I called Romell, telling him to meet me in front of our favorite grocery store, Betancas. I got there and just waited. So, I walked inside, bought apple juice and a pack of powdered doughnuts, went back to the corner, and waited some more. Romell was taking his sweet time. After finishing my doughnuts and juice, I reapplied my lip-gloss, still no Romell. Just about everybody was going in and out of that bodega, so I was growing impatient, until my girlfriend Pam walked up and decided to wait with me.

She always knew the dirt on everybody, who was sleeping with who, who was pregnant, who was notorious for cutting school, and who was just sent to a group home. This was juicy gossip back then, and once Pam was on a roll, she didn't stop. I was so engrossed in my conversation with her that I didn't see Romell approach, but I heard his voice.

"Aye, baby. You look good!"

Inside, I was screaming, but I turned around and softly said, "Thank you."

Without missing a beat, Romell said, "I wasn't talking to you." He grabbed Pam, leading her by the finger to the space between the buildings until he saw me walk off without him. He called after me so I half-walked, half-ran, trying to distance myself enough so that he wouldn't see the tears in my eyes. But he caught up, and when he did, he took one look at my face and handed me his starched handkerchief. I snapped it open and was about to wipe my eyes, until Romell whispered, "Chocolate, if you must eat powdered doughnuts, wipe your mouth."

♥ ♥ ♥ ♥

The music caught my attention again. Now, it was Mary J. Blige's "Be Happy." At first, I closed my eyes and snapped my fingers in my bathwater, swaying. And then, I joined in.

> All I really want
> Is to be happy
> To find a love that's mine
> It would be so sweet
>
> I asked for a sign
> From the sweet Lord above
> I know the answer is in front of me
> But when

I felt my hair sliding out from the hairpin into the water. I stood up and reached for my towel. There, standing in the doorway staring was Spider.

"How long have you been there?"

"Long enough." Spider said, cutting on the light. His skin was as tan as the basketball in his hands.

"One of these days, you should learn to knock."

"You know, at the label we say if you want to know what's on a person's mind, pay attention to the songs they sing. There was even a Candi Staton song something like that."

I thought for a moment. "Oh? Now, I'm a victim." Why couldn't he walk in when I was singing "Everlasting Love"? I was trying to set the stage for romance, and here he was trying to bait me into an argument. I sucked my teeth, then took the bait, "That reminds me. Who the hell is Asia? And why'd she call you?"

"I already told you; she's a friend."

"Why's this *friend* calling you?" I screamed.

"Lower your voice. Jeff is in the kitchen."

"How do you know her, Spider?"

"I met her through my man Lance. She's his computer hook up."

"Why is *she* calling on a new phone line? Do I have the number? Do I?"

"The new number at my mother's is for the computer, for

fax, e-mail, and Internet access. I faxed Asia from the computer, because I wanted her to hook me up with another one. She called the fax number back. That's how she got the number. I didn't give it to her."

"Why are you carrying on this friendship, knowing this woman is obviously interested?"

"Stop. I only called her because I knew we needed a computer to do my résumé."

"Then, why did she say it wasn't business when she called?"

"Maybe she *was* interested. Either that or she didn't want you to know what she was calling about. I *did* tell her I wanted to surprise my wife."

Every time he called me that, it threw me. I was speechless for a second. "Wife?"

"I said that to cool her off."

I gave him the evil eye for a moment and then said, "Well, how much was the computer, anyway?"

"Two hundred, and it has more memory and more features on it than my mother's."

"Your mother paid over two thousand for her Gateway. You only had to pay two hundred? Is that what your friend Lance paid, too?"

"I don't know what he paid, but he did tell me it was going to be four hundred."

"Are you sure there was no funny business going on between you and that woman, and that's why you sent that computer over to your mother's."

"You see, now you're thinking too much. The only reason I had her bring it there was because I didn't feel like arguing."

I had to admit. If a girl showed up here with a computer, Spider and I would have definitely had it out. I stepped out of the tub and blew out the candles. Then, I wrapped my hair in a towel. After Spider handed me another one, I asked, "Where did you get the money for it?"

"I haven't paid for it yet. Jeff told me he would give it to me because Asia was going to throw in a second one for free. I was going to give him that."

"Jeff borrows from you, Spider. Ain't nothing in this world free. And what do you mean *was going to*?"

It was hot in this bathroom. Spider used the bottom of his Knicks jersey to wipe the sweat off his face. "Asia says she can't get it anymore."

I shook my head. "Surprise surprise."

Now, he looked frustrated. "Any more questions?"

"Were you playing ball all day long?"

"Yeah."

"I can smell."

Spider laughed. "Well, not all day. For a while, I stood around watching Jeff blow his whole paycheck."

"Did he give you the money for the computer?"

"No."

I sucked my teeth again. "I only have the three hundred dollars. I was saving for a washer and dryer. Tee-Bo needs a crib, and now I've got to pay for a computer?"

"I could always owe her the money, until Jeff—"

"Get that thought right outta your head, Spider. You can't count on Jeff!" He shushed me, backed out, and looked down the hall. He came back with his finger pressed to his lips and closed the door, so I lowered my voice. "How did he blow his paycheck *this time*?"

"In C-lo."

"What's that?"

Spider sat on the toilet top. "A dice game."

"Jeff blew that much in a dice game?"

"That's not even the half of it," he whispered. "They're going to put him out of his apartment, because he's behind on his rent."

"Why'd you just watch him throw all his money away if his rent was behind?"

"He was ahead!" He shouted and then lowered his voice again. "After he aced out, he told me he has to come up with twenty-five hundred by Monday."

"So, what's the plan?"

"I don't know yet. We'll figure something out."

That was fine with me just as long as Spider didn't get any ideas about his insurance check. He knelt down, dipped his hand in my bath, and pulled the plug. The way he looked at me, I thought he was going to kiss me. Instead, he took his hand out and flicked water into my face.

"Hey!" I said wiping my face and blinking my blurry eyes.

He smiled. "Hurry up, so you can say hello to Jeff."

Wrapped in a towel, I walked into the bedroom and quickly jumped into my house clothes: my favorite

114

nightgown, the one with all the cooking stains on it, my old gray terry cloth bathrobe, and my fuzzy slippers. I heard the spray of the shower as I passed the bathroom on my way to the kitchen. Spider smelled like a dirty dog after he played basketball, but this was Saturday. I was all set to say hello and good-bye to Jeff, rush him out the door, and make love to my man, funky.

Once the scent of a fresh cut flower hit my nose, I knew I was definitely giving Jeff the boot. Spider had a single rose in a vase sitting on our small table. I smiled.

Because *Jeff* was in my kitchen; I quickly scanned the area. As usual, he had my Rubbermaid containers spread on the table as he invaded my leftovers. He had just warmed his plate in the microwave. I could still see the steam rising from his chicken and potatoes as it sat on the counter. I was glad he finally understood to use the stoneware. The last time Jeff had used my microwave, he warmed lasagna in my favorite container. When he was done, it had permanent tomato stains, and the cheese and grease ate a hole through the plastic. After looking around, I was satisfied that no damage control was necessary on my part, so I cleared my throat to make my presence known. Jeff surfaced from inside the refrigerator with a bottle of Mott's in hand. He put it on the table and gave me a warm hug.

"Whoa, Mia! You didn't have to get all dressed up on my account."

I laughed because my robe *was* on the raggedy side. Jeff was dressed to impress in black slacks, Spider's short sleeve silk shirt, nice shoes, and the back of his hair had a fresh fade. I started to ask where he was going, but I didn't care as long as he was leaving. "I should be saying that to you. How you doing, Jeff?"

Jeff pushed his long dangling curls back out of his eyes. "You know; can't complain. So Mia, what's up? Did the ol' man leave us all checks for fifty g's or what?"

I choked. "Did who do what?" I said after I regained my composure.

"I'm just messin' witchu, Mia," Jeff said with his toothy grin. Then, he added, "Seriously, my pops *did* have insurance?"

Now, I cut my eye at Jeff and put my hand on my hip.

"I'm just playin'," he said, pouring apple juice into a tall glass. He put the container back in the fridge and turned to me. "So, Mia. When are you gonna stop blockin'?"

"Dawn is seeing somebody right now," I said.

"What does that have to do with anything?" Jeff asked. I thought about that.

Jeff was short and skinny, with a sandy brown, curly mop top, and a face full of freckles; he worked at the Chicken Shack. I thought he was joking, but his green eyes were intent; he was a wide-eyed face full of teeth waiting for an answer. I bit my tongue and laughed to myself. Jeff always did have a sense of humor. He also had three four-year-olds, all born in November, and they weren't triplets. I knew better than to answer that question. "How's your mother?" I said.

Jeff twisted his lips. "*Ah-ight.* Change the subject." He soon added, "Lola is cool."

"Good. Tell Miss Lola I asked about her."

"No problem." Jeff sulked, and now I felt bad.

17

I WATCHED JEFF PICK AT HIS FOOD WHEN HE WAS usually a garbage disposal, so I knew he was disappointed. Kyle was everything Jeff wasn't. Sometimes it's better to politely change the subject.

♥ ♥ ♥ ♥

Dawn and Kyle were together for three years. I met him once, and that was by accident. I dropped by my sister's that day, because I was shopping in her neighborhood. Three months pregnant, morning sickness was kicking my ass. When I saw the Bentley parked in front of her building, I knew she had company. I rang her bell wondering. *Who is it this time? Was it another rapper or comedian? Football or basketball player? A boxer?* With Dawn, there was no telling. The only thing consistent was that she never dated hustlers.

Dawn looked through the peephole. Seeing no one, a few times she called out, "Who?" I answered, but I guess she didn't hear me. She cracked the door open and saw I was all doubled over. She stepped out barefoot. Her hooker shoes were in her hand, the lime green ones, suede, strappy, platform sandals with five-inch, spiked heels.

"I need to stay here for a little while. I don't feel so well."

"Hell no! I have company," Dawn said.

"I don't feel well, Dawn. Come on," I said to her knees.

"No. I am not gonna have you come up in here and bust up my groove. Stop being so dramatic and go home!"

"Dawn, I *am* sick."

"Yeah right! And, stand up, Mia. You know it is *not* that serious."

I slowly straightened, getting a better look at Dawn's yellow, silk mini-dress with its plunging neckline. Thin gold snake chains graduated from her cleavage up to her collarbone. Her lips were twisted in disbelief. I was soon to make a believer out of her. Once I stood completely upright, I lost my stomach, covering Dawn's silk dress and lime, suede, hooker shoes in recycled pizza and slushie. But after that, I did feel much better.

While Dawn was cussing and changing, I sat with Kyle. At first, I was trying to figure him out. He was wearing a tailored, white linen suit, with ornate, gold buttons, and not a stitch of jewelry, so I knew he wasn't a rapper. He smiled a lot and said little, so I figured he wasn't a comedian; they're usually pretty talkative and full of snide comments. He was tall and had a nice build, but he seemed too thin to be a football player and he didn't seem tall enough to be a basketball player who could afford a Bentley. His skin was as rich and smooth as peanut butter. The edges of his goatee were sharp. He had long, thin locks. They were the neatest I'd ever seen, but still too edgy for the corporate world, so I was puzzled. *He's too pretty to be a boxer. Maybe the car isn't his. Anybody could rent a car or shop bargain basement for a designer suit.* Then, Kyle pulled his sleeve back and checked the time. He did it in one quick motion, but my eyeballs snagged onto his diamond-face Rolex. And yes, I know this was uncouth, but I asked anyway, "Is that real?"

"Definitely."

"Where did you buy that?"

"It was a gift."

"Mmph," I said. "You must've made *somebody* happy." I watched him chuckle and straighten his lapel, even though it was already straight. *Maybe, he's an investment banker? Not with that hair.* I watched him shuffle his feet, dragging the soles of his expensive loafers across Dawn's white carpet. I looked down at my own bare feet and twisted my lips. My sandals were waiting by the door in the bin. Our own mother didn't walk on Dawn's carpet wearing her street shoes. If Dawn allowed Kyle to walk on her white carpet with shoes on his feet, he had to be loaded. "So Kyle, what do you do for a living?"

Kyle tucked his finger inside the collar of his light blue dress shirt and stretched his neck. His fingernails were neat and clean but too long. "I dibble and dabble in a lot of things. Mostly," he cleared his throat, "real estate."

"Nice!" I said. "Where do you invest?"

He laughed nervously, wrung his hands, and cleared his throat again. "All over," he answered. He peeked over at me out the corner of his eye. By now, I was on the edge of my seat; I had leaned forward and was nodding, urging him to explain. So, he took a deep breath and continued, "New Orleans, Rio, and Nevada." That said; I knew he had money. Dawn later filled me in; he was a virtual money tree with a Westhampton Beach estate. She had been seeing him for about two years at that point. Even now, Mommy still hadn't met him, but Dawn claimed that was only because he was out of town a lot. Dawn had yet to give us an explanation as to why she kept Kyle such a secret for so long. I mean, he was good-looking, well dressed, and wealthy; how could we disapprove? As far as I saw, he was perfect. Maybe a little too perfect.

♥   ♥   ♥   ♥

Hearing the ding of the timer, I pulled Spider's plate from the microwave, steam rising as I laid it on the table. "Spider, your plate!" I yelled. One by one, I stacked all my containers back into the refrigerator. Spider seemed to be taking his sweet time. "Spider!" I yelled. "If I wanted you to eat cold food, I wouldn't have bothered to warm your plate!" I still didn't get a response, but I watched Jeff finish with his dishes and rinse them.

I was trying to think of a tactful way to let Jeff know it was time for him to leave, when I was hit by the approach of *Obsession* cologne. Then, I heard Jeff say, "No khakis! That's what's up!" I turned around and looked as Spider stepped into the kitchen decked in a tight Romeo Gigolo black, muscle shirt and black slacks with his black dress lace-up shoes.

"Aye, Mia. Do you have a couple of dollars?" Spider said.

I walked over to the leather chair, spun it around, and reached inside the diaper bag for my change purse. I counted the money in it three times. It was the same three hundred dollars, no more, no less. I thought I was getting ahead by saving for the washing machine. With a sigh, I held forty dollars out to Spider, at first, but then I crumpled the money back into a fist.

"Can I talk to you for a minute?" I said, making my way toward the bedroom and almost losing my cool. He entered behind me. There he stood, smelling all tasty, tanned as copper as a brand-new penny, hair all glistening.

"Aren't you going to stay and eat?"

"I'll grab something later."

"Why don't you grab *me* now?"

"Stop playin', Mia."

I tightened my grip on the forty dollars. "No, Spider. Tell Jeff to go on without you. Please, I wanna spend time with you."

"Later."

Before I had the baby, I would have simply stripped. At the sight of my naked body, at least there was a fifty-fifty chance he'd tell Jeff he'd catch up with him later and later would never come. Still self-conscious about those last five extra pounds right around the middle since giving birth, I didn't think disrobing would have achieved the desired effect. That only worked when I felt sexy. I didn't want to lay any kind of guilt trip on him, but desperate times call for desperate measures. "Spider, you're killing me!"

He kissed me, Listerine on his breath, gently peeling the money out of my hand. "I'll take care of you when I get back."

"I'll be asleep!"

"I'll wake you."

"I'll be comatose!"

"Stop playin', Mia," he said, smiling. He snatched one of two sets of keys sitting on the dresser and walked out of the bedroom. Shortly after, I heard the front door close.

I just didn't get it. I was bathed in apricot bath oil. Maybe the raggedy robe wasn't the most provocative thing, but still, after a day of worrying, here I was spending my Saturday alone and horny, while he left looking and smelling his best. Once upon a time, I would've kept myself sane, by wearing one of Dawn's dresses, sipping Cristal in VIP amongst celebrities, and having her scream over the music, "Mia, he's buying! You better give that man a dance!" There was something about getting tipsy enough to kick off my heels and dance barefoot across a sticky floor, until I was wet with sweat that could make me say, "Spider who?" Even if it was three o' clock in the morning. Now, guess what? I didn't have that option. Yeah, Dawn invited me to a red carpet event, and I had a babysitter, but I didn't have the energy.

I removed my raggedy bathrobe, balled it up, aimed for the wastebasket across the room and sank it inside the wicker brim, knocking the basket onto its side. But, then I walked over, pulled my robe out, folded it, and stood the wastebasket back up. It didn't make any sense for me to trash my robe; I could still get a few more wears out of it. Opening the drawer to put it away, my pen stared back at me.

I had a better idea. I stuffed the robe in the drawer and grabbed my pen. Then I bent down and slid my arm between my mattress and box spring across the cold metal of my silver link bracelet right to what I was reaching for. I slowly pulled it out. I climbed into my bed and placed my purple journal on my lap. Smelling like my apricot bath oil only reminded me that I was alone. *I may be alone, but I'm not giving up, now. Just earlier, Spider called me his wife.* His exact words were, "Yo, Jeff. My wife said, 'Hi.'" I sighed. *It's just a matter of time, now. It's just a matter of time.* I opened my journal to the white satin ribbon that marked off the next blank page. Putting my pen to the page, I wrote a full poem and called it "It's Just a Matter of Time."

18

*I*T WASN'T LONG BEFORE I SLID MY JOURNAL BACK in place and turned out the light. Having missed about three feedings, my breasts were hard. Lying on my left side was painful. So was lying on my right. It was eleven thirty, almost time for Tee-Bo's midnight feeding. I stretched out flat on my back, closed my eyes, and inhaled a tasty breath. Apricot. I inhaled again. The flavor was different. I inhaled once more. This time, I allowed the breath to completely fill my lungs. But it wasn't sweet; it was salty. I opened my eyes. I was on the deck of a yacht surrounded by water and the sky was filled with stars. Romell's bowlegs were strolling toward me. White linen slacks hung loosely from his waist. Shirtless, his muscles rippled and his coffee-brown skin now seemed pitch black as moonlight beamed off his shaved head. I looked up into his face, and he smiled, revealing all three of his dimples—the deep one that pierced his left cheek, the subtle one on the right, and that comma just off the corner of his mouth. He gently placed his hand on the small of my back leading me past a row of deck chairs and into the gentle wind. It blew my white gown upward. Quickly, I smoothed it back down.

"I'm here for you now, Mia. Tell me what you want."

Romell's voice seems heavier than usual, I thought. I looked around and saw several women also with flowing white gowns, but they were walking around with these colorful drinks with tiny umbrellas in them.

"Can you go get me something to drink?" I said.

He nodded and then disappeared through a set of swinging doors.

I rested my arms on the brass rail and looked out into the frothy ocean. I heard a voice, "Mia, I know you were upset when I left."

Now, I was confused. I wasn't upset when Romell just left.

123

"This should make you feel better," he continued.

The heavier voice had me thinking, *Romell must have a cold or something.* I turned to him. He had a red drink in one hand and a yellow drink in the other. I chose the red and we toasted. Before I could take a sip, he kissed me. His lips were soft and his kiss was deep but I could taste liquor on his breath and he smelled like *Obsession.* The next thing I knew, a strong gust of wind blew my gown completely over my head. I don't know what happened to our glasses but, Romell's body pressed against mine. My sore breasts were about as obtrusive as a nine-month pregnant belly in a slow drag. I tried to pull away but he was all over me, touching and feeling. I felt his lips and tongue glide across my breast. That felt good. I closed my eyes tight and allowed my body to slowly fall to the deck in response to all the sensations it was receiving.

Wait a minute! I thought. *This is wrong. I have to stop him. We can't do this.*

But he began to lick me lower and lower. I grew more and more excited as he licked my belly button, my hipbone and down inside my thigh.

If this man is going to lick me where I think he's going to lick me, he can have me.

But then the licking stopped. I felt him slide right inside me as if he belonged, but I was too horny to stop him.

"Now, aren't you glad I came back?" he said, but now I was totally confused because this looked like Romell but sounded nothing like him.

"What is your name?" I asked.

"Stop playin', Mia," he said. "What's my name?"

"I don't know," I whined. He then went at it more vigorously. He was nowhere near as gentle as before. Now he was performing like he had something to prove.

"Guess!" The tone was harsh, but this time the husky voice was unmistakable.

"Spider?" I said.

"Open your eyes, Mia!" When I did, Spider's hard expression scared me. I held my tongue until he collapsed. He rolled onto his side. "Who did you think I was?"

"I don't know. I was in a deep sleep. So you can't blame me for not being aware of what was going on." I turned on my side and faced him. "I'm still upset with you."

He relaxed and lowered his tone. "What do you have to be upset about?"

"You slighted me by going out tonight, and that was like the third or fourth time you slighted me today. And to top it all off, you're going to question your mother about that check."

"Is that what's wrong with you? Fine, I won't mention anything then. You happy?"

"Yes. No! There's more. Stop dismissing me! If you care for me, be there for me like I'm here for you." That last statement got to me. A stream of tears flowed down my face.

"All right, Mia. All right. Shh, it's okay." He wrapped his long, strong arm around me, drawing me in. "Is that all?" Breath hinting of sweet liqueur warmed my ear.

"Just one more thing. Please, don't maintain any friendships with any women that I don't know about. My heart can't take it. And tomorrow morning you'll find two hundred dollars on the dresser. Pay that bitch off. I don't want you owing her anything."

"Mia, what are you worried about?"

"Spider, women try to be your friend because they're attracted to you, but I don't want any of those friendships to develop into something more."

"Do you honestly think I would let any female come between me and my family."

"You're a man, Spider. If the right pretty woman comes along, you might be tempted. So, please, watch it with these slick bitches!"

"Whatever," he said submissively.

"Is that a promise?"

"I guess," Spider yawned.

"So, you won't go back on your word?"

"A promise is a promise. If nothing else, I'm a man of my word."

I sighed, finally relieved. That was a close call. I should've known that was Spider. No matter what I saw in my dream, I was hearing a husky voice that didn't say "thank you," "I love you," or "I'm sorry." Who else would that be? I relaxed in the warmth of his embrace and for a moment was just giddy because everything had worked out. Then, Spider chuckled. "What's so funny?" I said.

"You crack me up."

125

"Why? Why am I funny?"

"You should know by now. I've never been a sucker for a pretty face. Stop worrying and go to sleep." Spider turned, facing the rattling fan. I put my arm around his waist, but my engorged breasts felt like rocks. I returned to my back. Listening to Tee-Bo's steady breaths, I knew he wouldn't wake. I closed my eyes and tried to relax, but then something Spider had just said started to upset me.

19

I SHOULD KNOW BY NOW, HE'S NEVER BEEN A sucker for a pretty face. Those words still stung the next morning. It was Sunday. I already did my grocery shopping, and now, I was attempting to bang out a perfect résumé on Spider's manual typewriter. *He's never been a sucker for a pretty face. What was he trying to say? Was that his way of saying he's never been a sucker for MY pretty face, or he's a sucker for my UGLY face? Did he think those words would put my mind at ease?*

I pounded a closed fist into the Smith Corona resting on the small leather ottoman in front of me. I finally had the thing typed past WORK EXPERIENCE with no mistakes, but forgetting to put the "o" at the end of Romeo, I typed Rome Gigolo. My mind was here, there, and everywhere. I snatched the sheet of paper out of the typewriter, balled it up, and tossed it into the wastebasket atop all the other crumpled balls. At this rate, I'd never finish. My concentration was shot. I had to put another blank sheet in, roll the carriage, set the margins, and tab the line all the way across. And that computer was over at the brownstone just sitting there. The telephone rang as I was marking the tab position on the ruler. I slid the ottoman out of the way and stepped over to the phone. "Hello," I said.

"Did you get that washing machine yet?"

"Hi, Mommy." I plopped onto the loveseat. It was seven thirty. I didn't expect Spider or Tee-Bo to wake for at least another hour but I wanted to keep this conversation short and sweet. "I should be able to get a washing machine soon, and I have a good feeling Spider will get me a ring soon, too."

"Wake up, Mia."

"Why are you being so hard on me?"

"Because, when you insisted on your plans for the pregnancy followed by the engagement, I warned you then

127

about doing it ass backwards, 'Don't bring a child into this world as a single mother without planning on raising it single-handedly.'"

"Mommy, give Spider *some* credit."

"You give your boyfriend too much credit. Now, he's got his baby, and all you have is an IOU. You can't bank on an IOU, Mia. You should know that. You're a bill collector."

"Spider's expecting a large check. That we *can* bank on."

"I know. Dawn told me."

That Dawn! I was so caught off guard by that one. "Well," I whined, "Spider is going...to go...and...and buy me my ring, Mommy. You'll see."

Her tone remained somber. "I hope so, Mia. But, remember what I always tell you."

"I know. Don't count your chickens. Why buy the cow? And I could lead a horse to water."

"All that's true, but remember insanity...is doing the same thing over and over, expecting different results. It's been ten years, Mia. And you still don't seem happy to me. That man may not be the best man for you. If I were you, I wouldn't put all my eggs in one basket."

I mumbled, "They're *my* eggs. Next, you'll be telling me what to do with my butter and cream."

"What did you say?"

"I said *that's* not the advice I need, Mommy. Don't you understand? I don't want another basket. I only want Spider! I can't live without him!"

"Stop saying that!"

I rolled my eyes. I wasn't even going to argue with her, but I knew I meant that. Being mindful of my tone of voice, I took a deep breath, and then said, "Okay, Mommy. I'll put it another way: Spider is the love of my life."

"That is a powerful thing to say about a man, but it ain't that powerful when you say it at the beginning of your life, Mia. I see where you're heading. I've been in your shoes myself."

"How were you in my shoes, Mommy? How!"

"I got your sister from a 'trust me' and you from an 'I promise' that's how! Needless to say, I raised you both *alone* until the next man came along and said, 'I do'."

"*I* am not going to be alone. *I* will do whatever I have to do to walk down the aisle, stand at the altar, and say those two magic words."

"Don't be so sure, Mia. Remember, I was sure at one time, myself. That's why I can see what you can't see. Right now, you're blinded by love, but *hindsight* is twenty-twenty. Now, what's going on with the baby's rash?"

"I took him to a specialist and got a new prescription."

"Is it working?"

"I haven't seen any improvement yet. And, I checked him thoroughly first thing this morning while he was sleeping in his stroller."

"Where did you take the baby this early in the morning?"

"Nowhere. I went grocery shopping at five this morning, but I left him here with Spider."

"Then why was he sleeping in his stroller?"

"He's sleeping in his stroller until I can get him a crib."

"Sleeping in the stroller? That's it! I'm on my way."

"On your way? For what?"

"I'm coming to check on the baby and buy him a crib."

"You can't come, Mommy!"

"And, why not?"

"I'm...I'm...pet sitting. Jackie's cat is here."

"Cat? How long will that animal be there?"

"A few weeks."

"Well, fine. I've got a catalog right here. I can have one delivered by tomorrow."

"No, Mommy! I'm going to get him a crib myself."

"Mia, you wanna do everything yourself, but I am letting you know, right now; I'm not going to stand by and let my grandbaby take a back seat while you bend over backwards for your boyfriend and his family."

"Okay, Mommy. But, what do you expect me to do?"

"Do something about my grandbaby's rash, Mia. And, get a crib or else I will be on your doorstep with my suitcase, and that cat is going out the window. Now, when the hell are you getting a crib for my baby?"

"Today, Mommy. Today."

"Good, I'll talk to you later, Mia. Call me if you need me."

She hung up, and I was numb. Just that fast, Tee-Bo went from being "the baby" to being her "grandbaby," and then to being her baby. Now, not only did I have to get rid of Tee-Bo's rash, I had to somehow buy him a crib and soon. Otherwise, I would have to deal with Mommy up close and personal. I did everything I knew possible to get rid of that rash. Nothing worked. I had sixty dollars. That wasn't enough to get Tee-Bo a new crib, but I had to get one quick. Telling Mommy a cat was here wouldn't hold her off for long because once Dawn crossed the threshold, all would be revealed.

Dawn couldn't hold water in a bucket. I remember when Dawn opened up Head to Toe with her best friend Imani. Imani asked me, "What's the best way to advertise?"

I told her, "Tell Dawn to keep it a secret." If I didn't get a crib, once Dawn got wind of it, Mommy was sure to find out, and if Tee-Bo's rash didn't clear, Mommy was sure to find that out, too. And, the last thing I wanted was Mommy at my house facing off with Spider. Spider couldn't stand lies, but Mommy was brutal. If she came over, she would have some honesty for his ass.

20

WITH SO MUCH WEIGHING ME DOWN, I NEEDED Romell, but discussing the same issues over and over made me feel like I was going around in circles instead of moving forward. I couldn't bring myself to tell him that Mommy chewed me out again for pretty much the same reasons. I wanted our next conversation to be about how I resolved everything. So, even though his wisdom would usually put everything in perspective, I didn't intend to dump my problems on him this time. We could talk about anything else. Really, I just wanted to hear his voice.

I picked the receiver up off my cube-shaped chest, which served double duty as an end table. I punched in Romell's area code but hung up; this wasn't wise. Spider was home. It was better to wait until later or go downtown to talk to Romell in person. I sat there a moment, contemplating, and then stood up. Stepping away from the loveseat, my floor creaked, stopping me. I was not about to let my squeaky floor give me away. Not if I could help it. I stepped and waited. Stepped. And waited. Stepped and waited all the way to my bedroom door, eased it open, and peeked inside. Spider lay in a twisted heap, eyes closed, and mouth open. He snorted. I dipped back behind the door and didn't move a muscle until I heard a smacking noise, then I stole a glimpse. Spider was smacking his lips as he rolled over toward the window. He grunted, and then I heard nothing but the rattle of the fan. I pulled the door all the way closed and crept back. Then, I dusted my bare feet off and sat Indian style. The way Spider looked, I figured he would be asleep for at least another hour. I sat the telephone in my lap and dialed. When Romell picked up, I whispered, "Hey."

"What's wrong?"

"Why?"

"Mia, I can always tell when something's bothering you."

131

"Nothing's bothering me. I—"

"I can also tell when you're hiding something. If you wanna tell me, tell me. If not, don't call me at seven forty-five in the morning. You know Sundays I sleep til noon." He yawned.

"I'm sorry. We do need to talk."

"What's wrong?"

"Spider said something that hurt my feelings. He is *so* unappreciative. I mean, really, I don't ask for much. What all do I ask for?"

Romell answered, "Love and respect."

"Don't patronize me, Romell Ulysses Goodwin." I laughed, "But that *is* all I ask for."

"Respect is like a boomerang, Chocolate. Give it, and it'll come back to you eventually."

I didn't know how to respond to that, so I made a joke out of it. "Like, I did not know that! Really? For real? Anyway," I said. "That's not the only thing that's bothering me. If I don't clear Tee-Bo's rash and buy him a new crib, Mommy will be our new roommate."

"Why don't you just buy the crib?"

"Low on funds."

"Come over. I can give you a few dollars."

It was not uncommon for Romell to flip his wallet open, peel off hundred dollar bills, and try to stuff them in my hand, starting twenty minutes of "you-keep-it-no-you-keep-it," because how could I accept it? Gift certificates at Christmas were one thing. Handing me cash was another. Don't get me wrong; I'd want that wad of cash. I was using my MasterCard to charge my phone bill, but I knew darn well if a wad of cash turned up at my house, Spider would pick that shit up, wave it in the air, and say, "What the hell is this?" And then, he would fold his hands across his chest and look at me funny. Then, I'd have no choice but to tell him one hell of a lie, knowing full well Spider hated lies, or I'd have to tell him the truth, which would hurt him. Sometimes even a wad of cash wasn't worth it. Besides, I was a grown-ass woman. I didn't need charity. "No. I have money. I'll look around today and see what I can find in the thrift stores."

"Thrift stores? Take the money and buy your baby a new crib!"

"No, I'll use the money I have and buy what I can afford."

132

"New cribs meet safety standards."

"Be that as it may, a used crib will be just fine."

"You mean to tell me, you would rather put your baby in a secondhand death trap than borrow a few dollars from *me*?"

"I'll know what to look for. I have a magazine article on crib safety. He'll be fine."

"Okay, Chocolate, if you say so. Your baby has eczema, right?"

"His pediatrician called it eczema. The specialist called it contact dermatitis."

"What did they do for it?"

"I got a prescription from each of them; neither worked, and the specialist told me not to put dark colors on him. Why so many questions?"

"I may be able to help you clear your baby's rash."

"Romell, in the past six weeks, I've been advised by a pediatrician, a dermatologist, and an orthopedic surgeon. As a last resort, I rubbed my baby down in cornstarch. What can *you* do?"

"Swing by with Tee-Bo; you'll find out."

"Fine, we'll drop by. I'd like to see this."

"Now, back to that crib. Are you sure you…"

"You don't give up, do you? Yes, I am sure I don't need a loan. And, I don't want you *giving* me the money, either."

"If you don't find a used crib today, how are you going to deal with your mom?"

"What?" I sucked my teeth. "I ain't got to worry about her. Shoo…I already told that woman that I'm cat sittin'. So—"

"Cat sitting? When are we cat sitting?" Spider interrupted.

21

SPIDER WAS AT THE ENTRANCE TO THE LIVING ROOM. I didn't know what he overheard or how long he'd been standing there, but his question hung in the air. My mouth froze, so I shrugged.

"We're watching Jackie's cat when she goes away to Hawaii?" Spider asked.

My heart was now a ticking time bomb in my chest; I could only manage a nod. Spider shrugged and walked over to the kitchen. He ducked but bumped his head on the corner of the arch anyway. Rubbing his forehead, Spider pulled the water jug from the fridge.

Through the receiver, I heard, "Chocolate. Chocolate? Hello. Are you still there?"

"I'll talk to you later," I whispered then hung up. I put the phone back on the chest and stood, turning toward the hallway.

"Who was that?" Spider asked.

I stopped. "Why?"

He raised a glass of water to his lips and took a sip. "I'm trying to figure out where you're going."

"Oh, I'm going around to different thrift stores to look for a crib for Tee-Bo."

"Who are you going to see?"

"Mommy?"

"Is that who you were on the phone with?" Spider said.

I nodded.

His eyebrow rose. "It's nice to see you and your mother getting along so well." He sat the water glass down, placed his hand at the waistband of his boxers and started scratching. "I saw the two hundred dollars you left on the dresser this morning. Why don't you take that back just in case the crib costs more than you have?"

"Pay that girl off, Spider. I should have enough."

"For a mattress, too? I don't want him sleeping on any

135

used mattress."

"I'll buy the crib today. And, I guess I'll pick up a mattress on Friday when I get paid."

"All right, then," he said.

I half smiled, walked into the bathroom, and took a shower.

♥   ♥   ♥   ♥

After I got myself and Tee-Bo ready, I went to every thrift store I knew and saw everything but what I was looking for. All kinds of typewriters, Crowns, Imperials, Royals. A CD Discman still in the package. Even a gynecologist's table complete with stirrups. No crib. I bought the Discman. I couldn't resist. It was only three dollars. I was tempted by a seven-dollar Panasonic word processor with a floppy drive, but I left that in the store, making up my mind to go to Dr. Snyder's at some point and type Spider's résumé on his computer instead. I needed to watch every nickel; car fare was seriously eating into my funds.

Romell's apartment was twenty-four blocks away from the last shop. With forty-seven dollars and fifty cents left in my pocket, I walked, pushing Tee-Bo's stroller as he slept. Clouds packed the sky like cotton. No sun. Still, in this humidity, I could barely breathe and the temperature felt like it was climbing. *Public transportation has AC*, I thought every few blocks. Then, I'd reach into my pocket count that same pittance, and press forward into the heat that rose from the ground ahead of me in waves. My denim mini exposed my thighs, but up on top, I was sticking to my fitted tee. Sweat trickled from every pore, and with my touchup long overdue, my edges rolled into knots. My hair was twisted out of my face, but every few blocks, I was using Tee-Bo's washcloth to wipe his sweat and mine. That was ridiculous, so I dipped into the first supermarket I saw.

I pushed the stroller through the automatic doors and the air was frigid. I looked to my left. There was a wire rack of circulars. I walk with my coupons, so I grabbed a circular and scoped out the prices. Veggies were seventy-nine cents a can. Here they called that a sale. Why would I do that? I was getting them for free. At my local supermarket, those same vegetables would go on sale, four for a dollar; I had a stack of coupons for seventy-five cents off of six cans, and I only went shopping on double coupon day: Sunday. Spider called me a thief every time I came home with two free cases. Same thing with the cereal; here the sale price was three dollars and ninety-nine cents. Where I shopped, the same box of cereal went on sale for a dollar ninety-nine. With my dollar coupons on double coupon day, they paid me a penny to take them, and even then, I still had the manufacturer's rebates to mail in. That's an extra dollar a pop. I hate buying postage stamps, but when those checks come in the mail, they add up. Last month I had forty-three dollars in rebate checks; that's how I bought my meats. *Seventy-nine cents for a can of vegetables. What a rip-off!* I shook my head and returned that circular to the stack.

I proceeded up the aisle. Looking straight ahead, the packages were only splashes of primary colors. Once I focused on the shelves, I noticed midtown supermarkets had a variety of healthy products not available in the South Bronx. Every other product was labeled low-fat, fat-free, low sodium, sugar-free, whole grain, multi-grain, or vitamin-dense. I walked into the meat aisle. There they had cuts of Porterhouse an inch thick. I walk over to the poultry. Their chicken wings had no yellow film. Just to the left were salmon steaks. I picked up a package and smelled; it didn't even smell fishy. When I reached the produce aisle, I got pissed off. All the fruits were picture perfect. The broccoli was the greenest green. The mushrooms were white, not brown. The peaches, firm but tender, had no holes or brown spots. And the tomatoes, where I live we only had one kind, the three pack wrapped in cellophane. Here they had like twenty varieties—grape, cherry, plum, beefsteak, yellow, green, sun-dried, Holland, Jersey. Granted, everything here was way more expensive than it was in the Bronx, and the healthy products cost a lot more than the regular, but I still felt slighted. The same variety and quality of goods should be available everywhere. I wouldn't mind paying a little more for quality, because when you think about it, what we save at the supermarket we eventually pay a doctor.

I stormed through the rest of the produce section and was about to storm out the store, but something caught my attention. It was a four pack of AA batteries sitting in a box marked fifty cents. I slapped a quarter on the counter with a forty-cent coupon and collected my change. I was mad that the cashier gave me back a dime and a penny, instead of fifteen cents, but I looked at the receipt and saw that they subtracted the coupon after they added the tax. As I snapped the batteries into my Discman, I knew the music would calm my nerves, and it did. I turned to my favorite station. No longer noticing the heat, I practically danced the rest of the way. I rang the bell. Romell opened the door, and I walked in, singing out loud.

"Chocolate. Chocolate!" Romell said, but it was a long time since I heard this song. I shushed him, singing.

> *I get so confused*
> *Because I love you both*
> *I swear it*
> *And if either love*
> *Walked away I couldn't bear it*
> *No no*
> *Oh how it hurts*
> *To try to chose between the two of you*
> *Cause I need the best of both worlds*
> *If love could*
> *Meet me at the*
> *Same place*
> *Same time*

I was holding my heart, pointing to an imaginary watch, and making all kinds of hand gestures when the radio station interrupted the song. *Right now, it's ninety-eight degrees, mostly cloudy, hazy, and humid. Highs will be in the upper nineties for the rest of the week with severe thunderstorms expected on Thursday for all five boroughs....*

I nearly broke my headphones pulling them down. "That was my favorite part!"

Romell shook his head. "Why do you love that song so much?"

"Why? That's Krystol. That's been my favorite song since high school. I still have the record but it's broken." With the headphones down around my neck, I heard the bass line to Mary J. Blige's song. I started dancing. "Aw shucks! 'Be Happy.' This is my anthem!" I put the headphones back on.

> *How can I*
> *Love somebody else*
> *If I can't*
> *Love myself enough to know*
> *When it's time, time to let go*

Sing

All I really want is to be happy
And to find a love that's mine
It would be so sweet

Romell snatched the headphones off my ears and yanked the plug out of the Discman. "I don't need an encore, especially when you're singing loud and off key."

I just cut my eye at him.

"That reminds me. Chocolate," he continued. "Why do you always ring my bell? You have keys!"

"Force of habit." I wheeled Tee-Bo's stroller over Romell's plush charcoal carpet, past his dining room, and to the semicircles of black marble, the rotating cocktail table that sat in the middle of his otherwise unfurnished living room. He still had his remote controlled wall unit; I guess he needed something to house his stereo system. It was nice and cool in here, but the ambiance was warm, ash gray walls, sporadically placed sconces, and recessed lighting. Romell's living room was nice bare. I couldn't wait to see what it would look like once it was refurnished. I knelt and wiped the sweat from Tee-Bo's face gently to avoid waking him, then I stood. "Can I have my headphones back?" I held out my hand.

He grabbed my wrist. "Will you please wear the bracelet I got you for Christmas?"

"One of these days. I'm saving it for a special occasion. Headphones, please."

"Special occasion? The bracelet is silver, Mia. Silver. You made me return the other one. Now, I want to see you wear that bracelet."

"Okay, okay, okay. Now, can I have my headphones back, please?"

He grunted. "Not if you're going to sing again."

I rolled my eyes and placed my Discman at the foot of the stroller. "Romell. Would you believe I was singing last night, and Spider almost had a fit?"

"Your singing has that effect on people."

I sucked my teeth. "Not because of my singing! Because of this internship at the record label, Spider believes paying attention to the songs a person sings will tell you what's on their mind. So, on top of everything else, now, I've got to watch the songs *I* sing around Spider. According to him, the songs I sing show what's on my mind or will manifest themselves some kind of way."

"That reminds me. My mom wants you to call her."

"How did that remind you of Mrs. Goodwin?"

"She says secular music corrupts the spirit. That's why she only listens to spirituals."

"Well, I disagree with Mrs. Goodwin, too. I love me some R&B music."

"That's fine. I'm not asking you to agree with her. I'm telling you to call her."

"Okay, okay. I'll call your mother. I heard you last night."

"Yeah, but last night your mind was on Spider Snyder. How *did* everything turn out?"

"It all turned out to be nothing. He explained; I listened. He went out; I got mad, and wrote another poem in my journal as usual."

"Let me hear a few lines."

"I'll tell you what I can remember." It took a moment for it to come back, but I recited:

> *Press on, press on*
> *Just keep pressin' on*
> *It's just a matter of time*
> *When you think you've taken all you can take*
> *Don't give up*
> *You must continue to strive*
> *It's a privilege of God to be alive*
> *Keep the faith*
> *Things will be okay*
> *It's just a matter of time*

"Wow! Keep it up; maybe one day you'll turn into another Nikki Giovanni or Maya Angelou."

I shook my head. "I love ego tripping, and I like to consider myself a phenomenal woman, but...I can honestly say my ink on paper will *never* be that good."

"Don't say that. You don't know what'll happen after you take a few classes."

I sucked my teeth. "What about *your* inner James Baldwin? I don't see *you* signing up for classes."

"I don't have time," Romell said.

"*The time has come for us to secure our proper place in society, because we, too, are entitled to prosperity. Pursue our dreams whatever they are. Once we make that decision, a little drive will take us far. Tomorrow's reality was yesterday's vision.'* Remember that?"

He laughed to himself. "How could I not? That's part of my high school valedictory speech. I'm surprised *you* remember."

"You should follow that advice, Romell."

"What do you mean?"

"All jokes aside, you should start circulating your résumé."

"Nah. Let's talk about something else."

I persisted, "Another company might give you what you want."

"I said I don't want to talk about it."

"Get a better offer somewhere else, and give those Livings & Moore people an ultimatum, Romell."

"My firm is reorganizing; I'm not going to make waves. So, forget it, Chocolate. I know what I'm doing."

"I know they are supposed to be so prestigious, and I'm sure they pay you well, but a glass ceiling is a glass ceiling! Romell, you are bigger than that!"

"Give them people an ultimatum, Romell. That's a glass ceiling, Romell." He was mimicking me. I didn't appreciate that, especially since he whined, sounding nothing like me. But then, he took a deep breath and resumed speaking in his normal voice. "Look, Mia. I already told you; I don't want to talk about this. How would you like it if I kept bringing up something you didn't want to discuss? You went crib shopping today. How much did you have to spend?"

"That's not important."

"Okay, here's a better question. What exactly did you find on your little scavenger hunt?"

"Well I...I saw...stuff."

"You shop in thrift stores, and I'm supposed to listen to you and piss away my six-figure fuckin' income? And I know Spider Snyder has a thing for junk, but I'd like to know what he had to say about this whole thrift store crib thing?"

"All right, all right! Truce?"

"Yeah, all right." Romell placed my headphones on the hood of the stroller. "That's fine by me. Now, let's do something about the little guy's rash."

I lifted my sleeping baby out of the stroller, ready to hand him over, but Romell hesitated. "Chocolate," He said. "Before I do anything at all, you *must* repeat after me."

"Repeat after you? Why?"

Romell cocked his head to the side. "Because, if you don't, this is not going to work," he said. I looked Romell up and down. "I'm serious," Romell added.

"Okay, whatever, Romell. Now, what am I repeating?"

"Say, I, Miss Love...."

"I, Miss Love...."

"Do hereby promise...."

"What's with the oath?"

"Do you want me to help you or don't you?"

My lips were tight, but I said it anyway. "Do hereby promise...."

"To trust Romell."

"To trust Romell," I sighed.

"I will not say a word...."

"I will not say a word?" I screwed my face up.

"Until he's done...."

Now, I shook my head. "Until he's done...."

"And I will not stop him...."

"And I will not stop him!" I snapped.

"No matter what," Romell said. I looked at Romell like he was crazy and pulled Tee-Bo close. "No matter what," he repeated. I rolled my eyes and looked straight up at his gray ceiling. "No matter what!" Romell said, raising his voice. I sucked every tooth in my mouth. He shrugged. "Fine, let me know how things go with your new roommate...your mom."

"Okay, okay. No matter what."

"Good. I knew you'd see things my way."

22

$\mathcal{G}$ PROMISED TO TRUST ROMELL, NOT TO SAY A WORD until he was done, and not to stop him no matter what. I shook my head with one thought in mind: *This remedy had better be good.* I continued to shake my head, until Romell lifted his gray undershirt over his head, pulled it off and tossed it to the floor. I bit my tongue. Romell stepped toward me. His dark skin had sheen, and this was no dream. I could clearly see his smooth chest was hard. Instead of a six-pack, his midsection had so many chiseled muscles up and down the front and sides, I lost count. Then, just below his belly button, silky hairs descended an inverted triangle of hard flesh that led into his gray cotton shorts. And these shorts hung dangerously low. Romell snapped his fingers. I looked at his hand, then his eyes. "Chocolate! For the third time, hand me the baby."

"Oh," I said. Romell looked at me. Then, he winked. I hoped it wasn't obvious, but I could feel myself blush, my heart pound and my palms sweat. I looked at Romell's hairy bowlegs. That was no help; he always had the thighs of an action figure. Focusing on his bare feet, I passed him Tee-Bo.

Romell held Tee-Bo up to his shoulder. "Chocolate, you told me the specialist said for him not to wear dark colored clothing. Did that doctor mention anything about detergent?"

"Um," I tried to look him in the eyes but couldn't help stealing glimpses of his stomach muscles. "Yeah, he said it might be caused by the chemicals in his detergent."

"Uh huh," Romell said. He walked past me down to the end of the hall. The instant he turned left, I fanned myself with my sweaty hands, stepped over to his thermostat and cranked up the AC. I hopped back in place just as Romell rounded the corner, returning with stiff-looking gray towels across his arm. A gray washcloth and soap dish were in his hand.

"What are you going to do with that stuff?" I asked.

"Never mind that," Romell said. He handed me the soap dish and washcloth then lifted Tee-Bo up off his shoulder and held him out. "Why do you have him dressed like this?"

"Why? That's one of his nicest outfits!" And it was. Tee-Bo looked good in red. The bold red and beige striped t-shirt brought out both his complexion and his green eyes. And if he wore the shirt, he had to wear the matching bib, and socks. The khaki shorts tied it all together. "He looks really cute."

"Uh huh."

"Why do you keep saying 'uh huh'?"

"Never mind that." Romell brought Tee-Bo back to his shoulder. "Come with me."

I followed him into the kitchen, cherry cabinets, granite countertops, a long island, stainless-steel appliances, six burners on his stove, a built-in microwave, a Sub-Zero refrigerator, a wine fridge, and not one, but two, dishwashers. I bust suds. "I hate you."

"Why?"

"All this and you don't even cook," I said. Romell didn't even own a pot.

He laughed. "Don't need to." Then, he nodded toward the refrigerator.

"I know. Take out. So what, showoff!" I said, expecting the fridge to be filled with Styrofoam containers. I pulled the door open, and my jaw dropped.

"Now, I prefer home cooking. Next best thing to a trip around the world." Romell said. The shelves were packed with plastic containers. Rubbermaid, Tupperware, recycled. Some were round. Some were square. Some had patterns. Some were clear. Blue tops. Red tops. Yellow tops. No two were alike. I shook my head. I could see Romell had at least ten women doing his home cooking.

I picked up the white container and looked through the clear top at some mushy stuff. "What the hell is this?"

"Oh, that's moussaka." Romell said. I screwed my face up so he explained. "Akasma, she's Turkish."

"You don't discriminate. Do you?"

"Hey, she's a dime."

"A dime?" She could be an Eskimo for all he cared. I closed the fridge. "You are so superficial. I'm surprised you

144

were never interested in Dawn."

Romell did a double take. Then, he squinted, shaking his finger at me. "You're still jealous of your sister."

"No, I'm not!" I wished I could be Dawn; there's a difference. I sucked my teeth. "You wouldn't be interested in Dawn no way. You don't like black girls!" Romell completely ignored my comment. He turned and started fingering the knob on his stove. So, I sat the container on another one just like it. Looking at all these containers, I wasn't about to open anything and sniff, but I was sure some of that mess had to be spoiled. I closed the door, shaking my head as a thought came to me. "You shouldn't be eating everybody's food. Even if none of that contains peanuts, any one of those girls could jack you up with a cross-contaminated frying pan. That's something you need to think about."

Romell froze and then nodded. "I feel you." Opening the oven door, he said, "Lower the thermostat."

"Why?"

"We're going to give your baby a bath."

"Oh no, we're not. I didn't bring Tee-Bo's bathtub; he could slip in the sink."

"We just have to be careful."

I shook my head. "A wet baby is a slippery baby. I know."

"Slippery, huh?"

"Very."

"Okay, I have an idea. Go, turn down the AC."

I gave Romell a strange look, but I walked back out to the thermostat and raised the temperature. When I returned, the kitchen was already warming up and Tee-Bo's eyes were open. Romell had lined one side of the double basin with a towel. His gooseneck faucet was spraying water and filling the sink. Romell was on the stool by the island. He had spread the other two towels across the granite top and laid Tee-Bo on the cushion of rough cotton. I cut off the hot water and ran the cold to cool the fixture, turned that off, and tested the temperature with my elbow. It was fine. Then, I ran my hand across the towel at the bottom of the sink. There was enough traction there; that was fine, too. Romell unsnapped Tee-Bo's shorts and pulled them off. He took off his socks and removed his bib. Romell undid the snaps along the shoulder of Tee-Bo's shirt, then slid his hands underneath it, gathered it up to his chest and froze. "You come do this part," Romell said. *Men.* I shook my head, stepping over, and tucked Tee-Bo's elbows into his sleeves. His shirt slipped over his shoulder, and then his head.

Romell ran his hand over Tee-Bo's undershirt. "Feel this," he said. I did. The Onesie was drenched. "Does he always sweat like this?"

I cut my eye at Romell. "No, only when it's hot!"

"Hot? We're in a heat wave. If he's sweating like this, you're overdressing him."

"If he doesn't wear enough, when we travel, the air conditioning will make him sick."

"Take off his undershirt, Mia." I removed the undershirt and diaper, seeing prickly skin from his face to his feet. "Hot, moist skin will aggravate a rash," Romell said, lifting my baby, while carefully supporting his head. The sink water rippled as he lowered Tee-Bo into it.

"Lather this washcloth and wash him."

"I only use baby wash, and I don't want to use this rag. I have Tee-Bo's."

"Just do it, please."

My lips grew tight. I didn't like his ordering me around at all, but while he held Tee-Bo, I placed the washcloth in the warm water, squeezed it, and ran it over the bar from the soap dish. I gently wiped, starting with his chest until swirls of suds covered Tee-Bo's body. Next, I wiped in the folds of his skin. Then, I rinsed the washcloth, squeezed it almost dry, washed his face, behind each ear, and under his neck. Afterwards, I rinsed Tee-Bo.

"Grab a towel. I'm taking him out," Romell said. I folded my arms. "What's wrong?"

"After I bathe Tee-Bo, I don't wrap him in anything but a fluffy, white towel. I have a receiving blanket in the bag. Let's use that."

"You agreed to trust me."

"I *trust* white towels. I can see if they're clean, like I can see those towels are way too rough for my baby's skin. Don't you believe in fabric softener and dryer sheets?"

"You also agreed not to say a word until we were done."

"Okay, Romell, but I'm letting you know right now. Whatever it is you're doing had better work." I removed one of the stiff, gray towels from the island and held it open. When Romell lifted Tee-Bo out of the water, I bundled him in the towel and began to pat him dry.

"Don't do that!" Romell said.

"Why not?" Now, my foot started tapping.

"Just hold him. Don't do anything else." Romell opened his bottom cabinet and bent down. My whole body loosened immediately. The top of his muscular ass, crease and all, had peeked out from the waistband of his shorts. His complexion was as rich and smooth as a perfect plum. There was not one blemish. From his booty all the way up his back, I didn't notice so much as a blip. And his back was so defined I wished I could just take my finger and trace the muscles as he fumbled around inside that cabinet. Romell stood up, closed the cabinet, and turned around holding a large can of Crisco.

"What's that for?"

"Tee-Bo's skin."

23

ROMELL SMILED AND WINKED. I WASN'T BLUSHING this time. He said he was going to use that stuff on my baby's skin. *Crisco. Crisco?*

"Romell Ulysses Goodwin, you must have space between your ears. Does my baby look like a pork chop to you? I'm outta here!" I stormed toward the living room holding Tee-Bo close; Romell was right on my heels holding that can of Crisco.

"Chocolate, wait! Please! You promised you wouldn't stop me no matter what!"

I laid Tee-Bo in his stroller, reached into his diaper bag and pulled out a diaper. I knelt down and slipped the diaper underneath Tee-Bo's bottom.

"Mia, this works. Trust me."

"You're no dermatologist! Who the hell told you to grease my baby with Crisco, anyway?" He didn't answer. I stood up and placed my hand on my hip. "Well?"

He looked away. "Jun Ko."

"Jun Ko? I'm out," I said and turned around.

Romell dropped the can, wrapped his arms around me, and squeezed like he was never going to see me again. Then, he whispered in my ear, "Don't catch an attitude. I'm only trying to help. Trust me. Just this one time, please."

Pressing against me, his body felt warm, so I couldn't help but calm down. "Romell, how do you know this is any good?"

He turned me around and looked into my eyes. "At the spa, Jun Ko's cream is made from Crisco."

"Then, why was it green?"

"She adds aloe vera?"

"Are you sure about that?

"No."

"Then how do you know for sure this stuff is safe for babies?"

149

"Jun Ko's sister is a pediatrician with a private practice not too far from here, and she said it was okay."

"That's all well and good, but how do you know this stuff gets rid of rashes?"

"Because, everything I'm doing for Tee-Bo worked for me."

"What do you mean?"

"I let my building's housekeeping service do my laundry and I broke out in a rash just like his."

I twisted my lips. "Okay, so what did you do?"

"The washcloth and towels I washed in a mild, fragrance- and dye-free detergent. No bleach. No fabric softener. I used nothing harsh."

"What about that soap? I told you I only use baby wash, because baby wash—"

"...has a fragrance in it. What I used wasn't soap. That was a moisturizing bar made for sensitive skin. You use baby lotion, too, right?"

"It's made for babies, right?"

"Yeah, but it's pink and smelly! Perfumes and dyes irritate sensitive skin. Now, if we apply Crisco while his body is still wet, that will seal in the moisture, and it's vegetable shortening. It won't clog his pores. Do this for the next few days, and stop overdressing him; the rash will go away in less than a week."

"Romell, if I let you try this Crisco thing and it makes matters worse—"

"Worse? Mia, look at me." Romell said, and I did...slowly. His smooth chest, broad shoulders, chiseled stomach, muscular thighs, and back up to the danger zone, just above cotton shorts that hung so low; I had to will myself not to look at the curly hairs peeking over his waistband. "Well, do I look like I have problem skin?" Romell asked.

His skin *was* clear. No doubt about that or the fact that he wasn't wearing underwear. "Ahem." I cleared the lump from my throat and said, "No complaints here."

He continued to plead. "I'm not experimenting."

I saw the concern in Romell's eyes. That drew my attention back to the matter at hand. I looked at Tee-Bo's speckled skin. Then, thinking about the possibility of Tee-Bo getting cradle cap, I nodded. "Do your thing."

Romell smiled and said, "You won't regret it." I sighed on my way to the kitchen. Romell screamed down the hall,

"Where are you going?" I waved, walking, so he added, "You'll have to do this yourself at home, too!"

"Whatever!" I yelled, turning the corner. The thought of what he was doing churned my insides. I just couldn't watch. I was getting sick to my stomach just thinking about it. Entering the kitchen this time, I noticed his wine fridge in the far corner. I decided to be nosy. It was full of Moët, Dom Pérignon, and Perrier-Jouët. I closed the fridge and pulled one of the sideways bottles off the wine rack, built into the counter space. According to the label, it was Napa Valley, Cabernet Sauvignon 1969, private reserve. I stuck it back in its sleeve and shook my head, walking over to the dishwasher. In it, a latte mug sat on the top rack. I rinsed it and looked at the espresso maker at the far end of the counter. That was a nice thought, but caffeine would be all in my milk, and Tee-Bo would be high and cranky. I filled the cup with water, popped open the microwave, placed the mug inside, and pressed its keys. The computer responded, "Beverage. Two minutes. Begin." I shook my head and watched the mug circle inside until the computer said, "Beverage. Hot. Thank You." For me, this was better than cable. Mine looked like an old television set. It had a dial and no turntable. I opened the door and carefully held the warm handle to avoid burning my knuckles.

I opened his middle cabinet. It was always packed with what I call grab and eats, energy bars, Pop Tarts, Wheat Thins, tuna, fruit, soups, and a lot of products certified organic by companies I never heard of, marked peanut-free, tree nut-free, and legume-free. As far as I knew, Romell was only allergic to peanuts, but he told me a lot of products contain scant traces of peanuts or peanut oil. I looked up at the top of the cabinet. Two boxes of Life. I looked at the bottom shelf. There sat a pair of large ruby stud earrings. I snatched them out of the way and checked out Romell's selection of herbal teas. He always stocked exotic teas. Now, he even had a new box of green. No black. I chose the lemon chamomile and dipped the bag. The aroma of lemons rose with the steam. Chamomile was supposed to be soothing. Good. I had a lot on my mind. I took a sip.

Spider already commented that I rolled Tee-Bo in flour. What's he going to say about the chicken grease? Hopefully, this rash will clear, and I won't have to explain anything. But if I want to keep Mommy off my back, I still need to find Tee-Bo a crib. I sipped again. *I can't afford a new crib, and I didn't find a used one. I don't have time left to look, because as soon as I leave here, I have to go to Harlem and type that résumé for Spider.*

"Chocolate!" Romell called. I walked into the living room, sipping my tea. Lying in his stroller on a gray towel, Tee-Bo was greased, diapered, and shirtless. I looked up at Romell.

"Okay, Chocolate. Here's a rundown. Everything that comes in contact with Tee-Bo's skin has got to be washed. Don't use any harsh cleaners. Only hypo-allergenic and bio-degradable. When you wash his clothes, wash them by hand, and don't use bleach or fabric softener."

"What about stain remover and dryer sheets?"

"None of that. Let them air-dry. The detergent should be mild, fragrance-free, and dye-free. You can find what you need in the supermarket across the street. Do you have money?"

"Yes," I lied.

Romell gave me a strange look then said, "Hold on to your money." He took off down the hall and disappeared around the corner. I continued sipping my tea. I had just sipped the last drop when I saw Romell rushing back toward me, clutching the bottles of detergent and household cleaner. In his hand, he held a small brown paper bag. "I can always run across the street and get more," Romell said, sticking the bottles in the basket underneath the stroller. He dropped the Crisco in the basket, then stood and stuffed the brown paper bag inside the diaper bag. Romell stepped back over to me. "Don't use soap. Use the moisturizing bar. Apply the Crisco while his body is still wet. And don't overdress him. Any questions call me. This rash is as good as gone, Chocolate."

"Okay," I said handing him the empty mug.

"I put some things under the stroller. Everything else you need is in the bag. You know I'll do anything for you, right?"

"Anything?"

"Yeah."

"Oh, okay. How about loaning me that Jaguar?"

"Joke all you want, but I'm serious, Chocolate."

"As serious as you are about your car?"

He shook his head. "Just remember what I said. Everything else you need...is in the bag. Now, it's up to you to get your boy a crib. All right?"

152

There was something in Romell's eyes that I couldn't interpret, but I said, "All right," placed my headphones around my neck, clipped my Discman to my waist, and steered Tee-Bo's stroller toward the door.

"Oh, Chocolate! I almost forgot."

"What now?" I said, turning toward Romell. Before I could even blink, he planted his lips on my cheek. I was stunned for a moment. Then, I took a step back and looked at him. "What was that for?"

"Trusting me."

"I need to trust you more often," I mumbled.

He looked at me. "What did you say?"

"You need...to drive that Jaguar more often."

"I take it out to get serviced."

"A few more miles won't kill it." I plugged in my headphones and placed them on my ears. "Oh, I almost forgot." I handed Romell the ruby studs then watched him squeeze them into his palm. He smiled, and all three dimples pierced his face. I shook my head. "You know you have too many women when they mark their territory like wild animals," I said. "What do you do with their stuff?"

"I mail their shit right back to them."

I laughed. "That's cold. Why not wait until they picked their things up?"

"I'd be up to my eyeballs in earrings and panties."

I opened the door. "You're a mess. Time for me to leave." I pushed Tee-Bo's stroller into the hall. I didn't hear a peep from any of the other three apartments on Romell's floor. I didn't even have the radio turned on. But, a song was on my mind, and when a song was on my mind, I didn't let it go. I gave in to the urge to sing. *"I'm going crazy. Same Place. Same time. I change like the seasons. I love you both for different reasons—"*

"Aye, Chocolate."

I looked back at Romell standing in his doorway. "What?"

"Save the free concert. This ain't Bryant Park!"

24

I ARRIVED AT THE BROWNSTONE SORRY I TOOK MY headphones off. *"At last...."* Dr. Snyder sounded as if she were in pain. Hearing that noise all the way downstairs, I stood in the foyer, listening to her wail for a good while after I let myself in. I put Tee-Bo in his infant seat and followed my bleeding ears right to her bedroom door. Now, I understood where Romell was coming from when he was complaining about *my* singing, but my singing couldn't possibly have been *this* bad. I knocked. Dr. Snyder hollered, "It's open!" Then, she started singing Etta James again.

I walked in, fighting the urge to run in the opposite direction. The room smelled like burnt plastic. "Hey, Dr. Snyder."

"Oh, it's you," she said. Her tall, thin body rested upright against the brass headboard, fingers gripping the neck of an eighty-proof bottle. Gray curls were mashed to her head. She fluffed out the top, and the black lace strap of her sheer nightie fell off her shoulder.

The air conditioning was full blast, but the fireplace was lit. That didn't make sense to me; it was almost a hundred degrees outside. I stepped around two heavy-duty garbage bags, smoothed the gold satin top sheet, and sat on the corner of her bed. Resting the infant seat at my ankles, I lifted Tee-Bo into my arms. "How's everything?"

She switched the bottle for the half-filled glass on her night table and turned the stereo off, but still sang her own tune, *"I've got a little bit of money, a little bit of time, a bottle of scotch, and a lot on my mind."* She raised her glass. Over articulating, she said, "I'm celebrate–ting. Would you like a cocktail, Baby?"

Baby? I knew then she was past drinking; she was drunk. Dr. Snyder never called me "Baby," ever. Then again, I never saw her sipping anything stronger than diluted Pepsi.

I shook my head.

"Oh, I forgot; you nurse. And, I know, he doesn't need *any*," she said, making sure she didn't slur her words.

I laughed to myself and watched her slurp that glass of scotch until she sucked in an ice cube, spat it out and smiled with her lips only. Frown lines creased her forehead. Deep wrinkles ran between her eyebrows. "I'm also tossing out a few things, as you can see. I made a promise that I would close this chapter of my life and move on and that is precisely what I'm going to do. I'm getting rid of *everything* that reminds me of Zachary. What brings you here?"

She looked at me and I paused for a moment, staring into her hazel eyes. That's when I noticed they were glazed, and the bags underneath were ringed with mascara that streaked her pale, thin face. "I came to type a résumé."

She looked at the digital clock on her night table. It read a quarter to four. "Today is not a good day for that. Why don't you come back during the week, *but* I do want to thank you."

"For what?"

"For not telling Spence about his check."

"You don't have to thank me."

"Yes, I do. If Spence would have stumbled across that check that would have complicated things, and what do you think Jackie would have done?"

"She would have opened the mail?"

"Exactly. And she would have told Spence. I knew you wouldn't do that, because you're trustworthy. That's why I asked you to sign for them, so I would have time to figure out how I'm going to break this to him. Our relationship is strained as it is."

I shifted around. "I don't think your relationship is strained, Dr. Snyder."

"Well, then you haven't spoken to Spence today." She laughed. "Ever since he started gallivanting with Zachary's son, he's been cold and distant. Spence never used to question anything I said or did. That bastard of Zachary's is a bad influence. He's been filling Spence's head with all kinds of nonsense. Why didn't I give Zachary a divorce? Why didn't I allow Zachary to see them? Why didn't I tell him Zachary was paying child support? And today, today, Spence had the audacity to call and ask me why there was no funeral."

"He did?"

"Can you believe that? Out of the clear blue sky. He never cared before, so I know Zachary's little bastard has got to be behind this."

"Dr. Snyder, what did you tell him?"

"I hung up."

"Spider should understand you need time. I mean, you're still mourning."

"Mourning?" Dr. Snyder narrowed her eyes. "I'm not mourning. I just need to buy myself some time. I have to somehow come up with an explanation good enough to satisfy that self-righteous brat and I can't think of one!"

"Why are you trying to conjure up something? You had Mr. Zach cremated because all your funds were tied up. Right?"

"Who told you that?"

"I assumed. Why? That's not the reason?"

"No! The reason I had Zachary cremated has *nothing* to do with money. Zachary had a good job. He worked for the State. Lola spent her life on Public Assistance; every dime she had was tracked by the city. That son of theirs is a gambler who squanders. Zachary was foolish, but he had no choice but to put all his money in his own name. It wasn't that much, but you better believe, as soon as I got word that Zachary died, I had my lawyer seize every penny."

"Dr. Snyder, you just said the reason had nothing to do with money."

"I don't need the money, Mia! But, why should that lazy whore have it?"

"Dr. Snyder, sometimes it's best to live and let live."

"This is not one of those times!" She poured herself some more scotch. "You're a sweet girl, Mia. I tell Spence all the time; you remind me so much of how I used to be. You're naive, like I was thirty years ago when I married my husband, except I was still a *virgin*." She sighed, and then continued, "I wore white. White *was* for the pure. Why tinker with tradition? Not everybody deserves to wear a white gown, you know. Not that you should concern yourself with that now. What's done is done. But don't worry, they make gowns in a lot of other pretty colors, and you'll have plenty of time to pick one out, before...." In the midst of rambling, she stopped and looked at me. "Can you keep a secret?" Dr.

Snyder smiled and leaned over.

"Yes," I said.

"So can I." She giggled and started humming. I had no clue what song it was until she sang out, "....*son of a preacher man.*" She rocked back and forth, and then took a swig from her glass. "Zachary's father performed *my* ceremony. Did you know that?" She sighed. "But weddings in halls are much more classy if I should say so myself. My reception was in a church basement. We went to Zachary's father's church every week; Lola was a member of that church, too. I was a different woman back then. Way different."

"What changed?"

"I did."

"Why?"

"You'd think it would have been the emergency visits to the gynecologist, but I loved Zachary. I kept forgiving him. It wasn't even Lola's pregnancies."

"Pregnan–cies?" As far as I knew, Jeff was Miss Lola's only child.

"Yes, Lola was pregnant more than once, and I was suicidal all three times Zachary's whore turned up pregnant. The second time she miscarried."

"Third time, too?"

"Not exactly. The third pregnancy, Lola was carrying twins, and she didn't know if Zachary was the father or if the father was the husband of a woman...who lived in her projects."

"Oh, wow."

"Yeah, too bad in life you don't get points for stupidity. I dealt with the situation by doing harm to myself. But, that other woman—"

"Who was that other woman?"

"Let's just call her Betty. Anyway, she handled things differently. With her, Lola wasn't so lucky. Lola was about eight months pregnant, when *Betty* waited in front of her building with a machete this long." Dr. Snyder spaced her hands, measuring about twenty inches.

"So what happened?"

"She carved Lola up like the Cornish hen that she is."

"And then what happened!"

158

"That poor woman was forced to serve time for attempted murder!"

"I mean to Lola!"

"Oh, that whore was alright, but the babies didn't survive. Neither did my marriage."

"What happened?"

"*Supposedly,* she was on her deathbed. Zachary blamed himself." Dr. Snyder's voice cracked. A tear made a black trail down her face. She continued. "It wasn't enough that my husband was messing around with that whore, and everyone knew it. It wasn't enough that her son looked exactly like Zachary with those same green eyes. My husband left me to be with her. *My* husband! He was supposed to be a righteous man, but he did *me* the way he did. After that, I left his church. I left all churches."

"Oh, now, I see. That's why you're an atheist."

"Mia, when Zachary left me, I wanted to die. You know what gave me the will to live?"

"What?"

"Making Zachary's life miserable." Dr. Snyder narrowed her eyes again and angry tears now flowed freely, collected at her chin and fell to her pale chest as black drops. "Lola may have had Zachary in life, Mia. But you know what?"

"What?"

Spider's mother clenched her teeth and said, "I got him in death." She reached into her night table, pulling out a lighter and a pack of Kools. She pulled one out and tapped the butt on her palm. "Cigarette?"

"No, thank you,"

"That's right. You nurse. Oh, I forgot. My grandson is in the room. I can't smoke, either." She tossed the lighter aside. It plopped on her satin sheet and bounced. She looked at the clock on her night table, perched the unlit cigarette between her fingers, and extended her arms. "Mia, pass me Little Tobiah, please."

"Why?"

"I need you to take these bags down for me before you leave."

I hesitated. As drunk as she was, I was not about to hand her my baby. "I'll buckle him in the infant seat," I said, and that's what I did. Then, I stepped away from Tee-Bo. I tried to step around the smaller garbage bag that sat closer to me.

My foot caught the bed frame, and I dropped right onto the overstuffed bag that was farther away. It was surprisingly soft, until my hand jammed into something. Pain shot up my wrist all the way to my elbow. Before Dr. Snyder could respond, I said, "I'm okay," shook it off, and stood, grabbing the Glad bag.

The bag wasn't heavy, but it was wide and that made it awkward to carry down Dr. Snyder's narrow staircase. I had to lift it up high. I was tempted to drop it over the banister, but I didn't know if anything in it would puncture the plastic. When I reached the foyer, I sat the bag down and unknotted it, peeling it open. A little voice inside me said, *what am I getting myself into?* But, I continued to look at what seemed to be just a bunch of rags, strips and strips of old, white rags. I sifted through them. As I pulled them apart and looked at them, I could see. Those strips were satin, lace, and crinoline. Some pieces were even embroidered. Some, adorned with sequins and pearls. Everything was covered in cinder and soot. I sneezed, and my heart sank. *Are these Mr. Zach's ashes?* This was Dr. Snyder's wedding dress, destroyed. And everything in this bag was shredded, melted, or burnt to a crisp. *Maybe these are cinders from the fireplace, but if she got rid of everything that reminded her of Mr. Zach this way, I wouldn't put it past her.*

Dr. Snyder was singing again as I twisted the neck of the bag and carried it out and down the steps. I set the bag up on one can and removed the metal lid from the other, but before I stuffed the bag in, I opened it again. Reaching through the fabric, I felt paper. It was part of a yellow triplicate copy. I pulled out all four pieces and arranged them on top of the garbage bag.

The form bore Mr. Zach's name, a seal from a university medical center, and the caption, Donation of Decedent. I didn't know what "decedent" meant, but I read all the way to the fine print, *"Once the anatomical donation process is complete,"* Anatomical donation, Dr. Snyder donated Mr. Zach's body to some medical college, *"the deceased is to be transported to the Wallingford Crematory for final disposition. Thereupon a death certificate will be issued. I understand two or more years may elapse before I am contacted."* This explained why she waited so long to file the insurance claims. She had no death certificates. *"All expenditures associated with the transportation and cremation of the deceased will be covered by the University and its affiliates. Inquiries regarding a donated body should be directed to the University's appointed coordinator."* Dr. Snyder checked the box at the bottom of the form that stated, *"I do not request the return of cremated remains."* I exhaled. *His ashes aren't in this bag. But, she never claimed them; that's just as bad.* Now, I slipped those pieces of paper in my back pocket.

I kept fishing. Near the bottom, there was a large, white book. I grabbed it, dusted off the leather-bound cover and looked at the front. Above an oval and in large gold script were the words "Our Wedding." The oval frame was empty. I flipped through the mangled pages, and they were empty, too. I stuffed the photo album back. The pictures weren't in there. They were burned up in the garbage bag. I pulled one out of the garbage. It was melted but I could see it was taken in front of a mirror. Her maid of honor I recognized right away, because she resembled Dr. Snyder. I knew that was Babs. Babs was a cocktail waitress. She moved back to Harlem this past spring. I first saw her from behind. She was wearing a leopard-print trench coat. I thought she was my age. The instant she turned around, it was obvious she wasn't in her twenties. In the photo taken maybe thirty years ago, her hair and makeup had her looking like a black, Raquel Welch. Babs was placing the veil on Dr. Snyder's head, while one of the bridesmaids held the huge bouquet of white roses. That bridesmaid was short with dark brown skin and chubby cheeks. Her pretty, round face looked so familiar; I stood, trying to place it.

"Is something wrong?"

I stuck the photo back, pushed the garbage bag down in the can, and spun around. My heart was beating a mile a minute. Dr. Snyder's friend, Babs, was standing there in a tight dress that exposed her breasts. She was carrying an overnight bag across her shoulder and a Blockbuster Video plastic bag in her hand. It was sad, but now her face bore more wrinkles than crepe paper and had an unnatural hardness that long, curly hair, red lipstick, and a smile couldn't soften. Staring at her, I couldn't think of a good lie to save my life, and it was obvious. "Oh, um, yeah! See, I dropped this bag. I was just putting everything back. Hi, Babs." I dusted my hands off on my skirt.

161

Her eyes told me she didn't believe me. She gave me a kiss on the cheek anyway, saying, "You'll have to *wash* that soot off your hands." Now, I knew how it felt to be caught red handed.

In the bathroom, lathering up and watching filthy water run down the drain, I couldn't help but think how much of a shame it was that Dr. Snyder was harboring all this resentment after so many years. Mr. Zach may not have been the best husband, but I met him. Spider and I went over to the projects where they lived, to visit him a few times right before he died. He smiled a lot. The first time we went, Mr. Zach actually tried his hardest to be pleasant, even though Spider wouldn't look at him, barely spoke, and didn't even sit down. He stood by the door the whole time. The only reason why he came was because Jeff was riding him about that for so long. Spider was still holding on to his anger. He couldn't warm up to Mr. Zach. Not then, anyway. And, even though Spider was being such an ass, Mr. Zach didn't say one negative thing about Dr. Snyder. In my opinion, he was a nice man. At least, he seemed that way to me. Now, it was clear why she didn't just bury the man. Mr. Zach was heavily insured. There was no funeral because Dr. Snyder wanted to spite Lola and Jeff by not giving them a wake, a memorial service, and a gravesite. She said she wanted to move on, but setting everything ablaze and sending it to the City Dump, that wasn't moving on to me. Moving on meant forgiving and letting go.

In the sink, the water was finally running clear. I cut it off, looking into the mirror. A lip print stained where Babs had kissed the side of my face. On my brown skin, this lipstick looked orange, and I couldn't wipe it off with just my finger. Dr. Snyder didn't have any Noxzema, so I rubbed on some cold cream and snatched Kleenex out of the box. A few wipes later, it was off.

When I walked back into Dr. Snyder's bedroom, Babs was standing there squeezing her hand. Dr. Snyder's eyes were still wet with tears, but now they were smiling at Babs, holding a whole conversation without words. Now, the vibe in the room was awkward. What was being communicated was obviously intimate. I knew I was on the outside of it. I just hope that I wasn't the subject, but I couldn't help feeling I was interrupting something, so I walked over to the plastic bag. "I'll take this down and come back for Tee-Bo," I said.

"No, Mia. That's quite all right. *I'll* take that down," Babs said.

Dr. Snyder was still staring at Babs, smiling with her eyes. I figured Babs didn't tell her I was snooping through her trash, but I knew she would. I picked up Tee-Bo. "Okay, you two. I guess I'll be going. I'll be back Wednesday, Dr. Snyder."

"My friends call me Mae Mae." Dr. Snyder glanced at me and then wiped saliva from the corner of her mouth. I noticed they were both wearing the same smeared lip color, but for the life of me, I couldn't remember if Dr. Snyder was wearing lipstick before, so I looked around the room for her drinking glass to see if there was a lip print on the edge. It was nowhere in sight.

25

*T*HAT WHOLE EPISODE MADE MY HEAD SPIN. I went home with so much on my mind that my music sounded like noise. I turned it off and pulled my headphones down around my neck. It was late, and I walked those dark blocks home from the train station, pushing the stroller in a daze. "Ain't nothin' on the ground, Mia!" I heard in a strange male voice. I stopped looking down and looked all around. I didn't see anyone else on the block. Only Red Beard. He stepped in front of me. "Pick your head up! You're blessed," he said. He was holding something wrapped in a towel. I was afraid it was a blade. Trying to maneuver past him, I accidentally rolled the stroller over his foot, but I got a better look at what he held in his hands. It wasn't a knife; it was a pigeon, a big one. It was upside down, and its feet were tangled in some kind of string that he was unraveling. I picked up the pace, half walking, half running to the stairs leading to the entrance of my building. The fact that Red Beard knew my name did not sit well with me, but he didn't follow us. That was a good thing because our gate was still broken, and we still had no doorknob. Just as I bent down to lift the stroller and carry it up the stairs, I heard, "Hey, Mia!" This voice was female and familiar.

I turned and saw Jackie. Her long, lanky body was well over six feet tall in her gladiator sandals. Wearing suede skorts, Jackie marched across the street like an Amazon, toting a pet carrier, of all things. My jaw dropped. "Jackie, you are *not* bringing me Joy!"

"Oh, yes I am. Spence told me you agreed to pet sit," she said, giving me a peck on the cheek and cracking her chewing gum in my ear.

I plucked a cat hair off her gold, crocheted halter top and noticed a few snags here and there. "I'll have to remember to thank him."

"Hey, Stink, Stink!" Jackie leaned down and rubbed Tee-Bo's belly. "What's with the funky towel?"

"Don't ask."

"You be buggin. Girl, I was out here for hours waiting for you. We were just getting ready to pull off because Mike has to use the bathroom," Jackie said chewing.

"How long has he had to use the bathroom?"

"About an hour."

"An hour? Tell him to come upstairs."

"Girl, he can wait. So, where are you coming from?"

"Your mother's."

"If I would've known you were over there, I would have dropped Joy off at the house."

"So I could ride the subway with a stroller *and* a pet carrier? No, thank you. I thought you weren't leaving until next week. What happened?"

"We changed our minds," Jackie said over the honk of Mike's horn. She then turned to the car and yelled, "Relax!"

"Jackie, tell Mike to come on upstairs and use my bathroom."

"No, girl. Trust me. He'd have your bathroom smelling so bad, you'd think something crawled up in him and died. He can wait. What was goin' on at my mother's taday?"

"Taday?"

"Yeeah, taday. Stop makin' fun of the way I tawk!" Jackie said.

I always got a kick out of her Harlem accent; it was so squeaky and cute.

"Well, *today* nothing much was going on, but between you and me, I think your mother needs a man."

"She doesn't need a man. She has Babs."

"That's not the same," I said. Mike honked again. This time, his horn blared. "Oh, you better go, Jackie. It seems like that man has to use the bathroom badly. We'll talk later."

She stuffed a bill in my hand and kissed me on the cheek. "Here's a hundred so that you can get Joy a new litter box and some litter, her bottled water, and her food. Her toys are in the kennel. She likes the ball with the bell in it."

Jackie walked up the stairs, opened the door, and sat the pet carrier just inside the entrance. Waving, she walked back down the stairs and across the street. She reached Mike's red BMW and then shouted, "Remember, Joy only eats tuna!"

"What brand of cat food was that again?"

Jackie stopped, turned around, and marched her way back. Mike honked his horn like he lost his mind, but she didn't care. Jackie stood in front of me, put her hand on her hip, and started talking with her neck. "Now, I know you never fed my baby cat food."

I remember Jackie was extremely particular about what she fed Joy, but I forgot what the damn cat ate. "Of course not, I'm sure I fed her whatever you told me to. What was it again?"

"Tuna! Joy only eats *real* tuna. Fancy Albacore...in oil, not water."

By now, Mike's horn was one continuous stream of noise. I knew I'd never fed Joy real tuna. I always thought she meant the tuna-flavored, fancy cat food, but I was not about to admit that. "That's right! Fancy Albacore. What brand was that again? Fancy Feast?"

"Tuna fish! Fancy Albacore! Mia, if you give my baby cat food, I'm gonna be pissed!"

"Jackie, I love you but back up. And, don't holler at me! Or the next time you leave town, Joy's gonna need her own plane ticket."

"Soorry." Jackie smiled. "Please don't feed her cat food; it makes her constipated. When she's constipated, she gets depressed. When she's depressed, she sheds. And when—"

"Okay! I get the picture. No cat food." Jackie hugged me and started back across the street. Mike finally released his horn. Just as she reached the passenger side, it hit me; I forgot to ask the most important thing. "Jackie, wait! How am I supposed to keep her off my furniture?"

"Just swing a broom at her! She'll back off! Or sprinkle some oregano around! It works like catnip! See ya!" That said, Jackie jumped into the passenger side, and the red BMW screeched as Mike pulled off. I sighed, picked up the stroller, and made my way up the steps.

26

ONCE I MADE IT INTO MY APARTMENT, I SAT ON the edge of my wannabe end table and rested the pet carrier on the floor. Joy meowed from inside and I opened the door. Joy took off, galloping across my living room before jumping up on my table and knocking down the vase with my single rose. When it cracked, I screamed, "Oh, hell no! You may do that at your mama's house, but you won't do that here!" I snatched that cat up by the scruff of the neck and slung that ass back in the cage. Then, I changed the vase, wiped the table down, and washed my hands. I had way too much decorative glass in my living room to let her have free reign. I had searched high and low for my collection of crystal, all cobalt blue. If I were to see so much as a scratch on any one of them, someone was going to catch hell.

I grabbed the stroller and pushed past the pet carrier. Joy mewed.

"Oh, shut up!" I said, feeling a twinge of guilt at not opening it, because I knew once Spider saw Joy caged up, he was going to have a fit. As much as Spider hated Joy, he didn't condone animal cruelty. But I didn't care what Spider thought at this point; I was just trying to save my glass. I pushed the stroller into the bedroom. Tee-Bo looked up at me. It was as if he knew I planned to keep Joy in kitty prison. My guilty conscience kicked in again. "Sweetness, I know I'm wrong for not taking Joy out. Just like I know I am wrong for leading Dr. Snyder to believe your daddy doesn't know about his money." I thought for a moment, and then laughing, I said, "In either case, hopefully, Spider won't let the cat out the bag."

I pushed the stroller into the bedroom and tugged the cord to the light switch. My back was locked. Carrying those bags and wrestling with the stroller all day had weighed me down. I placed my hands on my hips and stretched my upper

169

body around, until I felt a screaming pain in my lower back. My whole body jerked forward. Why did I get that epidural? Oh yeah. I remember why. When I was in labor, I was in so much pain; I wouldn't have even cared if my midwife went old school and stuck a piece of wood in my mouth. I actually begged Dawn to track a doctor down and drag him back to labor and delivery so that I could have that shot up my spine. Now with this sharp pain digging into me, spreading into my butt, stabbing me right there in my right butt cheek and shooting down into the inside of my right leg, I didn't even want to breathe, I just held still, taking short quick breaths. After about five minutes, I was able to stand up straight. Then, I pulled the diaper bag over my head and rested it on the dresser next to Spider's clip full of keys. Once in a while when he lost his keys, they turned up again. He misplaced them so often that I just glanced at the key clip and shook my head. Now, that he had two sets, I guessed that was a good thing.

I bent over the stroller, inserting two fingers into the front of Tee-Bo's diaper. These new Huggies were so absorbent I couldn't tell if he felt wet or not. I checked under his arms and around his neck for moisture. He hadn't been sweaty at all since we left Romell's. That was definitely a good thing, but I missed his baby scent. I cradled him in my arms. Having a newborn that didn't smell sweet was like having a new car without that new-car-smell. The only reason why I didn't douse Tee-Bo with powder was because Romell was adamant.

I kissed Tee-Bo's cheek. He turned his head and began to suck air. Then, he turned and tried to latch on to the crook of my arm. I placed my nipple in his mouth. Tee-Bo didn't nurse for long. Still on the same breast, he started drifting off. It was like he was sipping on knock-out drops. I knew then that he was feeling the effects of the chamomile tea I drank earlier. I wished I were so lucky. I was overtired and so sleep deprived I was a borderline insomniac. Tee-Bo stopped sucking. I tried to ease him off: he woke up, tightened his hold, and started again with his eyes closed. Tee-Bo's nursing slowed and then stopped. I inserted my finger into the corner of his mouth to break the suction. He released and latched right back on. It was as if he couldn't make up his mind which he wanted more: sleep or milk. He nursed and then stopped again. This time, I just left him there. He detached himself with a yawn. I straightened out the gray towel and laid Tee-Bo in his stroller for the night. I needed to wash everything that came in contact with his skin using that detergent Romell gave me. Now, with Tee-Bo asleep, this was the perfect time for that.

It wasn't easy sticking to Romell's instructions. He insisted that I wash everything by hand. The laundromat saved me time. I was so tempted to haul Tee-Bo's clothes right across the Concourse, but I didn't have any quarters. The bodega across the street never gave change; that meant I would've had to go to that supermarket all the way down on Webster Avenue to get a roll. So I hand washed, even though it took me forever to scrub everything clean. I was seriously fighting the urge to soak everything in bleach, spray the stains, and toss in a little fabric softener, but I stuck to Romell's instructions word-for-word, lining my shower rod with plastic hangers full of damp garments and all the backs and arms of all my chairs with wet blankets. Running out of places to hang everything, I hooked a wire hanger into the window fan and removed the last pieces—two of Tee-Bo's undershirts—from the top of Spider's suitcase record player. He didn't like me touching his record player, so I was not about to leave wet clothes there. I folded them across the last hanger, opened the top drawer of Spider's nightstand just a little, and hung that off the knob.

Inside the open drawer, Spider's promotional copies caught the light. I could play these now. I reached in and tossed the CDs onto the bed one after the other. Some were in plastic cases. Some were in cardboard sleeves. Most of them were still shrink wrapped, picturing the recording artist on the cover, all but one, which was unwrapped and in a white, paper sleeve. I grabbed my Discman and sank into my throw pillows.

I placed a CD in the player and hit play. The music was nice. Jazzy. I listened, expecting a female singer with a smooth voice. A hard-core rapper came on screaming and cussing. *Crap.* I took that one out and placed it back in the case. *Who made this?* On the cover was some rough looking man dressed in all black and posed with a pistol. I tossed that aside. All the ones that looked like rap I chucked aside, too. I spotted a young boys' group and snapped in the CD.

The voices sounded like the Jacksons but there was just a hip-hop beat. No music at all. *Crap.* I added that to the pile of rejects. *A girls' group. Where is there a girls' group?* I spread the CDs out. No girls' group. I removed the CD that was in the white paper sleeve, snapped it in, and hit play. The music was nice. *I hope no one starts rapping.* Without warming up, the female singer came right in.

> *Baby, you're the only one for me*
> *You could call me night or day*
> *Anytime you wanna stay*

I put the song on repeat, playing it over and over until I saw Spider in the doorway. "Hey, Spider. This CD is hot. Who made this?" I said, fanning the sleeve.

"One of the girls at the label," Spider said. His whole face was twisted in a grimace.

"What's wrong?" I removed the headphones.

Spider shook his head. "Jackie was here?"

"Yeah, she dropped the cat off," I said cheerfully, hoping my tone would lighten him up.

"I saw it in the thing out there, cryin'. When do you plan to take her out?"

"Never."

"You can't keep her in that thing forever."

"Maybe I can't, but I can sure try."

He half smiled. "What did you and Jackie talk about?"

"Nothing much. I told her I think your mother is lonely."

"I was just there. Trust me when I say she ain't lonely."

"Dr. Snyder didn't tell me you came by."

"I dropped by. You must've just left," he said slowly then shook his head. He bit his lip. A tear fell. He squeezed his thick eyebrows together. They formed an almost perfect "M" when he looked at me.

"What happened?"

"I went over to my mother's, and I heard strange noises, so I ran up to her room and opened the door."

"Was she okay?"

"Yeah, she was okay. She was *with* Barbara."

"With Barbara how?"

"How do you think?"

"Oh, wow. What did you do?"

"I closed her door and went into my room. I'm in there

playin' my game, and she comes in and tries to explain. I don't wanna hear that, so I told her, 'Just give me my check, so I can go. I have to help Jeff pay his rent.'"

"You did what!"

"I asked for my check!"

I hung my head and sobbed for about a minute. Squeezing my eyes tight, I let loose a deep sigh then looked at Spider, squinting. "What did she say?"

"She was inebriated; she said, 'Hell no.' So, I said, 'Fine keep it, then. I'll just have Home Life Mutual issue me a new one.'"

"Oh, no!"

"Yeah! She leaves, right. Then, she comes back with my check balled up in her hand, and she threw it at me. She told me to get the hell out."

I shook my head. "Oh, Spider. I am *so* sorry."

"I can't believe she didn't give my Pops a funeral when she had all that insurance on him. I can't believe that." Spider broke down in tears. I hugged him, kissed him on his forehead, and ran my fingers through his hair. After a while, he sat straight up.

"Are you okay?" I asked.

He nodded, looking at all the Ear-That-One promotional CDs scattered over the green top sheet. "Mia, when you get a chance, please put that résumé together for me."

"Oh, yeah!" I walked over to my nightstand, pulled two folded sheets of paper from under the clock, and handed them to Spider.

"What's this?"

"That's what I did on your résumé so far."

He looked at the papers, all his information written out on loose-leaf and his résumé on typing paper but full of typos. "Why did you have this underneath the clock?"

"To remind myself to make time to finish."

"You always seem to have time for everyone else, why do you need to remind yourself to make time for me?"

"Spider, I didn't forget about you. I spent all morning trying to get that finished, but I kept making too many mistakes."

"Yeah, I see. Look here." He pointed to the page, and I saw that, for his last job, instead of typing Romeo Gigolo, I typed Romell Gigolo. He looked at me, and all I could do was mouth an apology. Spider shook his head. "That's okay. You can retype this on the computer. It's in the living room. Hook it up later."

I stood. "I'll hook it up now," I said. Walking past the stroller, I noticed the front of Tee-Bo's diaper was soaked and ready to burst. *Poor thing.* I walked over to the diaper bag.

"What's wrong?" Spider asked.

"He's wet. So, I'm gonna—"

"Go ahead and set up the computer. I'll change him,"

"Okay," I said. Spider chuckled, so naturally, I said, "What?"

"At least, a few good things came out of all this."

"What's that?"

"Now, we can get Tee-Bo a crib," Spider said. "When Jeff drops by tomorrow, I can give him the money he needs to keep his place. And after all that, we'll still have enough left over for a down payment on a house."

"A house?" I wanted to pass out right there. I smiled and tears rolled down *my* cheeks. *A house. Wow!* Hearing Spider say those words was almost too good to be true. *Wait until I tell Dawn*, I thought then remembered what she told me about cashing that check. "Spider, if you need that cashed by tomorrow, you have to go directly to the branch that issued the check. If you deposit it, the check will take three days to clear."

"Okay."

"And just so you know, Jeff asked me if Mr. Zach had insurance. I didn't answer him."

"Good. Jeff overheard some of what I was saying when I was on the phone with you, but what he don't know won't hurt him."

"I understand."

I danced through the hallway, but when I thought about Dr. Snyder, I stopped cold. I passed Joy and sat on the loveseat. I knew Dr. Snyder must've felt awful. I had to call her, but I didn't have a clue what I'd say. I was supposed to run an errand for her next week, so my plan was to ask her about that first, and then explain why I told Spider about the insurance check. I picked up the phone and dialed Dr. Snyder. She soon picked up and said, "Hello."

In a low voice, I said, "Hello, Mae Mae?"

"Don't call me Mae Mae. You whore!" She was so drunk

that now, her words slurred.

"I may be a liar, but I am not a whore."

"What's the difference? Spence is making a big mistake!" Dr. Snyder slammed the phone. *I guess she doesn't need me to run that errand for her.* I sighed, but as soon as I placed the phone back in the cradle, I heard Spider. "Aye, yo! Mia!" He called out. I panicked. *Oh no! Spider heard me.* I started toward the bedroom.

As soon as I walked into the room, Spider said. "I thought you didn't have any money."

"I don't." Watching him hold out a wad of cash, I asked, "Where did that come from?"

"That's what I'd like to know," Spider said. "It was in this." He reached in Tee-Bo's diaper bag and pulled out a brown paper bag. The same brown paper bag Romell had stuffed in there right before we left. And I told Romell I didn't want any money from him. Spider looked at me as if I had the answer to the million-dollar question. Well, not quite a million. Knowing Romell it was at least a thousand dollars. "Well?" Spider said.

I knew then I needed to do two things. First, I needed to tell Spider one convincing lie. "Oh, um, yeah! That's Dawn's. See, she asked me to hold some money for her, to keep her from shopping with it." That was easy enough. Next, I needed to have a *little* chat with Romell.

27

*T*HE NEXT DAY WHEN I MADE IT HOME FROM work, I called Romell and got right in his ass. "Didn't I tell you I didn't want you giving me any money?"

"Hello to you, too."

"Romell, I distinctly told you not to give me any money!"

"Why should I listen to you? You don't listen to me."

"I do listen to you!" I said, startling Tee-Bo. His eyes widened in surprise as he swayed in his Fisher Price, battery-operated swing directly across from me. I sat up, pursed my lips, and made the kissing noise that usually calmed him. He settled quickly. I stretched back out on the loveseat, and in a softer tone, I repeated, "I do listen."

"Chocolate, you rebut everything I say and only absorb information through osmosis. You *never* listen."

"That's not true! I do listen!"

"Yeah? Since when? I'd like to hear this."

I searched for an answer. Spotting the swivel chair, I saw Tee-Bo's white, terrycloth, hooded towel slung over the brown leather. It was the only piece of his laundry still left hanging to dry. Now that I had my snappy comeback, I bragged, "Last night! Last night, I washed all Tee-Bo's clothes the way you told me to. I *did* listen."

"Bravo! First time for everything. I'm still waiting for you to call my mom."

"Stop hounding me about that. I'm going to talk to her." I almost believed that myself. Romell wasn't fooled though.

"Yeah, I know you are," he said. "Hold on, I'm putting her on the line right now."

"Rom—" There was a click in the phone line, then silence. *How does he do that?*

When Romell clicked back into the line, he sounded like a

ten-year-old. "Hi, Ma?"

"Yes," Mrs. Goodwin said.

"Mia is on the line."

"Well, hello," Romell's mother said. Her voice was as warm as baked bread.

"Hi, Mrs. Goodwin. How are you?"

"I'm doing well, but Romell tells me you've been under some pressure lately."

Now, repeating anything I said in confidence irked me to no end. Romell heard me complain about Dawn enough times to know that, so I was obviously annoyed. "Is that right?"

"Calm yourself," she said. "He didn't tell me much. That's why I wanted to speak to you myself. How are you?"

I sighed. "I'm okay I guess. Stressed...but okay. Mommy is on my back as usual."

"If that's usually the case, you should be used to it by now."

That made sense. I laughed and continued, "There are also Spider's family problems."

Romell immediately had his questions. "What? His brother again?"

"Romell, we don't need you *chiming* in." Mrs. Goodwin scolded.

"Sorry, Ma."

Again in her softer voice, Mrs. Goodwin said, "Mia, you are in a relationship. Sometimes family problems come with the territory."

"It's more than family problems. I'm going through so many changes with this man sometimes I don't know if I love him or hate him.

"That's not good."

"I know, but I am hanging in there. Doing my best, loving Spider with all my heart, and putting our relationship first."

"Now, let me stop you right there. No matter how deeply you love anyone, remember it is God you should love above all others. With all your heart, all your soul, and all your might. Put God first, everything else will fall into place. Put your relationship first, and it is sure to fail. All relationships go through changes."

"They do?"

"Yes, they do. And, do you know what you can do for

178

those changes?"

"No, what?"

"Put your hands together right now."

"Okay, they're together."

"Are your fingers intertwined?"

"Now they are."

"I find that when I am praying my hardest, my fingers lock into that two-handed fist. Looks like a hammer doesn't it."

"Yeah, I guess so."

"Well, that's your hammer. It can knock down walls and open doors. You have a Bible?"

"Yes."

"New International?"

"Yes, it's new. I've never even opened it."

"No. That's not what I mean. What version is it? King James or New International. Check. It should be on the spine."

"Hold on," I said. My Bible was in my bottom nightstand drawer. It took me half a minute to jump up and get it from the other room. I sat back on the loveseat and pinned the receiver to my ear with my shoulder. Reading the gold letters off the spine of the leather-bound Bible, I said, "Okay. It's the New International Version."

"Good. That's easier to understand. Here are some verses you should read. Get a pen."

I stretched the phone cord and reached for a pen, but the only scrap paper I had was the receipt for the CD player. I walked back over. "Okay," I said, ready to write on it.

"Read John 3:16...Isaiah 54:10...and Psalm 119:41." Mrs. Goodwin spoke slowly and clearly as I jotted the verses down on the back of the receipt. Then she said, "Mia, stay in prayer. And who knows, maybe one of these days, I'll see you in church." She paused for my comment; of course, I had none. So, after that brief, uncomfortable silence, she added, "You're always in my prayers, Mia. Don't be a stranger."

"Okay, Mrs. Goodwin"

"Goodbye, now," she said.

"Bye, Ma."

"Goodbye," I said. When I heard the click, I knew someone hung up, but I wasn't sure if anyone was left on the line. "Romell?" I said.

"I'm still here," he answered.

"Good. I have one question for you."

"Yeah?"

"If I don't want to hear a lecture from *my* mother, what makes you think I want to hear a sermon from *yours*?" I like having the last word, so of course, I hung up.

I felt it was noble of Romell to encourage me to talk to his mother *and* to try to loan me the money. Talking to his mother was one thing. Loaning me money was something different. Because Romell and Spider didn't get along, I didn't think it was right to accept money for Tee-Bo's crib. As Tee-Bo's father, it was Spider's place to provide for his son. So, no matter how noble the gesture, I had to be firm with Romell, otherwise his intentions would always outweigh my convictions. It was obvious Romell thought he knew what was best for me, but I decided what was best for me in my life, and I wanted my wishes respected.

I walked over and yanked the diaper bag off the chair. I reached inside and pulled out the stamped envelope addressed to Romell. Inside was a money order for one thousand twenty dollars. The extra twenty was for the fancy detergents. I licked the envelope shut, and lifted Tee-Bo out of his swing for a quick trip to the mailbox. Romell needed to stop meddling. If I wanted his money, I would have asked for it, and if I wanted Mrs. Goodwin's advice, I would have called her myself.

Even though I was never baptized, I still had that Christian upbringing. When we were younger, Romell's mother took all of us to church with her more times than I can count. But Mrs. Goodwin's answer for everything was reaching for her *Daily Word*. And, frankly, at this point in my life, I didn't want spiritual advice. Quoting scriptures and flipping through chapter and verse did not spell enlightenment for me; that spelled guilt trip, especially when, spiritually, I didn't know where I stood.

I bought the Bible only because Mommy told me there should be one in every home and I believed her. When I went to open it for the first time, Spider looked at me.

"What are you doing?"

"I'm getting ready to read the Bible."

He shook his head, and as he walked away, he said, "What's the point?"

So, I put it away. I hadn't touched it since.

Because I went to church often when I was younger, I expected atheists to be big hairy monsters, people so evil they were border-line demonic. When I met Spider, that myth was dispelled. As I got to know him, I understood that atheists are people who simply don't believe, and that doesn't necessarily weigh against their character. Spider was an atheist with a *solid* set of ethics. *Right is right, and wrong is wrong. Live by integrity. Then, by the natural order of things, I would have peace in my life. Treat people the way I want to be treated. Watch how people treat others, because more than likely, that's how they'd treat me. Do good things, good things happen. Do bad things, bad things happen.* He didn't believe in God; he believed in karma. This was simple enough to understand, and I had grown so accustomed to his way of thinking that, eventually, I didn't know what I believed, or if I believed at all.

Those times I exclaimed, "Lord help me," I had yet to acknowledge the existence of a higher being. It didn't matter to me one way or the other. I was who I was, and I wanted what I wanted. My main concern was getting my black man to marry me: the same black man who was resistant because he didn't want to end up like his parents—legally bound but in every other way uncommitted. Now, I was facing the possibility of Spider's view of marriage being further distorted by his mother's vengeance, and quite frankly, I didn't think prayer would help me now.

28

I RAN INTO JEFF ON THE WAY BACK FROM THE mailbox. Beneath his dangling curls, his eyes were as red as the corner stop sign. I started not to say anything, but walking with him back to the apartment, I could have caught a contact high from the stench of weed smoke rising off his uniform's orange, polo shirt. When I stuck the key in my door, I turned to him. "What happened, Jeff? You guys are spicing up chicken with Chronic now?"

"I look high?"

I nodded. "And you smell like a blunt."

"Ah, man. Lola is gonna have a fit."

"You're going to see your mother, and you were lighting up?"

"All day in the bathroom at the Chicken Shack. A little smoke helps me think."

"Right about now, you're genius," I said turning the key. I pushed the door, but it would not open. Something was blocking its path. I pushed, hearing something heavy dragging behind it. I held Tee-Bo close, stuck my face through the crack, and said, "Spider, I can't get in."

"Wait up! Wait up. Let me move this, then," Spider said clearing the doorway.

As soon as the path was clear, I stepped inside and Jeff stepped in right behind me. I looked at what was against the wall and screamed, "Woo–hoo!" I handed Tee-Bo to Jeff and jumped so high that both my feet kicked my butt at the same time. Then, I hugged the tall cardboard box that was marked "3-in-1 Convertible Crib." Next, I wiped away an imaginary tear, hugged the mattress covered in plastic, and grinned at Spider. He had his head tilted back with bloody tissue hanging out both nostrils. Drops of blood made a trail down his blue button-down shirt. He straightened up, took one of the tissues out, and quickly plugged it right back into his nose. There was a huge red knot on his forehead. "What the hell happened to you?" I blurted.

"Low pipe in the crib store."

"Yo, Spence. Next time, duck."

"Jeff, how many blunts did you have to smoke to think of that one?" I said, lifting Tee-Bo out of his arms. "Spider, you were right on time with this. What color is it?"

"White. I'll have it up in a minute. And, since we're talking about cribs," Spider said reaching into his pocket. He pulled out a fat bank envelope. "Jeff, go take care of yours."

"Yo, Spence. Before I take that, I want to know. Where'd that money come from?"

"Don't matter. Take it," Spider said.

"Spence, is this or is this not insurance money?"

Spider had his head tilted back, but I could see the tension pressed into Jeff's face. I held Tee-Bo closer to me and stepped out from between the two men.

Spider shrugged one shoulder and held the envelope out farther. "Man, you high. Knock it off and take the money."

Jeff shook his head. His long curls swung. "I won't take it until you answer me."

Spider looked at me. I looked away and buckled Tee-Bo into his swing. Spider grabbed Jeff's hand, slapped the envelope into it, and said, "What do you think?"

"That ain't right, man. That ain't right! At the very least, the old man deserved a decent burial," Jeff said, pushing his hair back.

"The arrangements my mother made may not have been much, but she stepped up when no one else did. She did more than she had to. So, I can't fault her."

Jeff exploded, "What! Are you *that* fucking blind? Lola borrowed money...from everybody. She was making the arrangements for the memorial service. For everything."

Spider furrowed his brow. "What do you mean Lola was making the arrangements?"

Jeff looked Spider in the eye and broke it down, "Lola was in the room with the funeral director; the contract was in her fucking hand, Man! Lola was planning the shit. Your mother showed up and threw her out." Jeff then spun around and punched the air. Long hair swung back into his face.

"My mother threw Lola out?"

Pushing his hair back out of his eyes, Jeff looked at Spider. "Your mother didn't wanna give him a service, and she didn't want anyone else giving him one, either. She deaded it."

"That's not possible! If Lola and the man were sitting down with the contract, as you say, my mother wouldn't have anything to do with that. Lola was Pop's common law wife."

"They weren't married, man! And, there ain't no such thing as common law in the State of New York. Lola tried to get an Order to Cease and Desist, but it was too late; Pop's body was gone. Your mother already had him cremated."

Spider sighed, clipped his thumbs onto the pockets of his khaki pants, and shrugged. "Well, there's nothing we can do for Pops now. What's done is done. I had nothing to do with that. That was my mother. That beef is between my mother and Lola. Not us. Jeff, take the money and pay your rent."

"I don't want anything to do with this money. This ain't right!" He held the envelope back out to Spider.

"Man, you're high and about to get evicted. Now is not the time to get a conscience."

"Come again?"

"Beggars can't be fuckin' choosers! You wanna get deep? Get deep when it's time to pay your child support or before you gamble away your rent money. Right is right, and wrong is wrong, but money's fuckin' money! And right now, you ain't got shit!"

Jeff pinched his nose. Next, he poked his lips out and drew them in tight. Then, he zipped the cash envelope open with his index finger, removed a crisp hundred, and looked at it. All the while, I was watching him closely. He sniffled, not once, not twice, but three times. I could tell he was fighting back tears. Jeff grabbed his crotch. And now, Spider and I were both staring at him anticipating what he would possibly say next. But, Jeff didn't look up at either of us; instead, he spat on the president and smacked the bill into Spider's forehead, throwing him off balance. Spider keeled over but quickly hopped back on his feet. He then hemmed Jeff up by the collar of his orange, uniform shirt.

"Spider, let him go!" I yelled, and Tee-Bo bawled.

"Stay out of this, Mia!"

"You wanna hit me, man. Hit me! You can't hurt me any more than I'm hurtin' right now," Jeff said, pounding his chest.

Spider punched the wall inches away from Jeff's head. That left no dent in the wall, but Spider shook his hand from the pain and let Jeff drop to the floor. He dusted himself off and got right up into Spider's face, "All my father ever meant to y'all was money!"

Spider waved his hand. "That's bullshit!"

"Bullshit? Y'all took all he had!" Jeff sobbed. "Lola used to sell her food stamps to buy me shoes, man. There were nights when all we had to eat was powdered eggs and government cheese, while your ass was in private school. Y'all never gave a damn about him!"

"*I* did!"

Jeff's eyes were red and glowing. "*You* couldn't stand him!"

"Only at first. I wasn't feelin' Pops in the beginning. And, maybe, I didn't know him as long as you did...but I loved him, too!" Spider said.

"If you loved him so much, where the hell are his ashes?" Spider didn't say a word as Jeff stared with a look of burning pain. "Where are his ashes, man? Do you know? Do you even care?" His voice quivered over Tee-Bo's crying. Now, I was steadily bouncing my baby. Part of me wanted to take him out of the room and calm him down, but my feet felt like they were glued to that spot. Spider and Jeff didn't even notice the crying or that we were still in the room. They were staring at each other. Even though Spider was two feet taller, his posture deflated. He looked like a wounded elephant, shrinking with his tissues protruding from his nostrils like bloody ivory tusks. I knew he didn't know the answer. That thought probably never even crossed his mind. The ashes were never important to him. He never once mentioned them to me. And now, his expression was a total blank. Jeff shook his head. "For the longest time, I took whatever I could get from you because I felt I had it rough because of you, and you owed me for that. But, you know what?" Jeff flung the envelope into Spider's chest, sending bills everywhere. "Fuck you and your money!" He stormed out, slamming the door.

29

$\mathcal{F}$OR THE LONGEST TIME, SPIDER DIDN'T SAY A thing. Neither did I. He didn't pick the money up off the floor, either, but stepped over it on his way to the kitchen. He tossed the bloody tissues into the trashcan, pulled a screwdriver out of the utility drawer, then grabbed the crib's box and dragged it. The cardboard scraped the entryway and turned up the hall toward the bedroom. I knew Spider needed his space for a little while.

Once I calmed Tee-Bo, I made it a point to flush those nasty tissues. Next, I plucked each bill off the floor, smoothed it out, and sorted it by denomination. Big bills on top. Small bills on the bottom. All the presidents facing the same direction. The hundreds, the fifties, the twenties, the tens. New bills always had a little funk to them, but I still loved the smell. I inhaled and then counted. Again and again. Two thousand five hundred dollars. I shook my head and took Tee-Bo out of his swing.

Walking into the bedroom, I saw the crib's instruction sheet folded in the corner with a pile of tiny clear plastic bags, along with the slats, spindles, frame, rods, wheels, nuts, screws, and the tools. Everything was neatly arranged around Spider. He was crouched on the floor. I sat the stack of bills right by him on my nightstand in front of his clock. The time was 7:38. It looked like I'd have a place to lay Tee-Bo once he was ready to go to sleep. So, I gently laid him on the bed, bunched pillows up against my headboard, and made myself comfortable. Spider never unfolded the instruction sheet. Matching pieces at random, he screwed them, unscrewed them and screwed them again without looking at the diagram. And he never breathed a word.

By the time he finally had the contraption standing, Tee-Bo was knocked out behind me. I'd propped my head up on my hand to keep myself awake. I dozed off anyway and woke up with a chin full of drool, a crick in my neck, and a numb left arm. The clock read 10:58. Spider was standing. With one eye closed, his eye of precision was examining his handiwork. Then, Spider licked the tip of his finger and ran it across the rail like he was the master carver who whittled it himself. He picked up the frame, lowered it into the shell, and screwed it in place. Then, he stepped back and studied it again. It was leaning to the side. I just knew Spider was going to do something else with it. But instead, he twisted his head as if that would straighten it and walked out of the room, returning with the mattress. As he laid it inside, I shook my head.

The frame was lopsided because one end was screwed in too high. One of the rails was screwed in backward, so the spindles on my side spiraled up and the spindles on his side spiraled down. I was surprised the crib was even standing. "It looks good," I lied. I looked at the metal rods, screws, nuts, bolts, washers, and wheels still on the floor, and then I tried to make eye contact. "I don't think you should have pieces left over," I said. He didn't answer. "Maybe you don't need these," I said. Still, nothing from the pouting man with the screwdriver in his hand. He didn't even look at me. "Oh, come on, Spider! Say something. Why are you mad at *me*?"

Now, he stared me down. "Why did you take up for him?" His voice was just loud enough for me to hear.

"Spider, Jeff is a hundred and twenty pounds with rocks in his pocket."

"So, what does that mean?"

"It means you're way bigger than he is. You get no cool points for kicking Jeff's ass."

"Don't you think I know that? I'm six-five, Mia!" Spider paced back and forth, shaking his head. "I'm a punk or a bully, a punk or a bully; I hate that!" He plopped on the bed. Then, he fell back on the mattress and laughed, "You know, he only did that shit because he knew he'd get away with it, right? Jeff's so small; anything I did would've made *me* out to be the heavy."

"You should still apologize."

"Apologize?" He sat straight up.

"Yes, Spider. You should call and say you're sorry."

"You buggin'! He knew I banged my head earlier, and he smacked me right on my bump. I *shoulda* snuffed him!"

"Spider, you never apologize."

"I'm never wrong!"

I slapped my own face in sheer frustration. "Spider, I'm sorry to say this, but your people skills suck. Jeff just found out that even though your father was disposed of the way he was, he was heavily insured. You picked that moment of all moments to insist that he take some of that insurance money. Then, you threw it in his face that he doesn't pay his rent or child support."

"Right is right, and wrong is wrong!"

"Timing is the key to everything, Spider. That only made Jeff angry."

"So what! That's what's up, and Jeff needed to hear it. A father is supposed to pay his child support! And, a man is supposed to pay his rent!"

"You don't!" I said, and Spider's jaw dropped. I figured that would prove my point. That's what's up, and *Spider* needed to hear it, right? I softened my tone. "You never have. And, as many times as Jeff seen me digging in my pocketbook, how dare you come out your face and criticize him, like your shit don't stink, when he's obviously upset about this whole situation. I'm sorry to say, but if I were Jeff, I would've smacked you, too."

Spider jumped up and flung the screwdriver. It hit his cologne bottles, knocking them over like bowling pins. He then snatched his keys off the dresser and clipped them to his pants. "Where are you going?"

"Out!"

"Out where?"

"You know where!" Spider stomped his way to the door. I heard it slam and the four clicks as he locked it.

30

I SAT THERE A MINUTE AFTER HE LEFT; THE BOOM of the slamming door and clicks of the front locks still reverberating. I have a ghetto door—an old, tenement building, heavy, metal door covered with years of paint, periwinkle on the inside, nasty gray on the outside...and it sticks. GHE–TTO. It used to have one of those clunky, steel, security bars, but I got tired of watching Spider trip over it on his way in. I knew sometimes you had to give the door an extra pull so that it would close all the way, but he slammed it; that wasn't necessary. I gave him a taste of his own medicine just to prove a point. I proved it. Now, his feelings were hurt. Boom! Click, click, click, click. It echoed in my head. That echo made the tick, tick, tick of Spider's clock sound like a time bomb. I was half expecting it to explode. *I guess this is supposed to be my fault, because Spider's never wrong.* I sucked my teeth, thinking. *He could stay mad for all I care.* Then, it hit me. He must've really been pissed at me. He was going to his mother's, and he was pissed at her, too. *Donkey Kong to the rescue!*

Spider loved that ColecoVision more than he loved me. There was never a speck of dust on it. He cleaned that thing with a Q-tip religiously before he even stuck the cartridge in. Once I got so fed up watching him do that, I hollered, "I wish you'd pay *me* that kind of attention!"

Spider was so into his game he paid me no mind. So I knew, once he got to his mother's house and started playing his game, he would focus on that TV screen like the fate of the world was in his joystick. Climbing a few ladders, jumping a few barrels, and saving a princess—I didn't know why, but these were things that always made him feel like a man again. And although I had my frustrations about that in the past, right about now, I was hoping he beat his high score.

191

♥　♥　♥　♥

That next morning, I opened my eyes. Through the crib's spindles, a gleam of light shone on Tee-Bo's hair. His breathing was steady. He didn't wake once during the night so I knew he had a good night's sleep in his new crib. I was so glad I had reassembled it after Spider left. What took Spider over three hours to screw up, my happy, black ass assembled in twenty minutes.

I took a deep breath, filling my lungs with Spider's cologne and a touch of lemon, but that didn't register. I yawned and stretched, expecting my arm to land on his shoulder. It landed on the mattress. I whipped my neck around. The sheets on Spider's side of the bed were still folded back and tucked tight. I sat up. His leather portfolio was resting on the edge of the dresser, and Spider was standing in the mirror adjusting his tie. The creases in his slacks were sharp enough to slice cheese. It was a little hot for the suit jacket, but he had every button on that double-breasted thing fastened. I started to sweat just looking at him. I could see his eyes in the mirror, so I knew he could see me.

"Why are you all dressed up?" I asked. He said nothing. He unbuttoned his jacket, looped the skinny bottom flap of his red tie through the designer's label, tucked it down between the buttons of his dress shirt, and refastened his jacket. In his reflection, I could see his furrowed brows and crinkled forehead. I knew putting on a tie didn't require that much thought. "What time did you get in last night?" I asked. In silence, he picked up the comb and ran it through his hair, smoothing it back. My lips grew tight. "Spider, did you go to your mother's?" I said, now raising my voice, and I waited. "Spider?" I said again but still waited some more. "Answer me!" I finally screamed.

"Where are my father's ashes, Mia?"

I swallowed hard. "I–I don't know. Ask your mother."

Spider looked at me. His eyes were icy. "I did. She told me to ask you," he said. I just sat there speechless. He continued, "Jeff and I argued about this. You were right there. You knew and said nothing." He then snatched his bag off the edge of the dresser and charged out. An *Obsession* cologne and lemon-scented breeze kicked back into the room. His dress shoes tapped hard against the floor on his way to the front door, which he slammed and this time, didn't even bother to lock. *I guess he didn't beat his high score. I was so sure, after a little Donkey Kong therapy, he'd come back as good as new. Boy, was I wrong.* I sighed, and then I remembered the last can of spray starch I purchased was unscented. The only thing we had in a spray can that was lemon scented was furniture polish. The man ironed his clothes with furniture polish.

Spider *was* right about one thing, I knew what happened to Mr. Zach's ashes, and I didn't tell, not even after he and Jeff argued. But, how could I tell him I knew what happened to his father because I was snooping through his mother's trash? I couldn't break that gently. No way. And, even if I could, why would I? When I told Spider how badly I want to get married. He told me, "We have issues." He has no money; I don't trust him; I'm supposedly loyal to everybody else but him; but especially, my relationship with Romell. Then, he went into this whole spiel about how he didn't want to end up like his parents. So, bearing in mind Spider already had his reservations about marriage, I was supposed to tell him what took place at his mother's? Was he stupid? Knowing Spider, I knew he thought I held back that information, because I was more "loyal" to his mother than I was to him, but that was not the case. Not at all. I just didn't want to give Spider one more reason not to believe in marriage.

What was I to do now? I glanced around the room, searching for ideas, from the prom picture on Spider's side of the dresser across my yellow walls to the apple green armoire that I converted to store our clothes. The daisy bouquets on both doors looked like decals, but I hand painted those myself in acrylic so they would look exactly like the ones on the white porcelain knobs I found in the alley when I was dumping the trash. There were enough for my armoire, dresser, and night tables, too. All this furniture was mismatched, but everything was painted the same shade of apple green and distressed, so it all looked aged. Our bedroom had a cottage feel. Even crowded with the crib on my side of the bed and the cradle over in the corner by the window, it was still a perfect retreat from a hectic day of collections, and I hated collections with a passion. I looked at my headboard; it was as plush as anything from *Better Homes and Gardens*. Now, I was convinced. If I could fashion a headboard that jazzy out of an old blanket, scrap wood, foam, a sheet, and buttons from an old suit, I could fix this situation. The only question was, how?

I looked. The twenty-five hundred dollars was still there on my nightstand. Not even an inch away, the clock read 6:22. The draft of Spider's résumé was still folded underneath it exactly where I left it two days ago to remind myself to make time to finish. Hey, after battling Romell and his Crisco, running into Dr. Snyder and her bag of goodies, having to explain a wad of mystery cash, and Spider and Jeff coming to blows, I was way too distracted to notice those papers under that clock. But, right now, I was ready to give Spider's résumé my full attention.

31

EFF WAS LIVID WHEN HE LEFT OUR APARTMENT. I was so used to Jeff kidding around; I had a hard time taking him seriously. It didn't help that he was in the habit of saying he was "just playing" even when he was serious. Then, soon after, he'd be grinning all over again. Grinning just like his father. The Snyder grin tickles. It made me fall hard and fast for Spider. That big, toothy grin on Spider nowadays was a rare occurrence like a full moon...on Valentine's day...during a heat wave...that just so happens to fall on a leap year. Now, Spider smiled without parting his lips. Jeff, on the other hand, flashed *his* Kool-Aid all the time. Jeff just wasn't Jeff, if he wasn't grinning. That's why seeing him so distraught was heartbreaking. It was Tuesday; a whole day had passed. I figured that was more than enough time for Jeff to calm down; by now, he would be a little more reasonable.

After work, I picked up Tee-Bo and went to the Chicken Shack looking for Jeff. He had called in sick and didn't pick up when I phoned his apartment, so I decided to head over to Miss Lola's even though I didn't have her phone number. That meant screaming alarms, two broken elevators and a nine-flight climb with a baby stroller. I lifted the knocker and tapped on her door. No answer. I knocked again. Still, no answer. I started rummaging through the diaper bag for a pen and paper to leave a note. That's when the exit door squeaked open, and I heard the scraping of bedroom slippers. I looked up. Miss Lola was taking steps toward me in her pink housecoat. Right behind her, Jeff's mop top.

He stepped around Miss Lola with his big grin. "Aye! Whatchu doin' here," he said.

"I came to bring you the money to save your place."

He stopped smiling. "Did Spence put you up to this?"

I shook my head. "Not at all."

"Good to see you, Mia," Miss Lola said wrapping her plump arms around me. She gave me a squeeze, and the top of her burgundy, braided wig tickled my nose. Miss Lola always reminded me of a brown-skinned elf. She had such a jolly face despite the keloid scar that traveled across her cheek and disappeared under her wig. She reached up, gave my face a gentle pinch, and then unlocked the door.

We walked into the living room. I parked the stroller to the side and saw pure fascination in Tee-Bo's face. Following his stare to Miss Lola's sofa, I could see the big red roses on the slipcover had him mesmerized. I took a few steps over and sat in the middle of the sofa. Jeff walked to the window and looked out. "As soon as I see Ray, I'm gonna run."

"Who's Ray?" I asked.

"The super. Aye, I appreciate what you're trying to do, Mia." Jeff said.

I pulled the money out of the diaper bag. "Here, then. If it's not too late."

He looked at me and shook his head. "I already cleared my apartment. That's *my* shit stuck in the elevator."

"I don't understand."

Jeff turned around and sat on the radiator. "This is my father we're talkin' about. Did you live with your father?"

I shook my head. "Never met him."

"That's why you don't understand. My pops didn't have much, but everything I needed he gave me. He taught me so much."

"Like what?"

Jeff sighed. "He used to always say, 'Good character, son. Some are born with it. Some develop it.' He taught me, that even though we make mistakes, we can turn our lives around, and that's deep. The old man was a giant; you just don't know. No matter what life threw at him, he smiled and made the best of it. My pops was a hero."

"Well then, I'm sure he would've wanted you to take—"

"Mia, you still don't get it. My pops wasn't just *my* hero!" He walked to the wall unit and grabbed a thick, navy blue, satin-covered book. He placed it in my lap and sat back on the radiator. The album was edged in white lace and had plastic pages that crackled. I split it open and lost my breath. Seeing Mr. Zach again, I was thrown off; he looked so full of life. His big smile and green eyes lit up the pages.

In one particular picture, Mr. Zach was standing with two other men. They were all wearing traditional dark suits, and their ties were exactly the same, black with white polka dots. "Why are they dressed alike?" I asked pointing.

On the coffee table, Miss Lola placed a pitcher of red Kool-Aid and three tall glasses next to it. Then she leaned over to see. "Oh, that. Zach was on the deacon board at our church," she said.

I kept flipping. I saw Mr. Zach dressed in a pale grey suit right in the middle of a semicircle of men in tuxedos. They were all wearing box-shaped hats. "Is this a church picture, too?"

Miss Lola looked. "No. That was the 75th anniversary gala for Zach's lodge." She shook her head and then smiled. "He was so upset with me that day."

The distant look in Miss Lola's eyes told me her mind was somewhere else. "Why?" I asked.

She pushed a glass over to me. "I'm a procrastinator, always have been. Zach was probably worse than me." She began to pour. I stopped her when it was half full.

"You guys were late?" I asked.

"That's putting it mildly. I waited until the last minute to do the laundry. Then, I took a nap and overslept. When I went down to the laundry room to empty out the dryer, all our clothes were gone. Zach had no socks and no shirts. So, I rushed to buy him some from Alexander's."

"Yeah, and by the time Ma made it back, she missed the dry cleaners. It was too late for her to get Pop's black suit."

Miss Lola laughed and a tear ran down her cheek. "When Zach came home, he just sat and sulked. He started not to go, but then he jumped up and said, 'Those people want to see *me*. Not my suit.' And, he reached in the closet and pulled that gray one out," she said.

I turned the page. "I see that in all these shots, Mr. Zach is standing in the middle."

"That's why," she said. "It's funny, that Zach started not to go. That turned out to be the best one ever. Just so happens, that year, they decided to give Zach the Distinguished Service Award." Miss Lola tapped the top picture, pointing to the crystal pyramid in his hands. Then she pointed to the man at Mr. Zach's immediate right. "You see him? That's Zach's best friend, Bubba. He planned the banquet that year. He rented a hall. It was catered. There was champagne, caviar, an ice sculpture, and there was even a swing band. Zach and I had so much fun," she said. And, I could see that from the next few pictures. Lola in her little pink dress standing with her arms wrapped around Mr. Zach. I giggled. He was so tall; she looked like she was hugging a tree. The two of them dancing. Miss Lola sitting with her head on Mr. Zach's chest. In all the pictures, both of them were wearing big smiles, especially her with her chubby cheeks. I paused, at first amazed at how thin she used to be, and then I noticed something. She looked exactly like the bridesmaid who was holding the bouquet in that picture I saw at Dr. Snyder's. *But, would it be tacky of me to ask?* That was the question on my mind when I turned the page.

There was greenery in the next series of pictures. He was tying a rope from tree to tree and then suspending backpacks from that line. Since it was obvious they were all in some kind of bush, I said, "Safari?"

"No, camping. That's Zach and his boys."

When I heard that, I took a second look to check for Spider's face. "His boys?"

"Yep, Zach was a troop leader...for almost twenty years."

"Wow!"

"Yeah, Pops volunteered at our community center, too." Jeff was holding his crotch; that let me know he was upset. I looked at his face. It was turning red. And so were his eyes. I closed the album and gave him my full attention. Jeff knocked on the side of the wall unit. "Pops built that. He taught the woodshop class." The side Jeff knocked had two frosted glass doors. The other end had rounded shelves. Lola had all her snow globes on it. In the middle section was the TV unit. The whole thing looked like solid oak. The grain was almost a perfect match for the coffee table. Not much detail, but a definite show of talent, considering it was handmade.

"I know Mae Mae was legally Zach's wife, and Zach *was* her husband, but he was also a lot of things to a lot of people," Miss Lola added. "And everybody wanted to pay their respects."

"Pops dedicated his life to helping others. That dragon lady robbed everyone who loved him. We never got our chance to say goodbye." Jeff looked at me, sitting with the cash still at my side. "So, Mia. You can put that away. No amount of money is gonna make everything all good. You feel me?" He still had a smile on his face.

I wanted to ask why Mr. Zach didn't write a will. That would've saved them all a lot of heartache, but I already had the answer. They never got around to it. Miss Lola admitted they were both procrastinators. They never expected Mr. Zach to drop dead. And now, Jeff's expression twisted, his grief was obvious. I finally understood. I never met my father, but had something similar happened to my mother, I would have been devastated. I sighed and leaned forward. "Well, Jeff. Maybe you should have a talk with your brother."

Jeff jumped up and shouted, "Fuck him!" He squared off and punched the wall unit. There was a simultaneous bang and crunch, then the crash. Jeff fell to his knees, clutching his hand. The wood where Jeff's fist landed had split, and half of Miss Lola's collection of figurines went flying. I wanted so badly to patch things up between Spider and Jeff, but seeing those snow globes fall to the floor, I gave up that thought. I didn't even touch that half empty glass of Kool-Aid. I got my baby up out of there.

32

*W*HEN I REACHED HOME AND STUCK MY KEY IN the lock, I was in tears. I leaned forward against the door. I could hear music from inside. My talk with Jeff didn't turn out the way I expected. My intentions were good, but I didn't know if I made matters better or worse. Smearing a tear away, I took a deep breath, and thought to myself. *At least I typed Spider's résumé.* I wiped my eyes again, sniffled, and straightened up. *I can fix this,* I reminded myself. On that note, I took a deep breath and turned the key.

It was after seven. I pushed the stroller to the side of the crib. Early evening light streamed through the bedroom window. The shades were up. Music was blaring and Spider was dancing around in his Fruit of the Looms to a Cameo song, of all things. Grace, he had none. Spider looked more like one of the Lakers shadow boxing, but he was jamming to his little suitcase record player. I thought the thing needed a new needle, but it was now playing fine with two pennies taped to the arm. Spider shadowboxed some more and spun around. Then, he really started to perform like he was wearing a red vinyl groin cup. Right there, in front of the window with a Right Guard aerosol can microphone, Spider sang, "*....back and forth.*"

I sat the diaper bag down and let loose a sigh. It felt good to see Spider in a better mood. His joy was contagious. I smiled, wrapped my arms around his waist and sang with him, "*Back and forth....*"

Spider stopped dancing and turned around. I kissed his shoulder, inhaling his cologne. His body was still nice and tan from his Saturday basketball game out in the sun. He looked so good; I wanted to just nibble him. "How long have you been home?" I asked. Spider shrugged. I released my hold and spun. *Cameo.* I loved this group. I especially loved this song. We had a routine to it in aerobics class back at

201

Howard. I sidestepped back to Tee-Bo's stroller. "You're in a good mood, huh?" I said smiling.

I was surprised to see Spider only return a halfhearted nod. The enthusiasm seemed to drain from his face, but he said, "Sorta."

I unzipped the side of Tee-Bo's diaper bag, pulled out the manila folder, and handed it to him. "If you're not in a good mood now, this should put you in a better one."

Spider turned the music off and looked at the papers. Confusion registered on his face. "What's this?"

"Your résumé."

"You never hooked up the computer, so where did you do this?"

"At work," I said cheerfully. I sat on the bed and continued to explain, "I snuck down the hall to Dan's office when he went to his board meeting. I typed it on his computer."

Spider raised an eyebrow. "Didn't you say your boss locks his door?"

I took Tee-Bo out of the stroller and placed him in the crib. I quickly checked the front of his diaper with two fingers. He was dry. "Everybody knows he hides his key in the rubber plant."

"You shouldna done that."

It was Tuesday. The clock read just after 7:30, too late to do laundry. I looked at Spider. "Nobody saw me," I said.

"Still shouldna have done that." His pager vibrated. He dropped the folder onto the bed.

"Why not?" I said.

"You risked losing your job, and I don't even need it." Spider's pager vibrated again.

I raised my voice. "What do you mean you don't need it?"

The pager vibrated right off the edge of the dresser. He picked it up off the floor and looked at the number. "I already got the job. I'll have to talk to you about that later." He reached into his drawer. Out came a pair of shorts.

"Director of A & R?"

"No. Associate Director. I'm also part of the distribution team and I'm the executive producer of our latest project. But I'll have to talk to you about that later." The khaki shorts were full of wrinkles. He shook them out and stepped into them.

"How about now?"

He pulled out his Knicks jersey. "I gotta cut out."

"You're leaving? Where are you going?"

"To the Factory," he said, slipping his jersey over his head.

"What factory? Why?"

"To see Suga." He knelt and looked under the bed.

"Sugar? For what?" I walked over to him.

"For Black Licorice....You seen my Hush Puppies, Mia?"

I was not going to answer that. Spider had those shoes since high school. He loved them. I hated them. Those old loafers were dusty and noisy. The right one had a hole in it and the left one had a split sole that squirted air every couple of steps. I knew exactly where his Hush Puppies were. I hid them in the newest shoebox and stuck them way in the back of the closet beneath a stack of other boxes. Ignoring his question, I said, "Black licorice, Spider?"

"Yeah, we're laying the 'Candy' tracks. My Hush Puppies, please."

"Candy tracks?"

"For the Web."

"Spider! I don't understand anything you said."

"My Hush Puppies! Where are my Hush Puppies?"

"That is not what I was talking about," I grumbled. He brushed by me, bent into the closet, and tossed his knapsack to the side. Next, he pulled out his wooden box of junk. Then, he went through shoebox after shoebox until he reached the one at the very bottom, snatched off the lid, and said, "Aye!" He clapped his Hush Puppies together.

"Sugar from the factory to make black licorice candy? What kind of freaky shit is going on at that label?" I asked. Spider plopped on the bed and slid his long feet into his tired loafers. "Now that you have your shoes, will you please tell me why these Twizzlers are so important?"

He paused, shook his head, and tied his dusty shoes. "I'll explain later. I connected the computer, Mia. Can you please type my marketing proposal for me?"

"We don't have a printer or any discs. That's why I didn't bother to connect it."

"I'll bring a disc home. Just save it to the hard drive for now."

Now, I gave a half-hearted nod. "Fine. Where is it?"

He grabbed his leather portfolio out of the closet and unzipped it, flipped through it, and pulled out about five pages. He then chucked the leather case back. It landed on his wooden box of junk. Spider stepped toward me, extending the papers. He stopped short and gave me a cross look. Over to the nightstand he went, slapped the papers down, and slammed the clock on top of them. "Remember to make time," he said.

Ouch.

He grabbed his knapsack. "Gotta go." Just like that, he breezed out of the room in his wrinkled khaki shorts, jersey, and those damn Hush Puppies. *Step. Squish. Step. Squish.*

He didn't scream or shout. It just seemed like he shouted, because his voice was so deep. He really didn't, but his tone was full of disgust. He was mad at the world, and I was the only one in the apartment with him who was not a baby or a cat. I wanted to fix things, but I could see I had my work cut out for me.

I wanted Spider to get the job, but the *plan* was I would come home and hand him his résumé. He would light up. I wasn't expecting him to thank me, but I was expecting him to show a little excitement. *Tomorrow*, he was supposed to get hired, call me, and ecstatically tell me the news. Then, we were supposed to celebrate with some wild sex and wine coolers. Well, maybe not the wine. But still and all, Jeff was supposed to call Spider and talk things through. And after all the smoke cleared, that's when I wanted to explain to Spider what happened at his mother's and what happened to his father.

Spider got the job but I had nothing to do with it. I wanted to be the one who saved the day. Not only did he get that job on his own, he was nowhere near as excited as I would have expected. And he was obviously still pissed at me. I threw my arms up and collapsed onto the bed, screaming, "Can this day possibly get any worse!" Tee-Bo jumped and started crying. That was all I needed. I was losing it. I realized then that I needed to talk to somebody.

I rocked, cuddled, and nursed a smile back on Tee-Bo's face. As for me, I had issues. Tension was throbbing all up in my temples. Every sound seemed to echo in my head. The lights made my eyes feel like they were about to explode. I stripped out of my restrictive work clothes and yanked my nightgown over my head. The neck caught on to my bun, which was a little too tight, sending a screaming pain to the back of my skull. So out came the hairpins one by one. Scratching through my kinky roots felt so good, but it did nothing to stop the pain. This was a hunger headache. It was dinnertime, so I cooked. With no appetite, I ate a bite or two, just enough so that I could pop a couple of Motrin.

The headache went away. Still feeling down, I soaked in a hot bath. Then I slipped back into my favorite gown. I thought that would lift my spirits, but afterward, I ended up stretched in bed, staring up at the light fixture in the middle of the ceiling until a tear crept out the corner of my eye. I wiped it away. More tears followed.

Now, more than anything, I needed to vent. For that, I only called one person: Romell. But I was usually very careful with what I told him about Spider. And I couldn't share much with Dawn. I loved her, but my sister could spread news faster than the free press. Right now, I needed to talk, but I still couldn't decide if I should tell Romell what was going on or not. I knew he and Spider hated each other, but if I didn't share what was going on with somebody soon, I'd go up a wall. I picked up to dial Romell, but there was no dial tone, so I said, "Hello."

And Romell said, "Hi."

I said, "You're gonna live a long time. I just started to call you."

He said, "Can you talk?"

That puzzled me. "Why do you ask?"

"You know why."

I had totally forgotten, but now it was coming back to me. "Oh," I said. The last time I called, I hung up on him when Spider walked into the room. "I can talk," I said.

"Where's Spider Snyder?"

I sucked my teeth. "Spider left. He's working for Twizzlers now; who knows *when* he'll be back. Why?"

"What are you doing now?"

"Right, now?"

"Yeah."

"Well, I missed the laundromat. So, I'm in my nightgown just lying here."

"Get dressed."

"Dressed? Why?"

"I want you to come to my house."

"Come to your house? Why?"

"I'll explain when you get here." He sounded nervous for some reason.

This was Tuesday night. I had to get up early in the morning to go to work. Romell was either out of his mind, or I was misunderstanding him. "When? Now?" I asked.

"No, next week. Hurry up and get here!"

I thought about it. Knowing Spider, he wouldn't get in until late, and I wasn't in the mood to stay home, so I said, "Fine, I'll get dressed. I'll be there in a couple of hours."

"Why so long?"

"Subway."

"Take a cab!"

"All the way downtown? Hell, no! You're lucky I'm coming at all! This is last minute! And I already told you about that shit! How the hell do you expect me to get out of my bed, fix my hair, get dressed, dress my baby, and come *all* the way downtown at the drop of a dime when—"

"All right. All right. All right! Take your time. Just get here."

I hung up the phone and thought for a moment. *Why was it so urgent for me to rush to his house tonight?* I called him right back. He had Call Waiting, but his line was busy. I called again. Still busy. *That was strange. He called me? That was even stranger.* I just knew something had to be wrong. I had been living in the same apartment for almost three years, and Romell never called me. Not once. My heart sank as the thought of all thoughts hit me: *something had to be seriously wrong if Romell called me at home.* I jumped out of bed and reached for my shorts. *Please, let him be all right.*

33

MY OLD, WHITE NIGHTGOWN WITH THE BIG purple number seven iron-on smelled like food and had permanent stains, but that didn't matter. I pushed it down into my shorts and didn't bother to put a bra on. I used to do that all the time. Growing up, I'd stuff my gown into my jeans and go. Dawn would scream at me. "Put some clothes on! You never know who you're gonna run into!" I could almost hear her voice now, but I was just making a quick run to Romell's to find out what was wrong. In two minutes, I had my bun in place, and I was out the door with Tee-Bo strapped on and the diaper bag full of diapers and bottles over my shoulder.

I passed the pet carrier and heard the most pitiful noise from Joy. There for two days, I had forgotten all about her. She sounded like she was dying. I knew for sure I didn't feed her. I lifted the cage and took a peek. Jackie's fat black tabby was as rank as smelling salts. Thanks to Spider, there were three opened cans of generic cat food. Light from the window glowed in her eyes like red flames. She wasn't dying, but I could tell she was not a happy kitty. I shook my head and sat the pet carrier down. Then I filled a small bowl with water, quickly unlocked the cage door, and pushed it inside. Joy pounced on that water like she had found a bottle of Evian in the Sahara. I didn't want Joy to scratch my hand, so I snapped that door shut and locked it. After I put the pet carrier back down, I shook my head and walked out of the apartment. *Caged up, eating generic cat food from tin cans, dehydrated, and no litter box: a far cry from fancy Albacore and her wicker, kitty couch. If Jackie could see her baby now, she'd kill me.*

As soon as I made it to the corner of 167th Street, I saw a cab. I was at Romell's in twenty-eight minutes flat. Outside his door I reached for the bell, but then Romell's voice rang in my ears, "Why do you always ring the bell when you have keys?" My set was in the side pocket of the diaper bag. I pulled them out, unlocked the door, stepped inside, and locked it. When I turned around, Jun Ko and I almost bumped into each other. She was just coming out of the kitchen wearing nothing but a red lace thong. In one hand she had a bottle of Dom Perignon. In the other, a can of whipped cream. I remember her being heavier. She lost weight; her stomach was flat. Her severe acne used to look like strawberry oatmeal. She'd plaster it with heavy foundation. Her skin had cleared. It looked smooth. I don't even think she was wearing makeup at all. And, her hair was now dark, all one color, and in a long, layered cut with bangs. I could feel tears sting my eyes, but as awkward and painful as this was, I forced a smile. "Did I come at a bad time?"

Jun Ko blushed, "No, not at all. Just let me run and put something on."

No sooner had she said that when Romell came running from out back screaming, "Hey, what's taking you so long? Let's do this!" He was halfway into the living room when we locked eyes. He looked as if he was about to turn and run, but like a deer caught in headlights, he froze. It was too late. I had already seen him. So, he just stood right there in his see-through, black, bikini drawers. It was a good minute before he thought to snatch the newspaper off his cocktail table and cover himself with it. "What are you doing here, Mia?" *He called me Mia.*

"You told me to come by."

"Well then, why didn't you ring the bell?"

"You always tell me to use my keys. Why did you tell me to come here, Romell?"

"I wanted you to give your keys to Jun Ko!"

I felt a ripping sensation, like a spear had gouged my heart. "Oh," I said. I wanted to throw those shits across the room but instead, held the keys out. "Here you go, Jun Ko."

Jun Ko stuck the can of whipped cream under her arm and stepped toward me. Her perfume was like a vanilla-scented candle, although I did sense a hint of insect repellent. She reached for the keys and her pink, lip-glossed lips smiled at Tee-Bo in his harness. "Hey, handsome! Your baby, his skin healed nicely, huh?"

Hearing that, Romell came running over to look at Tee-

Bo. "Oh wow! Yeah, it sure did. You never told me, Mia."

Again, he called me Mia.

"I guess I didn't," I said.

What's so bad was I had been so distracted lately that I didn't even notice the change in Tee-Bo's skin.

"Well?" Romell said.

"Well, what?"

"Aren't you going to thank Jun Ko?"

Of all people, Jun Ko had to be the one who provided the method and the one who pointed out that my baby's rash had cleared. And the cherry on top of this banana split was she was standing next to me—butt, booty-naked—with Romell who behind the sports section was still in his see-through, black bikinis. I was happy Tee-Bo's rash had cleared, but at the same time, I just wanted to die. My insides screamed. *Somebody just kill me!* I couldn't even fake the funk; I muttered a solemn, "Thanks."

Jun Ko's pink lip glossed lips smiled again. "No problem," she said, brushing her long bangs back behind her ears. Her large ruby studs sparkled. The same studs I found in Romell's cabinet two days before. *Those were Jun Ko's earrings I found in the kitchen.* I knew some woman was trying to mark her territory; I just didn't know who. Jun Ko turned to Romell. "I'll wait for you in the bedroom," she said.

Ouch.

Romell winked at her and in his smoothest voice said, "Okay, baby. I'll be there in a few." *Baby? Ouch!* Then, just as Jun Ko started off, Romell moistened his bottom lip and smacked her tiny hiney. And he didn't just smack her butt; he licked his lip and smacked it.

OUCH!!

She turned, smiled again, and then ran toward the back. Halfway through the living room, she dropped the whipped cream, turned, and picked it up. Her breasts barely jiggled. Those perky, little, titties had Romell's rapt attention.

I looked down at my own breasts, full of milk, sagging like water balloons. I was braless, in my dingy nightgown, and because *this* was the gown I always cooked in, I smelled like grease and garlic. "I gotta go," I grunted.

"Wait up!" Romell said as I unlocked the door. I turned and looked at him. "Drop by tomorrow, okay," he said.

I couldn't even respond to that. I yanked his door open

and marched down the hall. At the elevator, I banged on the up button then the down.

"Chocolate, what's wrong?"

"Oh! Now, I'm Chocolate. Now, I'm Chocolate!"

"Chocolate, wait!" He yelled, but I was not trying to hear him. When the elevator door opened, I stepped into it and pushed for the lobby.

34

*T*HE ELEVATOR'S COMPUTER SAID, "THIRTY-seventh floor. Going up." I quickly pressed again to change its course, but it was no use; it went all the way up to the roof. The door opened. In front of me was a set of glass doors. I stepped off and walked through them. Coming from the air-conditioned interior, the heat outside was stifling, yet it felt good against my skin. The top level of a fitness center was on one side and a huge Jacuzzi was on the other. Both were enclosed in glass. The paved walkway led me through the two structures. It forked at a large, unlit, stone fire pit and stretched in both directions with potted trees on both ends. Beige lounge furniture was topped with bright yellow, orange, and teal pillows. Walking halfway around, I stopped and glanced across the chest-high concrete wall. Across the East River, the reds, purples, and blues of dusk tinted the skyline and made the box-topped buildings of Roosevelt Island look like stacks of chips. The view was so breathtaking, I gasped. Then, I made tracks back to the elevators, past the lounge furniture, fire pit, Jacuzzi, and the fitness center. Any other time, this would have all seemed so serene, but feeling the way I did, the last place I needed to be was on anybody's roof.

I stepped into the next elevator and pressed for the lobby. It stopped on the thirty-seventh floor. Romell walked inside and the door closed. I didn't even turn in his direction. "Where are you coming from?" he said.

"The roof."

"Oh, I forgot. They offer all the amenities here. I've been meaning to take you on a tour. The sky lounge is hot, right?"

Sky lounge. I bet he didn't forget to take Jun Ko up to the sky lounge. "It's all right," I stared at the brass control panel. Two of the buttons were plastic, Alarm and Emergency Stop, which were black and red. The rest were clear. White light

211

already illuminated the one for the lobby. I pressed it again.

"Why did you rush off? I told you to wait."

My gaze went up the control panel to the small circle pattern of holes in the brass. Right above it was a large square pattern of holes. Two different sets of holes one right over the other, I had no clue what they were for. My elevator in the Bronx was nothing like this. It was a rickety box with no automatic door. We had to pull the outside door open and pull the inside gate closed, but right now, I swore mine moved faster than this one. "I need to go home. I have to type Spider's proposal."

"Interns have to do proposals these days?"

"No, Spider got a promotion," I said dryly and looked up at the digital floor indicator. *Twenty-nine. Twenty-eight. Twenty-seven. I wish this elevator would hurry to the lobby.*

"A promotion. Wow," Romell sulked. "Spider Snyder got a promotion and *I* can't get one. I wish these guys at Livings & Moore would just—"

"Dammit, Romell! Quit whining about your situation! Accept it or change it!" I banged the lobby button as if that would make the elevator go faster.

"What the hell is wrong with you?"

You know what's wrong. That's what I was thinking. I clenched my teeth. Seething, I said, "Nothing." *Nineteen. Eighteen. Seventeen.*

"Nothing? Chocolate, look at me."

"No. This elevator is so damn slow!" *Fourteen. Thirteen.*

"What's got you all bent out of shape? Talk to me." *Twelve. Eleven.* Romell pressed the Stop button. I expected the alarm to sound, but none rang, so I backed into the brass handrail and leaned into the raised oak paneling. He stepped directly in front of me and stooped so that our eyes were at the same level. "Are you going to tell me what's wrong?"

"No." I could feel my heart beating in my chest. I didn't know if it was my anger or that he was invading my personal space.

"We're gonna stay right here until you do."

I tried to turn my head but he gently guided my face back to his. Even though my nose was in his direction, I still refused to make eye contact, but I couldn't ignore his scent. He must've gotten dressed so fast he worked up a sweat. I inhaled, and my heart pumped harder. Whenever he perspired, he'd emit this musk that was so sweet, it was like a beckoning finger. To the walls, to the floor, no matter where I put my eyes, they kept finding their way back to him. They drifted up the tight, plain white t-shirt clinging to his chest, across the muscles of his arms and expanse of shoulders that hunched slightly forward even though he never slouched, up his smooth, brown face, and ultimately, to his slanted eyes. With his eyebrows raised, he peered so intently I closed mine. I could feel my heart pounding even harder still. Then louder and louder. I could almost hear it.

BEEP, BEEP, BEEP! The noise caused me to jump. I found the source, the control panel. Out the strange patterned holes came the distinctive British male accent I recognized immediately. "Any trouble?" An intercom. No buttons or anything. The strange holes were the microphone and speaker built into the damn wall. My elevator didn't even have an automatic door.

"No," Romell answered. "It's Mr. Goodwin from 3702, George. Everything is fine."

"Hi, George. It's Mia. If you don't mind, could you hail me a cab?"

"Consider it done," George responded. Then he added, "Can I be of service to you, Mr. Goodwin?"

"No, thanks. I just need a minute here to straighten something out," Romell said.

"Very well, sir. Understanding you are a bit excited, please, bear in mind; surveillance is wired for *sound*."

"Thanks, George." He turned to face me and gave me a dimple-flashing smile. "Are you gonna tell me what's wrong or is security gonna have to come and pry us out of this elevator?"

I almost smiled. "What? You're gonna hold a lady and a baby hostage?"

He laughed softly. "Hey, he's fine. Everything he needs is right here in this elevator." Romell's face seemed relaxed, but I looked into his eyes; they were concerned. He licked his chops and stepped closer. Now, only Tee-Bo separated us. Romell leaned in; his lips grazed my cheek and then, I felt his breath in my ear. "What's wrong, Chocolate?"

This sent a chill through me. My stomach knotted up. With my heart pounding, I opened my mouth. Some strange mousy sound came out. "You were using *the voice.*" I cleared my throat. "The voice."

He straightened up. "What voice?"

"The one you use sweet talking."

"I wasn't sweet talking." He turned around and released the stop button. We started moving again.

"Yes, you were!"

"No! I wasn't."

I was not imagining things. I remember when my voice had more bass than Romell's. I knew his voice like I knew my own. When at work or doing anything academic, Romell enunciated, carefully clipping words like a news anchorman. When he was upset, he'd lose the eloquent geek speak and would damn near mangle the English language. When he spoke to his "mom," his voice sounded boyish and whiny. When he was around another man, it went an octave deeper. When that other man was Spider, it went down two octaves. His voice only turned smooth and velvety for one reason: He was sweet-talking. And, he had the unmitigated gall to stand in my face and deny it. I cut my eye at him. "Romell, you were purring like a lion being stroked!"

"Shhh!" He pointed to Tee-Bo and continued in a whisper. "Okay, so I was using 'the voice.' What's wrong with that?"

I put my hand on my hips and stared at the wall. Then, I narrowed my eyes at him, squeezing tears. "I thought you weren't sleeping with Jun Ko."

"I am now. What's the problem?"

"Why Jun Ko?"

"Why does it matter?"

"I just wanna know. I'm curious," I said just as the elevator reached the ground floor.

The door slid open and Romell stepped out into the lobby. "Curiosity killed the cat," he said.

Right behind him, my footsteps tapped against the checkered marble tiles. My response, "Satisfaction brought it back. Why Jun Ko?"

Romell stopped and immediately faced me. "Shhhh! Bad enough we gave security an earful. Now, we're in public and you're making a scene. Don't embarrass me."

We're in public? There were all of about six people around. He made it seem like we were standing in a stadium. I glared at him and whispered. "Why Jun Ko?"

He sighed. "She's brilliant, sweet, and a lot of fun."

I stuck my finger down my throat and gagged.

Romell continued, "Besides that, she's the only person I know who can beat me at a game of chess."

"Chess? Seriously?" My mind flashed back to the sight of Romell in his see-through, black, bikini drawers. And here, I was the one who taught her how to beat him. Now, I know when I gave Jun Ko chess tips, I wanted her to see a different side of Romell, but not that side. I poked him in his chest. "She's no dime." Then, I brushed by him and walked over to the concierge at the front desk. Sweetly I said, "How are you, George?"

He was struggling with a sealed bottle of Motrin. He sat the pills on the counter next to his burgundy cap, started massaging his hand, and said, "A bit barmy, I'm afraid. This heat and humidity is *bloody murder* on my arthritis. Your cabbie is waiting outside. I would bite my arm off to be back in Liverpool right now."

I grabbed the Motrin. After a quick press-and-twist, I removed the safety cap, handed the bottle to George, and said, "Feel better." Then, I turned to Romell, rolling my eyes.

Romell was so confused his whole forehead creased. "What?"

"You heard me. She's no dime!" I passed Romell and spotted the new doorman way over by the seating area chatting with one of the residents. He didn't look up, until I was halfway to the entrance. Out the corner of my eye, I saw the blur of his burgundy uniform and white gloves rushing over, but I didn't bother to wait; I pushed the door open myself leaving my fingerprints on the polished glass.

Romell was right on my heels as I opened the door and sat in the cab.

"Jun Ko carries herself with dignity," he said. "That makes her a dime."

That statement made my blood boil. I sucked my teeth. "By what standard?"

"My standard! She's a dime! I never settle for less. You got a problem with that!"

"You want a dime? You want a dime! Find...yourself...a sistah!"

He leaned in, his squinted eyes fuming. "Thanks, Mia." He straightened up, looked down his nose at me with his head cocked to the side, and snapped his head back: the

215

fuck-you nod. Romell gave *me* the fuck-you nod. Then he said, "I can always count on you to put your two cents in."

I slammed the car door. That startled Tee-Bo and he started bawling. Gently bouncing my baby, I cut my eyes at Romell. "No. Thank you...for makin' me feel like two cents waitin' for change."

I fought my own tears until the cab driver pulled off. Then, the dam broke. My vision was blurred as I looked back. Romell was still standing in front of his building watching me move farther away. But once the taxi turned the corner, that was it; I lost sight of him.

35

*T*WO CENTS WAITIN' FOR CHANGE. THAT WAS LIKE our little inside joke since we were kids. So Romell knew exactly what I was talking about. When I was about nine, I woke up one night and heard Mommy crying. She was on the telephone. I didn't know who she was talking to but I distinctly remembered what she had said. "So what, his Mark VII has a telephone in it! I fell in love with Curtis, not that damn car...This is my fourth divorce? Oh, well...I refuse to spend my time with any man who makes me feel like two cents waitin' for change!" I told Dawn what I overheard and asked her what "two cents waitin' for change" meant. Her response, "It means you need to mind your business."

That was not the answer I was looking for. So I decided to ask Romell the next morning in the cafeteria. "What's two cents waitin' for change?"

Romell pushed his copy of the *New York Times* to the side and slid his tray away. Next, he reached inside his pencil case and plucked a napkin from the stack on my tray. He then put his nose to that napkin and started calculating. He jotted an equation, crossed it out, and scribbled another, over and over again until he looked up. "The only way that problem will have one only one solution is if someone pays two cents...and then, gets change back. The answer is a penny, right?"

Lights from the overhead fixtures bounced off the ripe Granny Smith that sat on my breakfast tray. I shook my head, grabbed my apple, and reached for a napkin. "I don't think Mommy was talking about money." I gave my apple a good polish as I filled him in. When I finished, I placed my apple on a fresh napkin and leaned forward. "So, what do you think that means?"

Romell put his finger on my Granny Smith. "You want that?"

217

My jaw dropped. "I was saving it for last."

"You can have my orange," he offered.

"I waited 'til all the oranges were gone!" I had first pick when the lunch lady brought the apples out. I made sure I chose the best one. That Granny Smith was perfect. No blemishes whatsoever.

"Well, do you want my orange or don't you?"

I sucked my teeth. "No, thanks. They're bitter."

That said, Romell grabbed my apple and began to polish it with his crumpled napkin with the math problems on it. There was a faraway look in his eyes for what seemed like forever. Then, he snapped his fingers. "Oh! Now, I get it. 'Two cents waiting for change' could mean a penny, or it could mean worthless."

"Men make women feel worthless?"

"I guess some do."

"Why?" I asked.

He shrugged his shoulders, eyeing the little green apple he had just buffed.

Worthless. At nine years old, I couldn't even begin to wrap my brain around that concept, but that definitely sounded like a bad thing. So I had to ask, "Would you ever make me feel that way?"

"What way?"

"Like two cents waitin' for change."

"No way!" Romell said. He raised the Granny Smith to his mouth.

In agony, I watched him bite into it with a loud crunch.

"Wanna bet?" I said, waving my outstretched pinky in his face.

Chewing, he shrugged and held out his. Together we locked fingers. "Can't break a bet when it's made."

He looked at me. "You're my friend. I would never do anything to make you feel bad."

"You say that now, but we'll see who owes who a dollar," I said.

Anyway, that's how it started. So now Romell owed me the dollar. It was funny. At nine years old, I was actually looking forward to winning that bet.

♥ ♥ ♥ ♥

I was still crying when I reached Head to Toe. The

hanging sign was flipped to the "Closed" side. The neons were off, but the inside lights were still on, so I banged on the glass. Through it I saw Park, the new girl I met the last time I came. After sobbing from the gut all the way there, I had a headache, my eyes were burning, and my nose was sore. Tee-Bo was crying uncontrollably, too. Park dropped the broom and ran to unlock the door. When she pulled it open, I bolted in, crying. Seeing me this way, Park's already broken English was now almost indiscernibly Korean. "Are...you...okay?" I was shaking so badly, I couldn't answer.

Dawn was in the shampoo room. She popped her head out, dropped whatever was in her hands and rushed over. "You got mugged?"

I shook my head. I didn't know where to begin. I stopped and took a deep breath, just to start crying all over again.

"Give me Tee-Bo," Dawn unbuckled the harness and passed Tee-Bo to Park. My sister's bangles rattled as she wrapped her arms around me. I was trying to fight the tears, but once in her arms, I couldn't hold it in. I broke down into an all out blubber. Dawn held me tight and rubbed my back. The best thing in the whole wide world to me was a hug when I needed one. Soon, I was calm, hearing Dawn whisper, "You wanna sit in the back and talk?"

I lifted my head and nodded.

She parted the curtain of translucent beads that hung in the back doorway, and we walked into the shampoo room. Dawn stepped over to the first sink, repositioned the chair, dried the seat with a hand towel, and I sat. "Breathe," she said. She had bent down, collecting rollers of assorted sizes and colors off the floor, dropping them into a bin. "Now, go on; tell me what's wrong."

Still sniffling, I said, "Romell called me two cents. He said I'm nothing but two cents...and she's his dime!"

"Who?"

"Jun Ko!"

"Wow! You even calling her out her name."

"That *is* her name! Jun Ko! It means 'pure child' in Japanese." I rolled my eyes. "I still can't believe how pretty her skin looked. Pretty skin and all, she's still not a dime. On a scale of one to ten, I'd give her a six and a half...an eight...okay, maybe nine. Oh, why did her damn skin have to clear up?"

219

"Stop talking to yourself and speak to me. Hold up! Romell called you what? No, he didn't."

"Yes he did! He made me give Jun Ko my keys, and then he started slobbing her down and groping her right in front of me. And, she was only wearing a thong, Dawn."

"A thong? What was Romell wearing?"

My mind flashed back to the sight of Romell in his see-through, black, bikini drawers. I looked at Dawn. Her interest was piqued. Her eyes were wide as I don't know what. I shrugged. "I don't know; he had something on, but Jun Ko was only wearing a thong."

"I'm surprised at him. He should know better than to go parading his naked girlfriends around you. And you had Tee-Bo, too?"

I nodded.

Dawn slammed the bin full of rollers onto the caddy. "I'm gon' cuss his ass out!"

"No!"

"He just called you a two-bit hoe, and you expect me not to speak on it?"

"Don't call him, please!"

The sound of Tee-Bo's crying approached until the beads clattered in the doorway. Park stepped through, rocking him, singing what sounded like a lullaby. It seemed familiar but wasn't in English. Park paused. "He's hungry," she said. "Do you have a bottle?"

Dawn tried to answer for me. "He's a titty baby."

"I have bottles," I said. Disposable bottles were inside the diaper bag. Two had formula. Two had breast milk. I reached my shaking hands in and pulled one out at random. I managed to snap the plastic cap off, but my hands were shaking so badly when I tried to squeeze out the air that Dawn took the bottle from me and passed it to Park. "You have to squeeze all the air out of the bag so that he doesn't get gas," I said.

"Romell's got you like this? Oh, hell no! I'm cussing his ass out for sure!" Dawn walked over to the wall phone, picked it up, and started dialing.

"Dawn, no!" I screamed. "Romell is not the only reason why I'm upset!"

Dawn stopped and looked at me. "All right. I won't call him." She hung up and pointed her bony finger. "But *you're*

220

gonna tell me everything." My sister took two steps forward then turned and picked the receiver back up. When she started dialing, I jumped up out of my seat.

"You just said you wouldn't call Romell!"

"Relax yourself. I am *not* calling your boyfriend." Dawn grimaced. I then sat back and watched her eyes go blank. She put that long fingernail in her mouth, so I could tell something was going through her head; I just didn't know what. Dawn came alive again. "Hey, Aunt Carole...Oh, sorry to interrupt your sleep...I need you to come to the salon and pick up Tee-Bo...I know, but Mia needs a break for a few days...Nothing too serious. My guess is it's just a little postpartum depression...Okay, see you in a few."

Out front with his bottle, Park already had Tee-Bo quiet. I was going through a lot lately, but through it all, I couldn't allow myself to freak out; I had to remain calm for his sake. And besides, I'd always thought women with postpartum depression wanted to hurt their babies; I just felt like hurting myself. "I do not have postpartum depression," I said.

"Maybe, maybe not, but your ass looks skinny."

"I hope so. Even nursing, I still can't seem to lose these last five extra pounds."

"Have you looked in a mirror lately? You look like you're on a crack diet! You didn't look *this* thin the last time I saw you. Are you eating?"

"Sometimes. Lately, my stomach has been bothering me."

"Uh huh, just as I thought."

"I am not depressed."

"Did you make yourself throw up?"

"Why would you ask me something like that?"

"Oh come on, Mia! You and I both know you used to be bulimic!"

"I was never bulimic!"

"What did you eat today?"

"Dawn! I am not depressed or bulimic or anorexic, okay! So you can stop giving me the third degree like I'm some kind of crazy person. I'm fine!"

"Denial ain't just a river in Africa. No matter what you say, Mia, you *are* stressed. It's harder to deal with stress when you have a brand-new baby, you're nursing, and your hormones are all wacky. To top it all off, you're not eating, and you look like you're not sleeping either."

221

I sucked my teeth. "All that is irrelevant. I don't think taking a break from Tee-Bo is the best thing."

"You need a break whether you think so or not, because right now, you're a mess. You're in no condition to take care of him! You're not even taking care of yourself!" She pulled on some rubber gloves, reached into the cabinet, and pulled out the tub of relaxer. She dropped it on the caddy next to me.

"What are you gonna do with that?"

"Kill two birds with one stone. I'm gonna do something to this bird's nest of yours. And you are going to tell me all that's going on. Now, start talking."

She tied a vinyl cape around me, sectioned my hair, and proceeded to smear base on my scalp; I explained the situation with Spider and his family, starting with the check. Every couple of minutes, Dawn would interject something like, "You know you should've never opened that envelope, right?" I'd nod, and she'd say. "Okay, keep going." I'd explain some more. "You know after you saw that check, you should've put it away and minded your business, right?" I'd nod and keep going. Again she'd interrupt, "You know you should've just let Dr. Snyder know you already told Spider about the check, right?" Again, I nodded and tried to continue. But, of course, Dawn stopped me. "Why were you searching through the woman's trash? The minute you saw Spider, you should've—"

"Dawn! I don't need you to tell me; I already know what I should've done. I knew it then!"

"Then, why didn't you just do the right thing in the first place?"

"I opened the envelope because I was sure it was a check, and the curiosity was killing me. At the time, I knew it was wrong, but I did it anyway. And, I had to confront Spider about the check. Because I automatically assumed he was holding out on me, I got pissed."

"Why didn't you tell Spider what went on at his mother's?"

"Because...I lied to Dr. Snyder. And, that's the reason why she felt she could trust me in the first place. When she started spilling her guts, I felt so guilty about not keeping her first secret, I figured the least I could do is maintain her confidence now."

"That's all well and good, but telling Spider about that

yellow paper would have been the right thing to do."

"I know that! I know! I was afraid, Dawn!"

"Afraid of what?"

"That Dr. Snyder would be mad at me, or worse—Spider would never marry me. I've always known what I should've done, but I did what I wanted. I couldn't help myself."

"You need Jesus."

"That's not funny!"

"That's not a joke!"

"You need help, and admitting you need help is not a sign of weakness; it's a sign of strength. We all need help, Mia. You are not the only one with problems. I have problems, too." She began to comb the relaxer through, and my scalp started to tingle.

"Dawn, don't hand me that. You're gorgeous. You have your own business, and your man drives a Bentley, wears Rolex watches, and has real estate all over the world. That's a recipe for happiness if I ever saw one."

"You think I don't have problems? Mia, every man I've given my heart to has either tried to use me or tear me down. All I've ever wanted was for someone, anyone to look deeper. That's why I shaved my damn head!"

"What about Kyle? Kyle is...." I hissed when I felt the sting of the chemicals. "Hurry up, Dawn this perm is heating up." Dawn nodded, and I continued, "Kyle is wealthy enough. How is he using you?"

"When I met him, he saw the body and chased me three blocks, begging to take me out."

"So?"

"So, I let him take me out to dinner, and I did what I always do."

"No, you didn't."

"Yes, I did. I ordered the most expensive thing on the menu, and all while I'm cracking my lobster tails, I'm looking him dead in his eye and reminding him, 'You know you ain't gettin' any booty.' At dessert time, I ordered a crème brûlée, and, of course, when the bill came, I pulled out my gold card and paid for both our meals."

I shook my head. "I could see how that would drive men nuts. Why do you do that?"

"If a man is about bullshit, I wanna know. I want to see his true colors immediately, and I want to send the message that I am not trading coochie for lobster."

"Then, what happened with Kyle?"

"That doesn't work when a man has real money. With Kyle, I learned a man could have money and still be full of shit."

"I don't get it."

Dawn spun my chair around, so I could face her. "Mia, Kyle kept showing me a picture of this house in the Hamptons, but he never took me there."

The relaxer wasn't in for long, but my scalp was now starting to burn; I winced. "Don't tell me he lives there with his wife?"

"No, the house in the Hamptons, he runs a gentleman's club out of that."

"A strip club?"

"Not exactly, it's upscale. Members only. All the members have a key. They offer humidor rentals, fine dining, live entertainment usually a jazz band, an open bar, spa services, Shiatsu and deep tissue massage, and a full staff of women dressed in lingerie."

"A gentleman's club? Don't dress it up! Call it what it is...a whorehouse!"

"No, it's only live adult entertainment like the Playboy Club. It's against policy for the hostesses to sleep with any member," Dawn stopped combing the relaxer through, "but shit happens." She looked at me. "Anyway, Kyle really ran me down that day, because he was looking to bring a new girl in. After our first date, he became interested in me for personal reasons. I had no clue what he did for a while."

"How'd you find out?"

"I got propositioned a few too many times."

"Propositioned?"

"Mia, he's made a name for himself, and I like to go out. It was only a matter of time."

I couldn't believe what I was hearing. "How did you explain all this to Mommy?"

"I told her Kyle is running an exclusive resort in the Hamptons, his family's business. That's all she needs to know!"

"How's it his *family's* business?"

"He runs it with his brother-in-law."

"His sister's husband?" I asked.

"No, his wife's brother."

"He's married, too?"

"Yes," Dawn said.

"That's why you never introduced him to Mommy!" I didn't mean to scream that out, but I couldn't help it. Dawn looked at me, and I watched her cast her eyes down to the floor. Now, it made sense. Why Dawn kept Kyle a big secret for so long, his very expensive watch that was "a gift" and why he always happened to have some emergency business meeting out of town whenever the time came for him to be introduced to our mother—it all made sense. Had Mommy taken one look at Kyle's Rolex, she would've known what time it was. Kyle never looked me directly in the eye. I should've picked up on that, but all I could do now was shake my head. For a while, Dawn just stood there saying nothing. Soon, the tingling of my scalp became unbearable. I squeezed my hand around the armrest of the chair. "Dawn! This is burning; rinse this stuff out."

"In a minute; it's not ready yet."

"No. Now!"

"All right," Dawn said. She turned the water on and reclined the seat. In seconds, she was running the hose over my head.

My head was stinging badly. The lukewarm water felt hot, but there was relief, feeling the nozzle scrape across my scalp. "Why don't you leave him alone, Dawn?"

"Mia, Kyle's so generous. Anything I want, he buys it. And sexually, no one ever made me feel the way he makes me feel."

"Practice makes perfect."

"He's loving, gentle, and—"

"He's a pimp."

"He's a restaurateur and a real estate mogul, *and* he loves me!"

"Don't you think he loves his wife, too?"

Dawn shrugged her shoulders. "Everybody has somebody, and if she knew how to work it, he wouldn't be all up in *my* face."

"Dawn, Kyle's married!"

"Separated!"

"So are my hands, but guess what." I sat up and locked my fingers. "They come together! And he's running...a brothel...with his wife's brother! So what, it's in the Hamptons, and it's upscale. It could be the best little whorehouse in the Hamptons, but it's still a whorehouse." Warm water oozed down my face, neck, and back.

Dawn passed me a towel. "Kyle is better than BOB!"

"Who's Bob?"

"My B-O-B, battery operated boyfriend! You want one?"

I pursed my lips. "That's an excuse."

"Ain't nothin' like being held, Mia!"

"By a pimp?" I shook my head. "Dawn, you are way smarter than this. And you are way too cute to be careless."

A tear crept down her cheek. "You right. You right. I know. I just can't let go. Not yet, anyway."

"Not yet? It's been three years!"

"I know; but we've been through a lot together, and we have made progress. Every time Kyle makes me a promise, he buys me a platinum bangle, and he keeps his promises, Mia. He keeps his promises."

"What kind of promises could he possibly be keeping?"

"He promised me he would move out. He promised he wouldn't date any more girls at the club. He promised...."

I covered my ears. "I don't wanna hear anymore! La, la, la...." Then, looking up at all her bracelets, I reached and grabbed Dawn's right hand. Her wrist to her elbow was lined with thin, platinum bangles, all in the same filigree design. I remember when she had only one or two. Now, she wore stacks on both arms. "Damn, Dawn! How many of those things do you have now?"

"Thirty-nine."

"Thirty-nine? Are you serious? Don't ask that pimp to promise you he'll get a divorce!"

"Stop calling him that! And Kyle can't get a divorce. He has vested interests."

"How many kids?"

"None. His father-in-law bankrolled his business."

Now, I was burping back puke, but this was serious. "Dawn, is he worth it?"

Dawn was quiet for a while, but then she said, "One of these days I'll say enough is enough. Just not today."

I heard that. There was nothing more to say. I leaned back and Dawn conditioned my hair.

The beads clattered in the doorway. Our aunt strolled in holding Tee-Bo. "Now, I *know* you didn't call me outta *my* bed so someone could have a day of beauty."

"No, Aunt Carole." Dawn reached over and gave her a hug.

Aunt Carole stepped back and looked at me. "What's wrong with you?"

"Nothing," I said.

"Don't believe her, Aunt Carole. Mia is stressed," Dawn said.

"I can see that. She looks thin. Get it together, girl. I know you don't handle stress too well, but you've got to learn to cope. This is the easy part. I wish all mine stayed this little. You should've seen how attached Tee-Bo's was to that Asian girl behind the counter; he started to cry when I took him away. Who is she?"

"Park," Dawn said.

"She was singing him the 'Itsy Bitsy Spider' in her language. Where's she from?"

"Brooklyn," Dawn said and Aunt Carole looked at her. "I mean Korea."

"Korean? Your nail business must be booming! When did you hire her?"

"She's my new partner," Dawn said. "I met her at the Beauty Expo and we just clicked. She's been handling all the nail business for about six months now."

Aunt Carole and I looked at each other. Dawn had opened the salon with her best friend Imani. As far as we knew, they were still partners.

"What happened to Imani?" Aunt Carole said.

"Things didn't work out," Dawn said. Aunt Carole and I stared at her. She looked down, then added, "Our personalities clashed."

Now, I was totally confused. Imani was not only sweet as pie, no one could ask Imani what she thought without her asking Dawn's opinion and automatically agreeing with whatever Dawn said. Half the time, they even dressed alike.

"Clashed? She was your sidekick since sixth grade. I can't even count the number of times she spent the night at our house."

"I know but right now, we're not speaking," Dawn said in a hushed tone; I immediately knew why.

I sighed and took Tee-Bo from Aunt Carole. I held and kissed him for a while before handing him back to her. Then, I took my keys out of the diaper bag. When I unsnapped the pocket and retrieved Spider's cash, Aunt Carole's eyes grew big. I shook my head. "It's not mine; I'm just holding it for Spider." I knew Spider wasn't thinking about this money right now. He was probably still pissed about being smacked in the head with a c-note. I stuffed the wad deep inside the pocket of my shorts.

My aunt sighed and chuckled. "Oh, for a minute there, I thought you hit the lottery." She kissed Dawn and me.

"Aunt Carole, do you have enough formula and diapers?"

"He has more than enough at my house. We'll buy anything else he needs."

"What about money?"

"Don't worry about that."

"Are you sure you don't mind watching him overnight for a few days?"

"Me and the kids, we got this. Spike and Teaira change him. Alicia feeds him. Yolanda and Delilah prepare the bottles. Stop worrying."

"All right, then, I guess that's it. Or, is there something I'm forgetting? No, that's it." I shook my head, took a deep breath, and handed Aunt Carole the diaper bag. I followed her all the way to the front and out the door. Then, I waited outside until a cab finally came, and I sighed as it pulled off. *This is only for a few days until I pull myself together.* I knew this was only temporary, but I still couldn't help feeling like a bad mother, like I was letting Tee-Bo down. I was nursing; he needed me. And I needed him. The one thing that kept me from focusing too much on my own problems was taking care of Tee-Bo.

When I returned to the salon, Park immediately locked the door and pulled down the shade. Then, she handed me a hand towel. In her heavy accent, she said, "Don't worry, girlfriend. In a few days, you'll be fine."

I smiled and nodded. Park was nice, but I knew that eventually, she, too, would bail on my sister. Soon enough, Dawn—so ashamed of herself she'd be looking at the floor—would open her mouth and announce, "We're not speaking." When Dawn looked at me again, her eyes would be watery, and she'd say, "Mia, this is not my fault!" Her confidence somehow would vanish. Her hand would start to flip back and forth. Now, she'd be looking to rally support. She'd soften her voice, and in her mildest tone, she'd say, "Girl, let me tell you what happened." That's when she would

228

commence to explaining how it really wasn't her fault that she revealed something Park confided in her. She'd demonstrate everything with hand gestures as if I wouldn't understand unless she twisted her wrist, pointed, and traced imaginary diagrams in the air. As soon as I stepped through the beads, I turned to my sister. "Now, Dawn. About Imani."

Dawn raised her hand and flipped that wrist back. Softly, she said. "Girl, let me tell you what happened." I knew it. She was ready to go on and on, trying to get me to side with her.

I stopped her. "Dawn! I may not know the details, but I can pretty much guess."

Her eyes started to water. "Mia, this was not my fault!"

"It's never your fault, Dawn! What kills me is you are the warmest and most caring person I know. I love having you in my corner. But, gurrrrrl!!! You need to learn to keep a secret!"

She chuckled and wiped tears away. "You're right. I'm gonna work on that." She nodded as if that was something she was seriously considering. "I am. I really am." That declaration was long overdue; still, I felt a nervous tremor in my stomach.

"Good," I said. Dawn sounded sincere, but I had just told her all about Spider's family situation and Romell. Although I didn't want to, I couldn't help but think the worst. I sat back. I didn't know whether to cross my legs or uncross them. My hands went from the armrest, to my lap, and back to the armrest. When I caught myself biting my nails, I had to say something. "Dawn, please don't tell anybody anything I told you tonight."

Dawn stiffened. "Now, I'm offended!"

"I'm not saying this to hurt you; I'm saying this because I know you all too well."

"Well, since we're spreading the knowledge, there's something I need to say, too."

"Oh, brother! Don't start! Again?"

"You got that right! Somebody needs to get through to you. With all that's been going on with Spider and his family, you didn't come running to me with any of that. But this thing with Romell, that's what reduced you to tears. You need to be honest with yourself about your feelings for him."

"What feelings?"

"Don't get coy with me, hooker! You know exactly what I mean! You love Romell!"

"Of course I love him. He's my friend!" I said.

Dawn twisted her lips.

"Romell is a *good* friend. No, he's my *best* friend, but he *is* just my *friend.*"

"Then, why did you have such a fit after seeing him with his naked girlfriend!"

"Because! For just once, I wish he would find himself a beautiful *black* woman!"

"Yeah, you!"

"No, not me! Anybody!"

"Okay," Dawn said. "I know plenty of eligible, black women. I can call somebody and hook the brother up right now." And she started marching.

Dawn wasn't that far from the phone. For me, the distance seemed like a hundred yards, but I dashed across the room, beat her to the phone, and wrapped myself around it. "You do," I said out of breath. "And you will die...a slow and painful death."

36

$\mathcal{D}$AWN DOUBLED OVER AND BACKED INTO THE wall, slapping her thigh. Then, she wiped the tears from her eyes before walking back to the sink, a good laugh at my expense. Afterward, she and Park busied themselves making me over. Park did my nails. Dawn did everything else. She blew my hair dry then took a deep breath and said, "Don't panic; I'm just gonna clip your ends." Of course I panicked because I knew she had the tendency to get scissor happy. She put her eighty-dollar shears to my hair and about three inches fell to the vinyl cape. I jumped up out of that hydraulic chair, screaming like it was hot. "I'm sorry but you have a lot of damage," she said.

I responded, "Why should I believe a bald beautician?"

We argued back and forth, but eventually, I sat back down. She clipped and my tears flowed. "Relax. I know what I'm doing," she said, but that didn't stop me from crying. So, my sister screamed, "Suck it up! If you don't want me to trim so much, get your touch-ups on time."

I was trying to grow mine to my behind. When I pinched and stretched, it almost reached my waist. Dawn knew I almost always wore a bun, because the less I fussed with it, the longer it grew. But as much as she loved to receive sympathy, when it came to hair, Dawn wasn't the least bit sympathetic toward others.

My sister started braiding when she was twelve years old. I remember seeing her early customers squirming and hissing as they sat in that hard wooden chair Dawn would place in the middle of our living room floor. She'd pinch each strand so tight, the scalp would pleat like my uniform's jumper. I'd give Dawn the eye to let her know she was being a little too heavy-handed. "I gots to braid it tight, so it'll last longer," she'd usually say. Still, Dawn always had more customers than she had time. And, she didn't loosen her grip

231

either, not until years later when she learned in a classroom setting that excessive strain around the edges could damage the follicles and cause the hairline to recede.

Dawn braided her way through college and beauty school. For years, she continued to do hair from home even though she was a licensed cosmetologist with a business degree. It wasn't until she finally saved some money that she took her knowledge and experience to the next level: her own shop. But with all she knew about hair care—styling for any length or texture, all the different weaving techniques, and methods of chemical processing—Dawn never understood the obvious. To some of us, the accumulation of hair on the head was more important than money in the bank.

Nope. When it came to hair, Dawn was never sympathetic. Now, seeing inches of my hair fall to the floor, I was in tears. Her way of combating this was to spin me around so that my back was to the mirror. I kept trying to steal glimpses.

"Mia, stay still in this chair, or I might make a mistake and cut too much."

That was all she had to say. For the first time ever, I sat perfectly straight without putting up a fuss. Eventually, I didn't even want to look in the mirror. I relaxed and let her get as creative as she wanted because when it came down to it, she always had a great sense of style.

My hair was spiral curled. Park did my fingers and toes. While I was still under the dryer, she cleaned and trimmed, filed and buffed, soaked and moisturized, and then she applied all the coats of polish. Once I was out from under the hot hat, Dawn sat me in front of the large makeup mirror and reclined the chair. Now I closed my eyes, sucked in my cheeks, and puckered my lips. Dawn plucked, dabbed, brushed, and patted. I was a little concerned, because all this seemed a little extreme for me. I preferred to keep my look basic: with a plain face and my hair twisted into my trusty bun, I always dressed in neutral colors. Still, Dawn went into her storage room and pulled out a top and two pairs of shoes. One pair was pointy-toe, cognac-colored, crocodile pumps and the other, black, wedge-heeled sandals. She flipped the cuffs on my shorts and even made me take off my nightgown, which was fine with me. It was drenched. She switched my gown for one of the tank tops she gave away at her grand opening. Then, she stood back, folded her arms, and a satisfied smile crept across her face.

There, with my back to the mirror, I felt nervousness build in the pit of my stomach, but I inched around toward the glass critic hoping this time, it wouldn't be so cruel. When I confronted it, I almost didn't recognize the person staring back. Thick, lush curls framed my face and spilled past my shoulders in long ringlets. The one time I applied makeup myself, I attempted to minimize my eyes with eyeliner. By tweezing my eyebrows into an arch shape, adding dark brown mascara, then bronze and gold shadow, Dawn exaggerated them. Now, they seemed to pop rather than bulge. Just by adding the right colors to the right places, she gave my whole face dimension. The bridge of my nose seemed sharper. My lips smoldered. I was top heavy, now that I was nursing, so the tank top definitely worked. It drew the eye upward off the stomach that wasn't as firm as it used to be. The high-heeled sandals and rolling the cuffs on my shorts exposed the curves of my legs. Subtle changes made a dramatic difference. I made Dawn show me step by step everything she did, and then she dumped samples of her makeup into a plastic bag with my nightgown, the crocodile pumps, and the flip-flops I had worn earlier.

On my way out, Dawn plucked a few strands and sprayed a few shots of spritz. She always had to make sure there was not a hair out of place. I hated that.

"Oops, I almost forgot," she said, running to the counter. She returned with a can of oil sheen and blasted me with a suffocating haze. When I walked out, she shouted, "Call me when you get home and let me know what Spider says!"

I stuck my head back in, "I plan to be busy tonight. I might even sweat out this hair. Call you tomorrow!"

I left Head to Toe late that night with a bright smile. It was way after hours, when the salon lights finally went off. The door was locked, and the gates came down. Dawn and Park closed up shop. For them, this was just another day, but I hoped, for me, this would be the start of something, anything.

37

*O*N THE WAY HOME, I PEEKED INTO EVERYTHING
that reflected until I finally walked through the
door. It was late. Very, very late. To my surprise, Spider was
wide awake with the bass of his suitcase record player
booming the way it had been earlier. At two o' clock in the
morning, our neighbors must've been too through with us,
but I was not about to make a stink about the noise. Not
when I was walking in at this hour. Instead, I stood a little
taller and walked a little prettier, hoping that Spider would
be so blown away by my new look that our problems
wouldn't matter for the moment. In the bedroom, he was in
his own groove singing "Choosey Lover."

I stood outside the door for a moment, listening. Spider
seemed to be enjoying himself. Deep down, I knew that would
stop the instant I walked through the door. Dawn called
Spider my eye candy. Lately, my eye candy was a crab apple,
but I was not looking to trade him in. She had her sugar
daddy. She opened her salon because while she was
spending his money, she was saving her own. Did that mean
Kyle was a better catch than Spider? Hell, no. Kyle was a
married pimp who was squandering his wife's family's
fortune on Dawn. She just couldn't see that. She couldn't see
her way clear in her own situation, so who was she to tell me
about mine? My sister needed to stop trying to convince me I
was in love with Romell, and start taking her own advice.

Romell was my best friend in the whole wide world. We
understood each other. Dawn mistook that as an attraction,
but friendship was all we had ever shared. I'll admit there
were times I found him sexy. Aw, hell! I always found him
sexy. He was a sexy person. That was his nature. He'd
moisten his lips, and my juices would start flowing. A wink
from Romell would send chills through me. And don't let him
take off his shirt. Whenever he'd just so happened to peel it

off, there was no such thing as taking a quick glance. He was dark and so ripped. The way his skin caught the light did something to me. No matter how hard I tried, I couldn't help but just soak him in like a sponge. His smell, his voice, his slanted eyes, his deep dimples, his bowlegs, his baldhead—I could go on and on. He was just a sexy person, but that didn't mean I was in love with him. We were friends. I was with Spider. *I have Spider.* I reminded myself. *I have Spider.*

I twisted the doorknob. My hips switched to the music in a seductive stride over to Spider. He was in bed, stretched out on his back. I stopped at his feet, thinking. *Now, strike a pose. Make it a sexy one. Make him want it. Make him squirm.* With my hands on my thighs, I squatted provocatively, so I thought, and leaned forward. There, ready for Spider's first words, I froze. Seconds passed. With a fling of my hair, I smiled. He stared at me with a blank expression. I didn't know how to interpret that, so I held my position. But now, my thighs were getting wobbly. I licked my lips and pursed them.

Spider finally opened his mouth. "Where's Tee-Bo?"

"I need a break. He's at Aunt Carole's for a few days."

"Is that where you were?"

"No, I just left Dawn's salon. See my shirt?" I stood and stretched the wrinkles out of my white tank top so Spider could read the rainbow print on the front; I'M A BEAUTY. Then, I turned so he could see the back, HEAD TO TOE. I spun back around. "So? What do you think?"

"You need a bra," he said and turned to switch the record player off. Lying on his side, he placed his hands under his head and stared at the fan.

"Spider?" I said. When he looked at me, I asked, "Aren't you gonna say something about the way I look?"

"You look fine," he said.

No emotion. No passion. I couldn't believe his indifference. Peas or Corn? Corn is fine. Should I wear the red or the blue? Either is fine. How do I look? You look fine. Those three words were monotone, flat, and plain. There was no inflection in his voice, emphasizing the word 'you,' the word 'look,' or the word 'fine,' so the statement was pointless. I would've preferred him to say nothing at all.

When I talked about Spider I'd always say, "Spider's so *fine.* He's *fine,* fine, *fine,* fine, *fine,*" not "Spider's fine." He was supposed to scream it, hiss it, moan it. *Oh, baby! You look so damn fine!* I might as well have been an old shoe, because hey, I looked fine. But then again, I didn't even get that much of a reaction. Spider saw his Hush Puppies and said, "Aye!" When the word "fine" is sung so that it lingers in your ear like a Ronald Isley riff, it means "sexy". When it's spat out like a cherry pit, it means "Okay, now leave me the fuck alone."

"Fine, Spider? Fine. Where's your enthusiasm?"

"I *said* you look fine!" He snapped.

I stormed into the bathroom, saw the scale underneath the sink, and pulled it out and stepped on it. One hundred and twenty seven pounds. Dawn and Aunt Carole were right. I had lost eight pounds in four days. How was that possible? I didn't look any thinner, or feel any lighter. I pushed the scale back and looked in the mirror. For some reason, now my face did seem a little gaunt. At least I didn't have to worry about losing those last five pounds. Sad thing was, even with the weight loss, Spider still didn't tell me I looked good. I remembered Spider calling me pretty Mia back in high school. What in the world did I have to do to get Spider to say I was pretty again?

I sighed and applied my cleanser, covering my nose, cheeks, and forehead with foam. I remembered step by step everything Dawn did. All I wanted was for Spider to say I looked good. I scrubbed my face, deciding hair and makeup would be part of my daily ritual until he did.

Skinny or not, I took heavy steps back to the bedroom, wrapping my shorts and tank top around Spider's money. At this point, I didn't know how to go about giving it back to him. So, once I was in the bedroom, I stuffed it into my night table's bottom drawer, so that I knew exactly where it was whenever he asked for it. The light fixture's beaded metal cord dangled over the bed. With a yank, I switched the light off. Outside the window, I heard the whiz of a passing car. I slid under the sheet. To my right was Spider's back. To my left was the empty crib. I snuggled up behind Spider, an attempt to spoon. There was something hard between us. I knew it wasn't him, because his back was to me. Whatever it was, it seemed to have a pulse. I flipped the sheets back and grabbed it. I held it up, and it ticked in my hand. "Why is this clock in the bed?"

"I just finished winding it," Spider said.

"This is a windup clock?" I reached up and tugged the light switch. Once my eyes adjusted to the light, to my surprise, I saw the brass key at the back of the clock.

Spider sat. "Mia you've been looking at this clock for almost eleven years. You didn't know that?"

"I always thought it was battery operated."

"Why would you think that? You never put a battery in it," he said.

I shrugged turning to the nightstand. It was bare. The papers Spider so rudely put there for me were gone. I sat the clock down and turned to Spider. "Where's the proposal?"

"I typed it myself," he said.

"Why'd you do that?"

"I couldn't wait on you. I connected the computer, typed the proposal, and saved the file to a disk. All I need you to do is proofread it. You still have that username?"

I hadn't used that in almost two months since I emailed a medical report to Dr. Snyder, but I said, "I guess so."

"Good. The Internet is already connected; the password is on the table. After you proofread my proposal, you can email it to me."

"Where did you save the file?"

"It's on a disk, Mia. The disk is on top of the monitor. Email the proposal before you leave tomorrow, please."

"You *could* proofread it yourself, you know. Just pay attention to the rhythm of the language and punctuate accordingly, like I showed you back in—"

"Are you gonna look at the damn proposal for me, or do I need someone else to do that, too?" Spider hollered. His hazel eyes threw daggers at me.

I didn't know what *his* problem was, but *I* definitely had a problem with what he just said. I called him on it, "What do you mean, 'someone else'?"

"I had to have a friend of mine type my résumé for me."

A nervous pain shot through my stomach. "Who's this friend?"

"Nobody you know."

"Male or female?"

"Female."

"You dirty dog."

"I am so tired of you calling me that every time you feel

238

threatened."

I waved my pointed finger in his face. "You no-good, dirty dog!"

"If I'm a dog and you're my woman, what does that make you?"

"Did you just call me a bitch?"

"Mia!" Spider snatched back the bed sheet and sat straight up. "I wasn't with anybody!"

I folded my arms across my chest. "Then, who typed the damn résumé?"

"The secretary at the label typed it."

I clenched my teeth. "Does this secretary have a name?"

"Pilar. Her name's Pilar."

"Pilar? What the hell is going on, Spider? Huh!"

He banged his fist on his thigh. "There's nothing going on! Why are you so damn crazed and insecure?"

"Insecure? You think I'm insecure? What do you expect, Spider? You never tell me you love me!"

He looked away. "You know how I feel."

"Whether or not I know how you feel is not the issue; I need to hear you tell me you love me. That is a basic need like food and water."

He threw his hands up. "Whatever! I love you; now, don't forget to proofread my proposal and email it to me tomorrow."

Now, a pain shot to my heart, and I zoned out. *I know back in high school Spider told me he wanted to find love. I distinctly remember him saying, "I want me a love." That's why I fell for him. Getting him to express his feelings nowadays is like pulling teeth. Why?* I looked at him. "Why don't you ask your girlfriend to do it?"

"What girlfriend!"

"You have so many; take your pick. Ask fast-ass Asia or your promiscuous licorice, Pilar."

"Besides my mother and my sister, you are the only woman in my life. I'm not like you." Spider said with a raised eyebrow.

I knew I was being challenged. My heart raced. I wasn't sure if it was out of fear or anger. "Whatchu tryna say?"

He narrowed his eyes. "You know exactly what I'm saying."

"Don't try to flip this on me. I've got more self-control

239

than anybody, but every time I turn around, you're involved with some woman!"

"Half the planet is female. Chances are I'm gonna have to deal with one once in a while. And, who are you to talk? Every time *I* turn around, you're involved with Romell!" He sucked in his bottom lip and bit it.

"Romell and I are not involved! Stop trying to flip this on me! I'm tired of hearing about you and all these different women!"

"I'm tired of this thing with you and Romell!"

There was a thumping at the bedroom wall, the common wall we shared with our neighbors. Their bedroom was on the other side. There were times Tee-Bo cried all night, and we didn't hear a peep out of them. Now, they were banging on the wall, obviously fed up. I brought my fingers to my head and massaged my throbbing temples. Then, I lowered my voice. "Stop it, Spider. Just stop it. There is no *thing* with Romell and me. But these women, I want you to leave them alone."

"Are you kidding? These females out here mean nothing to me. I can get another computer anywhere, and I can type for myself. I don't have a problem with that."

"Good. Then, it's settled." I yanked the light switch and snatched the sheet over me. I turned my back to Spider. Lying there, I felt no movement in the bed, so I knew he was still sitting up.

With a click, light filled the room again. "You ain't gettin' off that easily. I'm not done with you," he said.

I looked up at him. "What are you talking about?"

"Romell. I want you to leave *him* alone."

My stomach tied in knots. "Is that a joke?"

"Do I look like I'm laughing?" The expression on his face was stone cold. "I'm tired of you sneaking around here making phone calls, and then disappearing for hours."

A tear crept out of the corner of my eye. "There's nothing going on between me and Romell!"

"You forget you talk in your sleep," Spider said.

My heart nearly stopped. I couldn't help but consider all the possibilities, all the dreams I had. The last one I remembered had me and Romell on a boat, but I realized: if I had said something about Romell in my sleep, there was no telling what I said. I kept my cool. "And your point is?"

"If Romell is not in your bed, he's definitely on your mind."

"Romell is not in my bed, he's not in my head, and I don't talk in my sleep."

"You don't talk in your sleep?"

"No, I don't."

"All right! Then, there's no problem; we have an understanding."

"What understanding?"

"You don't have to worry about me and any other women, and I don't have to worry about you and Romell. Is that good with you?"

I couldn't look at him. Now, I had a headache, heartburn, and an upset stomach. I needed a Motrin and some Tums. I finally looked up. He was biting his lip. I could see small cuts on his lip where he had broken the skin. I watched as a thin line of blood ran across it and collected at the corners of his mouth. Slowly he repeated, "Is that good with you?"

I opened my mouth and gulped, but I was parched. My lips moved and nothing came out. I was stuck. No matter what I said, I was stuck, and then he hollered, "Is that good with you!"

"Okay, fine," I said.

"Fine?"

"I said fine!"

Now a smirk stretched across his lips. "Fine, huh. Mia, you don't sound very convincing. Where's your enthusiasm? Huh-ha!"

I don't know what he found so amusing. I was miserable. Oh boy, was I miserable. I usually like to have the last word, but my mind was a blank. Still, I refused to back down, and to say anything was to admit the obvious; I couldn't live without Romell. So, I said nothing, even though there was a hole in my heart. With Spider facing me, staring in my eyes, I stood firm and stared back as if I were unaffected.

38

SPIDER STOOD; I WAS STILL KNEELING IN THE middle of the bed, but we were locked in a staring match. Pulling one off takes more than just maintaining eye contact and not backing down. It means wiping away all signs of emotion and remaining stone-faced, which I did. For a minute there, I was working it. I really was. It was easy when I focused on all the girls who pursued Spider over the years and brought me so much grief. Then, I could plant myself and throw daggers right back at him, not a problem. But once I started thinking about what I was losing, it wasn't so easy.

Romell was the one person who could make me laugh when I cried. We talked about everything. He allowed me to vent when I was upset and always showed me things from a different perspective, yet he never judged me. He brought my mistakes to my attention and gave me advice without being an ass about it. He didn't remind me how imperfect I was; he encouraged me to be better. With Romell, I could do anything, be anything, say anything, and it was always okay. He called me "Mia" when he was pissed off. But, sooner or later, he'd say, "What's up, Chocolate," and I would melt all over again.

I felt a sigh coming on but took a deep breath instead. I knew I went too far. I refused to punk out, but was this fight even worth it? Not once in ten years did I ever confirm that Spider ever cheated. That didn't necessarily mean he was faithful; he could've just been very good at covering his tracks. Okay, maybe Spider wasn't screwing around. Half the time, this prude wasn't even interested in screwing *me*. At this point, it didn't even matter. I was losing Romell. The Pilars, the Asias, the Pamelas, Stacys, Lisas, Tonyas and every other whats-her-name that popped up over the years, right about now, I was almost willing to lock Spider in a room with those bitches in order to keep Romell.

The more I thought about that, the harder it was to breathe, the faster my heart raced, the more my adrenaline pumped. My hands started to shake. I balled them tightly and fought to remain firm, even though my head was pounding, my stomach was queasy, and my knees felt weak. Then, my eyes grew watery, but I still didn't budge. Once my leg started to wobble, that was it; I was done. The battle was over. I was visibly shaken. I realized I couldn't stare a man down when I was dying inside.

I climbed off the mattress and went to the medicine cabinet to do something about my splitting headache and nausea. I tapped two coated tablets out of their bottle, and popped them with a handful of water from the tap. Then I shook out a couple of antacids. Chewing the chalky tablets, I returned to the bedroom. Spider was sprawled out, facing the window. His long body took up two-thirds of our bed. I switched the lights off and squeezed to the edge on my end. My breasts were sore and full. I found comfort in an awkward position, chest up and legs to the side. The urge to sigh was inescapable. It was like my heavy breaths were connected to an automatic timer. Tears leaked, dampening my pillow. I shifted my face to a dry spot and closed my eyes, trying to figure out how I could ever manage to live without Romell. I didn't think I would ever find sleep. Somehow sleep found me, but not for long.

In my dream, Jun Ko and I were in a field of lavender, and she was strangling me with her thong. I opened my eyes, gasping in the darkness. Seeing the spindles of Tee-Bo's crib and hearing the ticking of the windup clock, I realized why: I was in Spider's embrace. During the night, he had gravitated to my side and wrapped himself entirely around me, drawing me in and holding me like I was his security blanket. What was *he* dreaming?

Less than two weeks ago, I thought Jun Ko was gay. Now, I realized I would have preferred her to be gay. That I could handle. There'd be no need to get upset. I'd just look her in the eyes and say, "No offense, I prefer one race and one gender. I love black men." And I do. Black men are so beautiful, because they thrive. In this whole wide world of ours, there's no comparison. None. No other man is as easy to love and as hard to satisfy. I love black men more than anything. In so many words, I'd make that absolutely clear. Problem solved.

Now, the reality of Jun Ko being straight, that was the real nightmare. I couldn't bear the thought of her spreading whipped cream all over my Romell or worse—him spreading whipped cream all over her. And he gave her my keys. For all I knew, she could've been moving in. And Spider wanted me to cut Romell loose?

I needed to think. It took a while, but I eased out of Spider's clutches and climbed out of the bed without disturbing him. I sat on the floor, crying silently. I wanted Spider to sever ties with his female friends, and I wanted him to marry me. But, above all, I wanted my friendship with Romell to remain intact. I needed to sort things out. I got on my knees and did that the best way I knew how; I slipped my arm between the mattresses and retrieved my poetry journal. This time, I took out my silver link bracelet, too: the same bracelet I'd kept hidden since Christmas, the same bracelet Romell had been bugging me to wear. It was a gift from him. Better yet, it was the exchange; I asked Romell to return the first one.

♥　♥　♥　♥

Every Christmas, Romell would give me a Macy's gift certificate. The first he gave me back in high school; it was fifty dollars. After he started making big money on Wall Street, he'd drop a five hundred dollar gift certificate on me like it was nothing. Me being me, I'd use the gift certificate to shop for everybody else. I'd get Mommy her perfume, and Dawn a gift certificate for the holidays and her birthday, February 14th. Anyway, the last gift certificate he gave me was for a thousand, so when I went to his place this past Christmas, that's what I expected, another gift certificate. In fact, I was certain of it. The only thing I wasn't sure about was the amount. At the time, I was about six months pregnant, so I was looking forward to using it for things I wanted for my baby. But, instead of my usual little red envelope, Romell reached beneath his seven and a half foot spruce for the pale blue, cardboard box tied with a big, blue, satin bow. The box was stamped Tiffany & Co.

"Aw, for me? You didn't have to." I heard about Tiffany's, so I was curious to know what was inside. Removing the lid, I saw another box inside. It was blue also, but velvet. Judging by the size and shape of the box, I knew it held a bracelet. I opened it. The sparkle was hypnotic. "Wow! A silver bracelet, I love it." About half an inch wide with a matte finish, it was concave in shape like one of the plastic cuff bracelets from Woolworth's that Mommy used to wear back in the day. It had no hinges but slipped on easily. I turned the bracelet around and around, struck by the way the large stones captured the white lights from the Christmas tree, refracting them in reds, blues, and golds. The stones alternated in a square, circle, and triangle pattern all the way around. "Wow, these CZ's look *real*," I said.

"That's because they *are*," Romell said.

That didn't register. I shook my head. "Real CZ's?"

"Don't insult me. Those are diamonds, Chocolate, bezel-set princess, round, and trillion cut, one-carat diamonds."

"Diamonds and Silver?"

"Platinum," he said, and he had this big grin on his face.

Now, I started to calculate. I had gone out on my own and done some window-shopping for an engagement ring. Actually, I pressed my face against the cold glass and drooled, but that's another matter. Anyway, on occasion, I did dare to venture inside, so I knew this: one-carat diamonds ran at least a couple thousand dollars, and those were the ones that were as cloudy as a cotton ball. These were as clear as drinking water, and there were nine of them. Then, there was the platinum. The funny thing about platinum was a little bit would cost a whole lot. So, I figured nine clear, big, white diamonds would cost about four thousand each. That bracelet had to cost a pretty penny. I shook my head and pulled it off. "I can't accept this," I said.

"You have to."

"No, I don't. I can't."

"Chocolate, I had a really good year. I wanted to do something extra special for you."

"That's what you said last year." I slipped it on and then off again. "I can't. Romell, I appreciate that. I really do, but if Spider saw this bracelet, I'd have to kill him. So, I can't take it." I handed it back.

"If you don't want this, what am I supposed to do with it?" Now, steam was practically shooting from his nostrils.

I shrugged. "Return it."

"To Tiffany's?" Romell said in disbelief.

I handed it back to him. "Yes, please return that to Tiffany's. The thought was beautiful. You don't even have to give me anything else."

"You know me better than that." He was walking in circles, licking his lips, but not in the flirtatious way he usually does. He looked like he was ready to spit fire, but that was not my problem. He took a deep breath. "I'm going back to Tiffany's. What should I get you as a gift, Mia?"

"If you insist on buying me something, buy me something simple and inexpensive like…" I thought about it for a moment then said, "silver. Spider wouldn't be upset if you bought me something silver."

The next time I saw Romell, he had a smaller, pale blue, cardboard box from Tiffany's. My stomach did flip-flops as I opened it. Inside was a blue velvet bag, and inside that bag was an adorable silver link bracelet, reminding me of the chains that threaded the short metal poles surrounding the grass back in the projects. I looked at the heart tag, stamped Tiffany & Co. and sighed with relief. "This is beautiful, Romell."

"It's perfect for you. They call it the *Please Return to Tiffany's Charm Bracelet*."

The way he said that, I could tell he was still upset but I smiled. "Thank you so much."

"You're welcome," he said and smirked, then added, "And, since Spider Snyder doesn't have a problem with silver, I had it engraved."

"Engraved?" I flipped the heart tag. Reading the words etched in the silver, my heart started beating faster. I was so touched; I had to collect myself, until I thought about Spider. Then I rolled my eyes at Romell. "You are such a piece of work," I said. Of all things, Romell had the bracelet engraved:

4 Ever

Love

Romell

He knew my whole purpose for asking for something simple was so Spider wouldn't get upset, yet Romell was determined to piss Spider off. There was no way Spider would read the inscription on this bracelet and not assume the worst. And I couldn't ask Romell to take this one back, because it was engraved.

♥   ♥   ♥   ♥

That's why I kept it hidden between my mattresses for so long. Now, outside my bedroom door, I squeezed my bracelet to my heart for a moment. Then I fastened the silver link around my wrist. Now that I was on the verge of losing Romell, it suddenly became precious, and I appreciated it like I never had before. I walked into the living room and glanced out the window. The sky, only beginning to pale, was barely casting light into the room, but I didn't switch either lamp on. That would've surely caught Spider's attention. I pulled the bistro chair out and laid my journal in front of the computer. I knew what I was supposed to do, but once my behind was in that chair, I just sat there. Slumped at the table, tapping my pen against the keyboard, I don't know how much time passed, but I did notice the room getting brighter and brighter. The silver bracelet glimmered against my brown skin, and all I thought about was Romell.

Romell needs to be with a black woman. I can't cut him off now that he's with Jun Ko. I straightened. *Maybe that's not such a bad idea. If I push the issue of his dating a black woman now, he'd probably continue to be with Jun Ko, and I'll have an excuse for avoiding him. If I avoid him for any length of time, not only would I buy myself the time I need, but also Romell would more than likely stop seeing Jun Ko permanently.* I smiled. *Once Spider's ink is on the license, all bets are off; I'll go right back to spending time with Romell. Until then, I'll just keep my distance. The worse that could happen is if Romell cuts Jun Ko loose right away, and that's still a good thing. Either way, I win.*

Okay, so now I can breathe a little easier. Romell needs to be with a black woman anyway. He needs to learn to appreciate black love. How could he grow up under the care of a strong and nurturing black woman and be so against dating one? It's like he's in an ice cream parlor. He'll try every other flavor, strawberry, vanilla, lemon sorbet, what about chocolate? What about black love? He needs to appreciate chocolate love. That thought gave me an idea. I opened my journal and put my pen to the next clean page. I tapped a rhythm on the tabletop, and the first words came.

You work so hard
Now I know why
It's because you like
The finer things in life

It seems you have all
Life's luxuries

My pen sped across the page then came to an abrupt stop, creative shutdown. *A word that rhymes with Luxuries— seize, keys, frees, sees, knees. Aha!* I focused again on the page and continued:

How is it you're missin'
What you need?

I stopped and tapped my pen. Again there was a brick wall right in the middle of my creative flow. *Black love is the way to keep a smile on your face; that is some corny mess. Black love. Ebony love, brown love. No, no colors. Flavors are probably better. Vanilla, strawberry, chocolate. Chocolate love. That sounds best.*

Chocolate Love every day
Can melt your fears away
And have you feeling new
That's what Chocolate can do

I repeated what I wrote aloud a few times to hear how it rang to my ear. After that, I had the rhyme pattern and the concept down; the rest of the words came easily.

So many women
You like them fine
In different flavors
Like you like your wine

Consider yourself
A connoisseur?
Sometimes
Less is more.

Chocolate Love every day
Can melt your fears away
And have you feeling...ooh!
That's what Chocolate can do.

Moet is okay
So is Dom Perignon
Caviar
And Filet Mignon
But really your lifestyle
Doesn't mean a thing
If you still feel incomplete.

I read what I had written. *That poem even makes sense. Wow!* I was impressed with myself. In one poem I summed up Romell's situation perfectly. I reread it. *I know what I'll do. I'll email it to him.* I turned the computer on. While it booted, I looked around for the password to login. Spider said it was somewhere near the computer on the table. I checked under the keyboard, under the mouse, under the floppy disk sitting on top of the monitor, and all around the floor. It was nowhere to be seen. I ran the software for the net and stared at the empty box when the curser prompted for the password. Not knowing what it could be, I was ready to wake Spider from his sleep. I stood, knocking my journal to the floor. Beneath it was a strip of paper scrawled with his cryptic handwriting. I deciphered it and keyed in the word letter for letter, f-r-u-s-t-r-a-t-e-d. I didn't press enter. Instead, I walked over to the other side of the room for the phone.

I dialed. As soon as Romell picked up, I asked, "What's your email address?"

"Why?"

"Why do you think? I wanna send you an email."

"You already have my email address at work. Is it business or personal?"

"Real personal," I said. "I'm gonna email you a poem."

"Just how personal is this poem?"

"It's about relationships. You've been with all kinds of women. I think it's time you heard my suggestion."

"Chocolate, I don't need to hear it! I already know you won't be happy until I'm with someone who's your height, your weight, and your complexion."

"Well, read my poem anyway! Now, what's your email address?"

"Send it to my job, Chocolate. You can also bring it to me when you drop by after work."

"What makes you so sure I'm gonna drop by?" I said.

"I want you to see my new sofa, and I *know* you wanna hear in person what I think of your poem."

I sucked my teeth. "Is Jun Ko gonna be there?"

"No."

"Okay. You just *might* see me."

I couldn't believe I said that. *Okay? You just might see me?* What was I thinking? I gave myself a quick snack on the forehead as soon as I hung up. *That was stupid, really, really stupid. Now that I've committed myself, I have to follow through. I have to go see him, because I already agreed; I'm obligated. I have no choice.* This was bull and I knew it, but I had to convince myself that going to see him was the right thing to do. Otherwise, I couldn't explain myself to Spider with a straight face.

I walked back to the computer and saw the strip of paper with Spider's password sitting on the table. Even more light had spilled into the room, and the scrap paper was angled a certain way. Instead of reading it only as characters, I noticed it as a word, frustrated, and I zoned out thinking. *Frustrated. Spider does have a lot on his mind lately. He and his brother weren't speaking. He just found out his mother is a lesbian. And, to top it all off, he still doesn't know where his father's ashes are. I was only focusing on what I was dealing with. Spider was going through a lot, too. That explains why he's been behaving like such a jerk.* I sighed. Then, I grabbed the disk from the top of the monitor, and placed it right next to the mouse, intending to take care of that proposal for Spider after I emailed Romell. But, just as I left-clicked SEND, the phone rang.

251

39

$\mathcal{J}$ACKIE SAID, "PUT SPENCE ON THE PHONE!" HER tone was nasty, but it didn't seem like her anger was directed toward me.

She was calling early in the morning from her vacation, so of course I was concerned. "What's wrong, Jackie?"

"Mia, I need to speak to Spence. Put him on the phone."

"Jackie, Spider's sleep."

"Wake his ass up!"

I pulled the phone away from my face and stared at it for a moment. Then said, "Jackie, first off...." I stopped and bit my tongue. She wasn't angry with me, so I refused to be drawn into this. I took a deep breath, shook my head, and walked over to Spider. His body was spread out diagonally across the mattress, chalky white circles dotted the green pillowcase, and Spider's face was still moist with saliva. I knew this was the first good night's sleep he'd had in his own bed in days. I looked at the crib note still crumpled in my palm. It was scrawled with Spider's password, frustrated. I was not about to wake my already frustrated man, so that his aggravated sister could holler at him from the South Pacific.

When I returned to the phone I said, "Jackie, he's out cold. He's been dealing with a lot lately."

"I don't care what Spence is dealing with! That is no excuse for him to cuss at my mother!"

"What?"

"Spence cursed my mother on the phone while she was at work. Mia, there is a lot going on with our family right now, and you're not family yet. Now, I need to speak to Spence!"

"Jackie, he's asleep! When Spider wakes up, I'll have him call you. Now, give me your number. Are you in Hawaii or Vegas?"

"Look, bitch. We wouldn't even be in this mess if you

253

minded your business in the first place. Put Spence on the damn phone, or else!"

When Jackie said that, I slammed the phone down. I didn't even care that she was calling long distance. My heart was racing as if I had just run or done some stair climbing; I was *that* angry. I was angry with her for speaking to me that way and even more upset with myself for not responding the way I would have liked to when I had her on the phone. *Who the hell does she think she is?*

The phone rang again. I snatched it back up and went off. "Now, *you* look, bitch. I don't know who you think you are, but I'm no punk. I'm from Melrose Projects. Come out your face like that again, you *will* see a side of me you've never seen before."

"Is that any way to answer your phone?" Mommy said.

I gasped. Tears trickled from my eyes and dripped off the tip of my nose. "I'm...I'm sorry, Mommy. I thought you were someone else. I'll have to talk to you later."

"Mia, stop crying. Take it easy and call me whenever you feel up to talking."

I smeared my tears. "Okay, Mommy. I will. I just can't go into it now, but there's a lot going on."

"I know. Dawn filled me in."

"Dawn already filled you in?" I said. That lit a fuse inside me.

"Yes, I talked to her this morning," Mommy said; her voice was full of concern.

Still, I remained there on the phone, fuming. When I opened my mouth, this came out, "Well, Mommy...here's something I bet Dawn didn't tell you! Dawn is...Dawn is...oooooh!!!" I slammed the phone down and covered my face with my hands. I didn't know which was worse, hanging up on my mother or saying what was right on the tip of my tongue—*Dawn is having an affair with a married pimp.* I snatched the receiver back up and punched Dawn's number in. As soon as she picked up, I hollered, "You can't keep a secret to save your life!"

"What's wrong now?" Dawn was pretending she was half asleep, but I knew she had just gotten off the phone with Mommy.

"You know what's wrong!"

She yawned. "Girl, Mommy dragged it outta me. Let me tell you what happened."

"I don't wanna hear it! I'm sick and tired of you being loose with my business and tight with your own!"

My sister came to life. "Mia, this is not my fault!"

"Dawn, you're a big mouth gossip, and that's why nobody likes you! I knew this was going to happen! I just knew it!"

"Well, if you knew this was going to happen...you're the fool for telling me your business!"

After that, I don't know who hung up on whom. I just remember unplugging the phone and marching into the bathroom. With the shower on full blast, I cried as the hot water beat down on me. I emerged from the bathroom in a billow of steam. The rest of my apartment felt air-conditioned as I got myself ready for work. The bathroom mirror was fogged, so I applied my makeup in the bedroom. Since I watched everything Dawn did when she did my face, *I* did a good job of it. At least, it seemed that way. For once, this mirror was kind.

I fluffed my curls, airing out some of the moisture that had seeped into my shower cap. My curls had dropped since yesterday's trip to the salon. Now, that my hair was frizzed, and the ringlets were loose, it looked more natural. That was a good thing. I went to my closet and grabbed something to wear, a fitted white blouse and a beige knee-length skirt. This outfit was supposed to be conservative, but I was fresh out of pantyhose. I looked ridiculous with my legs bare, so instead of tucking my blouse, I pulled it out, rolled my skirt a few times, and looked. That was much better. I stepped into Dawn's crocodile pumps and checked myself out again. Buttoned at my wrists, my sleeves seemed awkward. I rolled them. Now, looking back at my skirt and blouse, something seemed to be missing. I grabbed my brown leather carryall bag and wide braided belt out of my closet. Once I cinched that belt around my waist, I felt complete. I looked good even with the bare legs. I opened my carryall bag and started dumping in what I needed: keys, wallet, a pen, CD player, and Motrin. I sifted through the makeup and dumped in what I thought I needed to refresh my face during the day, the lip liner, and mascara. I snatched up the lipstick. Instead of dropping it into the purse, I pulled the top off and applied a little more.

"Who are you making yourself pretty for?" Spider said, sounding like a half-dead frog.

"Who do you think?"

He cleared his throat. "You don't want me to answer that."

At this point, Jackie, Mommy, and Dawn had worn me out. Since I didn't have energy left to fight with him, I figured I might as well apologize. I took a deep breath. "Look, Spider, about last night, if I said anything that upset you, I'm sorry."

In the bed, he shrugged, nodded, and rolled back over.

I threw my hand on my hip. "Well?" I said.

He looked back at me. "Well what?"

"Aren't *you* going to apologize to me?"

"For what?"

I looked at his wrinkled forehead and his blank stare, realizing that he felt no remorse for anything he said or did. I shook my head and whispered a solemn, "I give up." Dejected, I trudged out of the room and glanced back at him, only to shake my head again. My energy was zapped. My carryall bag was light, but it was as if the weight of the world was on me. I went limp, and my whole body felt heavy. I walked down the hall and leaned against the wall for support, wondering. *Will I ever hear a man apologize?*

40

*O*UTSIDE OF MY COLLECTION CALLS, I HADN'T SAID two words since I left the apartment. At the agency, my coworkers asked repeatedly, "What's wrong?" I wouldn't answer. I didn't feel like speaking to anyone. Besides, I had a headache, but even after my trusty tablets took it away, I still didn't want to be bothered.

After work, I walked from the West Side of town to Romell's. Every few blocks some stranger would call out, "Smile!" One by one, I fanned them all away, until doing that annoyed me enough to flip the last guy "the bird." He responded by calling me "a stank, conceited bitch." Strangely, that's what made me feel better. My logic: if he could mistake my sour mood for conceit, I must've looked good. I had totally forgotten that I was looking fabulous. I was reminded again when I reached Romell's.

He stood in his doorway gaping before he said a word. "Wow!"

"Wow, what?"

"I almost didn't recognize you. You look...you look...good."

"Is that supposed to mean I usually look bad?"

He smiled, dimples sinking—all three of them. "Nah, nah, nah, just not this...this...dayum!"

I rolled my eyes and brushed past him. "Where's your roommate, Romell?"

"What roommate?"

"Jun Ko," I said, walking past the dining room.

"I'm not tryna move her up in here."

"Why not?"

"Squatters have rights."

I stopped and turned. He had his head tilted to the side, and he was looking down before he looked into my eyes. *Was he just staring at my ass?* I sucked my teeth. "Okay, where's your *girlfriend*?"

257

"*Jun Ko* is at that spa of hers, and she is *not* my girlfriend."

"If she's not your girlfriend, why'd you give her my keys?" I strutted away, then added, "I know a relationship when I see one."

"Whoa, whoa, whoa! Time-out!" Romell shouted up the hall, his hands marking a "T," like a referee. He even whistled. "Relationship? I told you before: that path ain't for everybody. Jun Ko was just doing me a favor. In fact, giving her the keys was your idea."

My head spun. "What! What the hell are you talking about?"

"My sofa. Remember, Chocolate? Today is Wednesday; *I* told *you* I was having my sofa delivered today. *You* told *me* to call you when I needed the keys."

I thought about that. He did tell me he was having a sofa delivered, and I did tell him to call me when he needed the keys. For some reason, I still didn't believe him. I squinted at him the way he always squinted at me. "Is *that* why you had me rush all the way down here last night?"

"Why else?"

"Why didn't you just tell me you needed the keys for Jun Ko?"

"Because you don't like her."

I didn't know what to say to that. I sucked my teeth. "Well...why did you have me come here if you knew you had kinky sex planned?"

He walked away from me, then turned back, looked me in the eye and fessed up, "The plan was for me and Jun Ko to get together *after* you dropped the keys off, but since you said it would take you hours to get here, I told her to hurry over for a quickie."

"Romell, that was not right! I rushed down here thinking something was seriously wrong, and I found Jun Ko with her ass hanging out. I was hurt, angry, and...embarrassed! You lied to me! You're supposed to be my best friend, Romell! And *you* lied to *me*! What kind of shit is that?"

"You're absolutely right. I'm sorry."

"What did you say?"

"You're absolutely right. I'm sorry."

Whoa, I thought. *You're absolutely right. I'm sorry. What I wouldn't pay to hear Spider say those exact same words. Those five words would be even better than foreplay.* Spider was so accustomed to pointing out my faults that he never understood my pain, needs, or even tried to see things from my perspective. Romell connected to me in ways that I needed and in ways that Spider would never understand. Spider would never in a million years admit that I was right, and an apology just wasn't happening. The most I'd get out of Spider was a "Yeah, whatever." Even though it was very frustrating being left in limbo without closure, I accepted that as a man thing until now. "You're absolutely right. I'm sorry." Five mere words, but it seemed like I'd waited forever to hear them. I regained focus to notice Romell staring at me, witnessing my little mind trip. He winked.

I blushed then asked, "What's the wink for?"

"You were out there for a minute. I wanted to reel you back in," he said, smiling. Then he handed me my little ring with his two silver keys.

My assortment of keys was right in my carryall; I pulled it out and slipped the smaller set onto the tight split ring. I stood there for a moment with my head tilted down, thinking about how much I worried about his relationship with Jun Ko, and how I was now on the verge of losing his friendship. I was on the brink of tears and was blinking to fight them. When I realized that wasn't working, I cleared my throat so that Romell wouldn't notice my sniffles. Now that all my keys were linked together, I clenched them in my fist and looked down at Romell's polished black dress shoes. He stepped closer and I noticed the creases in his slacks. They weren't shiny and didn't smell like lemons. Those pants were dry-cleaned. He gave my chin a gentle nudge, lifting my head. My gaze rose with the blue pinstripes of his dress shirt right up into his eyes.

"What's wrong, Chocolate?"

I sniffled. "Rough day. That's all. How was your day? How are things over at Livings & Moore?"

He looked away. "They gave me my own office."

"What? Congratulations! What happened?"

He cleared his throat. "I went to Stevenson this morning and demanded a promotion."

"And they gave it to you?" I said surprised.

Romell nodded.

"Wow, I guess I'll come down to Wall Street tomorrow and check out your new digs."

"No! I mean nah. Right now...I've got to...to step up my performance. I need to work extra hard...you know...to prove myself. It'll be a while before I can have visitors."

"Is your number still the same or did they give you a different extension?"

"I don't know it yet. I'll give it to you later. Anyway, aren't you here to see the sofa?"

He grabbed my waist and rushed me into the living room. I saw his new sofa, and for a moment, I was speechless. I always knew he had expensive taste. Call me passé, but when he said "sofa," I was expecting to see something that resembled a couch. I couldn't believe my eyes. That thing was not a couch or sofa. It was more of an art-deco sectional comprised of ten individual, quilted, black leather seats. Elasticized leather strips connected them. Completely flexible, it wrapped around the living room. He had a throw across the back and four matching pillows spaced out on it. All were fur in a zebra print. Real fur, but I doubt they were from an actual zebra.

Romell pushed the sofa's middle section in and pulled the ends out. "See, it's a W." He straightened and stretched it making it appear longer; two of the pillows tumbled off. "See, I could twist, pull, and shape this sofa any way I want. What do you think about that?"

"What do I think?"

"Yeah."

I smiled and started singing the Slinky jingle, "*It walks downstairs....*"

"Very funny. Now, what do you really think?"

I giggled. "I'm serious. It looks like a big-ass Slinky. How much did you pay for that thing, anyway?"

"You don't wanna know." He was being evasive.

I pressed. "Yes, I do. How much?"

"Do you really wanna know?" He looked at me out the corner of his eye.

"Stop stalling!"

"Twenty-six thousand dollars."

"Twenty-six thousand dollars! For a couch?" I grabbed one of those throw pillows and commenced to smacking him upside the head. "You're nuts! Couldn't you find something better to do with your money than spend all that on a sofa?" When my keys flew out of my hand and landed behind it, I stopped bopping him, but he still heard my mouth. "I could furnish your whole apartment, my whole apartment, buy a new car, and still have something left over for Tee-Bo's college fund with that much money!"

Romell looked at me, as if I was selling bottled air. "You're kidding me, right?"

"No, I'm not kidding!"

"Well, Chocolate, I had to. I was getting bored with the look of the place."

"If you're bored and want to change things up, you don't go out and buy a thirty thousand dollar sofa; you buy some paint! $20 a can! And that's for the good stuff."

"That's actually not a bad idea. I wonder why I didn't think of that."

"You spend frivolously. That's why! I know how to cut corners, sacrifice, and make do."

He looked at me and shook his head. "Chocolate, there's nothing wrong with the way I spend money. You are just way too frugal." Then, he cocked it to the side, peering. "When was the last time you went away for vacation?" I looked away and didn't say anything. "Okay, when was the last time you treated yourself to something new without worrying about the cost?" I still didn't answer, because I couldn't remember. "All right, Chocolate, when was the last time you went out to dinner?"

I sighed and muttered, "When was the last time you saw a Slinky commercial?"

"Damn!" He laughed and shook his head. "You need to be more selfish."

"I don't know how to be selfish."

"That's exactly your problem, Chocolate." Romell shook his head again. "Okay, come with me," he said, walking toward the door.

"Come with you where?"

"Shopping."

"I am *not* going shopping with you!"

"Relax, Chocolate. Seeing how you once asked me to return a fifty-thousand-dollar bracelet, and you mail me a money order back every time I try to help you out, I am not going to buy you anything major."

"Okay, so what do you plan on buying me?"

"Just some music for that little CD player of yours. Spider

shouldn't mind that, right?"

I knew that was a trick question, but I went anyway.

41

*P*OOKIE'S JUKEBOX CARRIED EVERYTHING FROM eight-track tapes to CDs. The store was so narrow, customers had to squeeze past each other to get by, but it seemed much larger because the entire back wall that traveled the length of the store was mirrored. So, there we were in the R&B/Hip-Hop section of this record store where there seemed to be two of everything. Two long tables full of inventory. Two smock-wearing cashiers chewing gum and blowing bubbles. Two Romells dropping old jams into his basket. And two of me.

I plucked out shrink-wrapped jewel cases and tucked them back in place. None of which were alphabetized by title or artist, so this process was taking longer than I expected. As soon as I heard speakers thumping with the bass of Soul II Soul's "Back to Life," I was infected. My head was bobbing, and I sang along but mainly ad-libbed.

Romell interrupted me at the best part. "Why are you making up your own words?"

I stopped flipping through the CDs for a moment and turned to him. "I love this song. This one and 'Keep it Moving,' so I don't wanna hear it because I didn't say a word when you were jumping up and down to Kris Kross." I turned and went back to searching.

"You should learn the lyrics to this song that's playing."

"What for? It is not that serious. Now, let me know when you find anything by Mary J."

"Weren't you the one who told me to pay attention to the songs a person sings if I wanna know what's on their mind?"

"That was Spider's theory. What does that have to do with anything, now?" I shook my head, humming.

Romell chuckled. "I pay attention to the songs you sing, Chocolate. Now, I'm gonna hand you a few CDs. Let's see if you can figure out what's on *my* mind." He held out two CDs.

On top was the R&B group, Xscape, the first release with all its cuts. The other was an old single by SWV. I looked at Romell and shrugged. He laughed and let me in on the joke. "Chocolate, if you're tired of Spider Snyder, I've got an *Xscape* for you, and you can have this 'Right Here' if you want."

"*Xscape?*" I said. I turned to the back of the CD read down the list of titles. One of them caught my attention right away. I didn't know if Romell was serious or where he was going with this, but if he could play this game, I could play it better. I decided to throw that title out there. "Xscape. 'With You?' I never heard that before."

He reached into the basket and handed me the other CD, pointed to a song title on the back, and said, "'Do You Want To?'"

I snatched it and flipped it over to check out the front. "Xscape? That's <u>Off the Hook</u>." After a quick glance at the titles I added, "'Who Can I Run To?' and 'What Can I Do?'" Then, I folded my arms. I didn't think Romell had a CD in his basket that could answer that, so I was eager to see what he was going to do next. He pulled out Mary J. Blige's new single, "Be Happy." I giggled and spread the CDs out on the table. He dipped his dimpled face low and looked into my eyes. His eyes were smiling. My heart felt warm. So, I asked, "Romell, you're saying I can escape right here with you and be happy?"

He answered by licking his lips and raising his eyebrows.

I looked away, thinking. *First, Jun Ko. Now, me? Did Romell lower his standards?* I shook my head. It was hard to admit, but Jun Ko morphed. She really did look good. I just so happened to look into the mirror across from us and I realized. *My cuteness factor went way up! I'm curvy, styling. I'm...a dime. Damn, I am a dime.* I grunted as I thought about that. Then I mumbled, "He never settles for less." I looked back at Romell. His eyes were searching. I rolled mine away, mumbling under my breath, "This dirty dog."

"What did you say?"

I picked up two of the CDs and handed them back to him. In a cool shot, I said, "I'm not looking for any *Xscape*."

"Well, what do you want?"

"<u>My Life</u> and TLC."

He licked his lips, moaning, "Oh, I'll give you some TLC."

That sent a chill through me but I didn't let on. I folded my arms across my chest, turned, and cut my eye at him. "'Ain't Too Proud to Beg?'" I said.

"If that's what you want." He leaned over and his breath tickled my ear as he whispered, "Pal–eese, Chocolate. Please." I shivered and giggled. And while I was taking slower breaths to try to relax myself, he put the Heavy D & The Boyz CD in my hand. "This is *Heavy*. I got <u>Nuttin' But Love</u>."

I read the song titles and narrowed my eyes, "I guess you want me to have 'Sex Wit You' and 'Spend a Little Time on Top.'" My tone was filled with attitude, but he didn't seem to notice.

He held up a Tony, Toni, Toné, and said, "Whatever You Want."

I looked at it. I couldn't believe this was happening, and I couldn't even entertain the thought of any of this because my fears were louder than his sweet-talk. I sucked my teeth and handed them all back. "I don't care if this is *Heavy*! I don't wanna have "Sex Wit You," and like I said before, I'm not looking for an Xscape," I snapped.

He slammed Tony, Toni, Toné back into the basket and pulled out the Notorious BIG's album. Now, his face was tight. He smacked the CD down on the table in front of me. "Mia, I'm giving you 'One More Chance,' and that's a Biggie!"

"I know that's a *Biggie,* but I don't need it!" I looked around, until I saw Monica. I shoved "Don't Take it Personal" into Romell's chest and squeezed past him, storming out of the record store. At the curb, I threw my arm up to hail a taxi, wondering if I had enough for the fare. Reaching into my purse for my wallet, I noticed I didn't feel my keys. I ran my hand across the bottom. Nothing. I realized where they were. Taking a deep breath, I looked to my left. Less than half a block away a peanut vendor was roasting nuts from the cart, releasing a honey-sweet aroma, but the thought of eating the peanuts was not as appealing as the thought of hurling them at Romell and sending his ass into anaphylactic shock.

I looked back at the doorway of Pookie's just as Romell came stepping out, hands in the pockets of his black slacks, two plastic bags hanging at his left. Because he works out a lot, his posture's erect but his swagger seemed looser than ever. Still, I saw tension in his face. No dimples now, he had lockjaw. He looked at me, cockeyed. "No cab? Or did you just

265

realize you left your keys?"

I didn't answer that, and I didn't say a word to him in the cab; I tossed my head, flinging my hair back over my shoulder, twisted my body away from him, and crossed my legs. Romell tried to get my attention by whistling Marvin Gaye's "I Want You." When that didn't work, he started pelting my feet with pellets of used chewing gum wrapped in foil, seven pieces in about ten minutes. I figured he was chewing all that gum and spitting it out just to annoy me, but I kept my back to him the entire ride and walked ahead of him into the building. We rode up to the thirty-seventh floor in separate elevators. As soon as he unlocked his door, I bolted into the living room. Even in my slim skirt and croc pumps, I was Flo Jo. My leg banged into his marble cocktail table, sending it spinning around on its axis until the halves formed a circle. I dented my shin, but I wasn't rubbing my boo-boo. I jumped right on his Slinky sofa, leaned over it, reaching until I snatched my keys up off the rug. Then I made a beeline for the door, hoping I could run right out, but he blocked my exit. When I stepped to the left, he stepped to that side. When I tried to veer to the right, he kept right in front of me. I knew then he would not let me past; I had no choice but to get in his face, "What?"

"You don't wanna be with *me*?"

I shook my head.

"You *don't* wanna be with me?"

"No, I do not!"

"You show up in stilettos and a little skirt, and you expect me to believe you don't want me?"

"I did this for Spider."

"Well, Spider isn't here now. Is he? And, what about your poem?"

"What about it? I wanted you to know how I feel."

"Oh, so you admit you have feelings for me?"

"Pah–leese, Romell! That poem is about your situation."

"My situation, huh?"

"Yeah, that's the perfect solution."

"If you think you and I hookin' up would be the perfect solution, why don't you just say you want me?"

"Are you mental?"

"How long have you wanted me, Mia? How long?"

"Now, I *know* you've lost it. What makes you think I want

266

you?"

"Your poem! I've got it right here." He patted himself down, pulled a page out of his back pocket and unfolded it in front of me. "There! You say all through this how you're gonna melt my fears away and how you're gonna make me feel."

I looked, reading aloud halfheartedly, "Chocolate Love every day can melt your fears away and have you feeling new. That's what Chocolate can do." Then, I shook my head. "And?"

He smacked his baldhead, paced and then, banged the back of it into the wall. "Chocolate, your last name is Love!"

"So? I wrote this to motivate you to embrace black love."

"Stop it. The only black Love you want me to embrace is you."

Now, I read the whole thing through. I could see how he could make that assumption. The words "Chocolate" and "Love" were both capitalized all the way through the poem, but I didn't do that intentionally. That connection didn't even occur to me when I jotted the lines down; my mind was in a totally different place. I laughed, but he didn't see the humor in this, at all. His face was as stiff as steel.

I tried to explain. "I know how this looks, Romell, but that wasn't the meaning behind this. I meant chocolate as opposed to vanilla or any other flavor. Chocolate is a metaphor for black, and Love is just love, the emotion. Not my last name. That's just a coincidence."

"This ain't no coinkidink! I told you once before. You won't be happy until I'm with a woman who's your height, your weight, and your complexion. What I should have said is you won't be happy, until I'm with *you*. Why won't you just admit it?"

"Hello! I am in a relationship with Spider. Remember him? Real tall, kinda goofy, I *love* him. Seriously, I was not coming on to you."

He stood, huffing and puffing for a moment, then looked at me hard. "Did you eat any peanuts?"

"No! What the hell kind of question is—"

I didn't finish my sentence. The next thing I knew, I felt his warm tongue, stroking mine and tickling the roof of my mouth. I heard the crackling of plastic when Romell's CD bags hit the carpet. Then, my bag dropped to the carpet, and I backed all the way to the wall, but the lower half of me began to wind as if it had a mind of its own. He grabbed my behind, pulled me into him, and boy oh boy. Now, when I walked in on Romell and Jun Ko, and saw him in those see-through drawers, I knew then: he wasn't packing peanuts there, either. Now that he was fully hard, I knew he could poke a hole in me if I let him, but still, something inside me was aching for it.

I was so aroused, but it was as if the backs of my hands were glued to the wall. I couldn't bring myself to wrap my arms around him. To do so would've meant I was causing this to happen. As it stood, Romell initiated this. *He* was kissing *me*. Everything I was doing was involuntary. I wasn't stopping this, but I wasn't causing this, either. Technically, I wasn't responding. Kissing him back was only a reflex, a natural reaction to the stroke of his tongue, and the taste of spearmint, so *he* was kissing *me*. What I was feeling in my stomach I had no control over. This was my logic, and so by virtue of me keeping my hands to that wall and not "touching" him under any circumstances, I was *not guilty*.

Then, his hands started creeping their way up under my skirt. His lips left mine, traveled down my neck, and back up to my ear. "Chocolate, I need you," he whispered. I felt a jolt in my stomach—fear—next, my panties slipping off my behind. I opened one eye and saw Spider's face for a split second. That sent a chill through me, because in that instant, just like in our earlier staring match, Spider's hazel eyes bore into me. I shut mine tight now, but in my head, I could still hear his voice accusing, "If Romell is not in your bed, he's definitely on your mind."

Romell's face returned to mine. I felt his warm breath on my lips. He was panting, so was I. There was something in his eyes I'd never seen before. It scared me, because this part of me was supposed to belong to Spider. At Pookie's Jukebox, between those mirrors, it looked like there was two of me. Now, staring into Romell's eyes, I wished there were. He closed them and then moved in to kiss again, but I sealed my lips. Still, he licked, enticing me to open. He felt so good and smelled so good, but I pressed my lips tighter. I had to. My conscience was taunting me.

Romell backed up. It looked as if his eyes were reading mine. He smirked. I watched his eyes grow wide, him moisten his lips and then, wink. Now, I was totally confused. I had no clue what to expect until I watched his head take a slow descent. I lost my breath and almost suffocated as Romell gave me a gentle nibble where Spider's mouth had never been. But, if this were to happen, there would be no way I could claim *this* was involuntary. No, if Romell went down on me, I had to be a willing participant; there was no disputing that. And quite honestly, I was more curious than anything else, especially since I always had this inkling that sexually, Romell would just blow me away. So, deep down inside, there was this secret place in me that always longed for this, even if it were only just once. This was not Spider, but I always wanted to experience a man's tongue *there*. But then again, this wasn't just any man. This was Romell. He was the one collecting my panties in his teeth. This was Romell dragging them down my thigh. I was already tingling. This was Romell, not Spider. My panties were now at my ankles, and I didn't know what to do.

42

*I*T HAPPENED QUICKLY, BUT WHEN IT WAS OVER, Romell was on the floor. He groaned like I put a serious hurtin' on him. I always knew I had skills. But Romell was solid, all muscle. I'm no slouch, but realistically, I couldn't have hurt him if I tried. Romell was just overreacting, seriously overreacting. We were so close for so long that maybe our attempt to remain platonic was just staving off the inevitable. But, when and if things between us ever did turn sexual, this was also inevitable: something would happen that neither of us would ever forget. Romell just wasn't ready for my reaction. Quite frankly, neither was I.

My whole life, there had only been one kiss, one touch, one other body pressed to mine. There had only been one love. Well, maybe there wasn't just one *love*. Romell was in my past, in my dreams, and in my plans. So, Spider was right about that. Romell *was* on my mind. He was always in my thoughts, but he had never been in my bed, and that's why I slapped the shit out of him. Romell had my 99-cent-store panties down around my sister's shoes. I knew what was next, but I wasn't ready for it, and that's why I slapped the taste right out of his mouth. That noise cut through the air, bounced off the walls, and echoed. My hand hit the wall on the backswing, and now, my palm stung, and my fingers were throbbing. I shook my hand like it was rubber and then sucked my two middle fingers, two broken nails. I bit them off and spit them out. On my pinky, the chips in my polish had my airbrush looking like a Picasso, but that was the only thing I could think to do to prevent things from going any further.

Romell pressed his hand to his cheek and then examined his palm like he expected to see blood, all theatrics. Just like his staying on the floor was also theatrics. I didn't smack him to the ground. Romell was already down. He didn't expect to get slapped, so he lost his balance. He had no welts. He wasn't hurt. The only thing bruised was his ego. Now, he was trying to make me feel guilty. It wasn't working.

"Why didn't you just tell me to stop?" he asked.

I pulled my panties back up, instead of answering. When he was all over me, I was fighting with myself. I was horny, so if I had managed to utter the word "stop" at that point, it would have sounded more like I was begging for it.

"I can't believe you did that," Romell said, and he stood back up.

"I can't believe what you were trying!" I tucked in my blouse.

He stood in my face. "I'm *trying* to show you how much I care!"

My half slip was gathered somewhere; I reached up and snatched it back down. "I'm getting married!"

He grabbed my left hand and held it up. "That man ain't marrying you!"

That had long been the consensus from Mommy and Dawn, but I didn't pay them any mind. Now that those words were coming from Romell, my armor was pierced, but I refused to let it show. "Don't say that!" I pulled away from him and stepped across the rug to put distance between us. Then I faced him. "Spider is gonna put a ring around my finger any day now!"

Romell stepped closer, folding his arms. He dropped his head, squinting at me. "And, what if he doesn't?"

"I'll put a ring around his eye! But no matter what, I will never sleep with you!"

"Never?"

"Never! You will *not* turn me into another Rubbermaid in your refrigerator, Romell Ulysses Goodwin!!"

"What the hell is that supposed to mean?"

"You had a quickie with Jun Ko last night, Romell, and today, here you are pulling down my panties?"

"You were enjoying it! So, why fight it? You want this," Romell said, and I couldn't help but look down. He stepped closer, repeating, "You want this." Those words grew softer each time.

I backed into the wall. My body still felt the impression of his hands. I don't know why, but I started to shake and couldn't stop, so fidgeting, I pretended the purse, plastic bags, and folded poem scattered on the carpet had my attention.

"Look at you. You can't hold still. You can't even look at me." He stepped all the way up and boxed me in with both arms, leaving me squirming. In his frigid apartment, all I felt was his body heat. I turned my head, keeping my lips together. He leaned in, stroking his nose against my cheek and neck for a moment, and then he growled in my ear, "You want me bad, and you don't even have a clue how good I can make *you* feel."

I snapped my head back so fast I almost got whiplash. I looked him dead in his eyes. "Yeah, me and everybody else."

He backed up. "What's that supposed to mean?"

I walked over, snatched up my carryall, turned, and gave him the most evil look I could muster.

Romell hung his head for a good minute. Then slowly, he collected the two white plastic bags off the floor. I watched him pull a CD out of each bag and tuck them under his arm. He came to me, stuffed the bags into my purse, and looked in my eyes. "Don't you see? I want you."

All my life I wanted to hear those words from him. He never settled for anything less than a "dime," so to me, this meant I was unofficially inducted into the "pretty girl" club; but now, somehow, I wasn't even flattered. I snapped at him, "Can't have everything you want."

"You know you want me, too!"

"Romell, if you're not satisfied with ten women, I ain't fool enough to think you'll be satisfied with me. You can have your dimes; you just can't have all the others and me. I'll be a dime. But I refuse to be your penny!" Now, I felt tears; wiping them with the heel of my hand, I watched Romell's posture go limp. I didn't want to cry here in front of him, so I slung the strap of my bag over my shoulder and walked toward the door.

"Mia, wait," and it was strange; he sounded sad. I stopped in my tracks. "Stay, please? We don't have to do anything; we don't even need to be in the same room. I just really need your company right now."

His coaxing gave me more chills. He seemed sincere, but I still didn't turn around. I shook my head and continued to walk.

"Mia, please! Don't go. Stay even if it's just for a little

while." He rarely begged. I turned my head slightly, not wanting to look directly at him. Out of the corner of my eye, I could see him against the wall, head resting in the crook of one arm, while the other dangled. Something was bothering him. I could sense it. I wasn't sure if it was what had just happened or if it was something else, but *something* was wrong. I looked at the door only a couple steps away. That latch was calling me, sounding raspy just like Spider. I wasn't even supposed to be here. But, Romell needed me. Those few times he was vulnerable, I did everything in my power to make him feel better. I could do that then, because sex was never a threat. There was this invisible barrier between us: a line neither of us dared to cross. Frankly, I didn't know if I could comfort him now without crossing that line.

"Come on, Chocolate. Please."

His voice, now distraught, went straight through me. I dropped my head and sighed, ready to turn around. Then, reaching out for my hand, he said, "I promise I won't try anything." I knew him so well; *that* was enough to make me pick my head up, take steady steps, and close the door...on my way out.

43

*T*RAFFIC WAS LIGHT HEADING UP THE F.D.R. Drive. The air that blustered into the backseat blew my curls every which way, but I had no choice but to keep the windows open, sorry to be in the only yellow taxi with no AC. My sweaty body was sticking to the vinyl, but my mind, elsewhere, was way too distracted to focus; the map of Manhattan inches in front of me was actually a blur. A few times, I even caught myself unconsciously peeling back the edges. Sticker glue now coated the only halfway decent nail left on that hand. Out the window, a barge was coming down, now under the 59th Street Bridge. Moving slowly, it was barely breaking waves in the grey water. I could clearly see that because both the bridge and the barge were as big as day, but my mind was still where I left my fingernails, back at Romell's.

I promise I won't try anything. That would've worked for Spider, but then again, had Spider said that, it would not have been just another line. Spider never played games like that. If he said something, he meant it. He almost never made promises. He never had to. His word was good enough, especially since I had yet to catch him in a lie.

Romell, on the other hand, always kept a hidden agenda. Of all the men I'd ever known, he was the smoothest, but Romell wasn't always the smooth talker. Once upon a time, he was almost always at a loss for words. I had a smart mouth, so in high school, when he approached me with his 50 spiral-notebook-jagged-edged pages stapled together. A handwritten script full of pickup and rejection lines, it was the most pathetic thing *I* ever saw, but I understood Romell. Everything was a science to him, a formula that had to be figured out.

A little while? I know him. If things had gone Romell's way, Spider would not have seen me until morning. We

275

would have sat on that rug, talked, drunk something potent. Then, he would've claimed he needed a shower. *I promise I won't try anything,* top of page 27. *Nothing will happen that you don't want to happen,* bottom of page 27. Bottom of page 50, *I never said I was your man.* I shook my head, thinking. *That hard-on must've drawn blood from your brain. Hello! If you teach me your tricks, don't use those same tricks on me and expect them to work. Am I right or wrong? Outdated mating tactics. Typical. Who was he fooling with that?* Good thing I came to my senses. I was surprised he didn't follow me to the elevator, but I knew why he didn't. That ego took a beating. *Oh, well.* I knew he'd get over it sooner or later. Just like I knew if I didn't make it home before Spider, I'd have some serious explaining to do.

♥ ♥ ♥ ♥

I made it back to my building with light still in the sky. I love summer. A bright sky gave me a good enough excuse; I simply lost track of time. Ringing for the elevator, I looked over my shoulder to the stairwell. There, an orange Converse peeked out from around the corner. I walked over and sat down on the cracked step. Dressed in his Chicken Shack orange, Jeff was slumped forward, resting his head on his arms. His nest of light brown curls spilled over his knees, exposing the back half of his hair, which was faded to a hairline, squared across his pale, freckled neck. I nudged him awake.

He straightened out his body and yawned. "Damn, gurl. What hours do *you* work?"

I didn't answer that. "What brings you here?"

"I came to apologize," Jeff said smiling.

"I'm glad you decided to work things out with Spider," I said.

"Fuck him! It's *you* I wanna say sorry to." Jeff looked at me. My confusion must've registered on my face, because he continued. "Look, I realize all the times I was taking advantage, I was using *you,* and that ain't right. And, about what happened at Lola's, I'm sorry I shook you up like that."

"You didn't shake me up."

"Mia, your ass was shook."

"I wasn't afraid of you. I was afraid for Tee-Bo's safety. You broke all that damn glass when I had my baby in the room. So, if you're going to apologize, don't apologize because you think you scared me. Apologize because you put my child in danger."

"I hear you, and like I said, I really *am* sorry."

"Okay, Jeff. Just don't let it happen again. I know you're not coming up, so I guess I'll see you later," I said reaching to pull myself up.

"Wait!" Jeff said. "There's something else I wanna talk to you about."

"What is it?"

"Your sister."

"What about Dawn?"

"Yo, Mia. Ever since I met her at the hospital when Tee-Bo was born, I can't stop thinking about her. I had a long talk with her in the waiting room. She's got a good head on her shoulders, and her personality is just as beautiful as her face."

"Dawn's got two faces."

"Don't bad mouth your sister."

"Apologize to your brother."

Jeff rolled his eyes and spat through the banister into the stairwell. "Mia, I ain't dealing with none of them no more. I'm done! This thing with Pop's ashes is where I draw the line. Bad enough they did what they did to Lola."

"Who's they?"

"This crazy woman, Barbara, and Pop's wife, Mae Mae."

"Dr. Snyder? What did Dr. Snyder do?"

"She set Lola up, and Barbara tried to kill Lola."

"How did Dr. Snyder set Lola up?"

"She told Barbara that Lola slept with that crazy woman's husband."

"Well, did she?"

"Did she what?"

"Did Lola sleep with the woman's husband?"

"Don't matter! They were all supposed to be friends!"

"Friends?" Now it all made sense. That's why the woman in the melted picture at Dr. Snyder's looked so familiar. That was Lola when she was much younger.

"Yeah. And they cut my mother up bad. She's still suffering. She didn't deserve *that*."

I didn't know what to say. That was Lola in Dr. Snyder's wedding picture. Now, the whole situation made perfect sense. Dr. Snyder did say her friends call her Mae Mae, and Lola *did* call her Mae Mae. If Lola, Barbara, and Dr. Snyder were all supposed to be friends, and Lola was sleeping with both of their husbands, I can see why they flipped the way they did. Now, I understood why Dr. Snyder was so bitter. Maybe it was part guilt, but I still felt she needed to get over it; that was decades ago. I shook my head. There was more to this situation than I had realized. No one person gave me the whole truth. It had to be pieced together like my quilt, but I was willing to bet any amount of money that Barbara was Dr. Snyder's friend Babs. This situation went deep. Jackie may have pissed me off, but she was right about one thing: this wasn't any of my business. On that note, I decided to stay out of it. I looked at Jeff's sad, green eyes and shrugged. "I understand how you feel, and I'm sorry all that had to happen. But, you've got to realize they *all* made mistakes back then. So, it's best to just let the past be the past."

He shook his head. "It ain't that easy, Mia. I still don't know where Pop's ashes are."

"I understand, Jeff, but what can you do?"

"I don't know. I think I'll need me a blunt to answer that one." He looked at me and half smiled, then added, "But, Lola said I should just pray on it."

I stood and dusted off my skirt. "That sounds like a plan. Thanks for the apology, Jeff. Now, I really do need to get going."

"Wait, Mia! What about your sister?"

I shook my head. "Jeff, don't even waste your breath. My sister is a gold digger with a big ol' shovel."

"Maybe so, but not everyone would sign up to be your Lamaze coach." Jeff said. To be honest, Spider wanted to, but I was too afraid he couldn't handle it. After the stunt with the sonogram, I wasn't letting him anywhere near the delivery room. I looked back at Jeff. He pushed his long hair out of his eyes. They grew big, and their sparkle returned. "Dawn," Jeff paused, smiling. "She was there the whole time making sure you had everything you needed, and she kept those doctors and nurses on their toes. I see *that* as a beautiful thing."

I sighed. I knew Jeff was right about that, but I still preferred to be angry with her so I said, "When are you gonna cut that hair, Jeff?"

He twisted his lips. "You keep changing the subject on me! And what do you mean get it cut? I just got my hair cut."

"No, I mean a *real* haircut. You shouldn't be working around food with all that mess on your head. When are you gonna shave it off?"

"Never, I got all the hairnets I need."

"I still think that's unsanitary. I'm sure they're stressing you about your hair at work."

"Yeah," he sighed. "I think I'm gonna braid it. You know where I can get that done?"

"None of your baby mamas braid?" I snapped, watching him run his fingers through that mess of curls. He smiled again and shook his head. I smiled back. "I know a beauty salon."

"I ain't going up in a beauty salon to get my hair braided with a bunch of girlies."

"Trust me, Jeff. You're gonna *love* this salon. There's no place else like it."

He cut his eye at me in disbelief. "Can I get cornrows?"

"You can get crop circles if that's what you want."

He clapped his hands. "Aa–ight! What's this place called?"

I said, "Head to Toe." I didn't know if that was totally evil or the sweetest thing I'd ever done, but I could pretty much guess Dawn would cuss me out and Jeff would thank the hell outta me. I laughed, but even if Dawn did cuss me out, it would be worth it.

44

*B*ACK IN MY EMPTY APARTMENT, I SAT MY BAG down at the foot of the bed, dove onto the mattress, gathered an armful of pillows, and snuggled my chin into the pile. Alone and in silence, this was a good time to reflect. For a very long time, I felt things would work out just fine between Spider and me. Now, I wasn't so sure. I didn't know whether to fight or give up. I didn't know how Spider and I would work everything out; I just knew we had to. He was my whole world. Part of me felt like I was fighting a lost cause, but I had to fight, had to keep pushing, because that's what I lived for. If I didn't, there was nothing left for me to do but die. Fight or give up? Fight. I had no choice: my life depended on it.

With that on my mind, I pulled out my poetry journal, and wiped the tear from my eyelash. I cut my light on, crawled back into bed, and stared at the blank page; it was wide-ruled. I usually tried to camouflage my emotions with metaphors when I wrote in my journal. However, under the circumstances and as hopeless as I felt, hopelessness was what I wrote, even though my feelings were purged in poetic form.

We had yesterday.
Do we have tomorrow?
Should I celebrate?
Or drown my sorrows?
I wanna fight
When there's no wins,
Still I want you with me.

I'm hanging on
For dear life.
Nothing's working,
Now, I don't know what else to try.

We go through the motions
And pretend.
Is this the beginning of the end?

You're doing your thang.
I'm doing mine.
I wanna feel needed
And loved
Like the good ol' times,
But you ignore me.
That's how it's been.
Is this the beginning of the end?

Cold winter days,
Hot summer nights,
I felt so complete
In your arms,
As you held me tight.
Will you ever hold me
That way again?
Is this the beginning of the end?

I'd be okay
With what we had.
I realize our worst
Was not that bad.
Now, you have your goals.
I have my plans.
And, we're not connecting.
At least before
You and I,
We were talking
And not reading each other's minds.
Did you give up
When I gave in?
Is this the beginning of the end?

4 some reason,
4 some cause,
4 some strange reason,
It's just not obvious.

Please show me
What I don't see

What's the reason?
4 the problem

I closed my journal and slid it back between the mattresses. Then, I took a deep breath and sobbed. I hadn't felt this way in a long time. The last time I felt like giving up, I gave in. As a result, Tee-Bo was born. What was I going to do now? I didn't want to raise my son in a household with any other man, so I had to keep at it. Somehow, I had to draw strength from somewhere and keep on fighting for this relationship. *Spider didn't say I looked good. That's okay. Back in high school, he called me "Pretty Mia." I'll hold on to that. He doesn't tell me he loves me. That's okay, too. Back in high school, he told me he wanted love. Back then, he made me feel so special because he noticed me. I'll hold on to those memories and give this relationship all I have, once and for all.*

We were too close to getting married to stop now. Spider said we had issues. Now, I had to face them. One was money. That wasn't an issue now because of that big check he just received, and the record label just gave him a promotion, so I knew he finally would have a salary coming. Another issue was trust. He said I didn't trust him. That was hard. We just agreed to cut everybody else off, so I didn't have to worry about that issue, either. Then, there was loyalty. He felt I put everyone else ahead of him. That was funny; I had always gone out of my way to accommodate his family because I thought winning their approval would, in turn, satisfy him. But somehow, in the process, I managed to piss off everyone: his family and mine. Now, I didn't think there was anyone else I could even try to put ahead of Spider, except Tee-Bo. As for Romell, he had always been my very best friend. Now, we couldn't go back to being just friends. The curiosity alone would kill me. I had no choice but to leave him alone and make sure Spider never found out what almost happened. My silver link bracelet dangled from my wrist. It was funny how, after all the times Romell asked me to wear it, the one time I wore it when we were together, he didn't even notice. That was just as well. The engraved bracelet was a beautiful thought, but now I needed to let that go and focus on Spider and Spider only. I unfastened it and slid it back between the mattresses. So now none of our issues were issues at all. I just needed to convince Spider that we made progress so that we could hurry up and get married.

Spider didn't like me touching his old, suitcase record player, but I reached over and turned the radio on. Of course, every third station was playing "Be Happy." As much as I loved Mary J., I didn't appreciate her now. *"How could I love somebody else?"* How could I ever hear that again and not think of Romell? I needed to hear a song that reminded me of Spider. I changed the dial and heard James Ingram and Patti Austin, "How Do You Keep the Music Playing?" That was it. I left the station right there, lying on my bed, listening to the radio, until eventually, they played an old song by the Jones Girls, "You're Gonna Make Me Love Somebody Else."

I was singing or, better yet, screaming at the top of my lungs. I didn't hear Spider unlock the door or enter the apartment, but he walked into the bedroom with his dress shirt half buttoned revealing the scooped neck of his undershirt, his red tie in his hand. He cut his eye at me with a snide comment, "Who's the somebody else, your boyfriend downtown?"

This was exactly what I was trying to avoid. I massaged my temples, saying, "You're giving me a headache."

"Good. Now we're even. Sometimes being with you feels like a game of musical chairs," he said. "I don't wanna be left standing alone when the music stops."

I cut the music off. "Since you don't want to be left *standing* alone, when do you think we'll be *standing* at the altar?"

"I don't know about that. We have a lot of issues to work out. There are a lot of changes that need to be made."

"There you go again with these so-called issues. Why do you keep saying that?"

"Because, with you it's all or nothing. That's an issue."

Another issue? "I am not that bad. How is it all or nothing?"

He looked at me like I was crazy. Then he shook his head. "Why do you have such a problem with me having friends who are female?"

"Spider, once you start off sharing secrets, you end up sharing everything else."

"Is that what happened with you and Romell?" Now, he stared at me.

I was thinking. *Oh, damn. What does he know?* And even

though his hazel eyes felt like they were probing my conscience, I still managed to utter a cool, "Absolutely not."

"Then, what makes you so sure that'll happen with me? For all I know, you could've been with him tonight, but I trust you. I always have. So, it's about time you started trusting me."

Not the trust thing again. "Okay, Spider. I'll try, but it's hard. Especially since I know you were just with Pilar doing who knows what?"

"Mia, that was another all-nighter at the label; Pilar was just there taking the minutes."

"Why? Because you feel I didn't make time for you? Spider, you lied to me!"

"I didn't lie to you."

"You were supposed to go to your mother's. Instead you spent the night with some other girl? You lying, no good, cheating, low down, dirty, no count, trifling—"

"Mia, stop! Stop jumping to conclusions, and listen to me for once. You never listen to me, and that's another issue!"

"If it ain't one thing it's another! Okay! Okay, Spider. I'm all ears *now*. What do you have to say for yourself?"

"I didn't leave here to be with anybody else. I went to my mother's, but I couldn't get in. She changed the locks."

"She did?" Having those keys meant a lot to me. I sighed then looked up at Spider. "Is that why you called your mother and cursed her out?"

"Who told you?"

"Jackie called this morning," I said. Spider looked away as I continued, "I can understand you being upset because your mother changed the locks. But why did you have to go to that girl's house?"

"I didn't go to her house! I went back to the label. They were having an all-night brainstorming session. Pilar is the secretary, and she was there taking the minutes."

"The minutes?"

"Notes from the meeting. Afterwards, Pilar took the time to type my résumé for me."

I sucked my teeth. "It still seems like she was taking *my* time," I mumbled.

"That's because you assume the worst and don't pay attention to what I say."

"If I don't pay attention, it's because you don't say what I need to hear anymore. Back in high school...you called me Pretty Mia."

"I never said that."

"Yes, you did. You called me Pretty Mia the day you asked me to be your tutor."

"I would never have called you Pretty Mia."

I gasped, "Why the hell not?"

"Pretty Mia was the tall girl who wore that stink perfume and way too much makeup."

"If she wore too much makeup, why did you call *her* pretty?"

"Because she was always made up, even for gym class."

I shook my head. "Well, if I wasn't Pretty Mia, then who was I?"

"I would've called you Short Mia."

"I am not short!"

"I'm six-foot-five! You're short *to me!*"

"Okay fine, Spider, but that day, you *did* say you wanted love!"

"I didn't say that! I was fourteen years old!"

"Yes, you did! You told me if I was Mia Love you wanted me to be your tutor, and I asked you why. Now, I remember this like it was yesterday; your exact words were, 'Because, I want me a love'!"

"Huh-ha, huh-ha, huh-ha, huh-ha, huh-ha!" Spider was laughing so hard, tears were coming out of his eyes.

"What's so funny!"

"Mia Love is your name, stupid!"

When he said that, it hit me. *He meant "Mia Love," not "me a love." He was saying my name; he wasn't expressing an interest in me. He wasn't looking for love at all. All he had wanted was a tutor: He wanted me, Mia Love, to be his tutor, and that was all he wanted—a tutor.* I buried my face in my hands to try to stop myself from crying, but my nose was running. My face was all snot and tears. Had I known what he really meant back then, I would have acted accordingly. I wouldn't have spent so much time with him. Or made the first move to kiss him. And I definitely wouldn't have set my sights on him when my heart was set on Romell. Now, it made sense, why Spider never planned to marry me, and why he never told me he loved me. This relationship happened by accident. Not because he wanted me. A misunderstanding sparked the chain of events that led us to where we were at this point in our lives. So, what was reality now? If Spider never said that, who was he, and who was I?

All I'd ever done was try to be what Spider and everybody else thought I should be, but who was I really? Before Spider and I got together, my high school was my high school. After we got together, his college became my college, his major became my major, his life became my life, and his beliefs became my beliefs. My only goal was to love him the best that I could. I prided myself by believing a woman's love didn't get any better than mine. My only plan was for Spider and me to get married and buy a house. For that reason, I went out of my way to win his family over. To me, Spider became everything, my reason for existence, my life, and my future; he became the one I lived for. If what I based our relationship on didn't happen, what did we have? What was my purpose? Where was my life going? What would I cling to now?

Before, when he told me he never wanted to get married, my hopes were shattered. That was nothing compared to this. My entire life was all for nothing, especially since Spider found it so necessary to clarify; he gave no forethought to how this revelation would affect me. At the very least, he should've cared enough to spare my feelings.

Still with his tie in his hand, Spider leaned down and wrapped his arm around me. Now, after he'd just ripped my heart out and stomped on it, he felt the need to console a sistah. I could feel the knot of his tie in my back, "Mia, that don't matter. You know how I feel now."

I shook him off. "I know how you feel? How am I supposed to know you love me if you never say it?"

"Love is not what I say. Love is what I do."

"Love is what you do?"

"Yes. Every day I come home to you. I ignore all the flirting women out in the street, and I come home."

"You ain't doing me any favors, Negro! You come home to free room, board, housekeeping, laundry service, child care, and automatic bill pay. That's not love! That's convenience!"

"How could you say that? All right then, since this is about money, let me know what I owe you, and I'll pay you back."

"Fuck your money! If you really loved me, you would have married me a long time ago! Instead, you dangle that promise and use our issues as an excuse to try to change me!"

"Changes need to be made!"

"If you feel so many changes need to be made, start with your damn self!"

"Mia, we *do* have issues."

"So what! I'm tired of holding on and waiting for you to be totally satisfied. That'll never happen, so I'm not wasting any more time, Spider!"

"What?"

"I said I am not wasting any more time with you."

His brows squeezed together like an accordion. "You're not gonna waste any more time with me?"

"That's what I said!" I stomped over to the bedroom door and yanked it open. My hand went on my hip, and I pointed out. "Spider, you gots–ta go!"

He plopped on the bed. His tie fell to the floor, and he dropped his head in his palms.

So I screamed, "You heard me! Git!"

After a while, he rose from the bed and parted his lips, but there was a long pause before the words came out. "If that's the way you feel, then I don't wanna be here," he said, like he had a choice. He unclipped his keys from his slacks and tossed them on the bed. "I left the other set at work, but don't worry. I'll give them back to you." He looked around the room one final time. Then, he hung his head and sulked toward the door.

"Spider, wait!" I said. He stopped and faced me. I looked into his hazel eyes and watched the light wane as I said, "Don't forget to take that cat with you."

45

*T*HAT WAS THAT. I HEARD SPIDER'S FEET DRAG down the hall and Joy scamper inside the pet carrier. The front door squeaked open and then slammed shut. That's when I left the bedroom and made my way to the door. I peeked through the peephole. I didn't see Spider on the other side; he was gone. I put him out, and he was gone. Now, I started talking to myself. "I already know what Dawn's going to say about this but I did not just put Spider's ass out, because I'm stressed. I am not stressed! I put him out because I'm fed up. There's a difference. Stressed means I'm losing it. I'm not losing it; I'm just sick of him. I'm fed up; that's all. I'm fed up!" I locked all four locks, took a deep breath, and then threw my fist in the air. "Yes! That was invigorating! I should have a party."

I leaped onto the loveseat and smiled, staring into the ceiling's white stucco. It reminded me of Spider, nice to look at, but served no other purpose whatsoever. He wasn't a bad person; he was just hard to tolerate. One, he was withdrawn. I was always one to speak my mind. I needed communication. Not just complaints, I needed conversation. Talk to me about *my* interests. Ask me how *I'm* feeling. Ask me how *my* day was once in a while. He never did that. Two, he was insensitive. He didn't appreciate a thing I did. That made me feel my efforts were a waste. I was starved for a compliment, which led me to number three. As fine as he was, his greatest flaw was his lack of charm. He never flirted. He had the prettiest lips I'd ever seen on a man, but he never licked them, unless he was out of Chapstick. Those lips never whispered in my ear, sending chills through me the way Romell's did. And as dreamy as Spider's eyes were, he never winked; he just didn't do things like that. He didn't flirt. He didn't tease. His timing was always off. His idea of getting dressed was to throw on his jersey, khakis, and Hush

Puppies. He had no style, no sense of humor, and no zest for life. He was just...there. A gorgeous face, a six-foot-five-inch body, ripped with muscle, but not the least bit interested in sex on any day other than Saturday. And, that was Spider. What a waste!

Sadly, I was always aware of how Spider was. It was obvious that he was nonchalant the first time I saw him shrug his shoulders. It was reconfirmed every time I heard him say, "Fine, whatever." I just didn't know what to make of it; I couldn't tell if it was submission or disinterest. I recognized it as apathy around the same time I had also realized there was this wall guarding his emotions. But, by then, I was already in love with him; so of course, I made it my mission to be the one who would personally help him heal. But hey, I loved Spider. He had an innocence I had never seen in a guy; that was one of the reasons why I fell for him. I loved him, even though he was withdrawn, insensitive, and well...strange. He still had all his old toys. His Star Trek space ship, Evil Knievel, and Stretch Armstrong he kept in the original boxes. He wasn't particularly interested in cars. Only Spider could go to work, drive a Ferrari, a Bentley, and a Rolls, and still consider that a terrible day. He had strange ways and did all kinds of strange things, but I loved him. Because of that, if he couldn't marry me, at the very least, he should've appreciated me. I never got what I needed from him. After all these years, I had enough of that, but that was more than ten years wasted, and now, I had his baby to raise. So, I wondered. *What am I going to do now?*

All I knew was Spider. He was predictable. I knew his patterns. I knew his routines. I understood why he thought what he thought and did what he did. He rarely surprised me. I was only disappointed when I tried to turn him into what I wanted him to be. But I knew what he was. I had always known what he was; since I first met him in high school, he'd barely changed. We were together for over ten years, lived together, had a baby together, and even had a joint bank account: all this to break up. *This* was not supposed to happen. *We* were supposed to get married. No ifs, ands, or buts about it. Now, here I was twenty-six years old with no husband, no man, no money, no plan, a dead-end job, no degree, and a newborn baby. I couldn't help but think about that, at times out loud.

After all these years with Spider, I am not supposed to hunt for a new man. After ten years of ColecoVision, being his typist, and hiding his Hush Puppies, how am I supposed to move on to someone else? This is silly. I'm not going to even worry about that. I'll just do what everybody else does. I'll go out. If I meet someone that seems nice, I'll give him my phone number. Then, if I get to know him well enough and I find him attractive, eventually, I'll have sex with him. Just that thought gave me the heebee geebees; my skin started to crawl. *How am I going to sleep with a total stranger? I couldn't even get myself to sleep with Romell, and I've known him all my life. I couldn't sleep with Romell, and I've had a crush on him forever. And to top it all off, he's the sexiest man I've ever known. Still, I could not bring myself to give him some booty, Romell, of all people—sexy ass, lip-licking, panty-biting Romell. So how on earth was I supposed to climb into bed with some less than perfect stranger who, for all I know, could have a rusty butt and stinky feet? I can't. Romell is as sexy as they come. If I can't sleep with him, I can't sleep with anybody. I can't date. I've never been on a date before in my entire life. I've always been with Spider. So what the hell am I supposed to do now?*

Even if I could get myself to date, who would want me? I'm no striking beauty like my sister. And, unlike Jun Ko, I don't own a beauty spa and have a master's degree from Columbia. I am as regular as they come. I'm a collection agent, the only one at the agency who's been there for more than two years and has yet to advance to the legal department. Tears spilled down. *My ass is on written warning for taking so many days off to help folks out.* I chuckled and wiped my face. *I'm one step away from disciplinary and two steps away from suspension. There's nothing fabulous about me. I don't belly dance; I don't hang-glide; I don't have my pilot's license. So, who's going to want me? And what man in this day and age wants a ready-made family? Raising another man's child was popular back in the eighties. That was then, this is now. The days of the stepdad putting another man's child through college went out of style with the black leather blazers, tams, and skinny ties. So, I will never find a man, and I will never get married. I will be single until the day I die lonely, bitter, and depressed.* I punched my throw pillow and threw it across the room. That didn't help. I wished I were dead.

291

My eyes were teary, looking from the stucco down across my painted walls. *This blue is such a dreary color. This wall was supposed to be pink—cotton candy pink to be exact. There's no life to this color; it's a flat, ugly blue. I hate it. I wanted the color scheme for this room to be brown, cream, beige and cotton candy pink. I only painted it periwinkle because Spider thought the pink was too feminine. But the pink would have been the right color to soften up the browns from the leather chair and the chests, and that would have given this whole room just the right balance. I knew what the hell I was talking about. I had everything mapped out—soft color on the wall, accents throughout the room in a slightly darker shade of pink for coherence.*

"Periwinkle is damn near hospital blue; it's ugly." *I'll have to repaint. Then, if I do paint the walls over, I'll have to change the throw pillows. The flowers on the chaise are blue; I'll have to change that. And the crystal. I don't know when I'll be able to do all that. I work at the only company in America where the raises don't keep up with the rise in the cost of living. That's messed up, because Spider doesn't have a thing to worry about. He just came into money, and he just got a promotion. He's set. He can do whatever he wants. Me, I will always be short of either money or time, working two and three jobs to make ends meet, trying to be both mother and father to my son. Mommy did what she had to do. She worked it out, but I am raising a boy, that's not as easy. I will be struggling, but not Spider. Oh, no. Spider is going to go out and find somebody else, probably Asia or what's-her-name, Pilar. Who knows? He may even be with one of them right now. Whoever it is, he may not marry the bitch, but I'll bet he'll move her to a nice big house in the suburbs.*

That's okay though. My bills are paid. And if I ever need extra money, I could collect bottles. I sighed. *Going to the supermarket with a billfold full of coupons is bad enough; I don't want to be seen with black garbage bags full of dirty bottles. Then again, I could always wash them. No, the bottle thing is almost as bad as going down to the Willis Avenue Bridge with Windex and a squeegee. I could borrow a few dollars from Dawn, and I could always ask Romell for money. On second thought, I'd rather collect bottles.* I took a deep breath and slowly exhaled. *What am I worrying for? It's not like I'm in danger of getting evicted. Jeff got evicted and had to move in with Lola. Things are not that bad for me. But, if things got tough, I could always move in with Mommy.* I rolled my eyes. *I'd rather rent a room in Spider's basement. His house will be big enough; I'm sure. Forget that. I'd sell my tail. I wonder how the girls on Hunts Point are dressing. This is crazy; I am not going to sell my ass. Not like that's an option, anyway. I couldn't give it away with a coupon.* I closed my eyes tight and shook my head. "Stop it. Stop it! Everything is going to be fine."

Of course things are going to be fine…for Spider. He will be just fine in his house. I bet his house will have four or five bedrooms. A deck. A front lawn. A nice big pool in the back. A Jacuzzi. Yep, Spider will be just fine in that great big house of his. Poked out, my lips began to cramp from tension. I stretched them, moving them all around. Then, I sniffled. *That was supposed to be my house. Now, I'll never have a house. And, I'll never have a husband. That man took the best years of my life. I'll be stuck here, in this dump with my junkyard crap forever.* "Oh! I really wish I were dead." *It's not like I have anything to look forward to. I might as well get it over with right now.* "That's exactly what I'm going to do."

46

OW CAN I KILL MYSELF? THE ONLY QUICK AND painless way I know of is a gunshot to the head, but I don't know anybody who has a gun except Uncle Buster from Columbia, SC who's always shooting trespassers, so a gunshot is out. What are my other options? I could jump off a building, slit my wrist, or overdose on pills.

I am not jumping off the roof of this building. My building is only seven stories high. If I mess around and survive the fall, my ass will end up in a wheelchair. Then what? No, I am not jumping off this building. "Okay, then, I'll slit my wrist." I jumped up and went to the kitchen. I snatched open my utensil drawer, and pulled out the spatula, ladle, ice cream scooper, the nutcracker, bottle opener, meat tenderizer, the potato peeler, and my serving spoons. Now, all that was left in my drawer was the cutlery. I picked up my decorating knife and examined the rippled blade. I dropped it back in the drawer. *I ain't making no damn crinkle-cut French fries.* I grabbed my paring knife. Its blade had a straight edge, but it wasn't very sharp, so I chucked it back into the drawer. The sharpest knives I had were the tomato knife, the bread knife, and any one of my steak knives. My tomato knife would slice tomatoes paper-thin. My bread knife was so sharp; the first time I used it, I had given myself a nasty cut across the palm of my hand as I sliced a bagel. That taught me to stand the bagel on its end and slice downward away from my hand. So, I knew that knife was sharp. And as for my steak knives, even when I didn't tenderize, they sliced through meat like butter. I looked at the serrated edges of the bread and tomato knives. Then, I looked closely at the ridges and sharp stainless steel teeth of one of my steak knives and realized how drastic this was. "I ain't cuttin' myself for nobody!" I hurled the knives back into the drawer and slammed it shut.

All right, so what's in the medicine cabinet? I hurried to the bathroom and snatched it open. All I had was Motrin and Tums. "This won't kill me. And, if I mess around and try to overdose, I'll have to get my stomach pumped. That'll hurt." I closed my cabinet. *Okay, so I'm not going to kill myself, even though I know I told Mommy I couldn't live without Spider. I hung on for so long, because I felt without him I'd have nothing else to live for. Spider is fine, but not fine enough to cause myself any physical pain.*

I stormed into the bedroom. Seeing Spider's cluster of cologne bottles on the dresser, I knocked them across the room. Tears made their way down my cheeks again. *That ain't hurting Spider; I bought those.* I looked at his suitcase record player in the corner. The first time he saw me get too close to it, he had a titty attack. He snapped at me, "Don't touch that!" Well now, I marched myself over to his side of the room and knocked his little record player right to the floor. It came down with a crash and the top popped off. I sucked in a deep breath and blew hard. Now, I felt somewhat better. But still, I climbed onto my bed and cried some more.

Why am I so upset? It wasn't like I was happy with him. He didn't appreciate me. He was a jerk. We didn't kick back and enjoy each other's company; he frustrated the hell out of me. I didn't look forward to the time I spent with him. I enjoy my time with Romell. Romell's easy to talk to. I can talk to him about anything. I've always gotten along with him. He appreciates me; he tries to take care of me to the point where it almost sickens me sometimes. I took another breath. *And as far as charm goes, Romell oozes it. I thought I couldn't live without Spider. It's okay, though; I still have Romell.*

I laughed. *If Romell knew how I felt right now, I'm sure he would say something to make me laugh. Then, he'd find some subtle way of telling me how wrong I am. He lets me vent, and unlike Dawn, I don't have to worry about him repeating anything I say. He's my best friend in the whole wide world. And, Romell is the only one who calls me Chocolate. Chocolate Love.* I smiled. *Maybe, that's not such a bad idea. I did have that dream about him when I was twelve and all the other ones after that. Actually feeling his lips on mine was way sweeter than anything I'd ever dreamed. That kiss was a sugar rush. We were so close to doing it, too; he had my panties in his teeth. And Romell is so...sexy—his voice, his walk, his eyes, his skin; the way he smiles, winks, and moistens those lips. Sexy?* I laughed again. *He's scrumptious.* I now wiped tears from my face. *Crying...in bed—this is not the way I am going to spend the rest of my evening. If I must cry, I might as well put my tears to good use. If I spend tonight in bed, better Romell's than mine. And, I know his sexy ass is going to be all over me.*

I picked up the phone and dialed his number. As soon as Romell answered, I said, "It's over."

"What's over?"

"Spider and I broke up. He just left."

"He'll be back tomorrow."

"No, he's not coming back!"

"Trust me, Chocolate. He'll show up in the morning."

"What makes you so sure?"

"Only a fool would let a good thing slip away, and Spider Snyder's no fool."

"That's what you think! It's over! And, I don't want him back! Ever!"

Romell yawned, then said, "You say that now, but you two are gonna work it out." Not getting the reaction I'd anticipated, I opened up and let loose a wave of tears. Once my sniffles slowed to a steady rhythm of gentle sighs, Romell sighed, too and said, "Don't cry, Chocolate."

"Don't tell me not to cry! If anything, offer me your shoulder."

He paused, but then he said, "All right. If my shoulder is what you need, you're welcome to it."

"Okay," I quickly agreed. "I'll be right down." After I hung up, I took the fastest bath in history. I jumped in and out of the tub sloshing apricot-scented, oily water onto the bathroom floor then took slippery steps back to the bedroom. In a frenzy, I yanked my dresser drawers open and sifted through heaps of bras and panties. Thanks to Mommy's priceless advice on feminine hygiene, all my panties were cotton. The only decent bras I owned were nursing bras— ugly, white, orthopedic-looking nursing bras. None of this would be as enticing as a red, lace thong. Even Dr. Snyder had a sexy nightie. I owned nothing that was lacy, silky, satin, or see-through. *I could've sworn I had a plain black bra somewhere.* Rummaging through the odd assortment of scarves, wraps, and belts in my bottom drawer, I stumbled across my hot pink bikini bathing suit. I stretched the bikini top over my exploding breasts. Having missed so many feedings, they were sore and by now probably two cup sizes larger. The teeny, tiny, bikini top didn't look like it had enough fabric to cover the girls, but it was better than nothing. I slid into it. Then, I pulled out my one pair of Daisy Dukes and held them up. When Dawn insisted on buying these shorts for me, I looked at her like she was crazy. I swore I would never wear them. Now, I snatched off the tag. It was funny how never could happen so soon.

I tipped into Romell's, wearing a fresh coat of makeup among other things. His gaze traveled down my white tank top with my pink bikini strap peeking out, down my well-oiled, exposed legs all the way to the pointy tips of my pumps. He cocked his head and squinted. "Why are you wearing heels at this time of night?" he asked.

My voice steeped with innocence. "They match my bag."

I expected him to walk behind me so that he could check me out; he didn't. He shrugged instead and stepped quickly into the living room. He sat down on his sectional. I strolled over, and sat beside him. Leaning closer, I tried to cross my legs. The stiff denim of my shorts was gathering into my feminine parts and cutting off the circulation in my thighs as I tried to swing my leg over. I gave up that thought, returning my foot to the floor; but now, my greased legs stuck to the cold leather cushion. I shifted to the side and tried to slide a little closer to Romell—an attempt to snuggle on this sofa of his. The next thing I knew, the section I was sitting on tipped over; I had slipped. Friction between my skin and the leather caused a noise about as subtle as a blast from a whoopee cushion, and now, my body was wedged between the seats, caught in an entanglement of leather and elastic that was mashing my already sore breasts. I immediately looked up at Romell. I could tell this position was doing little for my sex appeal, but to make this seem less awkward, I flashed a smile. Romell didn't even crack one; so, ignoring the pain in my breasts, I struggled free and made myself comfortable on the floor where he soon joined me.

"You seem to be feeling better," he said.

"Not yet," I said. I unbuttoned my shorts, zipped them down, and let out a sigh of relief.

He straightened and inched away. "What are you doing?"

"The shorts are tight. I could hardly breathe." That was

298

an honest answer, but Romell still cut his eye at me suspiciously for a moment. Then he wrung his hands; his shoulders relaxed as he leaned forward. Through the fabric of his tight, white tank, the tiered muscles in his back were clearly defined. I sipped a breath and hissed. Romell whipped his head around. Now, his eyes were on me, so I sniffled. "Romell," I said. I then inhaled, releasing a deep sigh. "Why don't you play some music?"

He picked the stereo remote off the marble cocktail table. "What's good?" he asked.

I thought about our conversation at Pookie's Jukebox and smiled. I answered, "'Right Here'? 'Downtown'."

He responded quickly. "Chocolate, I'm not even going there with you. Not this time. Now, what do you wanna hear?"

I fought the urge to blurt the next thought that popped into my head: "*I Wanna Sex You Up*." Instead, I said something a little more subtle, "You can play some Marvin Gaye, Romell. 'I Want You'."

He shook his head, clicked the remote, and the ballad, "Dry Your Eyes," filled the room in stereo-surround sound. Swaying with the music, I eased my way to Romell's side, snuggled up, and rested my head on his shoulder.

The instant I wrapped my arm around his waist, he shut the power off and I slapped my own thigh in frustration. "Why'd you turn it off?" I shouted.

Once again, he inched away. "That's all you need to hear."

We locked eyes. I batted my lashes, moistened my lips, and panted, "I know The Deele."

"Yeah?" Romell snapped, "Then, you also know 'Two Occasions' played out." He tightened his lips. "You turned me down! Remember? Now, what do you want from me?"

Obviously, my subtlety wasn't working. Since he was challenging me to be direct, I obliged. "I want some TLC. 'Ain't Too Proud to Beg.' How about 'If I Was Your Girlfriend?' Hell, right now, I really want the 'Red Light Special!'"

"Stop it, Chocolate." He looked away, hung his head, and pressed a button on his remote. The song that played this time was the a cappella version of "If I Ever Fall in Love."

I sucked my teeth. "Oh! So, now you wanna play Shai!"

He giggled, but his eyes were moist when he looked back at me. "Mia, take your ass home."

Wow. My eyes brimmed with tears. These were real. "I

can't go home now."

Now he looked into my eyes. I was sure he noticed my tears, but still he shook his head, pointed to the door, and said, "Take your ass somewhere else; that's up to you, but you can't stay here." He stood up and cocked his head to the side. I waited for him to give me the fuck-you nod, but he didn't. So, for a moment, I just stared at his silhouette against the backdrop of his charcoal walls. Then, I focused on the bridge of his nose and his moistened lips that were now pursed in aggravation. I looked down, and I paid particular attention to his muscles, noting the pattern of the veins in his arm and shoulder. The cotton tank, stretching across the expanse of his chest, was on the verge of bursting at the seams, but it hung loosely at his waistline, revealing his dark brown flesh and the silky hairs that were always visible right over the elastic of this particular pair of cotton shorts. *He's not wearing underwear, again, but that doesn't matter.* I sighed and continued to record his every detail down to the grey carpet fibers between his toes. Then, I looked back into Romell's squinted eyes. He scratched his head and said, "What?"

My answer was solemn. "Nothing." This was the second time he made me feel like two cents. I started to say so. But now, that didn't matter, either. I stood, grabbing my purse and slowly walked toward the door. "Goodbye, Romell. Thanks for being *such* a good friend."

"Don't take this the wrong way," he said.

Without turning around, I said, "Too late for that now."

47

*H*OW ELSE WAS I SUPPOSED TO TAKE IT? LIKE I told Romell, I couldn't go home. I couldn't go home now or ever again. Nothing would be the same. There was nothing there for me now. I had failed...at everything. I stepped through the double glass doors of the sky lounge into the moist heat outside and took a good look. Scattered clouds stretched through the evening sky like tulle. In the still wind, somehow all drifted southeast—all, except a dense plume looming above. My heels clicked with each step across the paved walkway, until I reached the stone fire pit at the other end. The sun was long gone, and there were no stars; the moon was nowhere to be seen. Even searching the clouds, I didn't see any blurred circle of light or any portion of the moon, just darkness. Off in the distance as far as I could see, more darkness was closing in, making the flattened skyline of Queens resemble an industrial graveyard.

I took a deep breath, inhaling muggy air seasoned with salt from the East River. Then, I kicked my shoes off and knelt on top of the fire pit, hoisting myself up to get a better view over the concrete wall. My heart felt like it was twice as large; it was exploding out of my chest in heavy thumps that throbbed even more than my now rock-hard breasts. The porous concrete felt scratchy against my arms, but bracing myself, I peered all the way down. There were no obstructions. It would be a straight drop. I returned to my feet, picked up my pumps, and took a deep breath. Now, it was time to work up the nerve to do this.

I stepped out of the shadows toward a lounge chair that sat directly beneath a lamppost a few feet away. There, in the light, I dropped my pumps and then sat on the edge of the chair's beige cushion. Reaching into my carryall, I immediately pulled out a pen; I had to fish around for paper. Feeling everything else—my wallet, tangled headphone wires,

301

keys, the plastic bags from the record store Romell and I went to—I didn't feel one scrap of paper. All I needed was a tiny piece. I looked into one of the plastic bags, hoping it had a receipt in it among the CDs. It did. I pulled it out, placing it on my thigh. I was about to scribble on the front, until I took a look at it. Strangely, it had an itemized list of titles that caught my attention: *Ready to Die, Xscape, Jump, Right Here.* How appropriate. I paused for a moment then looked up. With a deep breath, I mumbled, "I just can't believe this is the end." That said, I flipped the receipt over to the back and began to write. My pen moved across the tiny white square leaving a teeny, blue ink trail of script to mark my last words:

> *So much for today*
> *There is no tomorrow*
> *Too many mistakes*
> *And too much sorrow*
> *Why should I fight*
> *When I can't win*
> *I just can't believe this is the end*

Those tiny words trailed all the way down to the bottom, all the way to the very corner. I flipped the receipt back to the front and read the itemized list once again: *Ready to Die, Xscape, Jump, Right Here.* My hand started shaking. I reached back into my carryall for the other receipt. I needed to write something that would serve as my will. I fumbled around inside the next plastic bag. Pinned beneath a shrink-wrapped, jewel case, there it was—the tiny slip of paper. I pulled it out and placed it on my thigh. My mind drew a blank. And then, I realized I didn't own anything worth anything. My whole wardrobe was outdated. I only wore costume jewelry and sterling silver, and every stitch of furniture I owned came from a thrift store. I took a deep breath and flipped the receipt over. There was an itemized list there, too. I couldn't believe what it said. In laser sharp text were two titles in this order: *Keep on Moving, Back to Life.* That was strange. A tear rolled down my cheek. I flipped that slip of paper from side to side in disbelief, over and over again as if the printing would somehow change. *Was this a sign?* I flipped both receipts, now rereading all sides. Romell bought these CDs back in the record store. We were talking about these very same songs earlier. I closed my eyes, trying to convince myself that this was a coincidence.

I pulled my CD player out of the bag and put on my headphones. I stuffed the two receipts into the inside pocket of my carryall bag, stood, took a deep breath, and walked barefoot toward the fire pit. Then, I reached inside my bag for some exit music—the one CD that would surely urge me to do this: "Jump." I fumbled through the CDs in my carry all; I didn't see it. I turned around and sat back down on the lounge chair. I stared up into the sky, but still didn't see one star. The cloud over me was not moving. I took another deep breath. Dumping the contents of my purse, I now searched for "Jump" or "Back to Life." Either one would make up my mind one way or the other, but neither was in the bag. I shook my head.

Standing back up, I reached over to the potted tree behind the chair. It looked like a small pine, but it was trimmed in such a way that the branches spiraled up. I pulled the carryall off my shoulder and hung it onto the tree. Then, I picked up the *Ready to Die* CD. Peeling plastic wrap away from the jewel case, I noticed the picture of the baby on the front. "Why in the hell would they put a baby on the cover of a CD called 'Ready to Die'? That is sick and twisted!" I stared at it. He was such a big, beautiful baby. Huge Afro. I smiled. My little Tee-Bo was still scrawny, long but scrawny, and I was supposed to be his next meal. My tears came again. I grabbed my purse and planted myself on the chair's cushion.

Okay, so now I wouldn't do anything stupid, but I still wasn't ready to go home just yet, so I snapped "Keep on Moving" into my CD player. Funny, I always thought the title was "Keep *It* Moving." I shook my head and turned the volume way up. I was wrong about the title, so instead of getting lost in the bass line once again, I paid attention to the words.

> *It's our time*
> *Time today*
> *The right time is here to stay*
> *Stay in my life*
> *My life always*
> *Yellow is the color of sunrays*

The right time is here to stay, stay in my life, my life always. I didn't even know those CDs were in my bag before, but I

303

listened to this song now. The words were so uplifting; I wished I paid attention to them sooner. As soon as I heard Soul II Soul sing the lyrics, *"Find your own way to stay,"* I completely burst into more tears.

48

*M*Y BATTERIES DIED. I DON'T KNOW EXACTLY when I fell asleep, but it was a cold, wet drop on my forehead that woke me. I smeared it from my face, wiped my eyes clear, and opened them, facing west. I gave myself a good stretch and noticed how the sky's once deep, dark blue faded into grayish purple clouds and then this band of red in the east. I took my headphones off and stood. Across the river, I saw the sun. Emerging through the crimson tint, it was orange. With each passing moment, it became brighter and brighter. This was the first time I'd ever seen a sunrise and right now, Queens looked like heaven. Nothing mattered but these colors on the horizon. Only God could make something this beautiful. It was then that I realized: when I came into this world I didn't have Spider or Romell, and when I leave this world I won't have Spider or Romell. More and more drops hit me, but this was the thought that was on my mind as I stood there watching a canopy of light rise and the sun disappear into the haze. Eventually, I looked down. Cool drops speckled my arms. Light rain also speckled my bare feet. Up above me, the clouds were dense. The air was only a tad cooler than it had been the night before, but a strong wind appeared out of nowhere, and I could actually see it blow; dust, gum wrappers, and cigarette butts gathered into a vortex of debris that swirled high and swept across the roof deck. And then I heard the crack of thunder. This was going to be a heavy downpour. I shielded my spiral curls with my arm, gathered my things, and made tracks back inside.

Not even two minutes later, I had my key in Romell's cylinder. I unlocked it and tipped in. I was only stopping in for an umbrella. Romell had an umbrella stand in his hall closet. It was tall and ebony with hand-carved, tribal warriors. His closet was all the way past his living room near his bedroom. I walked to the back quietly. The wheels of the closet's mirrored door squeaked in their track as I slid it open. Romell's umbrella stand had only one bleached wooden handle extending from it. I pulled the umbrella out; it was pink with a D&G logo etched into a metal plate on the handle. One of his girlfriends must've left it. I put it to the side, reached my arm all the way down inside the wooden tube, and felt around the bottom. There was nothing else in there, so I decided to check his closet floor. I got down on my hands and knees and fumbled around for a moment, seeing only galoshes, suitcases, a few Barron's and Pass Perfect study guides, Romell's gym bag, his briefcase, and his laptop—no umbrella. So, I backed my way out, stood, and then slid the closet door closed. In the mirror, I saw Romell behind me, bare-chested and dumbfounded, whispering, "What are you doing here?"

"I was looking for an umbrella," I said. "I found one, so now, I'm leaving."

"You can't take that one."

"The hell I can't!"

"Shhh! Lower your voice."

"Why are you whispering?"

"I have company."

My jaw dropped. Then, I whispered, "Who?"

"Akasma."

"That snooty bitch!"

Romell grabbed me by the elbow and whisked me through the living room all the way to the passageway by the front door. I shook my arm out of his grasp. "You trifling Negro."

"Why am I trifling?"

"You wasted no time gettin' that bitch up in here."

"Don't stand here and call Akasma names. You don't even know her."

"I know who she is! She's the one with the long, dark, wavy hair and the cleft in her chin; she wears the six-inch, patent leather pumps and Chanel sunglasses. The flight attendant. I know exactly who she is. She was coming to visit you once and saw me leaving your apartment. She asked me if I worked for you! She's snooty! At least Jun Ko's friendly! Jun Ko's a genuinely nice girl; I can understand why you'd want to be with *her*!"

"Wait a minute! You hate Jun Ko, too!"

Now, I couldn't look at him. He had every reason to believe that. I backed against the wall, folding my arms across my chest. "I don't *hate* Jun Ko. She's a nice girl," I grunted.

Romell stood in front of me. "If Jun Ko's such a nice girl, why don't you like her?"

"I have nothing against Jun Ko."

"Chocolate, any time I mention her name your whole demeanor changes. Now, tell me why."

I squeezed away from him. "I don't know, Romell." Hanging the umbrella's handle on my arm, I swung his door open. "You're smart. You figure it out."

In the hall, dragging my feet across the tweed carpeting to the elevator, I was in tears. To make matters worse, Romell stepped into the hall behind me, even though he was barefoot and wearing nothing but paisley, silk boxers. He looked at me with sad, sorry eyes and said, "Chocolate."

I wiped the blur from mine and looked at him. "What?" I said.

"That's Akasma's umbrella."

I looked at the logo on the handle. "Dolce. It figures." Now, even more tears welled up in my eyes and spilled over, running down my face. I stiffened my quivering lips and handed Romell the umbrella.

"Chocolate, why are you crying?"

"I'm crying, because I feel like two cents *waitin'* for change." I turned away and smacked the down button. Then, shook my head and began to chuckle.

Romell drew a deep breath. "Now, why are you laughing?"

"I'm laughing, because this is the third time you made me feel like two cents waiting for change, and you still haven't paid me my dollar."

"I don't owe you a dollar."

The elevator door opened, I stepped inside, and turned around. "Yes, you do."

"No, I don't, because if I owed you anything, I would have given it to you."

I pressed the lobby button and rolled my eyes at him. The doors were closing just as I said, "Wanna bet?"

In the elevator I sucked my teeth. The noise was so loud; it triggered a letdown reflex. Milk leaked into my bikini top and seeped through my transparent tank in wet, pink circles. I folded my arms across my chest until I'd rushed through the lobby and out of the building into the dim, early-morning light and the hot, salty breeze. Overhead, dark clouds ruffled the sky.

I hurried to the corner. *That was dumb; coming to Romell's was a dumb move. Why would I even try to jump from a man who doesn't believe in marriage to a man who doesn't even believe in relationships? That was stupid. Stupid. Stupid. Stupid.* The rain began to come down harder as I stood there flailing my arm to hail a taxi. I heard thunder. My once crisp spiral curls were now drooping. I reached into my carryall for one of the record store's plastic bags as that was to be my only head cover. The plastic bag ripped when I pulled it out. I grunted in absolute frustration, threw my carryall to the ground. *I don't know why I didn't go over that wall.* No sooner had that thought entered my mind than I heard the burst of thunder and the clouds opened and dumped on me. Not a sprinkle or a drizzle, this was torrential, whipping through the air in horizontal patterns; I was almost drowning in it. In an instant, First Avenue was a river, and both empty and occupied taxis whizzed by, plowing through. Now, I snatched up my carryall and reached for the only plastic bag I had left. Just as I shook it out to lay it over my head, I heard a screech and looked up; a taxi from the center lane swerved and skidded to an abrupt stop right in front of me with a splash. Nasty, dirty street water was in my eyes, all up my nose, and all in my mouth. And, what was left of my spiral curls was now sliding down my back in waves. I stamped my feet and hollered, "Oh, I'll be—"

49

*O*KAY. *I NEED TO START WATCHING WHAT I SAY.*
It dawned on me. Mommy warned me several times to stop saying, "I can't live without Spider." The problem was not only did I continue to say it, but I also believed that, just like I believed I couldn't live without Romell. That's what compelled me to do the things I did that led me all the way up to the roof of Romell's building. I once thought I had it all together. Everyone else seemed to be the problem: Spider was cold; Romell, superficial; Mommy, overbearing, Dawn, gossipy. Now, I recognized what was wrong with my life was not the fault of Dr. Snyder and Jackie, Mommy and Dawn, or even Spider and Romell; it was a direct result of my own thoughts and actions. I made my own decisions. There was no one to blame but me. *I* needed to change. I needed to change what I said and did because I *didn't* have it all together. If being on that roof deck brought me nothing else, it brought clarity.

Riding home in the taxi that had just splashed the hell out of me, I was a puddle, but I thought about what was right in my life. Spider had his way of being cold and inconsiderate, but he stayed with me, and there were many times when he had every reason not to. Romell was cocky and superficial, but if he and I never spoke again in life, I would still have a lifetime of memories to smile about. My sister—pain in the ass that she was—would always tell my secrets; however, there was never a problem I presented to Dawn that she didn't try to help me solve in one way or another. Dawn couldn't keep a secret, but she would always have my back. And, even though Mommy was overbearing, I never once doubted her love. And nobody was as on point with advice as she was. So, my sister's adage was right— Mommy *was* almost always right, and she ain't never lied.

Water was still dripping off of me when I stepped into my

living room. I didn't change out of my wet, nasty clothes; I didn't sit down. Before I did anything, I plugged my phone back into the jack and called Mommy. Once I heard her voice, I immediately apologized. "I'm sorry, Mommy. I'm sorry for hanging up on you. I was under a lot of stress."

"I knew you had to be if you could get flip and hang up on *me* like that."

"And I'm also sorry for not listening when I should have. You were right."

"What's wrong?"

"Why?"

"You sound like you were crying."

I hadn't shed a tear since I left Romell's. How she could still sense that I had been crying was beyond me. I took a deep breath. "I had a rough night, Mommy. Spider and I broke up."

"I am sorry to hear that. Do you want to talk about it?"

"Not now. I'll talk to you about it later, but you *were* right."

Mommy sighed. "Mia, I don't tell you what I tell you so that I can be right. I want the best for you. That's why I'm still upset about you not graduating, not because I wanted to show off. I rented a car and drove six hours in the rain to get to D.C., and when I got there and saw you were in the audience with me instead of on stage getting your diploma, I was flabbergasted. I'm still flabbergasted."

"Yeah, I know. I'm sorry."

"And I'm sorry for slapping you," she said. "That was uncalled for. But, try to understand: I've made too many mistakes in *my* life to raise a couple of fools."

Tears trickled down my cheeks. Now, I could see how she felt, and I understood why Mommy was so full of unsolicited advice. Experience brings lessons, and if nothing else, our mistakes make us experts on the subject of what not to do. After all I'd just been through, if I saw Tee-Bo on the verge of making some of the same mistakes I made, I would be just as unrelenting as she was. I wiped away my tears, and I sniffled quietly, but nothing got past Mommy. "Are you okay, Mia?"

I could hear the concern in her voice. "I'm fine now," I insisted, but I wasn't fully convinced myself, so I knew I had to cut *this* conversation short. "Talk to you later, Mommy. I wanna catch Dawn before she heads out."

"I wouldn't call her if I were you."

"Why not?"

"She's a little upset with you right now."

Now, I was confused. "What did *I* do?"

Mommy chuckled and said, "Right after you hung up, I called Dawn and asked her what the hell you were talking about, so Dawn went on to explain how soon Kyle is supposed to be getting his divorce. She rambled on for about twenty minutes, before I let in that you never told me Kyle was married."

"Ooh!" I giggled. "She told on herself, huh?"

"Yeah, so I'm warning you; if you call her for any reason before her brooding period is up, expect to get cussed out."

"Understood. I guess I'll have to wait to apologize to *her*. Love you, Mommy."

"One more thing, Mia. How did you get Tee-Bo's rash to go away?"

"The rash?"

"Yeah. What did you do for it?"

"There's a method with quite a few steps. Why?"

"It's back, and Carole said cornstarch isn't working. So, you'll either have to explain to her how to get rid of it, or go get him and take care of it yourself."

I sighed. "No problem, I'll pick him up tomorrow night after work. I might even pick him up tonight. Either way, I'll call Aunt Carole later and let her know for sure. I'll take care of it, Mommy."

"I know you will. I'll talk to you later, Mia. Call me if you need me."

After Mommy hung up, I sat there on my leather chair for a minute with both hands at my temples. *Man. I had totally forgotten to tell Aunt Carole what to do for Tee-Bo's skin. Dawn was right; I was stressed. Normally, my main concern is Tee-Bo. Lately, it seems like Tee-Bo's the last thing on my mind. And to think, I was even contemplating suicide.* I shook my head. *I'll never do that again. I don't care what I'm going through. I will tough it out, because if my life is for no other purpose, it's to be Tee-Bo's mother.* Thinking about that, I had to admit; despite all the breastfeeding, diaper changing, and all around caregiving, the reality of me being a mother never fully sank in. Somehow, it still wasn't real to me. But I had to think of it this way: as much as I craved Mommy's attention growing up, now, Tee-Bo deserved mine.

311

I don't like to think about it or talk about it, but I used to reach into the medicine cabinet and take some of Mommy's pills. I took the very first Humphrey pill because I thought they were vitamins. It made me burp for like fifteen minutes straight. After a while, I felt nauseous, my stomach knotted up real tight, and began to cramp. And then, the room felt like it was spinning. My stomach started retching, and I was gulping back this bitter taste until I couldn't hold it down anymore. I thought my stomach was empty, but I threw up anyway, and when I did, I saw what looked like yellow paint. That was bile, a taste I'll never forget. To this day, I think bile is the worst taste ever. But, when Mommy came home, she came straight into my room, sat on the edge of my bed, and put my head on her lap, rubbing my back and telling me everything was going to be okay. I forgot all about that bitter taste and remembered the attention I got. She asked me what I ate for lunch, and I told her, but I didn't mention a thing about that pill. And since I knew the pills wouldn't kill me, every now and then, I'd pop another one, two, sometimes three. Dawn always thought I was faking, but was convinced I was bulimic after watching some ABC Afterschool Special. But I was already skinny. I wasn't trying to make myself skinnier. Really, I just loved the fact that the chaos of everyday life would stop. I'd stay home from school, and Mommy would take off from work just for me. And when I'd stop puking, Mommy would make me ginger tea steeped from the actual root and a bowl of stewed chicken and noodles. And I loved stewed chicken and noodles. I think as a result of taking those pills, I got my first period two years before Dawn got hers, and she's three and a half years older. At ten years old, seeing blood in the toilet, I thought those pills burned a hole in my intestines. Mommy and I hadn't had "the talk" yet, so I called Romell first, thinking I was dying. Hysterical, I told him all about the Humphreys, and that I didn't want to die. I was only taking them to make myself sick for a little while. After the scare was over, he made me promise not to do "that" again. He never labeled it, but he still treated me like the least little thing that upset me would have me reaching for pills.

Anyway, that's something I chose to put behind me, but if getting attention was that important to me, I really should've been more mindful of Tee-Bo. He should've been my main concern. Instead of what was really the case, wanting to hurt Romell as badly as I felt he hurt me. There I was ready to throw myself off a building, and he called the next woman over. And, after the worst night of my life, Romell threw me out into the pouring rain, and left me ass-out with no umbrella. But, men will be men. I couldn't concern myself with Romell or who he decided to sleep with. My sole purpose was not for me to be here for Romell or Spider. It was time for me to worry about my son. Life is much too precious.

My crocodile pumps were cold and soaked down to the soles. I kicked them off and snatched them up by the heels. Making my way down the hall, my damp feet slapped against my old, wood floor. As soon as I approached the bathroom, I caught a whiff of that apricot oil along with something musty. I tried not to look, but couldn't help sneaking a peek anyway. The bathroom rug was soaked, so it was wet rubber I smelled. My clothes were still on the floor where I dropped them; makeup was all over the place. What disgusted me most was a soggy bar of Ivory soap still floated atop bathwater murky with soap scum, because I didn't bother to drain the tub before I left. I shook my head. That task was too overwhelming right now.

But, I was even more overwhelmed when I pushed my bedroom door open. I stepped over my towel into the room. Belts and scarves, panties and bras—everything was everywhere. I had forgotten I'd left in such a rush. Then, I looked into the mirror. The makeup was completely washed off my face. Through my tank top, my pink bikini was totally visible, as were my hard nipples. And, my spiral curls...I gave my hair a squeeze and water just ran from them. I looked like I'd just returned from Claremont Pool after being thrown in fully dressed. I flung my carryall to the floor. *I'm a mess. This place is a mess. There's no way I'm going to work today. That agency could write me up if they wanted to. At this point, I don't even care if they put me on suspension; I hate bill collecting, anyway.*

With a sigh, I brushed the heap of underwear away and flopped my soggy ass down onto the edge of my bed. I looked from the crib Spider originally assembled lopsided, to his record player in the corner knocked on its side, and to all my bras lying in disarray. Cologne bottles were everywhere. There was no way I could clean this mess and not think of

Spider or Romell. Besides that, I felt nasty. There was this layer of grit on my face, so first things first.

After I washed my face, I peeled off my top, the shorts, and my bathing suit. Then, I reached for the one thing that was sure to make me feel better—my poetry journal. I turned to a clean page, unzipped the inside pocket of my carryall and pulled out the two receipts. They were damp. The ink was smudged, but they were still legible. Line by line, I neatly copied the words from the first receipt into my journal.

> *So much for today*
> *There is no tomorrow*
> *Too many mistakes*
> *And too much sorrow*
> *Why should I fight?*
> *When I can't win*
> *I just can't believe this is the end*

Raising my pen to the top margin, I scribbled in the title, *I Just Can't Believe This Is the End.* The structure for this poem seemed so familiar. I moistened my middle finger and flipped to the last poem. Sure enough, it was very similar. I read to the ending.

> *Please show me*
> *What I don't see*
> *What's the reason?*
> *4 the problem*

Strangely, that poem was entitled, *Is This the Beginning of the End.* The poem I just wrote I titled, *I Just Can't Believe This Is the End.* That was so strange. There almost seemed to be a connection. I moistened my fingertip again and now flipped through all the pages. The titles seemed to be in a sequence that spelled out almost exactly what I'd been going through for the past few days. *Believe, It's Just a Matter of Time, Chocolate Love, Is This the Beginning of the End, I Just Can't Believe This Is the End.*

It was as if somewhere, deep down inside, I was predicting what was going to happen. I knew I was going to consider ending my life. Last night and since then, there had been a series of coincidences—the titles on the receipts just so happened to fall in an order that made sense; they also happened to reflect my own thoughts at the time. When I was looking for the "Jump" CD to play as my very last song that was not in the bag, and now the order of my very own poems. What was strange was how all this just so happened to fall into place right after Romell and I did our play on song titles in the record store and how all this also happened to fall into place right before I considered suicide.

Maybe this was all a coincidence. But then again, what if everything happens for a reason? If this wasn't an accident or a coincidence, what does this all mean? For once, I didn't have the answers. I didn't know what to make of any of this, but I knew who would be the right person to ask.

50

$\mathcal{S}$ITTING ON MY BED, I PICKED UP MY PHONE. THEN
I shook my head and placed it back. I took a deep
breath and exhaled. I felt uneasy; my stomach was churning
like a taffy machine. I laughed. "I've got to get a grip." I took
another breath and slowly released it. Somewhere from
outside, through the downpour, I heard a running motor
rumble. There was a hiss and then the squeak of brakes.
After what seemed like only seconds later, I heard the
grinding of gears and clattering between the hum of
hydraulics. Now, I knew it was a garbage truck. The Department of Sanitation is always prompt. Even in this nasty
weather, I could set my watch to them. Now, back to the
matter at hand, I picked the phone up, grunted, and placed it
back down, looking around me, but searching for nothing. I
was stalling, and I knew it. I had an idea of what I wanted to
say, but still, this wasn't easy. Especially since I had been
avoiding her. *Maybe I shouldn't even call.* I only reconsidered
for a split second, because I glanced at my journal and saw
that title again, *I Just Can't Believe This Is the End.* I
snatched up my phone and dialed. On the first ring, Mrs.
Goodwin picked up. "Good morning," she said. Hearing her
gentle voice, I smiled, and my eyes grew misty.

Now, after all the times I ducked her so I wouldn't have to
go to church, after taking her for granted for so long, and
even though I had yet to read a single Bible verse she
recommended, here I was being comforted by the mere sound
of her voice. Still, my own voice trembled when I said, "Hello."

"What's wrong?" she said.

"I just had the worst night of my life."

"Well, Mia. Weeping may endure through the night, but
joy comes in the morning."

I took a deep breath and then I asked, "Mrs. Goodwin,
how do we know if God is trying to tell us something?"

"God is always trying to tell us something. That's why we should read our Bibles so that we can know exactly what He says. Have you opened that brand-new Bible of yours yet?"

"No, I haven't."

"Why haven't you?"

"I don't know. No, I do. Mrs. Goodwin, I didn't know if I believed or not until this morning. Now, I think I do."

"Well, Sweetheart. That's something you definitely need to make up your mind about. You give that some thought, and I'll keep praying for you."

"You'll *keep* praying for me?"

"Yes, Mia. I've always been praying for you. You've been on my mind a lot lately, so I've been praying for you more than usual."

I didn't know how to respond to that. "Thank you," I said uneasily, then added, "Romell *has* been telling me to call you for some time. When I finally spoke to you, one thing you said was absolutely right."

"What's that?"

"All relationships *do* go through changes. Love changes. First, it's hot. Then, it's cold. It goes through its ups and downs, back and forth. You love 'em one moment and hate 'em the next. So, I can't take it anymore. I give up."

"Mia, love—as we understand it—changes, because we change. But, God is God all the time. He never changes. God's love remains the same, and His love endures forever," she said. My eyes started tearing. I wiped them dry and sniffled quietly. But then, Mrs. Goodwin asked, "Are you going to work today?"

"No," I sighed, "I don't feel up to it. Why do you ask?"

"Why don't you come to church with me? Midday service starts at noon."

"Not today, Mrs. Goodwin."

"Okay, Mia. Call me at work if you change your mind. And think about what I said, because living in this world unsure about your beliefs is like the love of your life and your soul mate being two different people."

Hearing her say "two different people," I was now afraid of where this conversation would lead. Quickly, I said, "Well, I don't have that problem. I have to go now. I'm late for work. I'll talk to you later. Bye."

I didn't mean to hang up on her, but it seemed she was

leading up to asking me about my feelings for Spider *and* Romell. Still, hanging up on her wasn't right, I knew better. *She didn't deserve that.*

I opened my night table drawer. Light hit the gold words embossed on the spine, New International Version. I reached in and pulled out my Bible. As I opened it up, the crisp, clean pages crackled. A receipt fell out. It was from the Salvation Army. *What on earth did I buy from the Salvation Army? Oh, yeah, the CD player.* The receipt was impressed with my own handwriting on the reverse side. I flipped it over and read it. John 3:16, Isaiah 54:10, and Psalm 119:41—those were the verses Mrs. Goodwin had given me. I moistened my middle finger. Snatching back the flimsy pages, I ripped a couple, but I found the first verse. "For God so loved the world that he gave his one and only Son, that whoever believes in him shall not perish but have eternal life" (John 3:16). And, the next one, "Though the mountains be shaken and the hills be removed, yet my unfailing love for you will not be shaken nor my covenant of peace be removed, says the Lord, who has compassion on you" (Isaiah 54:10). And, the last, "May your unfailing love come to me, O LORD, your salvation according to your promise" (Psalm 119:41).

This all seems well and good, but I'm still not sure. Mrs. Goodwin says living in the world unsure about your beliefs is like the love of your life and your soul mate being two different people. Maybe that's the case, but I don't have that problem. I don't have Spider; we broke up. And, if Romell and I can't be lovers, then we can't be friends, so I don't have him either. I may have thought Spider was the love of my life, but Romell definitely was never, is never, and will never be my soul mate.

51

I DON'T WANNA BE WITH ROMELL. DIMES—THAT'S all he wants. Dimes. I'm worth so much more, but Romell's so superficial; he doesn't see that. And, in a span of not even two full days, he went from Jun Ko to me and then to Akasma. And, Jun Ko's ass went running to his room with whipped cream. And, he put me out in the rain, too! Oh, I'll never speak to Romell's ass again. And as for Spider, when we broke up, he didn't cry, scream, cuss, yell, none of that. He just left. He was only mildly disappointed after ten years of us being together. Ten whole years. If that man cared about me, he would have been crushed. I'd bet any amount of money that he's lying up with some other bitch right now. If Romell and Spider can't see a good thing staring them in the face, then Romell can kiss one cheek and Spider can kiss the other. It's as simple as that. I don't know why I believed Spider. Having a baby for a man who's against marriage is a no-no. And, for the life of me, I can't figure out why I allowed myself to have that little crush on Romell. Getting involved with a man who can't even commit to a relationship is a definite no-no. Well, at least I learned my lesson. So now, I can forget about Spider. And Romell. I don't want either one. I don't need them. I just wish I could stop thinking about them.

Rather than focus on the negative, I made myself busy. I showered, shampooed my hair, put it in four big plaits, and tied it up. At the salon, Dawn had kept the perm in so long; it burned and now my scalp was scaly. But I didn't call my sister, bitchin'. Instead, I slipped on some rubber gloves and commenced to clean each room from top to bottom. That didn't take long. When I'm heated, I do everything faster, but faster isn't always better. I soon had my head in the oven, coughing from noxious fumes. Common sense should've told me: it's not wise to scrub an oven without proper ventilation. I cracked the windows, letting in some air. But, those toxins

321

still got to me. Bad enough my scalp was itching, now I was gagging. Because of a surge of adrenaline, this black woman forgot: she is not superhuman. So, my adrenaline buzz wasn't doing me a bit of good. The problem was I couldn't help but focus on Spider and Romell. Well, I had enough of being pissed off. I tugged off my rubber gloves, brushed my sweaty hands down my lucky nightgown, snatched off my scarf, and scratched my scabs.

I needed more of a distraction. In the living room, I opened my console and turned to an easy listening station. "You Gotta Be." I smiled and left it there. *Now, that's what I'm talking about!* That was exactly what I needed. I sang that song with Des'ree. Then I heard a noise and looked across the room. It wasn't the bass, so I turned the music down and stood still, listening. I didn't hear anything. In these buildings, there was always some banging going on: some-body's hammer, the pipes, ceilings, or bad-ass kids roaming the halls because they couldn't play in the rain. I turned the music back up. It didn't sound like the door, but I walked over, slid the cover off the peephole, and checked just to be sure. No one was there, so I went back to cleaning.

The only thing left to do was the polishing. I started with my bachelor's chest and ended with my console, which I always gave so much more attention to. Mrs. Goodwin had the same one years ago. Maybe that's why I fell in love with it. One particular morning, it had been there just sitting by the garbage truck, but waiting for me. I brought it in, and Spider had a fit, understandably. The glass was broken, but this was good wood, and it was all pine. I had gotten so excited; I soon stripped it and had it up against the wall. Later, replacing the shattered mirror and all the panes cost me big time. But in the inlay, there's my happy reflection. In retrospect, the console was exactly what I wanted. Good thing I won Spider over. Only a fool would refuse such a nice piece because of a little broken glass.

Okay. All the wood was done, now it was time for that mirror over the loveseat. I grabbed that mirror off the wall but forgot how tedious this process was. Scrubbing the scrollwork with an old toothbrush was a pain in the ass. I loved this mirror because it was beautiful, a little old-fashioned, but that was its charm. Now, hanging it back on the wall, the mirror looked like I gave up on it. The frame was shiny, except for a little tarnish, but I just didn't have the desire to stick with it. I was beginning to think sterling silver was a lot like Spence Snyder, too much work.

My two crystal candlestick lamps only took a second. They had ridges, so it wasn't like the fingerprints were visible. I grabbed a paper towel and wiped them just to be wiping them. But that wasn't the case with my crystal centerpieces. No paper towels for these two. I polished them with a lint-free cloth. First, the decanter: sleek, with rounded shoulders and a nice stopper. Then the fluted vase, it stood a little higher, long and lean. Both centerpieces were cobalt blue, with no chips, cracks, or scratches, but the vase was a gorgeous piece of hand-blown glass.

I wiped my forehead and took a long, hard look. Spider was always so indifferent about everything I did, but we came here with nothing, moving into four empty rooms and an echo. Every time I brought in something shabby and made it chic, that was my little victory. My loveseat with its camel back, my chaise with its Queen Anne legs, this mix of texture and color: periwinkle walls, the wood, the mirror, pillows, leather, upholstery, and the crystal; in this room all the elements came together. Here was my proof that even though I made some bad decisions, something was right about me. *My place is beautiful, even if no one else appreciates it.*

All right, enough of this light stuff, time to change the pace. I opened the console and tuned my radio past the static to an old Funkadelics song. I listened closer, snapping my fingers, then turned it up. It was their music, but some female was singing about being a freak. *This is hot!* I couldn't help dancing, and as soon as I caught onto the words, I started singing too.

The artist was Adina Howard. I had just finished scribbling her name on the back of my Modern Bride magazine when I heard a tap. *I thought I heard something earlier. I'd bet any amount of money that's Jeff acting stupid. Why didn't he just ring the bell?* "Just a minute!" I turned the music down and looked out the peephole. Again, no one was there. "Who?" I said, pressing my ear to the cold door.

At first, there was a hum. Then, trying to listen closer through the paint, I heard nothing. "Who!" I still didn't hear anything. Now, I tightened my lips. "If this is Jeff, I'm going to cuss your ass out." I quickly unlocked my door, swung it open, and stepped over the threshold, screaming, "Jeff?" But, the long, bowlegs I saw down the corridor, approaching me in full swagger, weren't Jeff's.

52

RAINWATER COVERED ROMELL'S HEAD. BEADS ran trails down his face. His jeans were soaked. Standing in front of me, he looked like a side of beef in his wet t-shirt. I kept staring. I always thought he didn't know where I lived, but then I remembered I mailed stuff to Romell, and I always wrote in the return address. I still couldn't believe I was seeing him. "How did you get here?"

He wiped his face with his bare hand. "The Jag's out front."

"You drove that convertible in this weather?"

"Top's up."

"Top's up? That car has never seen a speck of dust, let alone a raindrop. There's practically a monsoon out there."

"Shh! I need to talk to you, and I couldn't chance not catching a cab."

"Why didn't you call or wait until *I* called *you* like you always do?"

"I had to see you now."

"You just saw me a few hours ago."

He pulled my arm. "I need to talk to you."

"Okay, come inside."

"Nah, come down the hall with me. I need to talk to you...privately."

"Romell, if you want to talk to me privately, why are you asking me to come out into the hallway? Come inside."

He stepped back and looked at me. His eyebrows drew together, and he squinted uneasily. "Is...is your man in there?"

"Spider is not my man!"

Romell cut his eye and tried to glance past me. I sucked my teeth. "No, Romell! He's not here! I told you last night that I put his ass out."

I backed into the apartment and held the door open. As

325

soon as he stepped inside, I locked all four locks. When I turned, I saw he was in the middle of my living room. This was his first time here, but I didn't expect him to be looking around as if he were in a museum.

He walked over to my console. "This thing is solid. You're gonna have it for a long time." He knocked on the wood and turned around. "Your place is something, Chocolate. Who's your decorator?" I looked at him like he had a third eye. He looked back at me. It took a minute, but I saw the realization sink in; his eyes grew big, and for a moment, he couldn't stop blinking. He stepped to my chaise and stopped. Staring, he asked, "You don't have any idea how much this thing is worth, do you?"

"A lot I guess."

He responded, "If you need to guess, you *don't* know."

I shrugged, watching him shake his head and walk over to my loveseat, looking at everything again. Still in awe, he reached up to my crystal lamp and felt the blue silk lampshade. So I said, "Sometimes the most wonderful things fall right into our laps because someone else didn't appreciate them." For some reason, his head spun, and there was a strange look in his eyes that I couldn't read. Glancing away, I saw his Movado. The long hand was on the diamond and the short hand was where the ten should have been. "Romell, it's Thursday morning. Why aren't you at work?"

"I quit."

When he was begging me to stay yesterday, I sensed something was bothering him. Now I knew what it was. "You what? When?"

"Yesterday, but nevermind that. Chocolate, you and I, we've been friends all our lives and—"

"Romell, you didn't have anything else lined up!" I moved around the living room. "Why on earth would you quit your job? How are you gonna manage?"

"I'll be fine. Look, Chocolate. You and I, we got something that—"

"Fine? Hello, Romell!" I walked up to him. "That *is* a Jaguar parked outside. Your bills ain't like mine!"

"Chocolate, trust me. I'll be fine. I saved for a rainy day. Now, what I've been trying to say is—"

"Saved for a rainy day?" I pulled the sheers aside, yanked the cord to the blinds, and pointed out the window to the storm raging outside. "Did you save for this? How much do you need?"

"I don't need to borrow anything! Trust me. I'll be fine." He looked away and then looked back at me, smiling. He moistened his lips and softened his voice, "And, I owe you now as it is."

I walked over to him. "You don't owe me any money."

"Yes I do."

"No, you don't!"

"Chocolate, I never welch on my wagers. And, we *did* agree that if I ever made you feel worthless, I'd owe you."

"Romell, we were nine-year-olds."

"A bet's a bet."

"You don't have to pay me, Romell. It is *not* that serious."

"Nah, it is to me." He grabbed my wrist, reached into the pocket of his jeans, and pulled out a closed fist. Slowly, he released ten cold dimes into the palm of my hand.

Standing there with this fist full of cold, wet dimes, I said, "What the hell is this?"

"A dollar."

"I can count! Why are you paying me in dimes?"

"I wanted to make a point."

I shook my head. "What point is that?"

"I don't want you to ever feel worthless, Chocolate, because for you, I'll gladly give up all my dimes."

I shrugged and my eyes searched his. "What are you saying?"

"Let me know right now what it is you want from me, whether it's friendship or a relationship, and I promise you: I will make that happen."

"Romell, you should know by now. I want a husband!"

"Whoa, Mia! Come on! I'm taking a big step here. Work with me! I've never done the relationship thing before, but I wanna give it a shot with you!"

I smiled and shook my head. "Relationship?" Then, I cut my eye at him. "With me? Don't you have enough women to choose from?"

"I want *you.*"

"What happened? Did Jun Ko run out of whipped cream? Did Akasma say you can't have any more of her Turkish Delights?"

"Chocolate, don't be like that. I only feel things when I'm

with you."

"Oh really? So, I guess when Akasma was in your bed this morning, you weren't feeling things. And, when Jun Ko ran to your bedroom with that can of whipped cream, you didn't feel things then either, huh? Romell, take your ass home and flip through your Rolodex. Call somebody else. I got your number. You want all the comforts without the commitment. You're just as bad as Spider."

I headed for the door. When I reached for the knob, he grabbed my wrist and pulled me toward him.

"Mia! Look me in my eyes, and tell me you don't want me."

"I don't!"

He wrapped his arm around my waist and pulled me into him. He was already hard. "Look me in the eye and say that again."

I dropped my head to hide my smile. "Romell, why are you putting me through this?"

"Chocolate, I don't wanna put you through anything; I just wanna be with you. I want *us* to be together."

I eased back, folded my arms across my chest, and looked into his eyes. "Well, I'll have to think about that."

He smiled; his dimples deepened—all three of them. "Tell you what, why don't you come by my place? *You* and *I* could do some thinking. We can go straight to my bedroom and think. Then, we can take a shower, grab a bite to eat, come back, and think some more. Take another shower, go and have dinner, and when we get back, we could think for the rest of the night. And, after all our thinking tomorrow morning, we could shower, and I'll bring you home."

I shook my head. "All these showers...for thinking?"

"Hey, you know me. I've got a dirty mind."

I giggled, even though that line sounded like something he was probably practicing for years. When I looked back into his eyes, he winked at me and I got the strangest feeling, like a tickle in the pit of my stomach. And then I heard the voices, rattling off all the reasons why I should be disgusted, reasons why Romell could never be what I needed, reasons why this was all wrong; Romell was wrong for me; I was wrong for him. But I closed my eyes, listening only to the rain and breathing in his scent. After clearing my mind of every thought and every fear, the only thing that mattered was how I felt about him. He made my heart swell, and now it was bigger than me. That's precisely why I did what I did next. I tiptoed in and brought my lips to his.

He turned his face away. "Did you have any peanuts today?"

"Nope."

"No peanut butter, either?"

I shook my head, nibbled his bottom lip and then, his top. My tongue found his and breath sweet from peppermint. Change slipped through my fingers and chimed, hitting the floor. I placed my hand under his wet shirt. His skin was cool and damp, but this was the first time I had ever consciously put my hand on any man other than Spider. I hissed and ran my hand up to his chest. It was just as hard as his abs. My other hand tried to pull his shirt off. He grabbed my wrist. I opened my eyes. "What's wrong?"

He shook his head. "What if your man comes back?"

"Spider's not my man, and he's not coming back." I closed my eyes and inched back up toward his lips. I felt him pull away. I sucked my teeth. "He's not coming back! And, even if he does, he can't get in because *I* have his keys!" Still hesitating, Romell looked at me. Then, slowly he brought his lips back to mine. The next thing I knew, we jostled from wall to wall, all the way up the hall, leaving a trail—Romell's shoes, t-shirt, and belt. We burst through my bedroom door, backing in, until I fell, pulling him onto the mattress. I kissed him again, but now, his soft lips stiffened. I opened my eyes and saw him glance sideways at the crib. "Come on, Romell."

"Nah, Mia. I think we should wait."

"Romell, don't stop now." I said. He turned away and shook his head. I softened my voice. "Come on. I know you want some of this hot Chocolate."

"He turned and there was that same look in his eyes he had when he was about to go down on me in the hallway. A jolt of fear shot to my stomach. He reached up under my nightgown, and in one snatch, ripped my panties clean off. He dropped them, dug into his pocket and stuck a condom in his mouth. He tore it open with his teeth and spat out the edge of the wrapper. He got up and turned his back to me. His jeans dropped. I heard a faint crackle as the condom unraveled. And, before I could sneak a peek, he crawled over me. He reached down, probed me with his fingers and then, looked at them. I was so ready; those fingers were almost dripping. Romell stared into my eyes and eased himself inside.

Whoa. I took a sharp breath. Spider and I always fit together perfectly. This was different. This was definitely different. I could feel things shifting inside me. I exhaled in a slow whistle, and then, he started to move. "Wait!" I said.

"What's wrong?"

"Nothing. I just need a moment."

"A moment for what?"

"To brace myself." I looked into his eyes. He was still puzzled, so I added, "My garage is small, and your limo's a stretch."

He squinted. His eyes searched mine until they grew big, "Oh! Okay," he said half smiling. He dropped his face into my pillow. I felt him shake his head.

"Now, what's wrong with *you*?" I said.

"I can't." He looked over his shoulder at the crib. "This doesn't feel right to me."

"What? I can understand my discomfort, but what the hell is your complaint?"

"Not you! Us. Here. Now. I've got a bad feeling about this."

"Come on, Romell. Don't you want some of this?" He looked at me and shook his head again, but I was ripe. My heart, pounding louder than the tock-tick clock on my nightstand. I wrapped my arms around his waist. "Don't you want some Chocolate?"

"Nah, my instincts are never wrong. I know I tend to let my other head do the thinking, especially when I'm in this position." He looked at the clock, backed off, and sat on the edge of the bed, looking at the prom picture on the nightstand. "But not this time." He removed the condom and stuffed it in his pocket. Then, he pulled his jeans on and buttoned them.

Right now, every part of me had a pulse. I jumped up and turned the prom picture facedown. Tugging at his jeans, I begged. I was squirming. "Come on, Romell. Don't you want some of this hot Chocolate?"

He smiled. "Sounds sweet. Can I have some whipped cream with that?" Then, he had the nerve to wink.

I caught a flashback of Jun Ko on her way to his bedroom. My lips immediately tightened. I pinched him. "Why do you always try to distract me?"

330

He shrugged. "It always works."

I smiled, but I was way past frustrated. Every single time the chance to make love to this man seemed to present itself, something managed to prevent it from happening. This was a pattern. And right now, all those years of anticipation, all that pent up sexual tension spilled out of me. He wiped my tears away with his thumb. "Chocolate, come on now. You know I hate to see you cry. Save those tears for a rainy day."

"It *is* raining." I sniffled. "Maybe this is just not meant for us. You and I will never have sex, Romell."

"What was this?"

I shrugged. "I wanted this all my life." I laughed and wiped away another tear. "So of course, something has to go wrong. Something *always* goes wrong. Things like this never happen to me. Good things happen for everyone else, but they never fucking happen for me! I don't know if it's my luck, fate, destiny, bad karma or worse. I'm cursed. That has to be it. Why else would—"

"Stop it! Stop talking crazy!"

"It'll never happen! Watch!"

"Yes, it will!"

"It didn't a minute ago! It didn't last night!"

He sighed, "Last night was something different. Look, Chocolate. Sooner or later, that man is coming back here. If for nothing else, he'll be back to pick up his things."

The concern I heard in his voice brought me back. I asked, "When did you start caring about Spider?"

"I don't give a damn about him. I care about *you*. That's why when you and I get together, I wanna be sure you don't have any regrets."

I looked at him and sighed. Then, I nodded.

He zipped his jeans and said, "Put something on, and come with me back to my place. We'll pick up right where we left off. I promise."

I smiled. "All right, but I'm gonna need a minute to get myself together."

He looked back at the clock. "Chocolate, it's pouring outside, just throw anything on. Your clothes are coming right off as soon as I get you to my place, anyway."

I twirled my finger around one of my plaits. "I am *not* going anywhere with my hair looking like this!"

"Okay, okay." He shook his head. "Just hurry up. I'll wait

for you downstairs."

"Hold up, I'll walk you to the door." I stood, straightened my nightgown, and slipped on my fuzzy pink slippers. After removing the foiled edge of the condom wrapper from my bed, I then did a quick scan. Not seeing the larger piece, I crumpled the one I had and tossed it in the wastebasket. I stepped into the hall and watched him buckle his belt. He had already slid his feet into his shoes. He reached down, picked up his t-shirt, and pulled it over his head. Then, he took my hand, and our fingers locked. We stood there for a moment, just staring at each other. As we stepped into the living room, Romell looked around again. This time, he was nodding.

So I said, "I didn't need to buy a twenty-six thousand dollar sofa, either. I did my whole apartment for under a thousand dollars."

"Furniture, too?"

"Everything."

"I'm impressed. This is quaint, almost as cute as you are, if that's possible. I still don't see why you won't let anybody help you out. Your mom is a furniture buyer. Miss Anne could've gotten brand-new furniture...at cost. And, you definitely could have gotten a bigger place somewhere else. If you needed a down payment or something, all you had to do was ask me. Instead, you chose to be stubborn. You do know you're stubborn, right?"

I shrugged. "Just a little bit."

Staring into my eyes, he gave me a gentle kiss on the back of my hand. Then he squeezed it to his heart. "I wouldn't change you for the world."

When he said that, I looked away feeling myself blush. A mousy sound came out of my mouth when I spoke. "You go ahead to the car. I'll be right down."

He gave me a peck on the lips. "Make it quick," he said and peeled away. Just as he was about to release my hand, the top lock clicked. Romell looked at me and tightened his grip. I looked at the next lock. Watching the bolt disengage, I smacked my forehead at my own stupidity. Spider didn't only have one set of keys; he had two. I tried to tug my hand away from Romell's; he squeezed even tighter. Spider stuck his key in that third lock, and the friction was loud. My knees grew weak, and I felt like I was going to faint. Here I was, alone in my apartment with Romell, in my nightgown with no panties on. Now, Spider was unlocking the door, and Romell was squeezing my hand. The thumb turn on the bottom lock rotated, and my heart...my heart sank to my stomach. When I saw the knob twist, I closed my eyes and held my breath.

53

$\mathcal{S}$PIDER WAS COMING IN, AND ROMELL WAS NOT letting go of my hand. I got strength from somewhere, snatching my hand away just before the heavy door swung all the way open. The first face Spider saw was Romell's. Spider did a double take, and then his eyes grew bigger than mine. I watched the blood drain from his face, fading his copper tan pale. My courage came back. I got bold and took control of the situation. I rolled my eyes. "What the hell are you doing here?"

"I came to talk to you," Spider said.

Now, I didn't know which way to turn. Spider was left. Romell was on my right. I turned right. Romell's lips were tight and twisted to the side. This was the first time these two had been in the same room since high school. Now, they were men. Two bodies towered over me like skyscrapers, both drenched. Romell stood tall in his t-shirt and jeans; Spider, a little taller in yesterday's suit. But, despite all Spider's layers, Romell's upper body had more bulk. Spider was long and lean, but built like a strip of bacon compared to Romell.

Romell's velvety voice went way deep. "Mr. Snyder," he said. Then, he looked back and forth at both of us and said, "Miss Love?" The way he said it confused me. The inflection in his voice left me wondering whether he was asking Spider if he missed me or asking me what I was going to do. I froze because I didn't know what to say or do or what Romell would do next. Frozen, I watched Romell moisten *his* lips and lean toward mine. My quick reflexes kicked in. I snapped my head to the side, and he kissed me on my right cheek. Then, with a smirk, he looked Spider up and down and brushed past him. From the hall, he looked back. "Mia, I'll be seeing you."

I looked at him; he was squinting into my eyes and nodding. So I knew he was going to wait for me.

I nodded back. "Okay, Romell."

Then, Spider spoke. "Hey, Romell! I'll catch you later."

Romell squinted at Spider, then simultaneously, both Spider and Romell snapped back their heads. Romell looked at Spider for a moment and then casually swaggered off.

I locked the door and looked at Spider. His expression was blank. That was not good. Now, I had no clue what he was thinking, no indication of how he would react, and no idea what I should do to handle the situation. There was another problem; Spider wanted to talk, but I couldn't remember how Romell left that bedroom. So whatever Spider wanted to talk about, I had to make sure this exchange happened in the living room.

I grabbed onto Spider's damp sleeve and pulled him over to the loveseat. He snatched out of my grasp and started up the hall. I grabbed him again. He yanked away. "What's up with you? I have to use the bathroom."

"Oh, okay," I said. *So much for that.* I watched Spider walk into the bathroom. Then, I took off to the bedroom.

Hearing Spider use the toilet, I looked around fast. The sheets were rumpled. Smoothing them out, I felt a damp patch at the foot of the bed. The toilet flushed, and then the faucet ran. There was no time to change the sheets. I snatched the pillow off the floor and covered the spot. As I went to stand back up, I caught a glimpse of the foiled wrapper under the crib. Quickly, I knelt, snatched it into my hand and crumpled it up. I was just about to pitch it into the wastebasket when Spider walked in. So, instead, I tightened my fist and sat on the side of the bed, hoping that Spider didn't notice how hard I was breathing. Then, I eased the bottom of my gown under my thigh so that he wouldn't notice I wasn't wearing underwear.

"What was Romell doing here?"

"He had something important to tell me." Spider looked at me. His eyes weren't satisfied, so I added, "He just lost his job."

"Is that all? Because, it looked like he was up to something."

"Why are you here? You want your clothes? Your money? What?"

"I wanna talk to you!"

"Well, talk. And, make it quick."

"What's the rush?"

"I just wanna get this over with."

"I wanna try to work things out," he said.

"Why?"

"Where am I going? We've always been a couple!"

"It's over, Spider!"

"Mia, I'm not done. I'm not just gonna let ten years go down the drain, just like that!"

"The past ten years were a waste of time, Spider!"

"A waste of time? What about our son?"

"What about my marriage proposal?" I said.

He walked over and knelt in front of me, placed his hand on my knee, and tried to kiss my neck. I pulled away, saying, "What are you doing?"

"What does it look like I'm doing?" His sad eyes sparkled in the light. They were red and so was his nose. I could tell he was crying. The only reason why I wasn't fazed was because Romell had just left. I clenched my right hand even tighter around the condom wrapper. Spider leaned in to kiss my lips. I turned my head, and he kissed me on the left cheek instead. *Spider looks good, but I am not going to revisit old feelings, and even if I wanted to, I'm not wearing any panties. Wait a minute. Where are my panties?* I casually glanced around, but I didn't see them. He looked into my eyes, and the next thing I knew, his hand started creeping up my thigh. I brushed it away, and Spider whined in frustration. "Stop playing around! I miss you."

"You missed out."

"You're still pissed off? Okay. Okay, I fucked up! I didn't mean to hurt your feelings or call you stupid! Now, can we get past this?"

Spider's admitting he's wrong. That's a first. But now, it's too little too late. We could've gotten past this if my night was different or Spider had been about an hour earlier. I shook my head. "Are you going to take your things with you now, or come back for them later?"

"Mia, why are you buggin' on me like this? This shit is minor. You want a proposal? Fine, I've got a ring in my pocket. I wanted to wait until I could do this right, but here you go. I wanna marry you!" He grabbed my left hand. For a moment, I forgot which hand the condom wrapper was in, but it was in my right. Spider took hold of my ring finger and slipped on a gold band. "That's my mother's old ring. Is that good enough for you?"

The gold was pinkish. I think they call it rose gold. The old band was embossed with a motif of flowers. I looked up at him. "Hell no! That ring is jinxed!"

Spider laughed. "Your ring is at the jeweler's."

"What ring?"

"I got you an engagement ring. It's being mounted at the jeweler's as we speak."

"What jeweler? Where?"

"You forget the Diamond District is right around the corner from my job."

I twisted my lips. "You did that this morning, right?"

"No. I've had this ring on layaway for a year now. That's why I was bugging you about that résumé for so long, and that's also why I got the computer for you to type it on. I needed money to pay for the ring. I just got a promotion, but the label's only been giving me a stipend for carfare and lunch. So, all I could do was five or ten dollars here and there, and on the days I brought lunch in, I put five more on it."

"Yeah, right! Spider, I asked you the other day when we were going to get married, and you said eventually. You were *not* making payments on a ring!"

"I promised you we'd get married after Tee-Bo was born," he said, reaching into his pocket and pulling out a bunch of yellow receipts that were stapled together. He then handed them to me. There were a lot of payments written in, but the date on the top copy was August 4th, the day after I told him I was pregnant.

Spider looked at me. "A promise is a promise," he whispered. "Moments like this happen once in a lifetime, so I always wanted to do this right. Pop the question the old-fashioned way so I could always remember the look on your face. And, I knew if I skimped on the ring, your sister would never let you live it down. So, I picked out the nicest ring I could find. That's why I told you we would get married eventually. Making five-dollar payments, it would've taken me forever to pay for it. But, since I got the insurance check, I paid it off two days ago. I'm supposed to pick it up tomorrow."

I closed my eyes. Tears stung for a few reasons. One, I had no idea. Had I known, I would've made the effort to do his résumé, and I definitely would've been more patient. Two, there was no way I could accept this. If I did, Spider would definitely want some sex, and I was sitting here with no panties on. And three, I had waited so long for him to propose to me. And now he finally did, but Romell was downstairs waiting to take me back to *his* house. I was at a complete loss for words, so I opened my mouth and said what I was thinking, "Spider, why didn't you tell me you were making payments on an engagement ring?"

"Tell you? 'Aye, Mia. I got a down payment on an engagement ring, so when I pop the question, be sure to act surprised.' Doesn't that seem a little foolish to you?"

I sighed, looked at the antique wedding band on my finger, and changed the subject. "So, everything is okay with you and Dr. Snyder?"

He shook his head. "She gave me that ring a while ago."

"I guess she *is* pretty good at keeping secrets," I mumbled.

He didn't respond to that. I don't think he heard me. He took a deep breath, and said, "You know, for a very long time I resented Pops because I felt my mother was the victim in that situation. She had me feeling it was my place to right the wrongs in their relationship by living my life perfectly. But, that's not possible. I'm human!"

"We *all* are human."

He shrugged. "I just wish she could've been straight with me."

I wanted to say, *No, you wish she could've been straight.* What his mother did in the privacy of her bedroom was her own personal business. Even as uncomfortable as I was about homosexuality, had that been my mother, her being in love with a woman really wouldn't matter. I looked at Spider. His eyes were glossy. He was about to cry. His lips were parted. I waited for him to say something, even though the silence was getting stale. Eventually, he looked at me and said, "My mother told me where I can find Pop's ashes. Right now, that's all I care about. Enough about that, what day do you wanna make it official?"

I looked away. "I need to think about this."

"What's there to think about?"

"How can a marriage between us work when you don't appreciate me? You can't even tell me you love me!"

"Just because I didn't say it, doesn't mean I didn't feel it! Cause believe me, I had to appreciate your ass a whole lot to think I was going to pay for a ten thousand dollar ring five dollars at a time."

I blinked and quickly recovered, "Why wait until now to say so! If you care so much about me, why didn't you tell me before? What took you so...damn...long?"

He didn't say anything.

I shook my head. "Just as I thought, you don't love me. You just want to hold on to me the way you hold on to everything else, but I'm not going to be another relic from your past." I wrapped my fingers tightly around the ring and pulled it off.

"Mia, wait," he said. "I was afraid, okay."

"Afraid of what?"

He walked to the corner by the door and looked over. "You and your boy are so close, I was always afraid you'd wake up one morning and decide he's the one you want to be with. So, I held back. That way, if things ever did jump off between you two, it wouldn't hurt as bad."

"So, let me get this straight; you were holding back because you were afraid you were going to lose me?"

"Yeah, but I almost lost you anyway, because I was holding back." He laughed and said, "Kind of ironic, huh?"

I sighed and shook my head. "I love you, Spider, and you don't have to worry about me. I won't let anyone or anything come between us." I tried to put the ring back on but it slipped out of my fingers, hit the crib's rail and rolled under the bed.

He smiled and started toward me. Then, he knelt down and stopped short. He looked at me. "What's that?" he said.

"What's what?"

"Underneath the bed. Are those...your panties?"

54

I WANTED SO BADLY TO GET TO THOSE PANTIES
first; that way, I could scrunch them into a ball and
pretend they were laundry. But, Spider got to them before I
could. He held up my ripped panties, but I guess part of him
couldn't accept what he saw. He still felt the need to snatch
my gown up and look at my naked ass with his own two
eyes. Part of me wanted to stand my ground. Another part of
me wanted to run, scream, and hide. And, still another part
of me wanted to smack him and hightail it out of there.
Somehow, there was a part of me that believed I could
explain my way out of this. "Spider, it's not what you think."

"Don't lie to me." His voice was angry and quiet. "How
long, Mia?"

"We didn't do anything. Let me explain."

"How long!"

"Only this one time. And, it's not like you and I were
together."

"We broke up yesterday!" He sat on the edge of the bed
and dropped his head into his hands. Then, he started
laughing. "Ain't this about a bitch! *I'm* a lying, no good,
cheating, dirty dog, huh?" He looked back at me smiling, but
it wasn't a natural smile. It was more like he was baring his
fangs. I could see anguish burning in his eyes, but I could
only respond by silently shaking my head. "You've got more
self-control than anybody, huh?" Now, I could only respond
by dropping my head. Spider jumped up. He paced, beating
his forehead with the heel of his hand for a while, before he
looked at me and screamed, "Damn! Couldn't you at least let
the bed get cold?" He took a deep breath. This time he
inhaled through his nose and exhaled through his mouth in
a way that made his lips expand. Our prom picture was still
lying facedown. He picked it up, looking at it. He motioned
like he was about to throw it across the room but stopped

341

himself and sat it upright on the dresser. "I can't say I didn't expect this. Now, get dressed and let's go," he said.

"Let's go where?"

"The Justice of the Peace is up on the Concourse. We can take a walk over there, make it official, now, and then have some kind of ceremony for our families later."

"I'm sorry, I can't."

"What do you mean you can't? You can if you want to!"

"I don't know what I want right now."

"Do you want to get married or don't you?"

"No."

"What are you saying?"

"I'm saying, no. No, Spider. No."

"You wanna be with your boy?"

"I don't know."

He jumped up and knocked everything off the dresser. "Ten years, Mia! That fucking means nothing to you?"

By now, my tears were flowing. "It does, Spider. But—"

"But what!"

"I've known Romell all my life."

"You wanna be with your boy, Mia? You wanna be with your boy! Go right ahead!" He took his keys out of his pocket and threw them into my bedroom mirror. They hit the frame and the mirror shifted.

"Spider, don't do that! You're gonna break something!"

He bit his lip and looked at me with tears in his eyes. "Break something? Break something! You broke my fucking heart, Mia! You broke my heart."

Spider sat on the corner of the bed, covered his face, and broke into heavy sobs. I came over to him and he jumped up, screaming, "Don't touch me!" He then walked out of the room and down the hall.

I sat there on my bed, waiting for the front door to slam. It didn't. Spider's wind up clock ticked, ticked, and ticked. I hopped off the bed, slipped on my slippers, and listened. Nothing. I ran to my bedroom door and placed my hand on the doorknob. Then, I heard a series of booms and then, the shatter of breaking glass and Spider's ear-piercing scream.

55

$\mathcal{W}$ HEN I REACHED THE OTHER END OF THE HALL, my heavy mirror was facedown, and Spider was standing over my loveseat, shaking his right hand violently. The back of that hand was sliced open. Skin was just hanging. Blood was spurting, running down his arm, and dripping all over the place. Trying not to panic, I said, "I'll get you a towel."

Spider looked like he was about to bleed to death, but that didn't stop him from hollering, "Stay the fuck away from me!" He pulled his red tie out of his back pocket and wrapped it tightly around his hand. Then, he walked to the door, yanking it open so hard the knob left a dent in the wall. Just before he walked out, he screamed, "Bitches ain't shit!"

Blood was all over my loveseat. I could clearly see half a handprint on the arm. My living room—my poor living room—had broken glass scattered from one end to the other. His computer was on the floor sideways. My blue vase was on the floor, shattered. There was so much glass I didn't know what to do or where to begin. Where the mirror once hung, a patch in the wall was stripped down to what looked like cardboard. I lifted my mirror back off the chest. The glass was broken. Blood was covering the pieces. It looked like my seven-year run of bad luck had already started. I stepped carefully over to the door. I looked out into the corridor. There was blood on the floor, but Spider was nowhere to be seen. As soon as I locked the door, my phone rang.

"Chocolate, are you okay?"

I burst into tears. "Spider just left!"

"I saw him! What happened?"

"Spider saw my ripped panties on the floor and went ballistic!"

"What the fuck happened!"

"He trashed my place! He cut his hand and walked out,

calling me all kinds of bitches!"

"Oh!" I heard Romell exhale and then he chuckled. After that, he said, "He cut *his own* self. In that case, come on down, Chocolate. Let's go."

"I've got to do something about this room! There's blood and glass everywhere!"

"Don't even worry about that now. No harm done. Whatever he damaged, we can always replace. Take a ride with me downtown, and I'll help you clean up that mess when we get back."

"No! You go on, Romell. I...I need time...I need to clear my head. When I'm ready to talk, I'll call you."

"Are we gonna talk about us?"

"What us? There is no *us*."

"You've got to be kidding me! Listen, Chocolate! I'm begging you. Please, don't do this now."

"You don't even want me, Romell!"

"I want you more than I've ever wanted anything!"

"You didn't last night."

"I did, Chocolate!"

"You threw me out!"

"You weren't thinking straight, and I care too much to take advantage of you like that."

"You care too much? You care too much about *me*?"

"Yeah, last night, you were acting out, because you broke up with your man; all along, I knew he was coming back, so I didn't want to take advantage of the situation."

"So, last night you didn't sleep with me, because you knew Spider was coming back?"

"Yeah."

"And you didn't want to take advantage of the situation?"

"Yeah!"

"Today, you still *knew* Spider was coming back. So, you *were* trying to take advantage!"

"No, Mia! That's not what I was doing!"

"Then, what do you call it?"

He didn't answer.

"Romell, you play too many games."

"You want me to be honest with you?"

"Yes!"

"Okay! I saw an opportunity, and I jumped on it! That's the real! Last night, I wanted some ass, but that's all I wanted, Mia. You and I can't be fuck buddies! I learned *that* when you slapped me earlier. If I'm gonna be with *you*, I have to be ready to step up and be what you need. I didn't know if I could do that last night, but this morning, a gut feeling told me it was now or never. So, I spent half the morning parked right here in front of your building. First, I was just sitting in my car, checking for your man. Then, I was trying to make up my mind about whether to come up or not. And then, I was trying to figure out how I was gonna pitch it to you; because I knew I was gonna hear your mouth. I was so preoccupied with finding just the right words to say that a raggedy-ass, garbage truck came by and scratched the fucking paint off my Jaguar. But did I get upset? No, I locked my car and went to get change for a dollar...in dimes. This ain't a game to me, Chocolate. And I'll keep it real with you. Your ass ain't perfect! You're bossy, you're loud, and you got a fucked up attitude sometimes. But then again, sometimes you're the sweetest, most beautiful person I know. I love the way I feel when I'm around you. You're my heart, Chocolate. You! I could have anybody. I could have everybody! But I'd rather be with you, because no one else makes me feel this way. And I'll keep it really real. We ain't even fuckin' yet!"

"Do you really mean that? Or are you just telling me what you think I want to hear?"

Sounding as if he'd stopped just short of crying, he answered, "This ain't game! I wouldn't even be here if I wasn't dead-ass serious! I wanna be with you! I'll do whatever it takes! You and I will be *so* happy together!"

I wanted so badly to believe him. I squeezed my eyes tight. There were no tears, but I was one big bubble of angst. All I knew was that I wanted this feeling to stop. "What makes you so sure we'll be happy?"

"We're happy now!"

"Romell, there's glass and blood...all over my living room. *I'm* not happy right now!"

He laughed. "Okay, okay. I'll come up and help you clean that mess *before* we go."

"Romell! The man I've loved for the past ten years just crumbled right before my eyes."

"He'll recover."

"Romell! You don't get it! I can't! I can't do this. I can't be with you."

"You're gonna choose him over *me?*"

"No, I'm leaving you both alone."

"Fuck that! I'm coming up!" When I heard Romell say that, I slammed the phone down. It rang immediately, and I picked up only to hear Romell scream, "I'm coming up!"

"Don't you dare!" I slammed the phone down again.

Romell called back again. "You can't stop me!"

"Romell, if you show up at my door, I will spit in your face! I *don't* want to see you!"

I hung up again, but this time, I pulled the cord out of the phone. Making my way across the room, glass crunched beneath the soles of my slippers, even though I tried to avoid the bigger pieces. Once at the window, I sat on the radiator and looked out at Romell's black Jaguar. I didn't know if Romell would come up or go on home, and if he came up, I didn't know what I'd do. Because, no matter what I said, I would never spit at Romell. That's nasty.

Outside in front of the building, Romell stepped out of his car and shut the door. He walked halfway to the entrance, and then he turned around. The next thing I knew Romell tore out of his parking spot and took off down the street like it wasn't even raining. I don't know if he saw the stop sign at the corner or not, but he went straight through it. From my window, I watched his black Jag and a minivan collide at the intersection. The airbag deployed and the front end of his car crumpled like paper. He got out of the car and I could see his arms flailing as he argued with the other driver out in that heavy rain. But not only did Romell have the stop sign, he was driving too damn fast. He banged on his hood, climbed back in the car, and shut the door. Not too long after that I heard the bedroom phone ring. I grabbed the phone off my loveseat and pushed the wire back into the base. "What?"

"Chocolate, I need to come up."

"No."

"I was just in an accident!"

"You have a cell phone!"

"You're gonna leave *me* standing out here in the rain?"

"Good-bye, Romell."

"Oh, wow. You're really gonna do me like that?"

"I said good-bye, didn't I? Yes, I am being a bitch! At this point, I don't care if I'm being a bitch! I really don't care! Spider already called me all kinds of bitches! So you can go

346

right ahead and call me all kinds of bitches, too. Go ahead, Romell! I know you want to!"

"Nah. My mom raised me right. I would never stoop so low as to call any woman a dog. But I will say this: how could any man love and respect you if you don't love and respect yourself? Good-bye, Mia. It was nice knowing you."

56

I SAT IN THE WINDOW AND WATCHED ROMELL PUSH his car out of the intersection over to the curb. He then sat back inside and waited. I watched, but Romell's words hurt my heart. No, it was his tone. Normally, Romell didn't speak; he purred, and when he was upset, he'd yell and scream. That meant, on some level, he cared. Now, more so than his words, it was his tone that told me our friendship was over. He didn't argue anymore. His anger took him to a place where he had emotionally disengaged. Now, he was cordial.

This may have been hard for him to understand, but I'd had it. I wasn't allowing anyone to pressure me to do anything anymore. If I spent my life trying to make everyone else happy, I'd go crazy. Still, this is not the way I wanted things to turn out. I never wanted to hurt Romell. He'd been my best friend forever. I loved spending time with him. He was the one I was most comfortable talking to. He was drawn to pretty faces, so he never noticed mine; that *did* bother me. I'm a black woman; he didn't date black women. I had a serious problem with that, but I never wanted to see Romell hurt. I never wanted to hurt Spider, either. I always wanted to be the best thing that ever happened to Spider. I tried so hard to be everything he needed just so Spider would know he'd never find another woman like me. There were times I felt unloved, and there were definitely times when I felt unappreciated, but I never ever wanted to break Spider's heart.

A big red tow truck pulled up in front of the Jaguar and Romell stepped out of his car into the rain. While the tow truck hooked and hoisted his Jag, Romell stood on the sidewalk with his hand in his pocket and his posture bent. Even from my window, I could see he was sulking. I shrugged. *No matter what I decided, someone I cared about* would've been hurt. That's why I didn't plan any of this. I had a crush on Romell a very long time ago. Now, I know Romell and I sort of had sex, but that would never have happened if Spider and I didn't break up. That is the only reason why I let my guard down.

This is all Spider's fault. Spider should've told me he was paying on a ring. If he did, we would be together right now. But instead, his ass had me bending over backwards thinking I wasn't good enough to marry, and all along, he had the damn ring on layaway. Spider was broke. How was I supposed to know he had a ring on layaway? Then again, prom night, Spider gave me a ring. He saved up the money from his part-time job. He took me to the movies two weeks later. I went to the ladies room and took it off to wash my hands. That was the last I saw of it, but he did buy me a ring then, I should've known he'd buy me a ring now. It was understood that we'd eventually get married, but without a set date, to me eventually meant never. Bottom line is I can't blame Spider. We both agreed to cut our friends off. But, I didn't. Instead of typing Spider's proposal, I emailed that poem to Romell. Then, I went to see him. And, it's because of that "Chocolate Love" poem that Romell decided to cross the line. Just like I wanted my marriage proposal, Spider wanted his marketing proposal. And, if I would've just typed Spider's proposal like I was supposed to, none of this would've happened. I could've done that at any time, but I didn't. So how can I blame Spider? I sighed. Shoulda-woulda-couldas never did a bit of good. I guess at this point, it doesn't matter whose fault it is; I can't change the past. I've just got to find a way to fix this situation now.

The damaged front end of Romell's car was now completely elevated. He walked around to the passenger side of the truck and climbed into the cab. They pulled off. I didn't know what garage they were taking it to, but to me, the Jag looked totaled. I shook my head. How can I fix this situation? Maybe the situation doesn't need fixing. Who knows? Maybe Spider and I can still be together. It was always supposed to be just the three of us—me, Spider, and Tee-Bo. We weren't supposed to let anyone or anything get in the way of that. Maybe I should just page Spider and tell him I changed my mind. It wasn't like me and Romell actually had sex; we almost did. And, it's not like I felt anything deep for Romell *outside of my feelings for him as a friend.*

By now, my ass was numb, and pins and needles were radiating down to my toes. I stepped off the radiator, shaking out my leg and looked around at all the glass in my living room. *My work is definitely cut out for me here. I don't even know where to start. Compared to today, last night was fun and games. And last night I wanted to kill myself. Now, I know suicide is not an option. It's a good thing I already realized that or I would not have been able to deal with all this.* I sighed. *I'm going to put my house back in order. And when I'm done, I'll page Spider. As soon as he calls, I'm going to tell him I've changed my mind. We will get married like we're supposed to, and we'll be a family, just the three of us.*

Stepping around glass, I made my way to the kitchen, and got the broom. I tied a plastic bag around the bristles, slung a heavy-duty trash bag over my arm, and dropped the condom wrapper into it. I dragged the plastic covered bristles across the floor, and shards of glass scratched the wood. *I'm doing this for the three of us.* I reminded myself. Sitting the broom down, I moved the empty silver frame and carefully placed a foot-long shard in the plastic bag. And another. The third piece sliced my fingertip. It hurt like hell, but when I wiped the blood away and examined it, it was just a scratch, only about the size of a paper cut. I should have worn rubber gloves for this. I made my way to the medicine cabinet, and then into my bedroom.

I was trying to get through cleaning this mess by focusing on us three being a family again. Now, I had cut my finger. I needed a moment to regroup. I knelt near the bed and slipped my hand between the mattress and box spring for my poetry journal, but felt the cold metal of my silver bracelet. I pulled it out, fastened it on my arm and then retrieved my journal.

The ribbon bookmark was at my last poem, *I Just Can't Believe.* I turned the page back to *Is This the Beginning of the End* and read the last lines.

> *4 some reason*
> *4 some cause*
> *4 some strange reason*
> *It's just not obvious*
>
> *Please show me*

What I don't see
What's the reason?
4 the problem

I tilted my head, looking at the words. *4 some reason.*
What's the reason? 4 the problem. For; I consistently *substituted*
that word with the number 4. And, the funny thing is, I don't
know why I did that. Was there any significance? Or was it
just a mindless omission? I don't remember. There's me,
Spider, and Tee-Bo—us three. There is no connection, unless
Mommy or Dawn is the fourth element. Maybe I'm looking too
much into this. Sitting with my legs crossed Indian style, I
rested my head in both hands, thinking. *I am looking too*
deeply into this. Four could mean anything. We live on the
fourth floor. The Fourth of July is right around the corner. I
looked at Dr. Snyder's antique wedding band on my left ring
finger. Then the bracelet on my right wrist glimmered in the
light. I read the inscription. *4 Ever Love Romell.* The "for" in
forever was replaced with the number four. My conscience
read those words as a question. *Four; ever love Romell?* Now,
I had to honestly ask myself. *Did I ever love Romell?* First my
nose stung, then my eyes started tearing. *I always loved*
Romell. There was no use in denying it anymore. I was in love
with Romell; for that reason, he was that fourth element.
Romell was the problem. So, I couldn't consider getting back
together with Spider now or ever.

I can't fix this. This is a mess. My life is a mess. For so
long, I hoped to marry Spider and dreamed of being with
Romell. It never dawned on me that my hopes and dreams
were in opposition. Today is the day they all seem to come
true. Now what? I sighed. *Why couldn't Romell just notice me*
in the ninth grade before I met Spider? If only Spider had told
*me he put the ring on layaway, then I wouldn't have....*I
sighed. For so long, I'd envisioned Spider dropping down on
one knee and slipping a large diamond on my finger. In my
heart, I believed that would happen, until everyone else had
me thinking otherwise. Now, not only did Spider propose, but
he was also remorseful and appreciative. I saw with my own
eyes how much Spider loved me when he realized Romell and
I had sex. Instead of getting pissed off, he panicked and
wanted to marry me right away. As for Romell, he never
noticed me before; now, he noticed me. Romell didn't date
black women; now, he wanted *me.* And, Romell never wanted

a relationship ever; *now*, he wanted me. *Why did all of this have to happen now? Now, things will never be what they used to be. Why couldn't things just work out the way I planned? Why does love have to be so difficult?* I agonized over those thoughts until I remembered what Mrs. Goodwin said, "Love as we understand it, changes. God's love doesn't change." That was a concept I could only partially grasp. I understood about love, but I needed to find out about God.

I opened my night table and pulled out my Bible. Spider's wad of cash lay in a rubber band in the drawer. I closed it and opened the Bible at random. The first verse I saw caught my attention. "Therefore I tell you, whatever you ask for in prayer, believe that you have received it, and it will be yours." (Mark 11:24). I closed the Bible and smiled. *Mrs. Goodwin said, she's been praying for me. I believe that. I'm so glad someone was praying for me when I wasn't even praying for myself. That has to be the reason why I'm still here.* I grabbed my journal and turned to my last poem, *I Just Can't Believe.* I snatched it out and tore it up. Now, there was something I absolutely had to do.

I got down on my knees, clasped my hands together tightly, and closed my eyes. But I was afraid. I was too afraid to pray for anything specific, so I said the only prayer that came to mind, *The Lord's Prayer.* Over and over, I don't know how many times. My fists were clenched so tightly; my hands began to sweat. When I was done, I stretched the cramps out of my fingers, wiped tears from my eyes, and thought for a moment. *Mrs. Goodwin said living in the world unsure about your beliefs is like the love of your life and your soul mate being two different people. I couldn't relate to that before. Oh boy, did I understand that now.*

I wanted to call Mrs. Goodwin back, but I didn't want her to think I was calling because I wanted to go to church with her. I looked out the window. I needed a life preserver to go out in that rain. It was too bad out there to go anywhere, but there was still something I needed to ask Mrs. Goodwin. I took a deep breath. *I'll just make this conversation quick.* I picked up the phone and dialed her at work. She answered, "Fort Apache Outreach. Margaret Goodwin speaking."

"Hi, Mrs. Goodwin."

"Hello, Mia. What's wrong?"

"Nothing. I'm just curious. What do you do when the love

353

of your life and your soul mate *are* two different people?"

"You make a choice."

That wasn't the response I was looking for. "Oh, okay. I'll talk to you later."

"Is that all?" she asked.

"Why?"

"I thought you were calling to let me know you're coming to service."

"No way." I looked out the window into the pouring rain. "Not in this weather."

"Okay, dear. I'll be talking to you."

I hung up, thinking. *Make a choice. How? There's only one choice I can make. This will probably be the hardest thing I've ever done, but I gotta do what I gotta do.* I removed the silver link bracelet and placed it in my night table drawer. As soon as I could get to a Post Office, that would be mailed back to Romell. I then pulled the wedding band off my ring finger. I placed it in the drawer atop Spider's wad of cash. As soon as he came back for his things, I would give him back his ring and his money.

Now, I need to find the strength to move on. I'm weak, so I know I'll need some help with this. Maybe Dawn could keep me in check with this one. If Dawn checks up on me, that would definitely help. Dawn said, realizing I need help is not a sign of weakness; it's a sign of strength. She said I need Jesus. Well, I prayed so I'm good. I sighed. *Okay. I do need Jesus, but it's a mess out there. So, I am not going to church in the rain. And, only churchy people go to church in the middle of the week, anyway; I am not a churchy person. So, I am not going, I'm not. Not today. Not in this weather. No way.*

♥ ♥ ♥ ♥

Reverend Earl and old Deacon Thomas were standing at the head of the church. Deacon Thomas cleared his throat, and said, "Praise Him! Praise Him!" Then he bowed his head and sang the same prayer he always sang at this part of the service. "*Heavenly, Father, we are gathered here in this sanctuary today, and we want to say thank You! Thank you for waking us up this morning...in our right minds. For giving us life! And strength! You didn't have to do it, but You did. You are the Alpha...the Omega...the beginning, and the end. Father, I thank You that through You, all things are possible.*

All things! We humbly ask for Your continued guidance and protection this day and every day...in Jesus' name we pray. Let the church say, Amen! If there is anyone here in the middle of a crisis, I want you to know that God is the solution. If you feel it in your heart right now, come to Jesus...."

I felt numb, but a hand touched my shoulder. I looked up into Mrs. Goodwin's smiling, brown face and saw Romell's eyes and dimples. "Hi," I whispered and scooted over, making room for her full figure. Then, I looked again at Deacon Thomas.

He clapped his hands. *"Jesus is the only one who can be everything you need! He'll take your broken pieces, fix you up, and make you new...."*

Mrs. Goodwin gave me a squeeze. She crossed her long, thick legs, fanning herself with a stick fan of Dr. King that was probably older than me. "I knew you'd be here today," she whispered.

I was puzzled. "How? I told you there was no way I was coming."

Still smiling, she said, "God makes a way."

I smiled back, wiping away the tear that escaped.

"Does anyone here want to come to Jesus today?"

I looked around at the handful of people scattered throughout the church. No one moved. I then stood and squeezed by Mrs. Goodwin. My legs wobbled, walking down the aisle toward Reverend Earl and Deacon Thomas, but when I stopped at the altar, I stood firm and said, "I do."

I had always thought I'd say those words with Spider standing next to me. I had hoped at that time we'd be *here*. Knowing how unlikely it was for Spider to marry me in a church, I would've settled for the Justice of the Peace. But why should I settle? Neither Spider nor Romell were in any position to love me the way I deserved to be loved. And as different as they were, the one thing they had in common was that they both felt entitled to whatever they wanted, regardless of what anyone else had to say about it. If they could feel entitled, why shouldn't I? I had just as much right to my happiness as everyone else. Mrs. Goodwin said if I put God first, everything else would fall into place. So standing here now, I was more hopeful than ever. In fact, I made up my mind. One day I would stand at this altar again. When that day came, I'd know that the man standing next to me would be the right man for me. Who that is exactly, only time will tell.

LOVE CHANGES
Music Playlist

1. The Isley Brothers, "Choosey Lover."
2. Krystol, "Same Place, Same Time."
3. Rufus & Chaka Khan, "Everlasting Love."
4. Mary J. Blige, "Be Happy" from the album <u>My Life</u>.
5. Candi Staton, "Victim."
6. Etta James, "At Last."
7. Dusty Springfield, "Son of a Preacher Man."
8. Cameo, "Back and Forth."
9. Cameo, "Candy."
10. Soul II Soul "Back 2 Life."
11. Soul II Soul "Keep on Movin."
12. Kris Kross, "Jump."
13. SWV, "Right Here."
14. Xscape, "With You."
15. Xscape, "Who Can I Run To?" from the album <u>Off the Hook</u>.
16. Xscape, "What Can I Do?" from the album <u>Off the Hook</u>.
17. Heavy D & The Boyz, "Sex Wit You" from the album <u>Nuttin' But Love</u>.
18. Heavy D & The Boyz, "Spend a Little Time on Top" from the album <u>Nuttin' But Love</u>.
19. Tony, Toni, Toné, "Whatever You Want."
20. The Notorious B.I.G., "One More Chance" from the album <u>Ready to Die</u>.
21. Monica, "Don't Take it Personal."
22. Marvin Gaye, "I Want You."
23. James Ingram & Patti Austin, "How Do You Keep the Music Playing?"
24. The Jones Girls, "You're Gonna Make Me Love Somebody Else."
25. SWV, "Downtown."
26. Color Me Badd, "I Wanna Sex You Up."
27. Shai, "If I Ever Fall in Love."
28. The Deele, "Dry Your Eyes."

29. The Deele, "Two Occasions."
30. TLC, "If I Was Your Girlfriend."
31. TLC, "Red Light Special."
32. Des'ree, "You Gotta Be."
33. Adina Howard, "Freak Like Me."

LOVE CHANGES
Reading Group Guide

1. This story takes place in 1995 when Mia is twenty-five years of age, but memories from her teens and early childhood are still prevalent. In what ways have experiences from her past affected her adult decisions?

2. Mia's mother states, "I tell you time and time again, but you don't listen. You just don't listen! And when you don't listen, you suffer. Mark my words. Keep doing what you're doing, Mia, you'll keep gettin' what you got. Absolutely nothing." How do you think Mia's outcome would have been altered had she followed her mother's advice? How does this relate to your own relationship with your mother?

3. Although Mia nurses Tee-Bo, often it is obvious that her focus is not on her baby. What are the reasons behind this? How is her ability to properly care for Tee-Bo affected? Do you think this issue has been resolved by the final chapter?

4. Lack of communication is the obvious dysfunction in Mia's relationship with Spider. Which factors contribute to this lack of communication? How else is this relationship dysfunctional?

5. Compare and contrast Mia's relationship with both men. Why does she have feelings for both? What needs are addressed by each? Which is her primary relationship? Is Mia's ultimate decision inevitable? Did you sympathize with either Spider or Romell?

6. Music is a theme, as the songs Mia sings outline her struggle. What anthems serve as the soundtrack to your life? Is there a causative effect as well?

7. Mia has difficulty accepting Romell's preference for dating across cultural lines. How much of her anxiety is rooted in her own prejudices? What about her attitude toward interracial dating reflects universal themes and truths?

8. Discuss the role of faith in this story. Why did Mia finally pray? What about her experiences motivated her to cross her spiritual threshold?

9. Why are Mia's home furnishings important to her? How does her décor relate to her love life? How does Romell's décor relate to his? What symbols foreshadow the events of the novel's conclusion?

Coming
Soon

Chocolate Love

Here's an excerpt from the irresistible sequel to
Love Changes.

Chapter One

MY NAME IS ROMELL ULYSSES GOODWIN. NOW, WHERE do I begin? For starters, what went on at my mom's first doctor visit, I really can't say. I was there, but I only remember everything up to a certain point. There was a reason for that. Hospitals, I associate them with death and disease. Whenever I think of clinics: malpractice. That clinic was in a hospital. Why not see a doctor in private practice? Why have a procedure done in a clinic instead of the ideal: a nice, cozy, office suite with some magazines in the corner? My mom didn't have that option. Thank her HMO.

The odor was like Listerine, antiseptic and overwhelming. When I wasn't holding my breath, I was using it to warm my hands. *I've heard the excuses as to why they keep it so cold, but spare me. If low temperatures keep germs down, why have I always caught my colds in winter? Whoever controlled the thermostat in this place was obviously hell-bent on making this experience as unpleasant as possible. Even assuming the unlikely, that cold could somehow, in fact, kill germs, why would it still be necessary to "sanitize" with industrial cleaning agents powerful enough to singe nose hair? And another thing, nurses now wear scrubs. Those look like pajamas. Whose idea was that? If I ever see a petition to reinstate the short white dresses from back in the day, I'll be John Hancock.* All this was going through my mind, but I kept my litany of complaints to myself. However, they were necessary when my alternative was to torture myself with worst-case scenarios. My mom sat quietly on the examination table, her hospital gown "opened to the front."

This was my reality. My father was the truck driver found dead on Route 80, just outside of Iowa in 1978. I was nine. Because he was shot in the head and his cargo stolen, there had to have been more than one person involved. It was believed he picked up a hitchhiker. There were a lot of theories floating around as to what actually happened, but the murder remained unsolved. My mom's mother died young. My mom had two sisters. All three died from breast cancer. I mention all that only to make one thing clear. For me there was a period in my life where grieving never stopped; I just learned to shift focus. My mind can only operate in two directions. Going backward I'd find myself in a place where I couldn't function. So for me, lofty goals were crucial. This goal here might've been a little too lofty for me. I made the mistake of taking this woman sitting here in the hospital gown for granted. I expected her to always be around just like I expected the sun to come up every morning. Facing a possibility I couldn't mentally prepare for, I was trying my hardest to support my mom with strength I didn't have. My father wasn't here to do it. My mom didn't have any daughters. I'm her only son, so this responsibility fell on me. I could tell she felt uncomfortable about my being here for this, but I insisted. I didn't want her to have to go through this alone.

This hospital is located way uptown near the border, where the Bronx meets Yonkers. To get here, I showed up in front of Ma's building in a rented Benz, backseat filled with white roses. That gesture was intended to make her feel special, like this was Mother's Day or some other special occasion. Maybe I accomplished that. She seemed to be elated. After I hugged her, we got in the car. It was as if it were a normal day. On the way to the hospital though, this black Mercedes filled with all these flowers and especially their scent reminded me that there are only two occasions that call for this kind of pompous showboating and neither one is Mother's Day. My thoughts turned morbid. I felt myself tearing up. My first instinct was to pull over and clear that backseat. I saw myself yanking that rear door open and scattering those roses on the curb, but instead I remained cool and turned the radio on, which helped. I don't even remember the song; it was something loud and crazy.

My mom deserved better. Actually, she deserved the best because she's hands down the most giving person I know. I've watched her open our home to people, wear herself out for people, drive to the corners of the continent in a car with a hole in it for people, all the while not looking for anything in return or thinking twice about it. She made so many sacrifices for me; she had me fooled. I used to think we were wealthy. We lived in the projects, but I was wearing Bally shoes. I didn't know any better. I had everything I wanted and was in private school. I was an "only child" so I did what we only children do—I focused on myself.

I love my mom more than I could ever express in words. I'm not perfect, but I've always been a high achiever. And where my mom was concerned, I had long-term goals. I planned to take care of her financially *someday*. Buy her a mansion high on a grassy hill out in the suburbs somewhere, make sure she had a housekeeper or two, have her quit her job, travel. I wanted her to be comfortable *someday*. Eventually when that kind of money did start coming in, I got sidetracked. I started enjoying my own life. Women were a large part of that. It didn't take me long to realize the more money I made, the more options I had. By the time I regained focus and was ready to do for the woman who gave me life, she was already content living the life she was living—happy driving her station wagon, happy in her little apartment, happy working at the outreach center for a salary that only seemed to afford her public housing. I know this because I tried giving her all kinds of gifts. I even bought her a sports car. A brand spanking new Jaguar convertible. Anyone else would've appreciated such a beautiful car, but I ended up keeping it myself, because when I offered it to my mom, her response was, "Stop trying to buy me things I don't need! You wanna give me something? How about some grandchildren? I'm ready for grandbabies! Bring me some pretty little babies!" I already knew how she felt about having children out of wedlock, so her request was even more complex than it sounded. She already knew how I felt on the subject, as well. So last Mother's Day, I decided not to blow my money. I gave her one of those dime store picture frames. It came complete with sample photos of random smiling, multiethnic children of various ages. I handed it to her and said, "Wow! Look at those beautiful kids! You can't get any more adorable than that. They're models."

Getting smacked with a picture frame was worth a good laugh. But at the same time, I had made my point: No grandbabies from me, not in this lifetime. This was no reflection on her or "her parenting skills." I just didn't like kids. And now, whenever we made it out of this clinic, I hoped to make up for all the love she gave and all the sacrifices she made with that rented car, those flowers, and a City Island lobster.

Instead of sitting, I chose a space between the chair and some kind of large, scanning device. There I stood, taking inventory of everything in the room. A tray sat on the countertop. On it were several stainless steel tools half covered by paper towels, glass tubes, a small vial of clear liquid, and needles. Right then I felt a little dizzy.

"Are you okay?" Ma said.

"Of course I am."

"Are you sure you're okay? Whenever it was time for you to get a shot, I had to cover your eyes, so make sure you look away when the doctor does what he has to do."

"Ma! In case you haven't noticed, I'm a grown man."

"Appearances can be deceiving," she said.

I walked over and rested my arm on her shoulder the way I always did, and said, "What's tomorrow?"

Ma shrugged me off. "Quit leaning on me. You're heavy," she said. And then she smiled, "I was the one in labor for thirty hours. I know you'll turn twenty-six, but I also know you're afraid of needles."

"I'm not afraid of anything. I can handle this." Saying all the right things in this situation wasn't easy, especially when this crazy voice inside my head kept asking questions I already knew the answer to. *Why am I here? What am I going to do when he sticks her with that fucking needle?* I gave her hand a squeeze, kissed it before I released it, and returned to my spot like I was relaxed. I tried to stretch a bit but hit the scanner. My body was boxed in. Unfortunately, this gap was the one place in this room where I felt sure I'd be out of the way. I stood tall again and looked back over at her.

My mom didn't always have to put into words what she was thinking and feeling. Her expressions were really easy to read. Her raised eyebrows sent the clear but silent message: *I know what I'm talking about.* She was shaking her head. Her lips drew up at the corners and sealed in a way that said: *you can't fool me.* As if nonverbal communication weren't enough, she did in fact come right out and say, "You're doing a good job of hiding it, but I can tell when you're worried. There's no use in worrying about things you have no control over, so try to focus on something else. Have you finished that business plan?"

I was a stock analyst. At one time, I had too many clients. It had been a little over a month since I lost my job. "Not yet."

"Why not?"

"I'm a perfectionist."

Ma looked in my eyes and asked, "Did you ever start that perfect business plan?"

I shook my head.

She shook her head again and said, "Make an effort." And then she asked, "What about Mia? Did you call her?"

"My number hasn't changed. If she wants to speak to me, she can call."

"You know how stubborn she is. Give her a call and tell her how you feel."

"I already tried that. I'm not chasing her."

"I thought you couldn't stop thinking about her."

"That was last month. I'm not sitting on my hands anymore," I said.

"Romell, you have no real interest in marriage. You don't like kids. She has her child to consider. What really are you offering her? Try thinking of others for a change."

"Ma, I am! I told Mia I want to be her man. If that's not good enough, I don't know what is."

"It's always what you want! Stop thinking about yourself! Find out what *she* wants! Find out what she needs! You're so used to getting your way that you're not willing to sacrifice anything for anybody! It doesn't always work that way! This world doesn't revolve around you, Romell Ulysses. Don't you understand that?"

Now, my eyes were crossing, because this was not the

time to have this conversation; I had enough on my mind. I closed my eyes and rubbed my temples. Then, I said, "Ma, give it a rest."

She took a deep breath. "Romell, listen here. Everybody's not going to chase *you*. Now, I am only going to say this once. Don't let that girl slip away."